A Case for Conners:
By: Hugo L.R. Reed

Prologue: John Doe

A stiff breeze blew across the outdoor seating area that belonged to *The Green Harbor:* a local tea and coffee shop that had long since become the favored café of Doctor Josh Michaels. Doctor Michaels was an attending physician nearing his tenth year of work at Saint Anthony Hospital. Many of his collages had started to grow cynical and bitter after treating more addicts and liars than decent citizens. Somehow, Josh had managed to hold onto his optimism a while longer than many of his co-workers. Perhaps it was because he always held onto the hope that just one of his patients desperately needed his help, and he might actually be able to improve their life.

As the wind blew again, Josh drew his lab coat a little tighter around himself.

Well, he thought, amused. *They don't call it The Windy City for nothing.*

The February air was still hard and cold, which caused him to shiver a little. Still, Josh enjoyed the cold rush of air against his forehead and temples. For the dozenth time that hour he went over his new mystery patient in his head. He had yet to be identified—a male in his late teens or early twenties. He'd awoken early that afternoon after being comatose for a few months, but immediately there had been a few problems. As an experienced doctor, Josh was fairly used to problems: those who thought that they'd brought the bubonic plague back into society, people who tried to insist on unnecessary surgery instead of a simple regimen and treatment, and every single patient who seemed to think that between the Internet and "a friend" they had figured out their own illnesses.

However, memory loss was a tricky problem. Sometimes there was a driver's license or a family member or friend who could help reveal the person's identity. That hadn't been the case with his mystery patient. Still, the kid was incredibly bright and very alert. He'd been found in a bank that had apparently just been robbed. The police still weren't clear as to how the kid was involved. They hadn't labeled him a proper suspect, but he was considered a person of interest, which meant that he wasn't allowed to be discharged without being released into police custody. However, until he was declared conscious and in a sound state of mind by Josh, they hadn't been able to question him.

Of course, they'd had hit the first hurdle when the youth had awoken and it was clear he didn't know what his own name was, let alone why he'd been discovered in a bank. Honestly, Josh was surprised that the kid was physically fine after the beating he'd taken. His head had been bashed open after being smashed against the floor several times. He'd been brought in with several skull fractures, which were doubtless the cause for his memory loss. He'd also had a split lip, some internal bleeding, two broken fingers on his right hand, and a black eye.

The kid had been unconscious for almost four months without a single visitor. Nor had a missing persons report come in matching his description. While he'd physically healed up fairly well, Josh had long ago figured that the kid would either die or be left as a vegetable. Then at almost noon on the dot, the kid's vitals had picked up and he'd opened his eyes. As if that weren't enough, he started talking as if he'd known them for most of their careers.

The kid somehow put together the trauma he'd been through—at least so far as the extent of his own injuries—after only a minute or so of self-examination and had then thanked several of the nurses. He'd even called out which of them were regulars in charge of his treatment while he'd been unconscious. Josh had no idea how he'd been able to tell who they were, because the kid never even glanced at his own chart, nor had anyone told him much before he began to talk. He instantly seemed to understand everyone's position and quickly pointed out Josh as his attending.

When they'd asked how the kid seemed to know all of this, he'd only shrugged as if it were as simple as stating the sky was blue.

That single interaction had been driving Josh crazy for the past hour. Sure, some believed that a lot of what a comatose person heard could live on in their subconscious, but that was nothing like what this kid was doing. It wasn't like he was just guessing either. He genuinely seemed to have no idea what his own name was or what he'd been doing when he was injured. However, he had quickly worked out that he was the subject of an ongoing investigation and forbidden to leave his room.

That had been another thing Josh wasn't sure if he liked or not. On one hand, it meant he got to skip a very difficult conversation, which never got easier no matter how often he had to have it. On the other hand, the kid had no right understand things as thoroughly and quickly as he did. It gave Josh the uncomfortable feeling that the kid could somehow read minds, which was impossible of course. Still... it was disconcerting to talk to the boy.

The patient still wasn't permitted to actually leave the building, and after a slight moral debate, Josh had phoned the police and informed them that John Doe was up and talking. Josh sighed deeply. He took in the mixture of aroma from his hazelnut-flavored coffee and the crisp air that persisted, reminding everyone that they still had at least another month of winter weather to endure.

As he took another drink from the paper cup, Josh felt his cell phone *buzz* insistently in his pocket. Josh pulled it out and tapped on the screen a few times. The screen proudly displayed his long-time friend, Conner Castro. Conner was a cardiologist and had quickly become Josh's best friend at the hospital. They usually went out to drink together once a month or so and complain about things at work.

It was Conner who convinced Josh to buy the smartphone he was struggling with. The thing was still pretty new, released about nine months ago, and it was very high-tech compared to Josh's old flip phone. The idea that the thing only had a single button and relied on a touchscreen was something that fascinated him often. Still, that didn't keep him from wanting to chuck the thing off the roof a few times when it was being stubborn, like it was doing at that moment.

Eventually he got the phone to accept the call and let out a breath of relief.

"Hey Conner," Josh said as he lifted the phone to his ear.

"Hey Josh, glad I caught you," Conner replied, sounding a little out of breath. *"It's about your John Doe in 267."*

Josh sat up a little straighter, his body instantly prepared for action, even if he had no idea what he might need to do.

"Is he all right?"

"For now, yes. However the cops just arrived to question him and he's gone."

"Gone? What do you mean he's gone?"

"I mean he just walked right on out the front door. He apparently picked a pin from a nurse when she was checking on him and used it to pick the cuffs."

"How'd he get past security?" asked Josh as he hurriedly stood and and began the jog back towards the hospital, already knowing there would be nothing he could do at this point.

"Apparently he found and intentionally triggered a silent alarm on the third floor and waited until they left the doors before he walked out, cool as you please."

Josh felt his body freeze at that. This kid had somehow analyzed his situation, freed himself, dressed, and organized his own breakout in less than half-an-hour. That wasn't even considering that he couldn't remember anything and therefore had no way to know what the layout of the hospital was, let alone where the silent alarm triggers might be.

"Conner, what the fuck is that kid?"

"Honestly, I don't want to know. You'd better get back here though, the higher-ups are gonna rolls some heads before this is done and the sooner you ensure yours isn't one of them the better."

Part I: Origins

Chapter I: In a Name

A heavy breeze blew over the boy and he enjoyed the feeling of the May wind as it blew across his body. Early on after his escape, it had been cold and he'd shivered constantly. It had been a nonstop search for the chance to find some warmth. The discovery of a good pair of gloves and thick socks had been a lifesaver in the first few months. Now though, the weather was a little warmer. He couldn't be sure exactly what the temperature was, but the news report he'd caught at the coffee shop said they could expect to hit the high fifties. That was good news.

Warmer afternoons were good days to explore and find things and places he might need later. When he'd first escaped the hospital, he'd had nothing but the clothes on his back and a singular key. This key was promising, but had so far led to nothing. It was a small, brass key with the number 18 taped to it. It looked like a standard house key, only he had no idea what it actually went to. The key and clothes were in his room and he supposed they belonged to him, even if he couldn't remember owning them. The clothes consisted of a pair of jeans, a grey t-shirt, a black jacket with several different pockets, a cheap pair underwear and socks, and a pair of white tennis shoes.

With no other belongings, friends, or prospects, he'd had to keep on the move. He never stopped for long, only to rest. It was a week or so of movement before he really stopped. He'd found a burnt-out basement that looked like it hadn't seen use for at least a decade. The windows were broken out and the door didn't shut properly. Still, it had been a big improvement from the street.

That night had been the first time he truly slept. Prior to his base, he'd only slept a few hours at a time, and never stayed still for more than twenty minutes when he was awake. He'd been on the move constantly. He also didn't travel in a direct path. He didn't know why he'd been handcuffed to a bed in the hospital, but if cops tried to keep him put, it was in his best interest to keep mobile.

It wasn't hard to keep his movements random and erratic, because he didn't really have anywhere in particular he was trying to get to. So all he had to do was get away from the hospital or other areas he might be found. At first he'd thought to stay in the less populated areas of the city, and tried to move for the outskirts. It wasn't until he hit the Chicago suburbs that he realized his mistake.

He'd been stupid. In the middle of a crowd, dirty and smelly as he might be, he could blend in. Sure, in a lineup he'd be outed at once, but it was really hard to find one particular tree in the middle of a forest even if it was a different type of tree. However, the moment he was in a more casual environment, he stuck out in a very bad way. Among the more put-together crowd, he drew whispers and attention. That had been stupid. He'd fixed it soon enough and learned to never be more of an outsider than he could help.

What had been worse than the cold and the hiding was the hunger. He'd been able to deal with it for a while. He'd pushed his growling stomach away and ran, always moving. However, after the fourth day the hunger had gotten bad, and he rarely got the chance to drink anything. Sure, there were public buildings that had bathrooms and water fountains, but to really quench a thirst he would have to stay put—to stop moving—and he couldn't do that.

Then had come the coffee place. He hadn't fully understood transactions at first, but he knew enough to know he didn't have anything to trade for the food others had on them. His first theft had been a pair of blueberry muffins that had been placed on the counter of a coffee place. He'd only walked in the place to use the bathroom and wash himself at least a little. However, then he'd smelled the food.

He hadn't really intended to do anything about it, and had merely acted on instinct. As the person who had ordered the muffins went to pay for them, the boy ran up and swept the muffins into his pockets. It was hardly a subtle movement and instantly people had begun shouting and threatening to call the police. So he'd ran again, faster and faster. He had to lay low the rest of that day, hiding in an old sewer drain.

However, he *could* lay low, because he had the food. It was really good food too, not a bit burnt or moldy. They'd tasted wonderful. Even weeks later if he screwed his eyes shut, he could recall the smell of the pastry and blueberries.

When he'd been out the next day, an entire muffin left in his pocket, he'd seen a girl walking down the other side of the street. There was little remarkable about this girl, truth be told. It was pretty apparent she was a tourist because she often looked around, confused and lost. She also kept referring to her map frequently.

Of course, *he'd* been lost and confused at first too, but that hadn't lasted long. Once he'd been somewhere before, he remembered it. There was never a need for him to try and focus on where he was or where he was going. What fascinated him about the girl was that she had been carrying an empty plastic bottle with her, and tossed it into the trash. He'd seen a couple of these bottles around, but he'd never found an easy way to get his hands on one, but this seemed so perfect that it made him suspicious.

He'd taken a risk and staked out the trashcan for a couple hours, looking around for anyone that might suspect he would go after the bottle. But he could find no evidence that it was a trick. So, quick as a flash, he'd ran to the can and shifted through the paper and bags until he'd found it. Then he stashed the bottle and ran off, going twelve blocks before stopping and examining his gift. This was perfect; this made so much sense. He could carry the water and food *with* him when he was traveling now. This would allow him to go days without stopping if he wanted to, and it would be easy enough to find sources of water to fill the bottle as needed.

That night he'd discovered a new problem: freezing temperatures. He'd woken one morning to find that his bottle of precious water had frozen solid. That had taken a while to solve but eventually he found that by sleeping on top of the bottle, his body temperature kept the liquid from freezing into ice on cold nights.

So he kept moving. With food in his system and now able to carry water with him, he didn't have to stop at all. He could evade anyone that might be following him. He never actually saw anyone tail him. But if there *were* someone following him, he was sure they couldn't keep up: not without giving themselves away. Then a few days later he'd come upon his base, and he'd finally been able to sleep. It was a glorious day the next morning, with his mind sharp and his body able.

Sure, he was still a little hungry and smelly, but it was a step in the right direction. Food had been his next focus. This was a little bit harder because there was no clean answer for it. Unlike the water, he couldn't walk into just any building and get some food. He'd discovered some places that helped feed the homeless, like him. He'd tried a place like that once, but it had taken hours for him to get the food and it was too risky to be out in the open that long. So, he'd started foraging and stealing.

Honestly, it wasn't all that hard to do. He learned how to find those people who weren't paying attention, or families who seemed likely to throw away at least a little food. He found some bakeries threw out what he would've considered to be perfectly good food. Soon he was well-off enough that starving to death wasn't an immediate concern. That had been the first real step: survive. It had been harder than he'd thought it would've been, but he had managed it.

There had been mistakes of course—stupid mistakes—mistakes he made because he didn't know better. But he learned, and he made sure to never repeat the same mistake twice. He thought fast, he learned, and he adapted. Eventually, he'd found a way to make another big change to his home, which was a source of water. That one had been a little tricky for a while, but he eventually got his hands on a rain barrel. By siphoning water from the surrounding buildings a little at a time, he managed to store some in his little barrel.

This had helped when he felt things were risky because he could afford to stay inside all day if he had to. He could stay inside for a few days even, especially if he had a stash of food. It wasn't long before some of the other homeless noticed his success and began to come to him for food and water that they needed. While the boy made sure to never reveal his base to them, he did share his extra food and information with the others when he had some to spare. This didn't help some of the homeless: the gamblers and the drinkers for instance. But for those who were just trying to get by like him, things got just a little better.

So for a long, long time, the boy listened and learned. He learned about all sorts of things. He learned about jobs and laws. He learned about money and banks. He learned about shops and services. He learned so much that he thought even his brain might explode from all the knowledge he was soaking up. The lives of the homeless were a veritable stash of information, and if he were kind and talked with them, they would allow him to learn.

Soon, many of the homeless began to help him in other ways too. They sought out things he might need or found good locations for food. It was one of these men who had helped the boy get his water barrel. The man had smiled when the boy had accepted the barrel, and introduced himself as Frank. That had brought about a new problem to the boy: he needed a name.

That caused a morning's headache for him. He had sat outside his base in the May wind, carefully considering the names he'd heard. They were all odd and widely varied. Certain names were more common than others, but just as often someone would have a name that sounded like nothing he'd ever heard before or since. Even a few people he'd met were named for items or brands. So he picked through many of these names and tried to put them together in new ways. Many of these combinations were discarded instantly as unpleasant sounding. As he continued, he wished he had a pencil and paper to make his list. Instead he had to settle for viewing all the names in his mind. It worked in the end, but he still wished he could've physically seen the names instead of just keeping all the ideas in his mind. After twenty minutes, he went over the names he'd assembled and not discarded in his head.

Harold Norris
Steven Parker
Luca Varda
Conner Michaels

The last one made him pause for a bit. It was a combination of the names of two of the doctors he'd seen in the hospital, and there was a certain appeal in using their names for his own purposes. The names were close to what he wanted, but still not quite right. He switched the first and last name and considered it for a long moment.

"Michael Conners," he said aloud, letting the name roll off his tongue as the sound hit his ears. "My name's Michael Conners..."

It reverberated slightly and sent a soft wave of pleasure through him. This pleased him and he smiled to himself. Michael Conners it was then. Satisfied, he mentally began to think to himself in third person as an excuse to use his name and grow familiar with it. It wasn't that the name was anything especially fantastic, but it was his. That fact made it special to him. Michael leaned against the brick wall and reached into the pockets of his extremely worn jeans, and pulled out his key.

In the months since he'd fled the hospital, he'd examined this key dozens of times. Sometimes he even went to sleep examining it, as if it would suddenly reveal information about its use. Michael assumed that it must be some sort of safety deposit box or apartment key, but of course he couldn't remember what it belonged to. Still, he liked to hold the key when he was thinking hard about something. It became a calming ritual to him, as if holding a greater mystery over all the peculiarities of his life put them in a greater perspective.

Michael had also grown to appreciate his mind. It didn't take him long to understand he just thought faster and in greater detail than many others did. He did his best to hide that. He couldn't deny that it could be a good tool in a bad spot. He came to understand most people thought themselves smarter than the people that surrounded them. If he let them believe that, they would never suspect him.

Before long, he realized there were certain rituals that helped him think, and long walks along a familiar route had come to be high up on the list. Once he knew he would have food, water, and a place to sleep, it was no longer enough to simply survive. He needed more, even if he didn't fully understand what "more" entailed. But the conversations he overheard always hinted of a world far beyond the pieces he knew. There were people out there who studied science and mathematics all day, every day. There were people who built things and solved problems. There were people who had families.

So Michael began to take another walk that morning. He thought to himself while the calming breeze blew across his face and forehead. He began to walk a route that carried him through streets and blocks he was familiar with. He could walk without focusing on where he was going by this point. He never walked the exact same route two days in a row, and he would often double-back or do figure-eights in case someone was trying to tail him. However, he always stayed in a tight enough circle to know where he was. By taking these precautions he could think freely without examining the streets around him.

As he passed by a shop with several watches in a display case, he overhead a group of three boys around his age talking in a low whisper. Curious, Michael softened his footsteps and crept closer, listening carefully.

"…through the back. I don't think they got the cameras there yet," said one of the boys—a large boy with dark skin and a blue jacket.

"Betta than nuffin'," said another boy, a thin one wearing black pants and a white shirt. "We gonna do it or stand out here talkin' smack?"

This amused Michael. These boys were planning some sort of theft. Clearly they thought that it would give them something to trade because Michael couldn't think of any direct use for the watches that would help boys like these. However, at that moment a thought struck him and he peered around the rear of the building they were planning to rob. A quick glance told him all he needed to know. He walked right up to the boys, who stopped talking and glared at him.

"I wouldn't try it if I were you," said Michael, as if discussing something mundane. "They've got security cameras on the back door and front counter."

He pointed out the little black circle on the ceiling. The boys followed his finger and began to examine the other cameras within the store. From their placement it wasn't hard to make an educated guess as to where they pointed, even if Michael couldn't actually see the lens behind the black half-circle.

"Who the fuck asked you?" demanded the boy in the white shirt, poking at him with a boney finger.

"Easy now," said Michael and held up his hands defensively. "I'm just passing on the information. You do with it what you want, eh?"

He already knew it was the boy in blue he had to convince. He was better spoken than the other two, and clearly was the strongest thinker among the three. Michael had instantly understood that if he helped them with this score, he might just be able to manage a step up in the world. It would be the next move beyond survival: advancement.

"It's better than anything you've seen," said the leader to boy in white. "Now shut your mouth and help out."

A couple minutes later, Michael watched as the trio of boys came sprinting out, each with a case containing several expensive-looking watches. Michael sprinted alongside them, and caught up with the leader in a matter of seconds.

"I've got a hideout nearby," he said. "We can wait for the heat to blow over!"

The boy seemed to consider his words for a long moment, then nodded.

"Fine, lead the way."

So, for the first time ever, Michael showed his base to someone else. He welcomed three strangers into his burnt-out little hovel. They set their prizes in a corner and sat down, breathing heavily and examining him. Michael returned their glance. He was still breathing hard himself. It had been a while since he'd run that hard for that long. Still as best he could tell, no one had managed to follow them.

Then the boy with the blue jacket walked up to him and held out his hand. Michael took a second to catch on, then remembered the greeting he'd seen a couple of men give each other, and replicated the gesture with the boy.

"My name is Hunter," said the boy. "This is Flash and Barry. You looking to run with a crew for a while? You clearly know what you're doing a lot better than these clowns do."

Michael nodded, smiling softly to himself. It was time to step up.
"Yeah, I'm in."

Chapter II: Reactions

Michael jogged behind Hunter, Flash, and Barry; pleased that he was able to keep up with the other boys without completely exhausting himself. His supply of food and shelter did far more than provide mere comfort. It gave him strength and energy he hadn't had on the street. Before now, Michael had never really considered the prospect of joining a gang. It had always been about survival. He had contacts, even those he might consider partners in trade, but the idea of pulling jobs with a regular group? That was new to him.

However, now that he had the chance, it made perfect sense. It was a promise they could step up in the world. Survival had been a been a nasty fight for months. He'd made sure to win that fight too, but it had never been enough just to exist. There had to be more: a reason and a purpose to his life. He felt this was the first step.

After they ducked into an alleyway, the trio turned to face him, and began encircling him.

"Don't get me wrong, kid," said Hunter, a soft smirk on his face. "You're smart and I want you with us. But if you're going to roll with us, you're going to have to prove you can take a hit."

As soon as Hunter said it, Michael knew what was going to happen. They were going to attack him. They wouldn't seriously damage him or permanently injure him, but they wanted to test his fighting ability and prove his loyalty.

Very well, he thought. *Come and get me.*

His vision flashed red for a fraction of a second and it was almost as if someone were highlighting points of interest for him.
- *Unguarded left eye: damage would cause limited vision.*
- *Exposed collarbone: easiest bone to break.*
- *Left foot is too far forward: easy to trip and knock over.*

As he glanced at the other two boys, similar weaknesses flashed through his mind. All of this information came to him without conscious effort. It passed through his brain in the span of one long breath. Without knowing where the stance came from or how he knew what he was doing, Michael spread his feet shoulder-width apart and bent his knees slightly. He turned his body sideways and brought his hands up to his face, much like a boxer.

Michael did all of this without thinking about it and didn't even know exactly what he was doing. Rather, his body had acknowledged it was going to have to defend itself and moved practically of its own accord. Michael took another long breath, and Hunter moved forward. Hunter was fast, but sloppy, his stance was far too wide and too open. He choreographed his movements far too much.

As Hunter threw a right hook at him, Michael ducked under the blow and lay a fist in the boy's stomach. The blow connected hard enough to make Hunter drop to his knees, and Michael took advantage of the boy's injury to get the jump on Flash and Barry. Both were staring, distracted by their boss being laid out so quickly. Michael planted a heel kick right in Barry's sternum and heard the boy go down, hard. Flash moved and came at him. The man swung at him with wild haymakers.

Michael blocked the first swing, then the second, and kicked low. His blow caught the boy in the knee and almost forced the joint to bend the wrong way. Flash yelled out in pain and collapsed. It didn't look like he'd be able to return to the fight. Michael turned to Hunter, who had managed to get back to his feet after the first blow.

He ran at Michael again, and led with a flying kick. The blow was strong and quick. Again though, Michael saw it coming seconds before it happened, and side-stepped the blow almost automatically. He took the opportunity to land a strong kick in the small of Hunter's back, and forced the boy into the ground. Barry rose and ran at him. Michael held up his hands but Barry didn't move to punch him, instead he clutched both of Michael's wrists.

Michael felt confident what the next best move was, and leapt up, quickly planting the soles of his shoes on Barry's collarbone. Then he pushed off with the every ounce of strength in his legs, using Barry for leverage. Suddenly, Barry screamed and let go. The boy clutched at the spot in pain and backed away. Michael fell and managed to catch himself before he hit the pavement.

"Enough!" grunted Hunter into the asphalt. "That's enough."

Flash moved over to Barry, and leaned forward to examine the boy's shoulder.

"It's just a sprain," he said, after a long moment. "Nothing's broken or dislocated. You'll be all right."

While they all checked their wounds, Hunter glanced up at Michael, his eyes wide.

"Where'd you learn all the moves there, Jackie Chan?"

Michael shrugged, and decided to answer honestly, "I have no idea."

"Fine," said Hunter, still a little bitter. "We wanted to make sure you could take it, and you can certainly dish it out. You're in."

From that moment on, life changed for Michael. He no longer had to forage for food. Instead, they stole shipments of bread and fruit from stores. They got plenty of food to eat: so much that he had to poop almost everyday. He was filling out too. He was in better shape that he'd been even in the hospital. His chest and arms filled with muscles and he rarely got winded now. He was still lean, but he gained speed and strength. He was able to move faster and think quicker than anyone he knew.

He also learned skills with the gang that he wouldn't have learned himself. He learned how to talk to people and distract them. It was all about the right smile, the right phrase. He learned how to get a target to talk about whatever they were interested in. And while he talked to these people and distracted them, he learned yet more about the world. There was a lot left he still didn't know, but he was beginning to understand how things worked and how they were run.

He learned how to pick pockets, often emptying wallets of those who wore shoes worth hundreds of dollars. He began to learn how to pick locks, the complexity of tumblers and pins, and the finesse of the picks. He learned how to adjust to the delicate instrument in his fingers, and work by feel more than sound. He learned of street contacts and people who printed false legal papers. He even got a driver's license with his new name on it. That was something amazing to him and for a week straight, he feel asleep reading his own name.

Michael also gained a new understanding of legal and illegal, and especially of the police. He learned how quickly they responded to a robbery or theft. He learned which cops might be paid to turn a blind eye to small crimes. He learned which cops liked to punish or threaten those they had power over. He learned a sense of battle, and what it was to fight in a street war.

Michael learned too of those who ran things in the criminal world. He learned of the Italian and Irish mafia, many of whom had been around since the 1920's, and had only gotten more powerful and covert in their dealings. He learned what businesses they ran. He learned that there were things Hunter and the others could *not* do. He learned they would have to pay to run a crime in another gang's territory.

Three months after meeting Hunter, Barry, and Flash, Michael witnessed the most glorious sight he'd seen since leaving the hospital: the library. He knew of the building of course, but he'd never been inside. However, Michael was no longer the dirty, unwashed teenager who was too thin and too unnatural to fit in among the regular civilians. He was a charming, young man: a local Chicagoan and was—as far as anyone knew—a perfectly normal, law-abiding civilian.

So he got a library card and began to learn of many, many things. In fact, he was often up in the middle of night, reading on whatever subject had grabbed his attention. For the next few months, he learned. He learned of connected streets and buildings that left doors unlocked with back exits. He read and memorized maps of the city streets and the subway tracks. He learned so much, that even his mind would often pulse angrily with all the information it received.

Once he was read up on street knowledge, he began to study different things too: mathematics, biology, the basics of psychology, criminal history, electrical circuits and more. He learned so much that Hunter had taken to referring to Michael as a walking encyclopedia. Still, not a one of them could deny the effect it had on the group. They got away with everything, and often it was only because Michael had come up with some idea or remembered some fact that allowed them to act accordingly.

However, after four months with Hunter, as the city moved into autumn, Michael learned something new: the drug trade. Money was still something somewhat new to him, but he knew he didn't have enough of it to afford a house or a car. However, Hunter insisted that drugs were where real money was made, especially for people like them. So, Michael had agreed they should jump into the trade, and Hunter had found them a supplier for marijuana.

Unable to stifle his own curiosity, Michael had tried to smoke some himself the first night Hunter and the others passed a joint around. The result was a coughing fit that left his innards sore and burning, and an unpleasant fog settled over his thoughts. He'd immediately rejected any and all future offers of the substance. However, it couldn't be denied the the drug was lucrative. He couldn't help a nagging feeling in the back of his mind every time they did a deal.

He tried to tell himself it was just a fight or flight response, but deep down he knew that wasn't the case. Something about what they were doing didn't sit well with him. He pushed the feeling deep down and buried it. This was what he had to do. Besides, their customers were choosing to buy the drugs. It wasn't like they were forced or coerced.

That said, there was a danger in dealing drugs, primarily from rival gangs. Hunter said they should have guns on them at all times, especially during a deal. Barry and Flash were big fans of the weapons, but Michael didn't like it. The black metal felt like a knife that slowly dug its way deeper and deeper into his back. However strong his denial about the drugs might be, Michael couldn't help but admit guns really did only one thing, and it wasn't a thing he liked to think about. Even so, he couldn't deny the logic in making sure they had the guns on them. After all, the people they often dealt with had guns of their own, and there was no sense in crippling themselves.

His stubbornness and self-assurance died on the twenty-eighth day of October, as Hunter slammed a duffle bag on the table in front of the gang. Curious, Michael peered inside, and saw what appeared to be several white bricks wrapped in cling wrap. Then he realized what the bricks were.

"Cocaine," Michael said, more to himself than the others, but Hunter responded all the same.

"That's right," said Hunter, his mouth spread in a wide grin. "Time for the big league boys. Devinci's boys are trusting us for a drop and I think you should handle this one, Michael."

"I don't think so," said Michael, and hastily backed away from the cocaine as much as he could without actually getting to his feet.

"Oh?" asked Hunter, and his voice grew dangerously low. "Think you're above that stuff, huh? Well, let me point this out, smartass: you're only where you are now because of our wheeling and dealing. You've got the friendliest face of all of us and I don't want to spook this dude. Besides, we'll be covering you from the street. It'll be easy fucking peasy. So put the damn skirt away and do this."

There was nothing else for it, however much Michael disliked it. Hunter was their leader, and when he got angry like this, no one dared disagree with him. Michael nodded dismally and mentally groaned. It wasn't the first time he'd considered striking out on his own, and the impulse returned in force. However, he wasn't sure how well he'd be able to hide from Hunter. The police were one thing. They always had bigger fish to fry, but Michael doubted Hunter would be so easy to duck. Moreover, Hunter knew the way Michael liked to move and hide. He could find Michael if he needed to.

"Right," Michael said, forcing a smile. "No problem."

~*~

That night, Michael stood in a small, open area between a group of buildings with three different exits. He marked each one in his mind's eye, just in case he would need to get out quickly. The buyer was supposed to meet them at half-past eleven. Michael glanced at his watch, it was three minutes until the meeting time. That was cutting it pretty fine.

Michael was dressed in his baggy jeans and large hoodie. Frankly, they felt ridiculous, but the extra room made it easy to hide things... like the nine millimeter pistol resting in the waistband... and the brick of cocaine in his right pant leg... which they were selling for twenty-four thousand dollars.

Maybe they won't come, he thought, half-hoping. *Maybe they changed their mind.*

Against his hopes, a sleek, dark blue car rolled up and a man exited. He wore a fine suit and a hat that shadowed his face. Michael felt his heart rate jump up, and could hear it *thudding* hard in his ears. Another man in a dark outfit flanked him. One glance at this second man told Michael that he was armed and prepared to shoot if need be. Michael swore he felt the gun in his waistband grow slightly heavier.

"You from the Hunter?" asked the suited man, in a low voice.

"I am," said Michael, even as his voice stuck in his throat. "You have something for me?"

The man nodded and reached down. He pulled out a thick stack of hundred-dollar bills held together by a money clip. He tossed the clip to Michael, who quickly flipped through it. He pretended to count it while he tried to remain calm. After he finished flipping through the bills, Michael tucked the money into his pants pocket and pulled the cocaine out. His eyes flicked to the large man in black. As the man in the suit took the cocaine, Michael reached behind him. His hand grazed the handle of his pistol. His heart was pounding so loud he was amazed the man in the suit couldn't hear it.

However, as the man examined the brick, Michael heard a sudden noise behind him. A soft metal *clink*. Without thinking, he spun around and saw a dark figure up on the fire escape. The figure was bent down with one arm extended towards him, as if they were aiming. Michael's mind screamed danger at him and without thinking or asking questions, he moved. Quick as he could, he unearthed the gun and firing a warning shot at the figure.

Bang!

It wasn't until the sound of the shot echoed into the street that he saw the figure in fuller detail. The dark figure had been shadowed by the lit window behind him. Now he saw they were small... very small: child-sized. Michael saw the blonde hair and blue eyes of a small kid ten or eleven years old at the most. Then he saw the kid slowly reach up and grab his chest, where Michael's warning shot had clearly been *too* accurate, and blood began seeping from the boy's chest.

Then, the child crumpled and no one moved for a full second. In that second, which seemed to stretch on for years, Michael had one, singular thought run through his mind.

I just killed a child.

Chapter III: Rebirth

Michael froze for one full second. For one second the world stopped turning and nothing made sense. Then everything came crashing down on him as if he'd been hit with a sledgehammer. It was hard to breathe—hard to think. It was *impossible* to stay still. So he ran. Michael ran as hard and as fast as he could. He sprinted right into the main street and down the sidewalk. He stashed his gun and the money under his clothes without even thinking about it. He could hear Hunter yelling at him as he ran but the words didn't make sense.

Michael couldn't think. Because he couldn't think, he couldn't reason or find a solution. So he did the only thing he could and ran. He ran and ran and ran. He ran until his lungs felt like they would burst. His legs stung and he was covered in sweat. Yet still, he ran. Somehow, he felt everything that had just happened would catch him if he stopped, and he didn't know what would happen then. Would it break him? Would it kill him?

His brain physically hurt, and reminded him forcibly of the moment when he'd first woken in the hospital. He moved through the streets until his body hurt from all the running. Yet he knew pain, and could push through it. So, he kept running. He ran faster and farther than he ever had before. He ran right out of the part of the city that he knew.

He found himself among the towering skyscrapers and surrounded by people in suits and designer clothing. He saw shops that had bright, open doors with better cameras than those where he lived. He saw hotels that boasted bellhops and shining floors. He saw things he'd never known the city held, and finally collapsed against a wall. He fell to the ground and gasped for air while his lungs burned. His heart pounded so loud he couldn't even hear the people around him. However, the run had done one thing. He could think, at least one idea at time.

He'd killed a kid. Maybe not on purpose, but he *was* a killer. He threw his hand in his pocket and fingered his pistol… He saw the child from the alleyway collapse over and over in his mind's eye. His face began to sting painfully, and Michael thought it curious. While the October air was cool, it was a long way from cold and he'd lived through harsher weather. He reached up and rubbed his face only to feel the tears running down his face.

He was crying... that was new. He hadn't cried for as long as he could recall. Sure, things had been difficult but he hadn't ever been hit by something that made him cry. Crying was a waste of time and emotions. At least, that's what he'd told himself. However, now he realized he'd never been touched by what was happening to him. He'd fought to survive, of course, but it had never hurt him emotionally. Becoming a murderer though... that struck him in a way he had no words for.

So he acknowledged his tears and allowed them to became sorrow, and the sorrow turned slowly into despair. Looking around, Michael ducked into a smaller alleyway to hide while he wept. Now that he'd stopped moving, the tears were allowed. They wouldn't stop. So he stayed... for hours he thought. He wept and reflected.

The gun pressed against his waist and seemed to grow heavier and heavier until Michael pulled it out and examined it. He knew the gun intimately. He'd studied it and learned every piece of it. Michael had worked with it so often that he could assemble the weapon practically blindfolded. He'd become a decent shot, could feel every nook and cranny of the weapon, and could've recited the serial number that had been filed off from memory.

This thing was a dangerous device. It was as if he'd never really seen the weapon in his life. Yet it was the gun that had killed a kid; Michael had done that. So why shouldn't he pay for it? He lifted the barrel of the pistol to his temple. The cool metal felt more like a kiss than a threat. For the first time since the botched deal, his mind relaxed.

This... this felt right, and yet *that* thought made him pause. Killing himself might serve a sort of poetic justice, but more than that it would be peaceful. That appealed to him: the idea that things would stop and calm down after all the despair. However, there was another thought that held him back.

Shouldn't peace of mind be earned?

After what Michael had done, he certainly hadn't earned the right to peace. He had no idea *how* one earned personal or moral amnesty after the murder of a child, but it wasn't by running, hiding, or committing suicide.

So his mind began to formulate the beginnings of a plan. It put a fire in him that he didn't know could exist. It gave him a purpose. However it might be done, Michael knew he'd have to earn his peace of mind before he killed himself. That was the ultimate goal, and the only ending that seemed fitting. However when his time came, Michael swore that he would've at least made his best effort to balance his scales.

Purpose pulsating through his mind, he carefully wiped the prints off his gun and dropped it in a nearby dumpster. He was done crying, but that didn't mean he would forget what had happened. He also couldn't go back to his old home, not without being properly prepared. That would have to wait. For now he needed to calculate, theorize, and plan.

Michael decided to sleep in the ally that evening. He shook and shivered throughout the night. It bothered him that even the meager chill of the night got to him. He'd been through far worse than the mild wind before. His pampered lifestyle and proper base had made him soft... made him weak. However, he wasn't hungry and he had money: quite a lot of money, actually.

That was something. If he was going to stay in a strange place, he had to blend in. While his dirty clothes might've been fine for the slums, this part of the city didn't indulge in the same simplicity. And so, the first part of his plan fell into place.

- *Step 1: Get new clothes.*

Michael told himself that would be enough to start with. It was the beginning of a plan and a purpose. So he could rest. Still, he had nightmares filled with the sound of a child's scream and a pair of blue eyes that would never see the world again. When he woke up, he found he was crying again, and his lip was bloody. He must've bitten it in his sleep by accident.

Michael growled and wiped away the tears and blood.

Stop this! he growled at himself. *Pitying yourself isn't going to do any good. So suck it up!*

Navigating his way through the unfamiliar streets, he found a clothing store and purchased a few items. His new jeans were a classic straight fit, but after all his time in baggy clothing, they felt oddly tight. Still, the store clerk assured him they were a good fit. Then he bought a set of dull shirts. With a little luck, they would help hide dirt when he wasn't able to wash them. The shoes took a little time to settle on. He spent some time considering what he wanted to buy and settled on a pair of black converse with a white sole, providing a nice contrast in colors. They were comfortable but provided a nice grip and he could wear them all day without issue. Finally, as he was preparing to check out, he spotted something else.

It was a long trench coat, all black with red lining. It was very unlike anything he'd worn before, but he liked that. Plus, with such a long coat he could hide things if he wanted to. Now that his jeans weren't really suitable for the task, it seemed fitting to get a replacement. After paying a price that was ten times the cost of his previous wardrobe, he head back into the city.

To his pleasure, his new clothes were perfectly suitable. They were different enough that he didn't feel completely consumed by the crowd, but no one gave him a second glance either. After picking up some basic hygiene products, he found a park with a public shower and quickly cleaned himself. Even he wasn't daring enough to stay in a public shower a second longer than he had to.

After he brushed his teeth, Michael pulled out the razor and scissors. Michael knew that he hadn't really intended to rob Hunter or their benefactor when he'd run off with the money, but he had done it all the same. So, it would be best to change his appearance at least a little. So he cut the sides of hair shorter, re-styling the bangs to hang to the right. Finally, he carefully began to shave the scuff he'd gained on the street.

However, when he encountered his chin, he encountered a problem. Unlike his cheeks and neck, the angle of his chin was awkward and sharp. He tried to approach the problem from a few angles and ended up nicking himself twice. Persistence won out in the end, and he examined his look in the mirror. It was certainly different, but he had to admit that he liked it.

Michael cleaned up the mess of hair and products as best he could before he head towards the nearest library. While he'd grown accustom to his old library, he knew he wouldn't be able to go back anytime soon. Besides, this library would allow him access to a computer, and thus the Internet.

It took him a lot longer to understand the computer than he would've liked, but he also wasn't in much of a hurry to act. Due to the money, he could afford to lay low for a while now, and food wasn't a concern. He'd argued with himself over the prospect of renting a hotel room. In the end he decided against it because if he did, he'd quickly drain what cash he had on hand. There was no telling how much he'd need. It was best not to waste it on simple comfort.

Michael spent four hours on the computer that afternoon. A few people glanced at him every now and then, but no one seemed overly concerned with the loner obsessing over a computer. When he came to understand how to use a search engine, it took a lot of self-control not to get distracted and search everything he could think of. He managed to restrict himself to searching for answers to only his most immediate issues.

After his time in the alley he had come to a decision on what he really wanted to do. Working against the police had led him down the path that had killed a child. So he had to move in what was logically the opposite direction, and start enforcing the law. If he were diligent and not a little lucky, he might be able to help stop people like himself from hurting others.

However, this brought a complication of its own. The idea of becoming a policeman had some appeal, but it was grueling process and while his fake ID was pretty good, he still needed a lot of other illegal work done before he could do something as risky as trying to fool a cop with his credentials.

He would've needed a top-class forger for a social security number, birth certificate, and likely some proof of residence in the city. While he had some of that already, it would only fool a casual observer, and would not stand up to the high level of scrutiny that the police would put it under. It was an awful lot of paperwork to find in good quality. Michael may have had a decent amount of money, but good forgeries were extremely expensive. All of that aside, Michael didn't feel good about breaking the law to uphold it, even if he *could* find someone to do the forgery work without Hunter.

Options considerably limited, Michael decided to try his luck at getting a private investigator's license. It wasn't exactly the height of justice he'd been hoping for, but it was a good way to get started, and he could get a pulse on Chicago from a different side of the law. So after he came to understand the search engine a little better, Michael had found a small list of companies he could apply at. The library had even been kind enough to print out the results for him. They did charge the slightly insulting rate of a quarter per page, but it wasn't as if he had an alternative.

Michael spent the next two hours trying his best to gain a grasp of the differing laws on the country, state, county, and city levels. He certainly didn't have the time to memorize all the laws that existed on any of these tiers. However he had a decent grasp of the basics, and had a fair idea of where a private detective's line was drawn, legally speaking. He made a silent vow to himself to use the Internet again for his personal inquiries at a later date and closed his window. While he had sheets on several different agencies, the first thing he pulled out was a set of maps of the city.

The sight of the map brought the stymieing realization of just how large the city was. Of course, he'd recently discovered how one might be able to get lost within its limits, but he'd underestimated the true size of the place. Still, that would work to his advantage. Big cities made it possible to disappear. Every corner had needs. He would be able to work practically anywhere in a city as large as this one.

Michael poured over his list before pulling out a pen and scratching out several names. Upon further investigation, Michael had discovered that many firms primarily dealt with things like infidelity or frau. That was all good and well for them, but it wasn't the type of work Michael wanted to do. A cheating spouse didn't lead to drug deals or dead children, at least not usually.

Hope thus gained, Michael hailed a cab down. Never having done so before, it took a little observation to understand the process by which one determined if a cab was free and hailed down. Once he did though, he managed to flag a yellow car down and climbed in back.

"Where to?" asked the cabbie, disinterested.

Michael gave him address of the first firm he'd selected and the cabbie sped off. From the moment they moved away from the curb, Michael was grateful he had never attempted to drive. The physical movements seemed complexly interlinked and difficult to fully grasp without a clear view of the man's hands and feet. However, that was child's play compared to the way the driver weaved in and out of the traffic. He treated signs, lights, signals, and even the presence of other drivers as mere suggestions as he took the route to Conners' destination.

When the hellish journey finally came to an end, Michael felt his legs shake so violently he feared he would be unable to walk. He hastily paid the man before fleeing the car, which he now feared more than any gun he'd seen. Once there was solid concrete beneath his feet again it took more than a little effort to find the right address. Very few of the buildings were kind enough to provide something as significant as an address plate around their door. So he eventually resorted to knocking on doors to receive the addresses of the place. After a half-hour of trial and error, he found the right building and walked in.

His first impression of the place was instant displeasure. Most of the walls, floors, and ceilings were white and the place featured glass desks. While he supposed it gave the place a definitive style, it reminded Michael far too much of the hospital. As soon as that connection was made, he couldn't slip it. He wanted very much to run and escape the place. However, soon his logic triumphed over his panic. He began to breathe deeply to help slow down his accelerated heart rate.

Michael walked up to the main desk, behind which hung a large sign with the company's name emblazoned on it in golden, fancy letters.

Jackson and Prewitt: Justice and Fairness

Jackson and Prewitt had been the nearest company that hadn't been focused solely on boring cases. As such, it was his first hope of helping people. Michael walked in and saw several people wearing suits and ties and became very self-conscious of his converse shoes and t-shirt. On the street, no one seemed too concerned with his clothing. However in this place, he stuck out like an undercover cop attempting to infiltrate a high school.

"Hi there," said the receptionist, a pretty blonde girl with brown eyes and a small mole above her left eyebrow. "Welcome to Jackson and Prewitt. How can we assist you?"

"I'm here to apply as a private investigator," said Michael, trying to sound calm and collected.

She looked him up and down and Michael could see suspicion in her eyes. He had to exhibit a lot of self-control to resist the urge to growl at her. Still, he managed to hold his tongue and she eventually passed him a clipboard and several papers. The first two pages were entirely personal information, but luckily Michael perfectly remembered "his" social security number and address from the moment he'd been given it.

The next six pages were a sort of personality tester and tested basic understanding of the law. After about forty minutes, Michael returned the clipboard to the receptionist and smiled softly at her. She smiled back at him. After barely glancing at his information, she leaned forward as if to whisper something confidential.

"Look, Mister Conners. We appreciate you coming in today, but Jackson and Prewitt are looking for a... *certain* type of employee and we just don't feel you would be a good fit."

It took all Michael had not to yell at her. What exactly was the point of even letting him try and apply if they were just going to shut him down anyway? Instead of snapping at her, Michael slowly began multiplying numbers in his head. Simple mathematics were a concept he could keep focus on when he was growing angry. He found that focusing on the numbers helped keep his mind clear and his eyes dry. A few seconds later, he was calm, and he turned to the woman who was still smiling her sickeningly sweet smile at him.

"Your loss," was all he said before smirking slightly and heading out the door.

As he hit the street corner, he pulled out his stack of papers and crossed off Jackson and Prewitt. It was disheartening, but by no means a final straw. There were still a fair number of names on his list and he felt sure one of them would have him. They *had* to, or he could never set things right.

Chapter IV: Knighthawk Investigations

Michael did his best to approach the situation with all the optimism as he could muster. After all, Jackson and Prewitt was only one business. There were plenty of others. Only, his next would-be employer—Luca Vire—let him go with the vague promise to call if they wanted him. That sounded kind, but the tone in his voice made it plain he had no intention of hiring Michael. The next firm went just as poorly, as did the one after that, and the one after *that*.

His list of potential employers shrank rapidly. Michael walked to the next place and tried to keep positive. It different from the others, even at first glance. While many of the other businesses looked like major offices or had a floor rented out, this was a small hole-in-the-wall place. It looked like it might've been a firehouse once upon a time. However, it had clearly not been used as one in over a hundred years. It had an attached garage that would only hold a singular car, but the door was far taller than even the pickup trucks Michael had seen on the streets.

The building was made of brick and the old lettering on the window was beginning to peel and had faded somewhat. Even from outside, Michael could see that most of the main room was taken up by a collection of ten or so filing cabinets and a singular desk, which held several papers and files. A lone figure sat at the desk, hunched over his work. From this view, the man was little more than a shadowy figure, but somehow his presence demanded attention.

Halloween had come and gone, and the chilly November air had moved in. It left the streets cold and rough. As such, the office fireplace was roaring with a comfortable-looking glow that was to the man's back. It further accentuated his shadowy outline. A little afraid at the sight of this shadow of a man, Michael knocked twice on the door, unable to locate a doorbell.

"Door's open," came a slightly gruff voice.

Michael opened the door and stepped inside. As soon as he was across the threshold, he allowed himself a proper look around the office. Its interior matched the outside in that it seemed far less impressive than the other firms, but Michael found that he liked it better. This looked like a place where order and procedure came second to the work. The firm's owner—William Scott—had supposedly solved a great number of missing persons and murder cases alongside the Chicago Police.

Michael sat across the desk from him in a squeaky swivel chair that sank slightly under his weight. William was bent over a notepad and had written several pages of notes. Michael could only presume that they were in relation to a case the man was working on. The old man did not stop writing or look up at him. Michael took a moment to examine him in closer detail too. The website had not offered a photo of the man, but somehow he looked different than Michael had imagined.

William wore a blue, plaid button-up with a pair of sturdy jeans and brown, worn work boots. His shirt was clean but wrinkled, and seemed several years old. Physically, William was a bit of an oddity. He was a white man in his fifties or early sixties, with finger-length white hair and a thick, powerful mustache which came to the edge of his mouth. He was very thin, but something in his posture suggested he might've been able to charge right through a wall if he were so inclined.

The pistol at his hip was a revolver, and the holster was very worn, but bore the unmistakable style of a policeman's belt. The private detective badge that hung around his neck was old, baring several dings and dents. There was a cup of green tea to the right of the stack of papers that had begun to grow cold, and all the furniture in the room looked at least as old if not older than the man's clothes.

"So, what you here for?" asked William, still not looking up from his notepad.

"You're William Scott?" Michael asked, more as a confirmation than an actual question.

"Bill," said the old man and glanced up at him for the first time. "Call me Bill. I wasn't expecting anyone today."

"No sir… Bill. My name is Michael Conners. I was hoping to get a job as a private investigator."

The scratching of the pen stopped and Bill looked up properly, fully examining Michael. His examination was not cold, but it pierced right through Michael, as if the old man somehow could read minds.

"Why here?" he asked. "Plenty of places in the city to get a career started. Why here?"

"Well," said Michael as he tried to think of how to best phrase the issue. "Most of the places in the city are just small-time stuff:

people want proof someone's cheating, or that someone fudged some paperwork. I want to actually do something that matters."

Bill nodded.

"You wanna be a hero? Stop the bad guys?"

Michael shook his head and mentally rejected any description of himself as a "good guy."

"I want to…" he sighed and decided to put his cards on the table. "I want to help make things less shit. People get hurt and die out there. I can't stop it—not all of it. But I have to do something. I think this may be the best way to do it. Cops are bogged down with rules and red tape. I'm not after fame or a big paycheck. I just want to make things a little less shit if I can. Will you let me have a shot or not?"

Bill smiled and took a long drink of his tea. After too-long a pause, he set it down and looked Michael in the eyes.

"What exactly do you think I'm doing, son?"

That shocked Michael. Bill was unlike the other firm leaders and was testing his personality face-to-face, not with some standard test or series of questions.

"So, you want to make things a bit better…" said Bill matter-of-factly. "All right. I'll admit it's a little naive, but well-intentioned. I've done more with less. You have a P.I. license?"

"Not yet," said Michael. "Studying to get one now."

"Fair answer. What other obligations take up your time? You have a girlfriend? Family?"

"No. I'm a loner."

It was mostly the truth, even if he'd omitted a detail or two.

"What hours would you want?"

"Whatever hours you'll have me," said Michael. "I'm not here for a forty-hour work week and retirement plan. If I can help, I want to help."

Bill nodded.

"What do you believe, spiritually?"

That stopped him for a long moment.

"I'm sorry?"

"Do you believe in God?"

Michael thought back, unable to fully understand the question. He'd heard a few of the homeless talk about God, either to curse him or beg him in equal measure. He'd personally chalked it up to mental illness, never as something to seriously consider. However, Bill did not seem to be an insane man. Maybe he was a bit curt, but he seemed perfectly sensible and logical. Why would Bill put stock in Michael's belief or unbelief in this God?

"I don't," said Michael as he studied the man's face.

To his credit, Bill didn't seem disappointed or angry. Rather he seemed solidly resigned, as if he were accepting something he'd already suspected but hoped wasn't true.

"Very well, Conners. Grab a stack of the forms from the bottom drawer there. I'll take you on as a shadow until you get licensed. You get on my bad side or go against what I tell you and I'll kick you to the curb. I'd prefer that you believed, but I don't need to agree with your spirituality to work with you. But until you have half an idea what you're doing, it's my way: no highway. We clear?"

"Crystal, sir."

Michael went to grab the forms from the drawer Bill indicated.

"First rule," said Bill as Michael managed to get the drawer open. "Don't call me sir. It's Bill. I don't like liars or bootlickers. You want to get on my good side? Work hard and be capable. If you're lazy or incompetent, you can go elsewhere. So if we're not with a client, suspect, or cop, don't be afraid to ask questions. If you don't want to learn I can't use you."

Michael nodded and began filling out the forms and paperwork while Bill returned to his own files. Being that there was no obligatory personality tests, Michael finished the work fairly quickly. When he handed the paperwork to Bill, the old man examined it for a long moment.

"All right. While I type a bit, go ahead and sort these files into the cabinet over there alphabetically: last name first."

He handed Michael a tall stack of files with names written on the tabs. Michael immediately went to work. He moved to the nearest cabinet and couldn't help but grow slightly excited at the prospect of work. Bill began typing on a laptop. He occasionally checked his entries against Michael's paperwork and that made Michael nervous. Bill might not be as thorough as the police, but Michael had no idea how well his fake documents would stand up to a deeper look.

Still he did his best to push the worries out of his head and began sorting the files. After all, worrying about what Bill might or might not find wouldn't help him in any way. So he had better just to do the work and put it out of his head. After about an hour, Bill stood up and Michael finished with his files.

Bill opened a desk drawer and pulled out a silver badge with the number seven edged into it and tossed it to Michael. He caught it deftly and took two long seconds to examine the badge. It seemed oddly intimate to have a badge number that referred to him and only him. He clipped it to his belt and looked up at Bill.

"All right then," Bill said shortly. "Let's get to work. We've got an alleged hit-and-run down in Naperville. There's an officer who contacted me and asked if I wouldn't mind taking a second look. You do what I tell you, we'll get along great. All right, Conners?"

"All right, Bill."

Bill led him to the garage where an old, slightly beat-up truck sat. Conners climbed into the passenger's seat and took a quick moment to look around the cabin before Bill climbed in. The thing that most quickly caught his attention was a picture tacked to the dashboard above the radio. It featured someone who Michael could only assume was a younger Bill and a woman with long, dark hair. They were holding one another and smiling on a pier. They looked fairly happy. Although something was a little... wrong with the woman's smile. It seemed slightly chilling, as if her eyes were sending out ice beams that infected his bones.

Bill climbed into the cabin and Michael turned his gaze to the windshield, mentally preparing for the crazy journey he'd suffered at the hands of the cabbies earlier that day. Bill started the truck up, and Michael was greeted by a kind of music he'd never heard before. He found he was surprised by Bill yet again. While the man occasionally would pull suddenly into a lane or make a turn quickly, his driving was comparably sensible. His route seemed concise, and Bill was always sure to be in the appropriate lane a good amount of time before his turn. Michael had to admit it impressed him to see the difference in this man's maneuvers compared to the cab drivers he'd met earlier that day.

Throughout the majority of the drive Bill didn't speak, and Michael did not break the silence. Rather he took the opportunity to examine their route and the city around him. He watched, fascinated as the skyscrapers gave way to yards and family homes. It was actually very difficult for him to connect his mental picture of the streets and neighborhoods with their corresponding lines on his map of the city. On the map, a street was a simple black line. In reality, that black line had homes and shops attached to it. The city was just too large for his scope of the world.

What bugged him was that Chicago was also a very small piece of the state, and an even smaller piece of the world beyond. He couldn't recall every country he'd read about, but America was supposed to be a very large one. That considered, he had seen a map of the United States and Chicago wasn't even a dot on it. He'd found out where it would've been by comparing state maps to their country counterparts, but it bugged him to think that the small piece of the world he knew was nothing to the city, which was nothing to the country at large. It made his life seem somehow smaller than he would've liked.

As they pulled off of the interstate and started to resume something closer to a sensible driving speed, Bill turned the radio down for the first time since starting up the car. Michael made a mental note of some of the tunes he'd heard so that he might be able to determine the artist at a later point in time. The music was strangely pleasant. He'd heard music before of course, but he'd never really cared much for what he'd heard. However, this music was far more enjoyable and Michael hoped to hear more of it if he got the chance.

"All right," said Bill in a firm tone. "Unless I tell you to do otherwise, keep your mouth shut. We were invited here, but a lot of these guys can be hard-up, and there's no point in making things more difficult than they have to be. Got me?"

Michael nodded and Bill seemed to accept it. They pulled up to where a cop car and two officers stood, blocking off the road. As Bill stopped right in front of the officers, Michael unconsciously sunk deeper into his seat, wishing he had the ability to become invisible. Despite his logical mind, part of him feared these cops would somehow know what he'd done and would shoot him down then and there.

Each of the officers came up to one of their windows, and Michael got a clear look at them. They were both males. The first had faded brown hair and a mustache, though it was nowhere as powerful as Bill's facial hair was. He had a slightly tired look to him and there was a slouch in his posture that became permanent for older men. While his face bore wrinkles and lines, Michael would've guessed the man was in his late forties or early fifties. However, his eyes were dark and dulled from years of working on the force.

His companion was still fairly young, likely in his mid-twenties. He had dark hair and a bright wedding band shown on his finger, glinting in the light of the setting sun. His clothing and badge were still new, much like Michael's was. It made him feel a little less uneasy… but only just a little.

The younger officer tapped on the window and Michael obligingly rolled it down. As he did he caught the name *J. Hooper* on the man's nameplate.

"Sorry there," said the younger cop. "The street's closed off, folks. Got a hit-and-run down the road here. Afraid you're going to have to find a way around."

"It's all right, Hooper," said the older cop, who then turn and addressed Bill. "How you doing Scott?"

"Oh hanging on still," said Bill, smiling slightly. "How about you Dole? See you've got a new pup to follow you around."

"Yeah," said Dole. "Kid's fresh out of the academy. Still a little too green to know if he'll measure up, but he's trying. What's with yours?"

"New student," said Bill, jabbing a thumb at Conners. "Hoping he'll be able to show you how it's done when I finally retire."

"Yeah, you'll retire when hell freezes over," Dole said, laughing. "Kid got a name?"

Bill nodded to Michael, and he pulled out his license. Without objection, he handed it to Officer Hooper.

"Michael Conners," he said, trying to sound more confident than he felt.

Hooper examined his ID for a long moment before handing it back to him, and nodding at Dole.

"All right," said Dole. "Scene's down the road a little way; can't miss it. Don't break your boy too badly now, all right?"

"Please," said Bill, putting the truck into gear. "Gimme a month and my boy will dance circles around yours."

"I'll take that bet," said Dole, and he smiled as he waved Bill forward.

Michael waited until they were safely past the men before he turned to Bill.

"How do you know that man?" he asked.

"We worked together occasionally back when I was a cop," said Bill. "He's a decent man: one of the only ones I worked with. Half the time I got along with him better than my own partner. He's the one who asked me to have a look at this case. We don't officially work for the state, but you know enough of the right people and they'll let you have a look and say your piece. Sometimes that's enough."

"And if it's not enough?"

"You find ways to make peace with it."

Michael said nothing to that, merely logged away the information he'd received.

- Bill had been a policeman and still had good standing with at least one of the officers: Officer Dole.
- Officer Dole's new partner was Officer Hooper.
- Both now knew Michael's face and name.

He could handle that. This could work.

Chapter V: Driving Her Crazy

The first thing Michael noticed when they pulled up to the crime scene was the stench. Death had a defined scent to it. As they approached the scene, he gagged involuntarily. The overpowering smell drowned out any hint of life in the area. Death carried an aura along with its stench. Likely, there was something deep in human DNA that knew to flee from whatever had caused death to preserve itself. However, Bill and now he were to be defiers of evolution, and they head straight towards the greatest arenas of danger they could find.

"Our victim was Larry Kurtz," said Bill, snapping Michael out of his musings. "His widow is named Betty. We'll have to talk to her in a bit, but I want to get a look at what's going on here first."

Bill pulled his truck over and Michael half-stepped, half-fell out of the truck and got down on his hands and knees as he heaved horribly. He'd been on the street for nearly eight months. So he was no stranger to bad smells and rotting meat, but even his stomach churned at the stench.

"If you're gonna puke, make sure it's not near the body," said Bill, crouching down by the form of an older man who lay prone in the ditch. "Then clean up and come over here."

Michael took a moment, and managed to save a little face by keeping his food down before he made his way over to Bill.

"You all right there, princess?" asked Bill as he smirked at Michael.

"I'm good," Michael said, hoping he sounded more confident than he felt.

"Good, now take a better look," said Bill and he handed the younger man a pair of latex gloves. "What do you see?"

Michael took a long breath, and moved forward to examine the body in closer detail. While he looked, he did his best to think of the facts clinically instead of emotionally. The man's chest was caved in, causing several of the ribs to break and even protrude through the skin in places. He was covered in bruises and lacerations, including a particularly deep cut in the palm of his left hand. He as getting on in age, likely in his seventies or eighties; the damage made it hard to be sure.

Michael turned to examine the road and noted the absence of streetlights. If the accident had happened in the early hours of the morning, it was quite possible a driver wouldn't have seen the victim until the damage had already been done. The dead man wasn't wearing any sort of bright or reflective clothing. Additionally, several tiny shards of glass lay in the street. He didn't really know what to make of those.

"Hit-and-run," he said to Bill.

"You sure?" asked Bill.

Michael paused for a long moment. Bill didn't seem reproachful, or even as if he were warning Michael. Rather Bill seemed to want him to explain his thought; so he did. He explained the injuries and lack of streetlights. All while he talked, Bill listened. He allowed Conners to complete his thoughts without intrusion. Finally when he'd finished, Bill nodded a few times before speaking slowly.

"Not too bad. You've missed a lot too."

"How so?" asked Michael, trying not to sound defensive.

"For starters, the glass there is from a windshield. They make windshields out of safety glass so that it can break into several pieces without being likely to penetrate the skin. Keeps from causing too much damage in an accident."

"So? Isn't that consistent with a hit-and-run?"

"Yes and no. Yes, you're likely to find *some* glass if the windshield shattered. However, not only would our body in far worse shape, but most of the glass would've smashed *into* the cabin of the car, not out into the street. In a proper car accident, the car stops all at once and momentum carries the shards forward. For this, the car wouldn't have stopped unless the driver hit the brakes, and that likely wouldn't leave so much of the glass behind."

Michael examined the glass pieces on the road. There likely wouldn't be enough for an entire windshield, but there were still quite a lot of pieces.

"Plus there's the question of the cut on his hand. See how it's a lot deeper than the others?"

Michael nodded.

"Says it happened some other way to me, and I don't believe the universe it so lazy as to give me too much of a coincidence."

Michael examined the injury again, and again was forced to concede that Bill was right.

"Also, you've missed something that *isn't* here: tire tracks. Most people who were going to hit a pedestrian would slam the brakes, even if it were too late to stop. Our guy was hit clean through and through. There's something more to this."

"So what's the next step?" asked Michael.

"We need to talk to his widow. Police like her for this because his health insurance payout just went way up, and she's his beneficiary."

"They're thinking payout for motive. You don't agree?"

"Oh the motive's clean enough," said Bill and he opened the driver's door of his truck. "But I don't like the means. Think about it. If you lived with someone, you'd have ample chance to kill them. She could've poisoned him, switched medications up, stabbed him in his sleep, anything. She waited until he was walking down the road and ran him over? Doesn't fit well."

Michael nodded, seeing the logic in Bill's concerns. Not for the first time that day, Michael was forced to admit he wasn't quite as clever as he thought he was. However, that didn't mean he couldn't learn. So, he stuck close to Bill and went over the information they'd gathered so far.

About five minutes down the road, Bill parked in front of a yellow house with grey shudders and a red door. The place looked nice enough to Michael; somehow he'd expected the house to be… darker. Of course before it had become the house of a widow, it had been the house of Larry and Betty Kurtz, married couple. Bill walked in front of him while they traveled up the driveway. The little garden near the door was well-maintained, and boasted a small collection of flowers, though as none were in bloom he couldn't have hazarded a guess to what type. As they neared the porch, a man in a cheap, blue suit exited the house.

This man was around Bill's age, if not a touch older, and had white hair that was back from his temples. His face was clean-shaven and his green eyes had a steely look to them that made Michael feel uncomfortable.

"Scott," the other man greeted Bill scornfully. "Wasn't aware I'd asked for you on this one."

"Oh?" Bill began, feigning an innocence. "I wasn't aware I wasn't supposed to wait until you called. Well, that's just terribly rude of me and terribly inconvenient for you, unless you've actually learned how to do your job. Unfortunately, if I waited for you to realize you needed me before I got involved, your closure rate would suffer."

Michael was caught between the desire to laugh at Bill's jabs and complete astonishment at his goading of the man. True, Michael hadn't dealt with police properly, but he never would've thought to provoke them like this.

"Shove it Scott," said the policeman. "Not like I need you for this one anyway. Wife's getting half-a-million for the vic. Her car's smashed to shit and his blood's all over the hood. The D.A. will make this in an hour, piece of cake."

"Ah," said Bill, still seeming completely unconcerned. "Well, if it's all wrapped up, I suppose there's no harm in us taking a look around. Unless you're afraid that you've missed something."

The policeman scowled.

"Look all you want, but if you or your boy mess up my evidence, I'll nail you to the wall."

Bill grinned, and opened the door before turning and nodding to the cop.

"I always did miss the sweet talk."

Bill entered the house and Michael followed closely behind. They had walked into a living room that looked like it had been built and furnished in the eighties and had stubbornly resisted any and all change ever since. The television was a twenty-inch boxed monstrosity that still had an antenna atop it, and the rug was so old Michael was surprised it didn't send up puffs of smoke when it was stepped on.

Bill turned his attention to an elderly woman sitting on an old, green couch with a box of tissues in front of her on the coffee table. Her eyes were red and puffy and she looked disheveled and unkempt. It was clear she hadn't made an effort to keep up appearances. Bill sat down next to her on the couch, and Michael could feel a new energy radiating from Bill. Where he usually exuded power and control, he gave off the air of an elderly man in the park as he approached her. Despite the pistol at his hip and his earlier impression, Conners wondered if his perception of Bill hadn't been totally wrong. As he watched the couple seconds of interaction, he realized it was that Bill had somehow softened his very presence around the widow.

"Hello Missus Kurtz. My name is Bill Scott, and this is Michael Conners."

"I already told the other policeman everything I know," objected Betty, the sharp tone in her voice unmistakable. "You just won't believe me, but I'd never hurt Larry."

"No ma'am," said Bill. "I'm a private detective. I'm here because I believe you didn't kill your husband."

She looked up at Bill with watery eyes, and Michael saw a glimmer of hope in her.

"I'm sorry… Mister Scott, was it?"

"Bill, please," he said as he took her hand. "Betty, I want to help you, but I need you to answer a few questions for me first, ok?"

Betty nodded and Bill pulled a small notepad out of his shirt pocket. With a slow intake of breath, he looked down at the information he'd scribbled upon it.

"You increased life-insurance policy on your husband lately? Is that right?"

"Yes detective," she said. "But I swear I didn't kill him."

Bill nodded reassuringly.

"I believe you. Just need to make sure I have the facts right. What made you decide to change the policy?"

"Well… Larry had taken to going out with his poker buddies again lately. I don't normally like him to go out because all they do is drink until way too late, and he always insists that it will be fine, you know? It's just that he comes home so late that I worry when he's out there. I think about our sons, too. We don't have much money left. So, I told him if he wouldn't stop going out, I'd change the policy… just in case something happened. Honestly, I was hoping it would just help keep him home. I didn't really think…"

"I understand," said Bill. "Did you hear anything strange last night? Perhaps about the time Larry would normally get back home?"

"Actually, yes," said Betty and her eyes lit up slightly. "I do remember hearing a racket in the garage around that time. That wasn't all that strange, truth be told. Raccoons like to get into the bins, you know?"

"Right," said Bill and he quickly scribbled something on his notepad. "You said he goes out with his poker friends. This happen at someone's house?"

"Yes sir," she said. "I told the cops too: Harold Cartman. He lives up the street and my husband plays with him on Sunday and Tuesday nights. I hate him being out like that. I told him he shouldn't."

Bill nodded again, scribbling down the name.

"All right Betty, we'll need to talk to Harold and take a look at your car for a moment. Do you know Harold's address?"

She gave him the street and number, and Bill scribbled it down before motioning to Michael to follow him. Michael hopped up from his chair and moved with Bill out of the house and to the garage.

"She heard a noise in the garage, gets accused of a hit-and-run, and didn't think anything of it?" asked Michael, stunned.

"You'd be amazed at what people are willing to overlook, Conners. The number of times I would ask people to be on the lookout and they would not think twice about someone creeping around a house still infuriates me. A lot of crimes would be prevented if people were a little more suspicious. Then again, I suppose you can go too far and be the nosy neighbor that calls the cops over a car parked on 'your' side of the street."

"People really do that?"

"All the time. I started to keep track of those calls when I was a beat cop because it was funny at the time. I lost count of how many times I got that call somewhere in the forties."

"That's just... unbelievable."

"Truth is very often stranger than fiction, Conners."

Michael nodded a little, and tried to wrap his head around everything.

"So you think Larry was drunk when he died?" asked Michael.

"Probably. The police will get a report when the coroner is finished, but we won't have to wait for that if we check up on Harold, I'm betting."

"Shouldn't the cops be checking in on him too? Betty said she mentioned him."

"They should, yeah. But sadly I know that bastard we ran into—Gerald Stilts—and he's more concerned about closing cases than being right. We were detectives in the same precinct back in the late seventies or early eighties. Rising up in the ranks sometimes requires you to play ball and rub shoulders with certain people. Stilts was willing to play ball and I wasn't. Eventually, he made sergeant and not too late after that I had a fight with my partner and left the department. Stilts and I never saw eye-to-eye. I wanted to help people and he wanted to look like he was doing his job."

"What happened to your partner?"

"He… had a good mind but was too glued to the letter of the law. We had a case where morality and legality butted heads; you'll find a few of those. I did what I felt was right, and he couldn't deal with it. We came to blows over it. Never spoke to me again. I quit within the week to start up private practice. Stilts took him under his wing after that. Stilts always was an opportunist bastard."

"Well," said Michael, smiling a little. "Glad you can be civil with him now instead of pissing him off."

"Always find a way to enjoy what you do, Conners."

"You never tried to speak to your partner again?"

"Looked him up a time or two. He's a lieutenant, last I looked. But old men can be really stubborn about closed doors, kid."

They entered the garage through a side door, and Michael felt around for a light switch. After a few idle slaps, he found one and flipped it on. As a soft light filled the garage, Michael instantly saw the large piece of evidence the police must've been convinced by. It was a four-door luxury vehicle sitting in the middle of the room, and its windshield was in a thousand broken pieces. Many of the shattered glass pieces still hung there, loosely connected, but most of them were missing. Michael felt confident that if one were able to recover all the pieces from the road, the windshield could've been put together like an absurd murder puzzle. The idea made him slightly excited at the challenge of it, but he reigned the impulse in. After all, he already had one difficult puzzle in place.

"Let's go have a look at the hood," said Bill.

"The hood? I thought you said the glass would be smashed into the compartment?"

"It should be, but I'm betting that whoever smashed the windshield did it by standing on the hood and striking down at it with a bat or golf club."

Michael nodded and together they walked to the car. As they peered at the blue coating, it wasn't too difficult to make out the black shoe marks on the edge of the car. What was also evident was that there was a bit of blood on the hood, and Michael had little doubt it would match Larry's.

"So they smashed the windshield, gathered up the glass, and left it at the scene?" asked Michael. "Why would they do that?"

"To frame the wife," said Bill, rubbing his great mustache. "What bothers me is 'who' more than the why. The door and windows haven't been forced. The cops might be selectively blind but even they wouldn't ignore that."

Nevertheless, they double-checked the doors and windows. As Bill mentioned, they were still in good shape. They piled into Bill's truck and drove up the street to Harold Cartman's house. It was only a few blocks away, but if Larry had been drunk, Michael imagined it would've been a very difficult journey on foot.

Instead of knocking on the door, Bill went immediately to the car, which was parked outside of the garage. Bill bent down over the grill and hood and nodded, pulling out his cellphone.

"Hey Dole, it's Bill. Yeah listen, you should send someone down to Harold Cartman's place to arrest him. He's the hit-and-run on Larry Kurtz. Larry convinced Harold to help kill him to frame his wife for raising the insurance policy."

Bill talked for a short while afterwards, giving the address and specific pieces of information that would be needed to help Dole close the case. Then, he shut the cellphone and motioned to Michael.

"So, case closed?" asked Michael.

"Almost," said Bill. "How did I work out what happened?"

Michael smiled, grateful that he was given the chance to learn and improve instead of just being dragged along without any clue of what it was he was doing. He examined the front of the car as Bill had. It didn't have any blood on it, but there were several points where the coating on the car had been worn away, as if stripped down slightly. It took Michael a couple minutes to understand, but eventually he caught on.

"He's been cleaning the front of his car," said Michael. "But he hasn't been using the right soaps and has been scrubbing vigorously. So he's stripped some of the coating away by accident. So, *Harold* ran over Larry, and helped frame Betty."

"Good. And…"

"And Harold shouldn't have any real reason to want Betty in trouble, even if he *did* have a reason to want Larry dead—which it doesn't seem he did. However, with Betty changing the life insurance policy around, Larry had a reason to be really pissed at his wife. So, if he got drunk enough to hatch a really stupid plan…"

"Then Harold might be convinced to help out for a bit of a payoff, and it wasn't as if Larry was concerned about leaving money behind for his wife anymore. Besides, they were already playing poker. It'd be easy enough to disguise a payoff as a particularly lucrative poker streak."

"That's… impressive Bill."

"Don't worry," said Bill, smiling at him. "You'll pick it up soon enough, Conners."

"One thing I still don't understand though," said Michael. "Why give credit to the police? I mean, you basically solved this thing solo. Why give them the credit?"

"A couple different reasons," said Bill. "One: it's far easier to operate if people don't know who you are. If you get put in the paper too often, it's not good for a low profile. Two: if they get the credit for it, we sometimes get paid as consultants. The pay isn't enough for steak every night, but it's enough to help get by. Three: if you let the cops have the glory, they're more likely to let you loop in on future cases. If you're a glory-hog they'll try to shut you out so they can save face."

Michael nodded, thinking over what Bill had said.

"So it's all about solving the cases?"

"It's about helping people. Come on, Conners. We've got paperwork to do."

Chapter VI: Question the Stars

Within a week of working with Bill, "Michael" was a name that he all but forgot. He was "Conners" day in and day out. Truth be told, Conners came to appreciate hearing his last name over his first. It added a layer of formality and respect when they met with police or clients. Yet when Bill used it, the name seemed to be akin to a term of endearment. Bill wasn't exactly a sensitive man. In fact to an outsider, Bill could often seem cold or gruff.

However, after seeing the man almost every day the past week, Conners had come to understand Bill a little better. Bill wasn't an unemotional or unfeeling man, rather he was very internal. He didn't display his thoughts or emotions and often took time to think before bringing something up. In fact, Conners was under the impression that Bill almost never said anything without giving it some careful consideration. That was interesting, because Bill was possibly the first person Conners had met that liked to think as much as he did. During his time on the streets, Conners had assumed most people thought like he did. Time revealed that to be untrue. He considered the chance his injury had affected him and changed his thought pattern, but without remembering how he used to think it was impossible to reach a conclusion.

Regardless of the cause, Bill was a man who thought and was careful, just like him. It was a relief he didn't know he'd needed.

Once Bill had come to understand the way Conners thought and worked, a few of the walls between them had come down. Bill started to show Conners how he worked through evidence and testimonies. He also started to allow Conners to theorize with him, and this was a gift Conners held in high esteem. Being allowed into Bill's inner thoughts was like being permitted to access to a sacred resource, and needed to be treated as such.

Speaking of sacred resources, Bill had been particularly generous where his treatment with Conners was concerned. True, Bill didn't pay him much, but he always paid promptly without any issue or protest. However, once he discovered Conners had no home, the old man had cleared away a space in the storage area above the office for him. He'd supplied Conners with a second-hand mattress and a small desk for paperwork. The far kinder gift was the aging computer Bill had turned on and connected to the Internet for him.

The Internet was easily the height of luxury for Conners. It was information unending literally at the tips of his fingers. So a routine was quickly established; Conners would work with Bill from eight in the morning until six in the evening and the two would part while Conners would research whatever he took interest in, all the while listening to textbooks on tape that would help him with the private detective licensing test. Honestly, studying for the test was easy. Once Conners had heard something and paid attention, he could recall it as needed.

What aroused far more interest was the wide wealth of information on the Internet. At first, much of it seemed conflicting, and he quickly learned to verify anything he found that seemed suspect. However, he came to understand much of what he'd been lacking during his time on the streets.

As soon as Bill paid him for his first week of work, Michael used the money to buy another set of clothes and food for his little space in the flat above the office. He'd also signed up for a gym membership that offered a monthly fee. Truthfully, he had little interest in working out, but the opportunity to improve his cardio would be welcome. What he really relished was a way to shower and clean himself, and for ten bucks a month it was a hard bargain to beat.

Not everything in his new work life was bliss and upgrades. Conners soon found a part of detective work that he did not enjoy: paperwork. The stacks of files seemed to be unending, and they had to sign statements for everything. They had to confirm what they'd seen, what they'd touched, what they hadn't touched, where they'd been, where they hadn't, and much else besides.

"Honestly, it's not normally this bad," Bill had said as Conners signed off on one of the many papers. "It's always worse if it's an open case. For cold cases or closed ones you take pro-bono, there's very little to write out, if anything."

"We gonna have to sit this out in court?" asked Conners, gesturing to his statement for their first case together.

"I doubt it," said Bill. "At least I certainly hope not. Hate going to court proceedings; could never stick my head up my ass for that long. Figured that's half of why lawyers charge so much. Honestly, the D.A. doesn't usually care to bring someone like us in. Private detectives aren't as credible as policemen, and the cops don't like admitting they needed help on the case. So they're more likely to just take credit for anything you find. Works out better for both sides, honestly."

Bill stretched and looked up at the clock. Seeing it was past two in the afternoon he stood.

"Come on, Conners. Let's grab some coffee."

Conners smirked at Bill, standing up from the small desk Bill had cleared for him.

"You asking me on a date, boss?"

"Very funny. Don't be a smartass."

"I'm just saying, you're taking me out to a coffee place. I assume you're paying for the overpriced drinks. I mean, if you're expecting me to put out, I'm sorry to tell you I'm not that kind of gal."

Bill rolled his eyes.

"It's good to learn about one another. There's tons I still need to teach you. Plus, if I can get you to shut up for a few seconds, I think you have the makings of a decent detective in you."

That did make Conners go silent for a moment. When he next spoke, it was quiet but he knew Bill could hear him.

"Thanks."

Bill didn't speak again throughout the entire walk to the coffee place. It was commonplace for him to be silent for long periods of time, and so Conners didn't interrupt. However, as they were walking back towards the office with two large cups of coffee, Bill suddenly spoke out again, as if the long pause between them had never happened.

"You never did tell me," said Bill.

"Tell you what?" asked Conners, feeling his heartbeat speed up unrelated to the caffeine in his system.

Bill sighed.

"Serving on the force for as long as I did lets you in on a few things. You get some extra senses. I can just feel when a driver is carrying a gun long before I see it, I know by looking in someone's eyes whether they're liars, and I know when I'm looking at someone who's killed before."

That made Conners' heart stop cold.

"I… I don't…"

"Don't bother lying," said Bill. "I've watched you for a week, Conners. If you were a serial killer or a sicko I wouldn't have put up with you. Still, if we're going to keep going, I do need to know what happened."

Conners considered lying, or changing events, but already knew it would do no good. The fact was Bill was very good at what he did, and if there was any chance of salvaging this relationship, he would have to be honest. So he told Bill about everything. He didn't hold anything back or conceal his history… at least any of it that he knew. All the while, Bill stood silent, listening intently. The old man's face betrayed nothing, and his steely gaze burnt a hole into Conners' head.

He explained the cocaine deal, his accidental shooting, and his desires to fix something in the world. He was even prepared to explain his plan to kill himself, but Bill didn't seem to need to hear it. He placed a hand on Conners' shoulder.

"I'm glad you told me," he said kindly. Then his face grew hard. "I took you on because I believe you're a decent person. I believe you when you say it was an accident and that you mean to do whatever might be done to set things right. However, let me make one thing clear: You hurt another kid—ever—and I'll kill you myself. Got me?"

Conners nodded. It was firm, but hardly unfair.

"Crystal, Bill."

"Good. Then we don't need to talk about this again."

Bill climbed into his truck and Conners followed him. For a long while, neither spoke as Bill drove straight through the city traffic. Eventually Bill broke the silence.

"You were honest with me about your past, and that deserves some recognition. You could've lied to me, or tried to at least. So, I'll return that respect. Firstly, I always knew you weren't who you said you were."

Conners felt his heart turn to ice for a moment, and then logic caught up with him. If Bill meant to turn him in for it, he would've done so already. He took a long breath and tried to calm down a little, even if it didn't help much.

"Your license isn't horrible, but a decent background check quickly reveals that it wasn't actually printed by the state. Only teenagers, undercover law enforcement, and criminals use fake ID. Since you look to be in your early twenties, that took out the first; and I very much doubted the second. Meant it wasn't a hard guess. I took you on because I believe you when you say you want to make things a little better. I can teach you the techniques and how to think, but I can't teach you compassion or morals."

"If morals are a prerequisite of the job, I think I'm disqualified," said Conners softly.

"I don't think so," said Bill, though he didn't elaborate. "I'm getting older now, I had a wife for about a year. The divorce was quick and nasty. My wife of all of four months really came out of her shell with a string of affairs. I tried everything I could think of: counseling, prayer, limiting exposure, and others. Nothing really took for more than a couple weeks. After a while, I knew that even though I loved her, I could never end up raising kids with her."

"Did you ever have children?" asked Conners, curious.

"No, no. I always wanted a little girl, but by the time we had a home ready, the affairs had begun and afterwards… Well, things never lined up right, I guess. She still contacts me every once in a while: Kelsey, my ex-wife. I always tell myself I won't answer when she calls, but it's hard to completely cut out someone you loved, however screwed up they might be."

Conners thought through what Bill had said. As far as he could recall, he'd never really had someone in his life that he loved. Sure, it was possible that he'd loved someone before the hospital, but he still couldn't recall anything from that point of his life. He did understand the science of love well enough and had read countless articles about the illogical responses love would cause in people. That didn't stop the shock that someone as smart as Bill could fall to something like sentiment.

"Now, we've got a cult out in the sticks I want to look into. Supposedly, several non-believers are getting shocked to death when they attend. Allegedly not a crime, but I've been a firm believer in the smell test, and this don't pass it by a mile."

Conners nodded softly, trying to shift his focus in thought to the current case.

"Who's our client on this?" he asked.

"We are," said Bill. "If you see something wrong, Conners, don't wait to be asked to fix it. Just fix it."

That had perhaps been the biggest change in the time he'd been working with Bill: moral understanding. At first it seemed like a confusing and unrelated set of rules to him. However, as time passed he'd began to understand the center focus of all Bill's morals. Bill didn't hold the law of the government as a priority, but rather the protection and care of the average citizen. It didn't matter to Bill if someone smoked weed, but he would be furious if someone was a drunk driver. It was a slow process, but Conners was starting to understand it: just a little bit.

As Bill drove on, Conners quickly found himself moving out of the parts of the city that he knew and was familiar with. However due to his studying of the maps, he understood roughly where they were and where they were heading. Bill drove on, stopping only to gas up the truck and for some dinner from a gas station. Conners actually appreciated Bill's dog-like determination where casework was concerned. It meant they didn't waste time or have long, uncomfortable moments.

Bill insisted he wasn't a great teacher, but Conners privately disagreed. Bill had a method of teaching that resonated with him. Bill would often let Conners try his hand at something first, and then correct him where he was mistaken or heading down a wrong path. The result was that he quickly picked up on the key work of investigation, and rarely had to be taught the same thing twice.

As they drove on and on, the tall buildings and skyscrapers gave way to homes and suburbs. These in turn gave way to open country and tall fields along the highway. At first, the high driving speeds had scared Conners, and he'd maintained a death-like grip on the sides of his seat. However, once they were out of the main city, he found that the unending horizon of the country made their speed feel far more reasonable.

Soon, the sun had disappeared from the sky and Conners looked up, stunned by the sight of the open night sky. Within the confines of the city, he'd seen the moon and plenty of stars. That was horribly inadequate preparation for the millions of stars he could see now. It made the night sky less of a dark blanket and more of a canvas for millions of little lights. The night sky was a painting that would've costed an artist several years of their life. He felt himself seized by a strange desire to sleep out under the beautiful sky and examine the stars for hours. He also found that no matter how he tried, he was unable to fully commit the stars to memory. There were simply too many and their placement was too erratic to recall perfectly. Yet in that chaos and randomness, there was also a beauty and a desire within him. What exactly the longing was he couldn't have said, but it was more sincere than anything he'd ever felt.

"Never seen the night sky like this?" asked Bill, suddenly drawing Conners out of all his musings.

"No," said Conners, softly. "I never knew there were so many stars. How many are there?"

"No one's sure," said Bill. "Scientists aren't even sure that the universe has a definite end to it, as of yet."

"I'm sorry?"

"Some theorize the universe just... keeps going."

"Until what?"

"That's just it. There is no 'until.' It just is."

Conners tried to wrap his head around that idea, and found it impossible. Sure, he logically understood what infinite meant. However, that was very different *understanding* infinity. Somehow his brain just couldn't fully grasp the concept of no beginning and no end. Everything started somewhere and went until there was no more of it, didn't it? Sure some things could be frighteningly huge. He could grasp the idea of millions of planets and stars. Even if that would be incredibly vast, it was still a finite amount of space. However, the idea that the universe might not end... That was a scary thought.

Conners couldn't explain why the idea of unending space was scary. Perhaps it was because it introduced the idea of impossibilities in an otherwise possible universe. Life was complicated, he had no delusions about that, but everything he'd seen was possible. An incredibly complex system allowed his heart to pump blood through his body and carry oxygen to his brain so that he could think and survive. That was complicated, but he could grasp it. However, infinity: no start and no end, that was beyond complicated. It was impossible. Yet, some who had spent their whole lives to the study of that universe theorized that it was, in fact, the truth—despite its impossibility.

So, Conners did the only thing he could ever think to do when his mind couldn't solve something. He let the thought go and tried to immerse himself in the moment. It was far more difficult than he figured it should be, but it was possible. The sky, not yet black, provided a soft blue background to the millions of lights. He knew many stars were so far away that humans would likely never get near them, regardless of how good technology got. He'd considered the possibility of life on other planets once before, but the idea of it quickly got way too complicated to realistically theorize with. Sure, logically it was possible that another single-celled organism had landed on another lump of rock or water, and had evolved over time. However, earth had been built on such an incredibly fragile set of circumstances that Conners had no clue if it would've been possible to replicate that on other worlds.

"Do you believe in life on other planets?" Conners asked, somewhat suddenly.

However, Bill didn't look at him askance or even consider the question for any great length of time.

"Nope," he said, simply. "The bible teaches that as humans we are children of God. To me, aliens wouldn't fit in with that and I'm not sure has an answer. As such, that's the conclusion I draw, but a lot of people argue over it. All-in-all, I don't really concern myself with it. I focus on what I can change and try to change it for the better."

Conners nodded, considering Bill's words. The idea of just doing what he could made a sort of sense. Still in the back of his mind he couldn't let go of those queries of the impossible.

Chapter VII: Sheep to Slaughter

Conners didn't know exactly when he'd drifted off to sleep. However, when he woke up, he saw that Bill had stopped driving and the night sky had gone from blue to black. Dazed, he looked over at the dim green light of the clock displayed on the truck's radio. It was ten minutes to midnight. He stretched and glanced around, slightly confused. They were in a parking lot that had roughly thirty cars in it, and Conners could see no people or building for the owners of the cars to have vanished into. Bill chuckled at Conners' confusion.

"Where'd everyone go?" he asked, indicating Conners should try his hand at deduction.

Conners nodded and hopped out of the truck, rubbing the sleep from his eyes and looking around. He forced his sluggish brain to focus and work as it was supposed to.

"It's possible but not practical that a bus or shuttle would've picked them all up from this spot."

"Good. Why not?" asked Bill, standing by the truck.

"There'd be no reason for a bunch of people to drive to the middle of nowhere and then get picked up to drive somewhere else. We're not near any gas station or any city or town, so far as I can see."

"Correct."

"Since this certainly isn't a community parking space, there is something specific about this spot. The ground here is also concrete, not gravel. So there was a bit of money that went into this."

"Very good. So what do you see?"

Conners took a long look around and saw nothing that stuck out to him. However, what did catch his eye was the truck with lifted suspension in the middle of the lot. He studied it for a long moment. It would've been very hard to climb into that truck, even for a young man like him. Drawn more by curiosity and impulse, Conners inspected the large vehicle. What surprised him was that it looked as if the truck hadn't moved recently. There were no signs of earth or dirt in the tires and the entire vehicle was stone cold, as if it hadn't moved for a long time. Sure, part of that was the November night, but it went beyond the simple surrounding cold. Conners had a sneaking suspicion that the truck hadn't been moved in several months at least.

Curious, he tried all the doors and found they were locked. So, he crouched down under the truck, which really only required him to bend a little, and examined the ground beneath it. To his surprise, he saw a round hole about three feet in diameter directly under the truck. He quickly moved out from under the vehicle and called out to Bill.

"I found a sort of manhole under the truck. It's literally an underground group."

"Very good," said Bill. "You're learning. Now, let's go see how this whole thing works."

Bill reached into his glove box and rummaged around for a long second before walking over to Conners and holding something out to him. Conners reached out on instinct and froze as he realized Bill had handed him a pistol. Bill was sporting the same revolver Conners had seen when he'd met the old man.

"Bill," said Conners nervously. "I can't… I mean… Not after…"

Bill silenced him with a look.

"I get why you don't want to," he said, solidly. "But you need to do this, Conners. You're one of those blessed with intelligence and ability. If this is where you want to apply those abilities, you're going to end up coming under fire sooner or later. Not every cop has to fire their gun in the line of duty, but they all carry one."

Conners shook a little, but nodded and took the pistol. It was a Glock .43, with a six-round magazine. Conners slowly felt along the edges and ridges of the gun, familiarizing himself with the safety and magazine release. Then Bill handed him two spare magazines, which Conners placed in his right coat pocket. It helped slightly counterbalance the immense weight of the pistol in his left chest pocket. He'd worked out what the deep pocket in the coat was for ages ago, but he'd never intended to actually use that pocket for a gun. He couldn't help but feel the heavy thud of the metal weapon against his chest with every step he took.

More out of instinct than anything else, Conners tried to recall the gun's serial number from touch, only to realize that the weapon didn't have one.

"No serial number?" he asked.

"If you ever *do* have to kill someone again—and I hope you don't—you can wipe the gun and ditch it if you have to. Not a nice thought but it's always better to be prepared. However, that being said, don't pull it out unless you mean to shoot, and don't shoot unless you need to."

Conners nodded while his heart *thudded* painfully in his chest. Bill went down the manhole first, and Conners could tell there was a ladder from the way Bill moved. So he climbed down after him without hesitation. It was strange, but he would've sworn he could hear some sort of strange crackling as they descended the ladder. However, he couldn't locate the source of the sound, and wondered if he wasn't just hearing things.

As they reached the bottom, Conners half-expected to hit a sewer tunnel and filthy water. However, they stepped onto the smooth stone floor of a corridor about four feet wide and ten feet long, ending in a tall ornate door. The centerpiece of the door was a large, detailed eye in the center of a triangle. The eye was bright blue, and had a horrible piercing effect, as if Conners were actually being watched by the thing.

"The Eye of Moloch," said Bill softly. "Also called the Eye or Horus or the Eye of Providence by the Freemasons. This is going to be a dangerous one, kid."

Bill knelt down and clasped his hands, praying fervently and quietly. Conners did not interrupt Bill as he prayed, and silently tried to apply his will to Bill's prayers. Conners didn't actually believe in God, but if Bill was concerned then this place was a level of dark not to be trifled with.

Eventually Bill stood, took a deep breath, and knocked on the door three times. Conners could not see any handle, nor did he hear the door unlock or unlatch. However, it slowly swung open, seemingly of its own accord. Conners felt every muscle in his body tense up, preparing to flee as they had no idea how to fight what they were facing.

"Easy kid," said Bill, a slight shakiness in his own voice, before muttering softly. "I am a servant of the divine God of the heavens and earth and I shall have no fear, even though I walk through the valley of the shadow of death."

That sent Conners' fear into high gear. Conners had given little study to religious icons and terms. However, the term "valley of the shadow of death" hardly conjured up pleasant images. As they entered the room, Bill's prayer all but flew out of his head.

They'd entered into something that reminded Conners of the old gladiatorial arenas in ancient Greece, albeit far smaller. Instead of a bunch of citizens of an ancient civilization, they were surrounded by several dozen beings in heavy black cloaks and hoods. Conners looked from person to person, trying to make out any defining characteristics. In the deep shadows of their hoods, each being he laid his eyes upon was interchangeable with the next. They were less people and more silent black guardians of the darkness itself.

Conners felt the blood in his body freeze, as if he'd suddenly dropped into icy-cold waters. He could no longer feel his feet or his hands. He lost control of his movements and stumbled, almost falling twice. He only managed to continue forward by staring at his feet so he could tell when he'd hit the ground. Bill seemed to be virtually unaffected by the horror that had gripped Conners, and he couldn't figure out how the old man was managing it so well.

Then there was a horrible scream and Conners spun on the spot, looking for the source, but saw nothing that seemed to be the cause of the noise. No one else moved or reacted, not even Bill. In fact, Conners got the horrible feeling that he was the only one who heard the scream at all. That thought caused his mind to race. Logic and order quickly gave way to disorder and chaos, and it made him incredibly anxious. The gun in his coat pocket seemed to be growing heavier and heavier, practically dragging him to the ground. He had to remind himself to breathe and could almost hear his heart strain with the effort required to send blood through his body.

A man separated himself from the throng of cloaked and hooded figures, and walked towards them in calm, measured steps. An ornate, golden broach was pinned at his throat and his clothing beneath the cloak was made of fine silk. The man's shoes were leather with a rubber sole. Even at a quick glance, Conners felt sure they would've cost more than most people spent on engagement rings.

"Welcome gentlemen," said the man, spreading his arms wide, as if moving to embrace the whole room. "We are so pleased to receive you. I am called Yusuf. I am the instruments of the gods!"

The man moved forward and actually did embrace Bill.

As they touched, the old man growled, *"Get your hands off me!"*

Yusuf wheeled back as if he'd been burnt by Bill, even holding his own hands in shock. He regarded Bill with a dark glint in his eyes. Instantly, the feeling of cold in the room intensified ten-fold. Conners fell to his knees, unable to keep upright under the oppressive atmosphere. He found himself whispering softly, but wasn't aware of what he said until the words hit his own ears.

"Please... please, let's leave."

Bill did not seem to hear him, and addressed Yusuf.

"How do you kill them?"

"Detective," said Yusuf, as if Bill were a particularly dangerous but valuable animal. "They are merely found unworthy by the gods. I do nothing."

Bill responded, but Conners didn't hear what he said. In fact, for several long moments, he couldn't hear anything at all. His vision was growing darker and darker and the world around him seemed to fade away faster and faster as he tried to hold on to it. His breathing became rapid and short, and it felt like he was no longer in control of his own lungs. Conners fell onto all fours, hitting the metal beneath him hard enough that he heard a hollow reverberation underneath him. He could still feel that same strange *thrum* of energy, but his brain was too paralyzed to connect it to anything.

He heard the scream again, but this time it made sense to him. This was a scream he'd heard over and over again as he lay down to sleep. Without having to turn his head, Conners could see a small blonde child standing in front of him with a bullet-hole in his head. Conners moved away from his vision of the child, more rolling than turning to his side suddenly there was a splitting pain, as if he'd been pierced by a knife. He clutched at the spot but there was no wound.

All at once it felt like his nervous system was set on fire. Everything was gone in the blink of an eye. There was no room, no figure, no sound, no child, only the immense pain and he could do nothing but scream and twist. Conners lost track of time as he writhed and twitched on the floor. He could smell burning but had no idea where or who he was. He was not under an abandoned lot, tracking a killer cult. He was nowhere and he was nothing. Then... for perhaps the very smallest fraction of time, he could see something. There was a vision of a man in front of him. The man had smooth, slicked-back brown hair and stubble on his jaw. His eyes were also brown, though much lighter than his hair, and they were wide... dangerous even.

Suddenly Conners was back, and he was on the cold metal floor, pain ebbing through his entire body. He had to look around for several long seconds to try and understand what had happened. Neither Yusuf, or any of those cloaked figures in the stands seemed to have been affected as he had. However, Bill was also on his back, a pained expression on his face, even as the old man reached for his revolver. Then, a thought occurred to Conners and he glanced back to Yusuf's shoes. Just as he recalled, the man's shoes had thick, rubber soles on them, and suddenly the metal floor and the thrum of energy made sense.

He opened his mouth to call out to Bill, but suddenly found his tongue locked to the roof of his mouth. An icy wave of water, fear, and dread crashed over him. It made him feel as if he were drowning in a dark ocean... He was cold and wet and alone, and there wasn't a single thing he could do about it. A small figure appeared in front of him: a child with blonde hair and blue eyes. Conners felt tears come to his eyes and he tried to speak to the child but the words only came out as a flurry of bubbles.

However, he heard the child's voice, and instantly knew it was the child's, although he'd never heard the boy speak.

"Why did you kill me?"

Conners tried desperately to explain that he hadn't meant to, that it had been an accident, but his pleas went unheard.

"You shot me dead. You are as dark a monster as the ones you're trying to hunt."

Then between them, a small glint of metal appeared. Instinctually, Conners reached out to grasp at the spark of light. His hand grasped the handle of the Glock, which felt pleasantly warm. In the darkness and the wet, Conners examined the gun. Hadn't his plan always been to kill himself in the end? Sooner or later, wasn't all of this work going to come down to this moment anyway? Why shouldn't he get on with it then? What was it he was really waiting for? What penance could be paid for his sins?

He lifted the barrel of the weapon slowly to his temple.

"Is this fair?" asked the boy, coaxing him on.

Conners nodded softly. This was what should be done. He began to slowly tighten his grip on the trigger and then heard an earth-shattering *bang*. For a long moment, he waited to die. However, he was slowly growing warmer and warmer, not colder. The damp and the dark were fading away, replaced by the metal floor and the surrounding cloaked figures. Conners looked around and felt that he was not injured. He shifted and stood and saw Bill pointing his revolver at Yusuf, who was laying on the ground. Blood seeped from a bullet wound in the man's left arm. Several feet away lay a strange remote with a large switch on it.

In that moment the calm broke and all the figures in the stands began to run in different directions, many fleeing the room through the door Conners and Bill had entered. Bill turned and sprinted to Conners as quick as he could while not letting Yusuf out of sight.

"Kid!" he called in a panic as he pulled Conners up. "Kid!"

Conners patted himself down quickly, feeling no puncture wound or injuries. He wiped the tear stains off his face and realized the gun was in his hands. Nervously he nodded.

"I'm not hurt," he said, his voice soft and very shaky. "He's electrified the floor. That's why he's not hurt. His shoes…"

"I know," said Bill. "If your phone still works call the cops and then help me guard the entrance. I'll make sure Yusuf doesn't move."

Conners did as Bill asked and an hour later, local cops showed up to help place any remaining members in cuffs. Most of them had fled when Bill had managed to get a shot off on Yusuf. However, a solid half-dozen were arrested, including Yusuf. Both Conners and Bill were able to give some description of what the cops had to look out for in the future.

Then, they were thoroughly examined by several EMT's. Eventually, they were cleared to leave of their own volition, though were told they should rest for the next few days. After he was left alone, Conners sat next to Bill and spoke softly enough so the local police and EMTs couldn't hear them, still wrapped in a shock blanket.

"I'm sorry, Bill."

"No," said Bill, his own voice slightly croaky. "I'm sorry, kid. I shouldn't have put you through that. You had no way of handling something like that. I *knew* the moment we went down that manhole that there was a demonic energy over the place. You have nothing to apologize for. This was my fault, and mine alone."

Conners had no response to that. Bill might not blame him for what had happened, but Conners didn't agree. He should've seen—

should've been faster on what was going on. Why hadn't he realized it was an electrical current when they'd first seen the room? It should've been obvious. Still, that didn't explain his visions or the panic that had gripped him.

"While we were down there," he started slowly. "I... I saw... things."

"Yusuf was a satanist, Conners. Some of them have the ability to make you see things. What you saw... what you heard... you can't let it take you down or it can consume you. You've earned some rest. I need some too, come to think of it. We'll take a week easy or so. You're going to be all right, ok?"

Conners nodded, but didn't speak. Regardless of what Bill had said, he knew he *couldn't* have had a demonic vision. That would mean demons were real and there was yet more he couldn't control, and he just couldn't accept that. Maybe the electricity had hit a spot in his brain and that combined with the amnesia had caused his visions or something... Hopefully, that was what it was.

Chapter VIII: Lawrence

After helping close down the cult, Conners and Bill had taken a couple days to recover and relax a little... at least as much as either of them was capable of. However, before long they'd gotten back to work. At first, Conners constantly made small mistakes or missed some small detail that connected all the pieces of a case correctly. However, Bill was always patient with him and showed him what he'd missed.

Bill also made sure to give Conners a chance to do better with each new case. And their casework continued to come almost as fast as they could handle it. They handled anything and everything that interested either of them. They handled dozens upon dozens of fraud cases, disappearances, thefts, and of course murders. Time began to run by faster than Conners could've tracked if he'd cared to.

Within a half-year, he'd taken a proper citizenship test and gotten his private detective license. Shortly afterwards, Conners had found a small apartment near the office and taken the space for himself. Case files, written theories, and printed articles lay everywhere in his small apartment. Yet the space lended itself to a strange sort of organization, even if no one besides Conners would ever be able to navigate the mess.

And the work continued.

One thing Conners quickly found himself amazed with was the fact that Bill seemed to personally know someone in every profession, especially where any sort of law enforcement was involved. Bill frequently would call someone who was merely described as an old friend. These old friends included policemen, an F.B.I. agent, a criminal lawyer, a car mechanic, a street informant, a forensics expert, and many others besides. More than once, Bill was on such good terms with someone that they were more eager to help out the old man than they were to deliver the information to their superiors.

Still, Conners had started to earn his own keep with Bill. Being younger and still in good health, Conners could often understand things and see them in greater detail than Bill could. His mind was slightly faster too. While Bill's experience and understanding kept him ahead of Conners during cases, the younger man was closer and closer to falling in step with Bill each time. They both knew it wouldn't be long before Conners was a better case worker, and Bill celebrated the fact, often being eager to help bring him along in his studies.

So, they continued to take work together. Winter came to a close, and spring to replace it, which was quickly replaced by summer. They handled tons of cases then, and Conners even got on a first-name basis with a fair number of the patrolmen. Several of their cases were ones that had long gone cold, or else had convicted someone incorrectly. Many of their activities meant that they ended up talking to or working with policemen. Luckily, Bill was an expert negotiator and no one was particularly eager to make trouble for someone who was making them look good.

Bill and Conners almost never received public credit for their part in the casework, which neither particularly minded. Honestly, it was less hassle to let someone else deal with the courtroom drama and talk to any of the news teams who were interested. They got to solve cases and Conners was relieved to see that for the first time in his life, he was helping people. He preferred things like missing children's cases or clearing someone of a murder, but even solving a cold case or finding out who was guilty in a recent one could often bring closure and relief to a family member or friend.

So people talked, and a few of the public began to understand that the police didn't always mention the efforts of the two detectives from Knighthawk Investigations. It was mostly mentioned by word-of-mouth or a few small message boards online. Still, it did cause them to gain a few more clients and soon Bill and Conners didn't have much time between cases at all. Usually within a week of one case being closed, they received another, or found a cold one that peeked interest.

They ended up getting work outside of Chicago too, traveling to St. Louis to help track a serial killer the police were trying to find. They'd even received a letter of thanks from the state governor for that. Soon enough, summer yielded to fall… which in turn gave way to winter again. Bill and Conners celebrated his one-year anniversary and Christmas together. Bill had opened up with him during the year too. They were both somewhat emotionally despondent, but could be open with one another without fear of reproach or judgement.

Then almost two weeks after welcoming in the year 2010, things changed a bit. Conners examined his new mustache and goatee in a small mirror, running his fingers through the growing hair. While he still wasn't sure exactly how old he was, Conners' best guess was that he must be moving into his twenties now. It had been a journey-and-a-half to finally get documentation, and passing the citizenship test had been the easy part. Still, when they'd had no other information to go on, they eventually agreed to allow him to use his chosen name and had doctors examine him and assign him an age. According to his ID, he was twenty and that was probably close—within a couple years at most.

Nevertheless becoming an actual living person in the eyes of the state meant that he could more easily get things for himself, and the apartment had been a huge stride in that direction. He'd also found several tools to help occupy his hands when he was thinking particularly hard, and usually had a Rubik's cube, cigarettes, and a small stash of Jolly Ranchers packed away in the pockets of his trench coat, along with an assortment of tools for his detective work. Getting a smartphone was also a big jump for him. Bill personally didn't care for anything more complicated than a flip phone, but when Conners discovered that he could connect to the Internet with one, he'd become very interested in the device. While he'd gotten a fairly solid grasp on the world around him, he was still fascinated to learn more and the Internet seemed to have all the information anyone could ever ask for.

As Conners moved away from the mirror, Bill opened the door to the office and stepped in, shaking the snow out of his hair and off his coat.

"Nice to see you made it in, old man," said Conners, smirking slightly.

"Please," said Bill. "I've been through worse than a little snow. Old geezers like me got used to that when we were kids."

"Oh right," said Conners, spinning around in his chair while he lit a cigarette. "You had to walk twelve miles through the snow, uphill, both ways."

Bill scoffed and sat down at his desk, pulling a file out from within his jacket.

"Put that out. Smells like a teenager's car in here. If you ever figure out how to shut up for a moment. You'll see your new case."

Conners got up and walked over, curious about Bill's wording.

"*My* new case? You not accompanying me on this one, boss?"

"No," said Bill, smiling back. "Afraid I lost the leash I usually tether you with, and I can't be bothered to chase you around all day anymore. What? Nervous you might screw up?"

"Hardly," said Conners, taking the file in his hands. "Just wanted to make sure you weren't losing your step. Should I have the nurse send over your slippers and robe too?"

"For your information," said Bill. "I have a meeting today. Besides, if you're ever going to really grow, I can't hold your hand forever. You'll be fine, kid."

Conners looked over the file. There was a man who had been reportedly found dead in an alleyway by suicide, with a knife wound across his throat. That was already a little suspicious to Conners. Firstly, cutting to commit suicide was more often an act done by women than men. Men tended to be more direct and lethal in their suicide attempts, trying to make everything stop. They preferred guns or jumping from a rooftop. Typically, it was women who were more dramatic with their suicides, usually taking pills or slitting their wrists. Secondly, even if the man had decided to cut himself, the arms were a far more common choice, cutting across your own neck was awkward, although not unheard of. Still, it was more than worth a proper look.

Conners closed up the file and tossed it onto his desk, nodding to Bill.

"All right boss, I'll have this thing closed soon."

"I'll hold you to that," said Bill, smiling as Conners closed the door and walked off, hailing a cab.

~*~

As he exited the cab onto the crime scene, Conners felt himself grow extremely excited. It was somewhat involuntary, but he'd learned to encourage the process because when he actually started examining evidence it meant he would get a huge adrenaline rush. It caused the world around him to slow down and allowed him to pick apart evidence or body language far faster and easier than he might've done otherwise.

As he approached the police tape, he recognized the officer: Leo Narvaez. Leo was an officer he and Bill had run into while they were solving a series of drug store robberies back in August. He looked up and waved slightly to Conners and Conners returned the gesture. Leo was a decent enough man, but he didn't have a lot of drive or intuition. Still, Conners didn't mind working with the beat cop.

"Hey there, Conners," said Leo, as he got near the officer. "You coming in on this one?"

"Howdy Narvaez. Yeah Bill said he misses you and wanted me to check in."

"Oh, how sweet," said Leo, sarcastically. "You can come in. Watch the homicide team though. They're already at it."

"Appreciate it," Conners said. "Who we got today?"

"The old man is Higgins. Bit of an ass honestly. He's lead on this one. His partner's Lawrence. She's a bit intense, but all things considered, she's all right."

"Thanks."

Conners glanced down the alley and saw the homicide team standing over the body, talking softly with one another. As he examined them adrenaline flooded his brain. The world slowed down. His brain began examining the duo, noting things quickly of its own accord. When this happened, he could almost see words popping up with the information that he'd concluded, as if his vision had a computer overlay that would tell him things.

The man was far older—Conners surmised in his late fifties—and wore a dark grey three-piece suit with matching hat. His tie was a dull red that was faded with age and he wore no wedding ring around his left ring finger. However, Conners could tell that he had been married long ago. Likely the wear of the job and the man's own bitterness had led to a nasty divorce.

The woman appeared to be near Conners' own age. She had tan skin with light brown hair and vibrant green eyes. She wore a tan jacket and white button-up shirt along with jeans and a pair of laced-up boots that Conners suspected were military surplus. Both had badges hung around their necks. They finished their conversation as he came up to them.

"Might not have been able to get his hands on a gun," Higgins was saying. "Or might've just been into the pain. Who knows?"

"Michael Conners," Conners said as a way of introduction. "Knighthawk Investigations."

"Fucking hell," hissed Higgins, standing up and pulling a cigarette from his pocket. "Can't you wannabes give the actual police five minutes to do their job?"

Conners sneered at the man, but inwardly felt the thrill of a back and forth coming on. After all, working for over a year with Bill had caused the old man's behavior to rub off on him a fair bit.

"Well, I could," said Conners, almost conversationally. "But that would require that you can actually *do* your job, and that's just not a chance I'm willing to take."

The woman—Lawrence—examined him closely, as if trying to size him up.

"Bit of a loudmouth, aren't you?" she asked, raising an eyebrow.

"Oh but there's so much more once you get to know me," Conners said, spinning around with his arms spread wide, as if displaying a new fashion.

Lawrence moved forward and Conners reacted instinctually. As her left hand moved forward slightly, he caught it by the wrist and saw her smile a little, impressed with his reaction.

"I'm not your average, good-looking, incredibly intelligent private detective."

"Maybe not," Lawrence said, softly. "But you talk too much."

He suddenly felt her boot hook behind his left ankle as she pushed him back a little. Unable to catch himself quickly enough, he fell to the ground. He had to admit, she wasn't too shabby. Instead of getting mad at him or trying to pull rank, she'd simply tricked and tripped him. She had a good mind. They'd done well to make her a detective.

"Sergeant Jessica Lawrence," she said, stepping back as he started to get up. "This is Detective Louis Higgins. So, what are you here for, besides being a mouthy kid?"

"Lawrence," said Higgins, firmly. "I don't like this kid, either. Still, upstairs said we should bring him along. Just try and make sure he stays out of the way."

"Well," said Lawrence, looking back to Conners. "How about it, private detective? Show us something, if you're as good as you think you are."

Conners smirked at her and went to examine the body.

"Sure thing sweetheart," he said, softly. "And the name's Conners."

"And mine is Lawrence; call me sweetheart again and I'll break your face."

"Well that *would* be a shame."

Conners slipped on a pair of latex gloves as he knelt next to the body and began examining it, letting his excitement spill over into a small rush of adrenaline. The man's neck had been slashed open, almost from ear-to-ear. The cut was about an inch deep and very fine, which meant it was very likely a knife or something with a fine edge. Also it was a singular, long cut instead of a stab, and the man didn't have any defensive wounds or skin under his fingernails. It was likely he'd been killed from behind: an assassination. That suggested that it was a hit, not a mugging and it made suicide seem even less likely.

Conners dug through the man's personal effects. The wallet and keys were both expected and not at all helpful. He did check the phone quickly, but saw no calls that seemed unusual. While there were a few that only listed a first name, they didn't seem to be especially important to him. Nevertheless he mentally logged them away in case he needed them later. What was far more interesting was the box of matches alongside a pack of cigarettes.

Bar matchboxes were an older custom and while it wasn't still in practice everywhere, it was something that could be used to make sense of some of the deceased man's habits. Conners couldn't see a lighter anywhere, though several of the matches had been torn out so it was likely the man knew he would've been able to get a matchbox from his bar. Conners checked the location, and smiled softly.

The Left Hand

It was the name of an old Italian mob bar a few blocks away. Supposedly the name derived from a Biblical passage of not letting your left hand know what the right was doing, but Conners had never understood the verse or cared to try and make sense of it. What interested him was that the bar was known to host a few illegal card games. That combined with a knife kill meant it was hardly a difficult puzzle to put together.

What was a little more interesting was the idea of why the man would've been killed. Of course, debts seemed the obvious answer, but mobsters usually didn't kill someone who owed them money. After all, dead men can't repay debts. So, instead it made far more sense to kill someone who had stolen from them. Conners figured it was far more likely this man had cheated them at cards, or perhaps just been uncommonly good, and they had decided to recoup their losses as it were. It would also explain the missing matches and cigarettes. After all, it did not take long to lose money at a table, but no one likes to leave if they're winning.

Conners mentally went through the list of known mobsters that would handle something like a theft, and had four solid suspects before he'd even stood up.

"So," said Higgins, with the unmistakable air of contempt in his voice. "What's your incredible deduction?"

"Not much," said Conners, standing and removing his gloves. "He'd had a big win last night over at *The Left Hand*. Probably cheated, though I'm not entirely sure. Either way, point is he was likely a regular there, and was in a habit of winning often. I imagine he ended up sweeping a bit too much from them and they decided to recoup some losses. I can give you a list of suspects right now."

Both of the detectives stared at him, as if expecting him to claim that it was a joke. When he didn't, Lawrence spoke.

"You're completely serious?"

"Well as fun as you are to mess with, I'm afraid I like my pretty little face just the way it is."

"So," said Higgins. "You're saying we can just skip on over to a pub and get a confession, right?"

"Oh hardly," said Conners. "Italians guard their own fiercely. No, you'll have to get ahold of the note or text the man used. My money would be on a note. *The Left Hand* is run by the Moretti Family, and they tend to keep things pretty old school. You could do worse than to check their garbage, but honestly a home search would be better. Mobsters don't like to ditch anything unless they have to. More likely he's taken the knife home to clean it thoroughly. However, if he still has work to do, he'll need time before he's done. Knives are easier to deal with than guns but you still need a really thorough scrub job if you're going to lose the blood."

There was silence for a long moment before Higgins spoke again.

"Nice try kid, but you've got a while before you really understand the way all this works. We'll head to the bar, you just keep back and out of trouble."

"Actually," said Lawrence. "I'm a bit interested in what he has to say. After all, running down a list of names can't really hurt, can it? What if I run a quick check of the names with him and you follow the bar lead?"

Higgins seemed to consider it for a long moment. "Whatever," he finally said. "Better you than me."

Chapter IX: Flames

Conners leaned back while Lawrence began to search the police database for the names Conners gave her. He had to admit that the police's ability to conduct quick searches on people's history and residence made him a little envious. It was much more work to acquire someone's address from a friend or co-worker, or even just to follow them. His wonder was only put out a little by his fear at being in a police car. At least he was allowed to ride in the front.

"It'll take a little time before we can get a warrant and search the homesteads, but it's a good first step."

Conners rolled his eyes. Warrants were just a bunch of legal tape that took up time, and if criminals were suspicious or experienced they knew how to use that time.

"No harm in checking out the places ahead of time, is there? I mean, we could at least see who is and isn't home."

She examined him curiously, and seemed reproachful. However underneath her distrust, he sensed her desire to solve the case and catch their bad guy. It made Conners smile inwardly. He didn't even have to push her on this, because she wanted it almost as much as he did. All-in-all, this Lawrence might not be too bad a cop to work with.

"Fine," she said. "We'll hit them up, but you follow my lead on this, ok?"

"Of course ma'am," he said, giving a mock salute.

She started up the car and pulled into the flow of traffic. What surprised Conners slightly was that while Lawrence was clearly used to navigating the streets and the insane amount of cars that made up the traffic, she wasn't so efficient as the cabs around the city were. Granted, she didn't break any traffic laws unlike he often saw the cabbies do, but he couldn't help but feel that a talented cab driver would've cut their time in half.

Their first visit turned out to be a bust. While the tenant was home and he allowed them to search the apartment, they found nothing particularly interesting or incriminating. The second man had an alibi that was fairly airtight, considering he'd been at a party with friends and had been caught on a dozen or so cellphones.

It was the third residence—an apartment in a slummy part of town rented by Lucas Viggo— that changed things up. Lawrence knocked on the door several times, but there was no answer. Conners listened carefully but couldn't hear anything. Lawrence shrugged and turned from the door.

"Guess we'll have to come back with the warrant," she said softly.

"Really?" asked Conners in mock surprise. "But didn't you hear that?"

"Hear what?" she asked, leaning towards the door slightly.

"Well, I would've sworn I just heard a woman scream," Conners said, pulling out a set of lockpicks. "Now, that could mean anything. Perhaps he left a television on, or a computer video. However, if a woman really *is* in danger there, are you willing to just let her get hurt, detective? Don't your lot have a law about doing no harm?"

"That's doctors!" she said, exasperated. "And there was no scream!"

"Oh? But I'm sure I heard something," Conners said, pushing the pins of the lock into place with a smooth motion.

"Are you insane?" Lawrence hissed. "I could arrest you here and now!"

"Jury's out on that," he said softly, opening the door. "I guess I'm just banking on you wanting to catch the mobster who slit a man's throat open more than you want to bag me for picking a lock."

Lawrence appeared to consider his words, seemingly chewing on her tongue for a long moment. Despite his confidence, Conners couldn't help but feel that she really *might* arrest him for his little stunt. Granted, breaking into a house was only considered a crime in Chicago if one could prove intent to burgle or commit some felony, which he didn't, but she could certainly arrest him for it if she wanted to. In the end, her curiosity won out and she shook her head softly.

"You're nuts," she said. "But if we make it quick… Just don't touch anything. If you find something, it's evidence. You got me?"

"Copy sergeant!" he said, impersonating a gruff military figure.

They both moved throughout Viggo's apartment. The inside was nearly as filthy as the outside, covered in layers of dirty laundry and half-eaten food. Conners could hardly be surprised by the disgusting oder that clung to every inch of the interior, or by the two rats he came across while examining the place. Neither the bedroom nor kitchen revealed anything of interest, aside from a pile of dirty dishes that would've put a college dorm to shame.

However, when it came to the bathroom, Conners knew they'd struck gold. The fiberglass bottom of the tub was stained pink from Viggo's attempt to wash out the blood, and there was a white shirt drying above the drain. The fan was going and likely had been for some time, but it was not nearly enough to erase the smell of bleach, just distinguishable over the general stink of the place.

"Moooom!" Conners called to Lawrence, holding his nose. "I found some of that stuff you told me not to tamper with!"

Lawrence re-appeared quickly and reached for her phone, hitting the speed dial before lifting the phone to her ear.

"Hello? This is Lawrence, badge number 1-3-1-6."

As she put out an order to lookout for Viggo, Conners began to mentally picture the scene, committing every detail of the area to memory. He doubted he really would be needed for the court case. Given the mountain of evidence, it would be easy for the police to wrap everything up, but he'd rather have the info and not need it. Besides, Bill liked thorough reports anyway.

Lawrence ended her phone call and looked up at him, as if he were a painting at an exhibit that required a fair bit of thought.

"Well," she finally said. "Thanks for your assistance."

Conners looked at the hand she held out, and clasped it.

"Thanks for not being a pain in the ass."

She rolled her eyes at him, sighing, "And here I was… *almost* impressed."

"No, I'm serious," Conners said, smiling. "You let me get involved, listened to me, and didn't stop me from walking around a few lines. I appreciate that. If you need a set of hands on anything else interesting I'd be happy to help."

What surprised him almost as much as her was that he was speaking sincerely. He'd had a far more difficult time skirting around cops who were too concerned with the letter rather than the spirit of the law, and knew if her partner had come along they wouldn't have gotten the case closed like they had. It was a relief to see a cop who genuinely just wanted to put bad guys away. It forced him to consider what his own life might've been if he'd been able to become a cop. He pushed the thought away and examined Lawrence.

She looked at him quizzically, as if she were trying to solve a puzzle or problem.

"Right, I… I *might* just take you up on that, Conners. Anyway, if you don't mind, there's about to be a ton of law enforcement all over this place, and I feel like the less they talk to you, the better… for now."

"Afraid to introduce me to your protective family?" he asked, smirking. "As long as you're not ashamed of me."

"Shut up."

"I mean, because I really thought we were getting somewhere special, and I'd hate for this to be ruined just because daddy doesn't like me."

"Do you only have two settings: helpful and smart-ass?"

"No!" he protested, winking at the police detective. "That implies I can't do both at once. I'll have you know: I can multi-task. Honestly, you're probably right, and I'd rather not get grilled for hours on the same stuff. So I'll make my way on home. Here's my cell though… just in case."

"Right," she said, pocketing his business card. "Just in case."

Conners head out of the building, grateful to breathe in the (comparatively) clean air, and hailed a cab to take him back to the office. Along the ride back, he pondered Lawrence. She was very odd, all things considered. But he had to admit he'd liked working with her. Besides, she was far more fun than that stick-in-the-mud, Higgins. Luckily, the case hadn't been too difficult. Anytime they started working with new people it was best that they made a good impression, because that introduced the chance of getting more work. Bill would be happy. It was his first solo case and he hadn't done half-bad either.

However, he was suddenly snapped out of his musings as the cab stopped so suddenly that his face smashed into the back of the driver's seat, causing Conners to grasp his damaged nose in pain. Grimacing as he peeled his face off of the cheap leather, he leaned around towards the cabbie.

"What was that about?" he growled.

The cab driver turned to him, white-faced and pointed out the windshield. Conners rolled his eyes and looked up. At first, he didn't understand exactly what it was he was seeing. It was just a huge glare of blue and red lights against a huge orange light. Eventually, as his eyes adjusted to the sudden influx of color, he realized what he was seeing. They had arrived back at the office, and it had been set ablaze.

The first thing that registered in him was panic. He could feel his heartbeat had at least tripled in frequency and could swear the world around him had been placed on pause. Why wasn't anyone doing anything?! Firemen were spraying into the flames, applying oxygen masks and hoses, but no one actually seemed to be checking if there had been anyone inside, and Conners didn't see any sign of Bill by an ambulance.

He wasn't even aware of opening the door or taking off his coat. All he knew was that he needed to get to Bill. Surely, *surely* the old man had found a way to get out before everything had gone up in flames. Hadn't Bill mentioned that he had a meeting that day? He hadn't mentioned the time, but Bill *must've* been out of the office when the fire had gone up! Conners sprinted pell-mell, flying over the barrier the police were placing and right past the officer who tried to stop him.

Logic and rational thought were leaving him. He only knew that Bill *needed* to not be in the building. Maybe none of these idiots cared enough about an old man to help pull him out of the flames, but Bill deserved better than that. As he reached the fire, the wave of heat crashed into him almost like the shock-force of a grenade. However, Conners pushed right on through his body's screams to stop. He dropped low to the ground, crawling quickly along the floor like a frantic spider. The office, which was more familiar to him than his own bedroom, was filled with fire and black smoke. His eyes burned and watered, and he had to close them frequently, navigating as much by memory as by sight. Despite his low position on the floor, Conners felt the smoke build up in his lungs and he coughed several times. He inhaled nothing more than dirty air and ash, but he ignore the pain and pushed onward.

Conners shoved aside a chair that must've tipped into the flames, ignoring the burnt wood and finally reached Bill's desk. The old man was still there. It was almost as if he'd barely moved since Conners had left that morning; as if any moment he would smile and laugh.

What are you doing, kid? Trying to give yourself a tan?

However, Conners did not need even half-a-second to see that Bill would never greet him. There was a bullet hole in Bill's temple, and dried blood clung to his face and shirt. The old man had been dead long before the flames had begun to eat at him. Conners felt himself tearing up again and it had nothing to do with the smoke swirling about him. Bill was a good man, and a much better friend than Conners deserved. Yet despite that, Bill had ended up dead... and he hadn't been around to do a thing about it.

No, instead been off playing out some *stupid* fantasy of fixing something. He couldn't believe he'd been so stupid! Why hadn't he stayed and defended Bill?! Why hadn't he been smarter? Been faster? If he'd solved the case quicker he would've been back ages ago, with plenty of time to stop this! He'd been too slow, too stupid.

Against his instinct, Conners reach back and slapped himself across the face, hard. It stung and hurt, and helped him refocus. Things were dark, but he knew he couldn't leave Bill here to burn as if he'd never existed. It wasn't about a burial. Bill wanted to be cremated anyway, but he didn't deserve to be erased by a fire that would conceal his murder. Conners ran around the desk and hoisted the old man's arm around his shoulders and began to pull and drag him across the floor. Luckily, Bill was fairly thin. Regardless, the smoke and ash were getting to Conners. He felt his mind start to spin and forced himself to stay as low as he could.

If only he could reach the door. Surely it couldn't be far. Yet every inch seemed to take several minutes, and every foot an hour. Still, Conners refused to let Bill be dishonored by leaving him to burn. The idea that his murder might be written off as a simple accident was an insult that struck him on a personal level. He kept pulling, doing his best to avoid the fire and smoke, but the building was burning faster and faster. The firemen outside did all they could, but the flames were clearly winning the battle. Conners gave a last tremendous heave, and felt the cool breeze of the outer world upon his back. He was near the open door when a pair of arms wrapped around his torso and began to pull.

Conners did his best to pull with the stranger's arms, but refused to let go of Bill's body. He didn't let go until the heat faded away. Then Conners completely collapsed into the snow, shivering, freezing, and burning up all at once. For several long moments, he existed only in a black void, unable to make sense of the world around him or tell which way was up. Then, like a flash of lightening, he heard a voice. It was unpleasant, low, and slinking, as if it belonged to a snake.

"I'm going to give you one chance, and only because I admire your balls in doing this. Get out and I won't kill you."

There was a flash of cold and he was back. Pain flooded through him and his back felt as if someone had been trying to skin him alive. Something was pressed over his mouth and he reacted instinctively. He tried to push it off for a full second before he realized it was an oxygen mask and he was in the arms of a fireman. He waved at him to show that he was conscious and the man removed the mask while Conners coughed violently.

"You're one damn lucky kid," said the fireman. "We thought you were gone for sure."

"Yeah," said Conners, coughing again. "I'm ok… thanks…"

"Well kid," said the fireman. "We didn't get to you. We were gearing up when she pulled you out. She's as crazy as you are, but I guess someone's looking out for you."

Conners glanced over to where the fireman pointed, and was astonished to see Lawrence sitting there, holding an oxygen mask to her own mouth.

"You'll need to go to the hospital for an examination and some treatment for your back; you got burned a bit, but you should be all right."

Conners nodded and looked around for Bill's body, and saw it lying in the snow, not far from where his own imprint lay. A few police were examining it and Conners stumbled over to them, still hacking and coughing as he did so.

"Wait!" he managed to call out. "Wait! He's my friend!"

They looked hesitant, as if about to deny his request. Lawrence waved at them and they stood aside, allowing Conners to examine Bill's dead body. The flames had burned the left leg badly, but Bill was mostly whole. Somehow this brought him a bit of relief. His examination of the body didn't really take very long, in spite of his emotions going haywire. Bill's wallet wasn't touched, though his cellphone was missing. The pistol around his hip was still there and hadn't been fired. However, a note lay in the man's shirt pocket, written in a woman's neat hand.

2859 N 7th st.

Conners scowled and pocketed the note before reaching down and placing a hand on Bill's shoulder.

"I'm sorry Bill," he said, so softly only he heard the words. "I'm so, so sorry. I need to do better... I *will*. I promise."

He stood up again, retrieved his coat and sat next to Jessica Lawrence, who was perched on the back of an ambulance. She was still holding an oxygen mask. She offered it to him as he sat next to her and he took the mask, catching a proper breath again before passing it back.

"I'm told I have you to thank for my life," he said, trying and failing to sound humorous.

Lawrence shrugged softly.

"I figured you would do something crazy, and I'm a cop. Protect and serve and all that."

He shrugged, not feeling up to another joke or mocking statement.

"How'd you know what happened?" he asked.

"Radio," she said simply. "Heard that the fire had been responded to, and recognized the address from your card. Didn't take long to realize that you'd be panicked about it and all. They said your boss was shot."

"Right temple," said Conners. "I think the person was facing him, making it a left-handed shooter. The round was small-caliber, I'm sure ballistics will reveal it."

"All right. Anything else?" she asked.

Conners seriously considered telling her about the note now residing in his jeans pocket, but thought better of it. Lawrence might be a good cop, but she was still a cop and this was far too important to leave to anyone else.

"No," he said firmly. "That's all I know."

She nodded again.

"Don't worry," she said. "I promise we'll find out who did this. We just need you to recover and relax for a little while. I'll make sure you know anything the moment we do."

Conners nodded. He silently took another hit off the oxygen mask and knew that he couldn't trust what she'd just said in the least.

Chapter X: Retribution

As Conners left the hospital, moving carefully so as to try and avoid hurting his back further, Lawrence walked alongside him. Completely disregarding his insistence that he didn't need a babysitter, she'd been at his elbow ever since they'd left Bill's office... or what remained of it anyway. The old man's body had been taken by the police for an autopsy. Several cops had taken a moment and assured him that they would find out what had happened, but privately Conners had doubts.

Part of it was he'd been doing their jobs for them for around a year. Conners had little trust in the law's ability to help solve crimes. The other part was because they didn't know about the written note he'd found in Bill's shirt pocket. Conners had tried to convince himself that he'd taken it because there was no proof it meant anything. However, the truth was that he didn't *want* the cops to find Bill's murderer. He wanted to find the woman who had killed the old man himself. Conners didn't really know what it was he wanted from them. He didn't really want to kill them, and arresting them wouldn't be satisfying. He just wanted to see them, and understand the why of it.

So he kept the note. As they exited the hospital, Conners made to call for a cab, but Lawrence stopped him.

"Given your relationship to William," she said slowly.

"Bill," he corrected her.

"Bill. Given your relationship with him and your profession, we need to keep you under watch for twenty-four hours."

"I'm sorry?"

"Conners, you're extremely rash and you're used to looking into things yourself. We don't let cops handle cases that are too close to them, and this is much the same thing."

"Well that's very flattering, but you really don't have any legal right to keep me under watch."

"Actually, I do. You have three choices; you were released into my custody because I assured my lieutenant that you would be easier to keep out of trouble under my watch than you would be in a holding cell. So you can either spend that time in a jail cell, under hospital watch, or with me."

Conners scowled. As tempting at it was to accept the cell just to spite her, his rational brain won that argument. Try as he might, he also couldn't convince himself to accept the hospital watch. It would have been too much of a reminder of his old life and getting examined and questioned by the staff was bad enough. Besides, if he fled hospital care this time he *would* have a legal name and papers attached to him.

"Fine," he said, already considering when he might have a chance to slip away.

"All right. Get in and I'll take you to my place."

"Wait, why your place? I do have an apartment."

"And I'm sure it's a perfectly lovely place, despite the disgusting state it's probably in. However, I don't really feel up to crashing on a couch and I highly doubt you have a second bedroom."

Aside from her assumption on his place's cleanliness, she wasn't wrong. His apartment was barely big enough for him and didn't even have a single bedroom. Rather his bare-basics apartment had a single living room/kitchenette and a bathroom. He usually pulled his mattress up against the wall during the day and would pull it out to sleep on at night. Lawrence really *couldn't* have stayed at his place if he'd wanted her to, and he didn't want that in the first place.

"You *do* have a spare bedroom?" he asked, slightly surprised.

"My sister and her son like to visit from time-to-time. After the time is up we'll discuss if we need to make other arrangements or if you can go about your own way."

Conners nodded. Twenty-four hours was a long time, and even police detectives needed sleep. It would hardly be difficult. She would presumably sleep for six to eight hours. He might have the whole case wrapped up by then. Lawrence's place turned out to be a fairly nice apartment on the outskirts of the main city. She'd also clearly taken a large interest in personal decorating. He noted a decent number of photos adorning the walls.

He saw a picture featuring Lawrence and a woman who was almost exactly identical. Conners took this to be the aforementioned sister. Both were being hugged by an elderly woman he figured was probably their mother. There was another photo that appeared to be from Lawrence's graduation day at the police academy. There were no photos of her father, nor anyone that might've been a significant other. She was unattached, dedicated to work, and a family-indicated person.

There was another photo by the bathroom that surprised him a little. It depicted Lawrence being pulled out of a river by a smiling older man with several people gathered around.

"What's this one?" he asked, pointing.

Lawrence looked up at the photo he indicated.

"A picture from my baptism. My mom took the picture and refused to let me take one of all of us because she couldn't stop crying. Don't know what she intended to do if I ever got married."

Conners chuckled softly. He'd read about baptisms but didn't fully understand the concept. To him is seemed eerily similar to a drowning that went incomplete and everyone celebrated. Still, he'd learned from Bill not to question too much when it came to religious beliefs.

Instead he sat on the couch and Lawrence began doing something in the kitchen. He leaned back, and felt this head hit the wall as he stared dully at the ceiling fan. He caught himself following the rotation with his eyes while his mind spun like a top. What would Bill say if he saw Conners now?

Come on kid. What are you waiting for? You have a clue to go on. Hoping my killer can get away with it if you sit on your hands long enough?

"I'm sorry," Conners whispered, not even sure what he meant by it.

He didn't know if he was sorry for letting Bill die, for not having caught his killer, for leaving him in the first place, or for being stupid enough to run into a burning inferno just to pull Bill's dead body out. Nothing made sense right now, and it was driving him crazy. Lawrence reappeared a few moments later, holding a steaming cup of hot chocolate.

"Drink," she said. "It'll help. Spare bedroom's the first door on the right there. You need extra blankets or anything?"

"No," he said, accepting the cup from her. "Hey, I just wanted to say thanks... for helping me. You certainly don't owe me anything."

"It's good," she said, nodding kindly. "I'm gonna lock the door and turn in for the night. There's an alarm, just in case you had ideas."

Conners held up his free hand in mock-surrender.

"I get it," he said, already working to think of a way around this new snag.

"Goodnight," she said, closing her bedroom door behind her.

Conners waited until he heard her breathing deepen, and Lawrence passed into true sleep. Then he got up and went into the kitchen. After rummaging around for a little while, he went and found a pad of paper and a pencil. The fact was Lawrence *had* been kind to him. So if he was going to break her rules, he owed her an explanation... if she woke up before he got back, that was.

Hey sweetheart, (not actually here so that whole "breaking my face" thing doesn't have to happen, right?) Got a lead on what happened to Bill. Would've told you, but you would've stopped me from going. Don't expect I'll be gone long and if anything comes up, I'll loop you in.

Conners.

It was short but that was probably for the best. After all, too long a note would only give her more information and he wasn't sure he wanted her to know anything more just yet.

Getting out of the house without detection was a hair harder than he'd expected. It turned out that Lawrence's alarm system not only covered the door, but the windows in the main room and the spare bedroom. However, he got a lucky break in the bathroom. Admittedly, the window was very small and if he weren't so lean, he wouldn't have been able to even attempt to slip through it. However, he also knew that people tended to forget about their bathroom windows beyond making sure no one could peep in through them.

So, after several long minutes of careful contortion and standing on a painfully thin edge, he managed to navigate his way out of the window and dropped down into the grass eleven feet or so below him. Getting back up would be an issue, but not one that couldn't be tackled. Besides, all decent plans required a bit of improvisation.

He jogged to the main road and hailed a cab. Luckily, Chicago had such a busy nightlife that the driver merely looked happy to get a fare from someone who wasn't drunk. Conners gave him the address and let his mind run through its process while the man drove. Unfortunately it was basically impossible to start putting any puzzle pieces together just because so much of Bill's life had been unknown to him. So when they reached the building, Conners felt he was no better than when he started.

As it turned out, the address in Bill's pocket led to a very tall building that Conners would've taken for an office, save that there was no security or janitorial staff present. Before he went in, he quickly smoked a cigarette, and tried to calm his racing heart. He had assumed the building was locked up and he'd have to break in somehow. But he was surprised when the door opened easily and he was granted access.

The ground floor was large and open, causing his footsteps to reverberate. There were several murals and pieces of art carved into the wall that made Conners think of an abandoned art display. At the end of the floor was an elevator with a post-it note stuck to the front.

It simply read: *Top Floor, Michael.*

That sent a chill through him. Bill's killer knew him, which meant they knew what he did for the old man. This in turn meant they had likely waited until Conners was actually out of Bill's office before attacking. That was at least a little calming because it meant they didn't want to kill him too. Still, Conners didn't know who would have that much personal interest in him... Perhaps someone from his past life, but then why not call him by his old name? Unless they knew he wouldn't remember?

He shook himself. There was no point trying to theorize this early. He *needed* more information. He pressed the button for the elevator and a few seconds later it opened. Conners pressed the button for the top level—33—and tried to ignore the music that filled the compartment as it moved upward quickly. It was not like most elevator music, designed to calm people down or entertain them. It was ominous and unsettling. Before long, the elevator stopped and the doors slid open.

Conners found he had stepped into something like a grand dining hall. The majority of the room was taken up by a large black table, which could've seated over twelve people very comfortably. The floors were polished to a shine and hanging from the twenty-foot high ceiling was an ornate chandelier, sparkling like diamonds.

"Michael Conners," said a woman's voice and Conners turn his attention to the speaker. "It is good to finally meet you properly, dear."

The voiced belonged to a woman who appeared to be in her late fifties: perhaps early sixties. She wore a black silk pants suit with a pressed, white shirt and a thin tie. Her hair was jet black, curly, and fell just past her shoulders. She sat at the head of the table and had some type of meal before her on a cast-iron plate next to a very full glass of wine.

"Please, sit," she said, taking a long sip of her wine.

He couldn't help but notice it looked uncomfortably like she was drinking blood.

Looking down, Conners saw a note written in the same hand as the elevator note, showing his name. Whoever this woman was she had a control or power fetish. As Conners took his seat at the far end of the table, he glanced down and saw a covered tray with a dome that appeared to be true silver. As soon as he was properly seated, a man dressed in a fine suit came and removed the plate cover, to reveal a high-grade steak and fresh green beans on a similar cast-iron plate. Then, the man poured wine into a glass, setting it just above his plate.

Conners growled, looking down at the food. It was clear this woman expected him to play along. However, it wasn't as if he'd been searched. What if he just drew his pistol and shot her dead, here and now? He might not be a crack-shot, but surely he could manage that much. She didn't *seem* to be wearing a vest. However, he couldn't deny the burning curiosity in him. He wanted to know who she was and what her story was as much as he wanted to shoot her.

There was also the fact that she hadn't been openly hostile towards him. Of course, he didn't trust anything about this woman, but if she'd wanted to have him searched, or put under gunpoint, she certainly could've done so long before now. As he sat examining the food, she spoke out.

"It's not poisoned," she said, a soft laugh to her voice that did nothing to relax him. "And if you *do* decide that you're going to shoot me, you might as well abuse my hospitality before you do, no?"

Conners felt as if she'd slapped him. He was sure his face had remained impassive. He hadn't touched his gun and it was safely concealed behind his back. How did she know he even had the weapon? The look in her eyes had suddenly turned ravenous, as if she were a lioness about to pounce on her prey.

"Surprised?" she asked sweetly, seeing his face. "You can't be around dear William for so many years without picking up a few things. He really *did* have a knack for it. Didn't he, boy?"

"W-who are you?"

She sighed, as if somewhat disappointed by his question.

"Really dear, I had hoped he'd finally found someone special. It took him so many years to finally find a protégé. I had to admit, I was excited when you started examining me when you walked in. That wasn't half bad. But 'who are you?' Really? It's so drawl, dear. I am William's very dearest friend... or at least the closest thing to one he is capable of having."

Conners mentally shook himself, trying to clear his head of the fog that seemed to have come over it, as he struggled to think faster. Whoever this woman was, she *really* knew how to play his game. He was going to have to perform at his peak.

"It's Bill," he said, solidly, and that thought gave him strength. "His name was Bill, not William. You're the one... aren't you? His ex-wife; Kelsey."

She smiled softly.

"Now *that's* better. Kelsey Richards, the one woman would could ever tame the insufferable William Scott. I'm pleased you've heard of me."

Conners mentally processed her words and recalled what little Bill had said about her.

Definite narcissistic personality traits, he thought to himself. *Likely some sadistic qualities with hints towards extreme rage and a vindictive streak.*

"I've heard you were a bitch and don't know how to make a relationship work."

Anger flashed across Richards' face, and for a split-second, she appeared positively murderous. The pupils of her eyes almost seemed to elongate and grow into slits. Then, with a blink of her dark green eyes, it was over and there sat the prim business woman.

"So I know why I brought you here, but why have you come, Conners dear?"

"I wanted to see the woman who killed Bill," he said simply. "I wanted to know the person I'm going to hunt down."

"Oh, so you *do* mean to kill me. That's good to know. Why not do it right now then? I doubt William would've let you go unarmed for so long."

"He didn't," said Conners, pulling out his pistol.

Up until that second, he hadn't been sure exactly *what* he intended to do when he met Richards. He didn't know for sure if he wanted to kill her or run screaming. However, something solidified in him in that moment, and it was almost as if he could hear Bill's voice, whispering in his ears.

Do it right, kid.

"I'm going to arrest you," he said, clearly. "Not today, and likely not soon. However, there will come a time when you're sitting across from me in a courtroom and I will bring you down. You'll blow these words off, even as you'll remember that I said this. Then, the day will come and I will destroy everything you are. When it comes, I want you to remember this: Bill was a good man, and better than you ever deserved. And even if it wasn't directly, it will be his teachings that bring you to justice."

"How scary," said Richards. "I *can* see where you got some of his insufferable behavior. Well boy, all I can say is that I hope you're as good as that fool thought you were. The way he went on and on about you was disgusting. So, go and do your worst. Just know that I've been playing this game for a *very* long time. There's a reason I haven't lost yet. Goodnight."

Without another word, Conners rose and head back to the elevator, feeling the woman's eyes drilling a hole in the back of his head.

Chapter XI: A Wake

As it turned out, getting back into Lawrence's apartment undiscovered hadn't been all that easy. In fact, a more honest way to put it would be that he never had half-a-chance of accomplishing it. His best bet would've been to use a ladder, but even if he'd had one, there was no way to then get rid of the tool either quietly or satisfactorily.

Smash.

Of course, even if he *had* managed to do so somehow, it wouldn't have eliminated the much larger issue that Lawrence was already awake when he re-entered the apartment. The sight of the police detective dressed in pajama pants, a long t-shirt, and with her hair loose about her face had seemed harmless enough at first. Then had come the yelling, and dishes started flying like a hurricane had gone off in the armchair she rested in.

"Complete! Inconsiderate! Jackass!" she shouted, hurling a fork at him which he only just dodged as it went clattering off the countertop. "Didn't even think! Not for *one* moment! You could've been killed! You could've been captured!"

"Lawrence!"

Smash.

This time a coffee mug exploded over his head.

"No mention of where you went or what you were trying to do! Did you think I was *kidding* when I told you to do nothing? Do you have *any* clue how dangerous that was? You risked your life against a homicidal manic, not mention you nearly blew the *entire* case for what?"

"I only wanted…"

"Shut up!" she shouted, and Conners would've sworn he heard a dog bark above them. "You are the *biggest*, most *egotistical* ass I have ever met! Did you even think how much risk that put *me* in? You were released into *my* custody, Conners. If you'd gotten hurt…"

Lawrence trailed off into a long string of Spanish he couldn't have begun to follow. She collapsed into her armchair and Conners slowly peaked out from the tray he'd been using as a make-shift shield. He felt a stab of guilt as he saw the pained expression on her face. The truth was that he *hadn't* thought of the risk she'd been put in. After all, they weren't all that close and he'd been so focused on Bill's murder that he hadn't really taken the time to process how much she'd helped him. She'd been nice enough to help him avoid a much nastier watch, and his weak thanks had been made immediately invalid by his actions. Bill would've been disappointed in him for it.

Thinking of Bill meant he could almost hear the old man's voice again.

That woman saved your life while you were being an idiot and this is how you want to repay her? That's poor form, kid. You need to do better. Now, pull your head out of your ass and apologize to her like a man.

"Lawrence... I'm sorry," he said, putting as much earnest feeling into his words as he could. "I didn't think about what it would mean to you. I know you did this to help me and I betrayed that. But please tell me you can at least understand why I did it."

She ran her fingers through her hair, pulling it back.

"Of course I get *why*," she said. "I understand what you wanted. It doesn't change the fact that you almost gave me a heart attack. You're... good at investigation work and honestly, I want you to succeed. Bill sent a note to my lieutenant about you and he spoke highly of you. It's why you were allowed in on the Viggo case and you were what Bill said you would be. I guess I just wanted you to be a success story."

"I'm sorry?"

"It's a part of being a cop," she said, almost staring into the distance. "You see so much crap and so many lies. It's very easy to become jaded and feel like everyone's going to let you down. My counter is to try and find the good where I can. It's the best way I have to stay human, and it makes things hard if someone betrays that. You did what you did because you wanted to do right by Bill. I get that... more than you might know. Still, if you really want to do the right thing, I need you to work *with* me."

Conners considered her words. It was a better deal than he deserved and why shouldn't he work with her? She was already a better cop than most he'd met and he couldn't deny that she had earned the right to his trust when she'd saved his life and then spoken up on his behalf to her lieutenant.

"Ok, deal," he said, sitting on the couch. "I promise. Just please keep me in the loop as much as I do for you."

She nodded and looked around at the mess.

"Got a bit of a temper?" he asked, smiling softly.

"I get it from my mom's side. My grandparents on her side were both Hispanic. Bit of Latin temper, I guess."

"Well, I'll help you clean up and share what I found."

So they began to sweep up the shards of china and recovered the pieces that were still whole. Meanwhile Conners told Lawrence everything he'd been keeping to himself about Bill's death. He told her about the note and about Richards. To her credit, Lawrence never interrupted. She instead logged away everything he said. After he finished, she asked a few clarifying questions. He expected that she might continue her earlier tirade but she didn't. She'd said her piece about his stupidity and didn't feel the need to express it twice.

"I'll see what we have on Kelsey Richards. I know a bit about her business, but no more than the next person. Supposedly, she's very well connected. I think they do business with Kingston Inc. right now."

That name sent a flash through Conners' brain. It was like suddenly getting bashed in the back of the head by a baseball bat. Yet, in the flash of pain his brain dug up a single name.

James Kingston

He had no idea who that was or why he would've remembered the man's name. He made sure to mentally file it away and look into it later. Something in his past was related to James Kingston... but his mind would give him nothing more. Conners growled slightly and rubbed his temples, unsure if he were more frustrated at his own locked-off memories or at his behavior towards Lawrence.

"I appreciate that. I can't look any further into her at the moment anyway. I've got to give this some space before I act, or she'll outsmart me."

"I'm surprised you're willing to admit someone *can* outsmart you."

"I know I'm not *always* the smartest person in the room," he said, smirking slightly. "Just most of the time."

She rolled her eyes and held up a butter knife threateningly. Conners held his hands up in a mock-surrender.

"I do have to make the arrangements for Bill's funeral though. Most of it should be covered, but can't trust them not to screw something up. Is your custody of me relinquished or are you going to put me in cuffs?"

She looked at him critically for a long time, as if weighing the options. Finally, after a pause that was more than long enough to make him uncomfortable, she nodded.

"If I find out you go after her without our say-so, I will arrest you."

"I promised," he said simply. "Besides, I sort of liked working *with* you. Can't have us at opposite end of things, can I?"

He adjusted his coat and walked out of Lawrence's place, so tired that he could've slept on the cab ride home.

~*~

The next week was extremely busy for him. This was largely due to two separate issues. The first was Bill's cremation and funeral service. While the old man had planned a fair bit of his funeral, there were still a ton of details that had to be ironed out, and Conners had never discovered how little he cared about several things. He spent the next few days answering questions on things like catering, cloth colors, pictures for the bulletin, and seating arrangements. It was all just so incredibly tedious. It was as if Bill's actual death came second to his funeral.

The second issue was his moving into a new apartment. He had no question now that he wanted to continue the detective work, which meant he would need an office. Even with the old office gone, he still had a few offered cases that people had mailed in, both on the Internet and through snail mail. So, he had to get a new apartment and turn it into an office.

The place he eventually chose wasn't as drab as Bill's office had been. The walls weren't lined with filing cabinets for a start. That was one advantage Conners' understanding of technology brought him; everything he documented was contained within a computer and a couple backup drives.

So instead of a desk and computer, his studio apartment featured a couch opposite a couple armchairs with a few pictures of the city sights. Personally he didn't care for them but the saleswoman had assured him that it would make the place a little more relaxing. After recovering Bill's badge from his body, Conners framed and hung it over his kitchenette countertop. It was a small act, but one that made him feel that Bill was not forgotten in his work.

The place was admittedly small, but just as large as he needed it to be. It also boasted many things he deemed useful, such as a large glass case filled with several different bullet casings from all sorts of handguns, rifles, and sub-machine guns. He'd intended to actually have the bullets and several of the guns to match, but Chicago's anti-gun laws made it almost impossible and he'd been forced to settle in the end.

As Wednesday the 20th finally arrived, Conners dressed in a good pair of jeans, his grey shirt, and his black trench coat. Most people dressed up for a funeral, and Conners had no doubts that those who did show up that day would do so. However, he found the idea offensive. After all, Bill had never dressed up for anyone and this was the uniform he'd worn with the old man for well over a year. It seemed only fitting to wear it to his funeral. It vaguely reminded him of the soldiers who wore military dress to the funeral of one of their platoon mates.

Bill's wake was a relatively small affair. His body had been cremated before the ceremony and his ashes were placed inside a pewter urn, which now sat beneath a large picture of Bill. Bill's life, focused as it was, had left him with only twenty or so people who attended his wake. Most were older men involved in some branch of law enforcement. There were a couple police officers, one lieutenant, an FBI agent who sat towards the back, three people who Conners could only surmise were past clients who had read about his death, and others of a similar caliber.

As the person who was closest to Bill in the end, Conners stood to deliver a speech. He didn't intend to go on for very long, and already knew what he wanted to say. Still, the demand on his emotions was something he hadn't completely anticipated. As he stood, he felt tears leaking from his eyes and a lump formed in his throat as it became harder to focus or speak.

I'm going soft, he thought, morbidly. *I never would've been like this before Bill. It's weird, but I guess it's better. It's what Bill would've said was better anyway.*

As he acknowledged that in his own mind, he could almost hear Bill's voice again.

You can do this, kid. It's part of humanity. You connected to me deeply enough to miss me. That's a good thing.

It made it just a little easier to focus his mind: just a little easier to know what he needed to do. He wiped the tears away and pulled out his speech, clearing his throat.

"Bill was many things in his life. He was a cop, a husband, a private detective, and one of the smartest men who ever lived. However, he was a man of faith above all else, and that showed in everything he did. He affected the lives of those around him, and refused to accept a comforting lie. He was also a man who cared more about the caliber of a man's character than his achievements. I can remember meeting a physics professor who was supposed to be at the forefront of his field, and Bill told him he was an incompetent ass with an ego that would dwarf the entirety of the United States congress."

He chuckled softly at the recollection, and could hear a few of the people in the audience laughing along with him. It made things a little easier: a breath of reprieve from the sorrow enveloping the room.

"Bill was a better man and a better friend than I deserved, or could've asked for. I will always be grateful to him for that."

With that, he nodded slightly and pocketed his speech before returning to his seat.

The ceremony was wrapped up shortly afterwards and they were released. Many head to collection of beers or food. Conners found he didn't have any inclination to join them. He'd never been drunk and the idea of making his own mind sluggish didn't appeal. Besides, it felt like his stomach could turn and force him to be sick at any given moment. A few of the attendees came up to him, mumbling their condolences. Conners shook their hands and promptly forgot their words. It wasn't like they would help anything now.

It was a little odd when a man in a brown suit with a bad hairpiece came up to him, examining a piece of paper.

"Are you Michael Conners?"

"Yes," he said, curiously.

"Sorry, Hugh Windsor. I'm part of a legal team who handle the matter of the last wills of the deceased. We were part of the team who handled Mr. Scott's last will and testament."

"Oh... thanks?" Conners said, having no clue what the man wanted from him.

"Well, I'm here because you are listed as a beneficiary in Mr. Scott's will."

"Oh!" said Conners again, suddenly understanding. "Sorry. What do you need from me?"

"Well Mr. Scott left several items to you, and I need you to sign saying you consent to their ownership and delivery."

Conners accepted the piece of paper and saw a small inventory of items. He didn't give the list more than a passing glance before signing at the bottom.

"Finally, this letter was entrusted to our firm to pass along to you."

He handed Conners a thin letter with Bill's handwriting on it. He accepted it as carefully as he could. His hands shaking as if he had tremors in them.

"I'm sorry for your loss," said Windsor before turning and heading out.

Conners ran his hands rhythmically over the note, as if he could commit the feel of it to memory. He held a piece of Bill's life in his hands. Somehow, it felt that by not opening it, he could extend the old man's life. After ten minutes of standing comatose in the corner of the room, logic and curiosity superseded his reverence. He opened the letter and immediately saw the old man's writing at the top. It was almost like walking into the office and hearing Bill's voice all over again.

Hey kid,

If you're reading this, seems like time or someone finally got me out of the game. I want to tell you a few things and for whatever reason, it's easier to do it like this. Maybe it's because I don't know how you'll react. I hope they mean something to you. I want to tell you that I'm proud of you. I know you never did the work for my sake, but I've seen you grow in your skill, your drive, and your heart over our time together. I hope you continue all that. Heaven knows, there's more than enough crap in the country for there to be use for a good detective like you. Trust your instincts and you'll end up all right, kid.

That having been said, don't do as I did and lose yourself in the work. I was so destroyed by my marriage that I ended up bitter and alone until the day a strange kid made his way into my business looking for a job. You may be unsure and unused to others, but you do have a decent heart. I hope you find friends to share it with. Life is too short to live it all alone. Take that from an old man who learned the hard way.

Regardless, you'll be moving forward without me hollering at you. That's as it should be. No one can really grow if they don't get out on their own eventually, and you have a lot of potential. There isn't much I had left to teach you as a detective anyway—at least not that practice won't give you. There are other things I hope you'll pick up, but those are never things that I could've forced you to learn.

I never had kids, and though we never talked about our views on each other much, I always hoped I'd have a son who was like you. You're clever kid, and you've got a decent heart, even if it's buried under a few layers of smartass. So, I'm leaving whatever it is I have to you, including the business. It's not popular, but more than a few people heard the name in my time... perhaps a few more have since you started with me. All the same, it's yours now. So use the company as you think it should be used. I'll make sure I leave you my book of contacts. If you tell them you're taking over for me they should be willing to help you out.

I also hope you can find a way to cleanse your own soul. I always have hope for you, kid. I like to think that regardless of what you say, you're searching for God... albeit in your own way. I just hope that you end up finding him. Just know that if you do, I'll be waiting to join you in heaven. It's one wild trip up here, kid.

Take care,
Bill.

Conners slowly traced the lines of the letter, feeling the effort that had gone into the handwritten note. Each slash on the paper felt like just one more second where Bill had not died, instead had only gone on a trip for a while. Moving slowly and carefully, Conners folded the note up just as it had been presented, and placed it in his inside pocket, already knowing this would be the most important thing he could receive from the old man.

Chapter XII: Prodigal Son

Conners stretched back and placed both his hands behind his head, smiling to himself as he placed his feet on the table in the center of his apartment. So far, he hadn't taken a case since Bill's funeral... mostly because he hadn't legally accepted ownership of Knighthawk Investigations and couldn't legally have a practice until he did. However, the universe had apparently decided it wasn't content with allowing him to keep out of work, and so had brought him a case from the police that he would be permitted to consult on as an individual. To top it off, it was Jessica Lawrence who brought it to him.

"It's a fairly straight-forward case," she said, as Conners looked through the crime scene photos. "But that means it's something they won't mind you consulting on, and it could be good publicity for you. Plus if this goes well, they should let you help with future cases."

"An internship?" asked Conners, smiling softly. "Is sleeping with you also part of my tryout?"

"All at once I'm regretting my choice."

"No I get it. One solved murder is a fluke. Two cases is indisputable proof I can do your jobs better than you."

She rolled her eyes at him.

"It's not like you've got anything else on your plate right now."

"What makes you think that? I've got a few different cases crying for my attention."

"If that were true, I wouldn't have found you here."

He lost the smile at her words. She was completely right, of course. If he'd had a case he would've been cracking down on it, not lounging around his office.

"It's nice to know you're already this focused on me, Lawrence. Honestly all this flirting is incredibly flattering."

"You wish," she said, standing up. "You want the case?"

"I'll take a look. Never know, maybe it'll turn out to *actually* be interesting."

He walked with her to a wine-red muscle car parked outside his building. It surprised him for a moment when Lawrence climbed inside the car and motioned to him to get in. As he did, he glanced around at the vehicle, still a little taken aback.

"What?" she asked, seeing his curiosity. "You didn't think *all cops* drove patrol cars, did you?"

"You were driving one when we worked the Viggo case."

"My baby was in the shop that week. Now I'm all settled. Officers have to drive a patrol car, but detectives are usually permitted their own vehicles. This is my personal ride."

"Really?" he asked, growing more and more surprised by the moment. "I didn't think you'd drive something like this."

"What *did* you expect?" she asked, smirking. "A bright pink mini-cooper? My cousin was a car mechanic and I learned early on how to handle things like changing a tire or the oil. After dad left, I'd just hang out at the shop. I started to pick up some things and would help him out from time-to-time. I actually found it to be great stress relief when school was getting to me. Fifteen years of that and I managed to get my own ideal car and start fixing it up."

"I guess I just never thought of you as a car person," he said, honestly.

"You're smart, Conners, but you don't know *everything* about me."

He nodded in agreement as she started up the car and Conners nearly jumped in his seat as the engine exploded into life. Lawrence began to move through the traffic tapping on the steering wheel in time with a song that was playing on the radio. Lawrence was clearly a skilled driver too, often flying through yellow lights at the last moment and moving through lanes with a lot of skill and practice. Still he thought he would've preferred a cabbie, or even walking. At least they were less inclined to risk his life.

Lawrence drove on through the city and into the suburbs, and finally out into the much wider country. The drive wasn't nearly so long as the time Bill had taken him to the cult grounds, but he still had to slap the sleepiness out of himself. As he took a look at the surrounding scene, Conners reached into his pocket and unearthed a Jolly Rancher, which he promptly unwrapped and popped into his mouth.

The crime scene was a farm with a gravel driveway. The property itself covered twenty acres or so and bore signs of regularly worked ground and livestock. He saw several wire fences containing goats, chickens, a few cows, and even a llama—who was currently perched atop three bales of hay and spitting at a patrolman who was stood too close. The sight made him chuckle softly. To the west was a decent-sized garden with several rows that all lay empty in the January cold. Finally there were two buildings: a two-story house with a small balcony in the back, and a large barn that was open at the end of the driveway.

"Victim's this way," said Lawrence indicating the barn.

Conners nodded and followed her towards the barn and as they reached the police tape, the officer who had been spit at by the llama stopped him.

"It's all right; he's with me," said Lawrence. "Conners, this is Officer Miller. Jake, this is Michael Conners."

"*Detective* Michael J. Conners," he corrected her.

"Yes, *Private* Detective Michael J. Conners. He's an ass, but he's been useful before."

Officer Miller chuckled and moved back so Conners could enter.

"You always find the strange ones Lawrence. Can't say I've heard of this guy before."

"It's all right," said Conners, smiling as if they were friends. "I've never heard of you either, and I doubt I'll remember you once this is wrapped up."

The cop frowned and looked as if he were about to retort, the corners of his mouth twitching. However, he seemed to think better of it and merely motioned for them to move forward and examine the scene.

As they entered, Conners felt his excitement rush outward like a dam that had just burst, and a flood of adrenaline hit him as he looked around the slightly dusty barn. The first thing he saw that annoyed him was the abundance of footprints on the floor that disturbed the gathering dust. While there was clearly a path that was often traveled, many other sections of the barn looked as if they'd gone untouched for at least several months or even a few years. However, given the parade of police-issue shoes that had galloped all around the floor, it would take far too long to examine the floor for any useful evidence, if any even would've existed.

A thick rope that must've been regularly used to lift bales of hay hung from a pulley system put into the rafters. The rope had been cut halfway down, with the body that had presumably hung from it laying on the ground beneath it. The dead man appeared to be in his fifties, with thinning salt-and-pepper hair that lay flat on his head.

His clothing was all quite sturdy and old, baring the unmistakable marks of having been repaired and patched by an inexperienced hand. Several tears and buttons had been sewn in place with a different colored thread, and while they were sturdy, they did stick out sorely against the originals.

His hands were thick and callused, baring the small scars that were common for those that did a lot of work with their hands. The truly interesting thing was the man's neck. At first glance there was simply a deeply-lined mark just below the jawline, as was fairly common with hangings. However, within the mark was a much thinner and deeper line. Most likely it had been made with a much finer line, about as thin as picture wire. Such marks were not uncommon in cases of strangulation, though the fact that it had been done so high up on the neck suggested either the killer was at least six-and-half feet tall, or a premeditated act that was meant to mimic a hanging. Conners mentally filed away the information for later.

The man's fingers and teeth held the unmistakable stain of a heavy smoker and from the slight aroma that hung around him, Conners would've bet he smoked weed as much as cigarettes. However, he couldn't smell any alcohol on the man, and his boots didn't bare the wear and tear of drunken stumbling.

The rest of the barn held little of interest. Aside from some standard tools and a few bales of hay and feed; there was a stand-up ladder that lay on its side, presumably used to help hang the man, and an aging television in the corner that had a system so old Conners couldn't place it.

"His name's Jacob Carter: age 52," said the officer who had greeted them. "Coroner says he probably died around two in the morning. Obvious cause of death is suicide by hanging."

"Nope," said Conners, leaning against the doorframe of the barn.

"What do you mean?" asked Lawrence, as she looked at him curiously.

"Oh," Conners said, feigning nervousness. "I wouldn't want to embarrass Officer Whatshisface here. Plus I always get so bashful in front of others."

"Just tell us."

"You're no fun anymore," he sighed, pointing to the body. "There's a second thinner mark around his neck where the noose dug into the skin. He was strangled before he was hung up. More likely the killer only knocked him out. It takes a little while to fully strangle someone to death. However, what the strangulation didn't do, the hanging did."

Lawrence crouched down and examined the man's neck, standing up a moment later and nodding to confirm what he'd seen.

"Good eye, Conners," she said. "Carter had two boys: Luke and Lars. Lars was the one who called us in. He said that he thought Luke might've been involved in his dad's death. We'll have to bring them both in and talk to them."

Conners coughed unconvincingly.

"*What?*" Lawrence asked, and he could hear her roll her eyes.

"Only that we could do worse than to search the house."

"They've already searched it; there wasn't anything suspicious."

"No," said Conners. "They didn't *find* anything. Which is why I am suggesting you and I search the house."

"If I say yes will you shut up and help?"

"And here I thought I was already being helpful."

She sighed and waved to the officer who had waved them in as they made the thirty foot or so trek to the back door of the house. The wood that made up the back porch was old, and more than once it *creaked* worryingly as they walked upon it. However, once they entered the old house, it was different. The floors were all hardwood, but swept and cleaned fairly well. The kitchen was very small, even by the standards of most Chicago apartments. There was *just* enough room for a stove, sink, refrigerator, and a set of cabinets. There was a singular bedroom on the ground floor, and a quick look inside revealed that one of the sons likely used the room, as several posters depicting women were spread about the walls… the most modest of which were wearing swimsuits.

Conners searched the bedroom carefully, but turned up nothing interesting. There were several clothes: all of which were sturdy and roughly washed. There was an old stereo with a few dozen cassette tapes in a tower next to it that boasted several rock bands: primarily from the eighties. There was also a drum set in the corner that was poorly cared for and had several clothes and papers strewn atop it. In the closet was some type of reptile terrarium, though no reptile lay within it. Then there was the full-size mattress that lay upon the box springs on the floor, with a messy slew of bedsheets in a pile atop it.

Eventually, Conners satisfied himself with the room and glanced over at Lawrence, but she hadn't found anything that interested her either.

They head into the main room which had a small iron fireplace and a stairway to the bedroom upstairs, which Conners immediately began to walk up while Lawrence spoke to the two men sat upon the couch. The master bedroom—such as it was—had room only for a queen-size bed, a chest of drawers, a small television set atop the dresser, and an old guitar upon a stand in the corner.

Curious, Conners went to the guitar and examined it. A brief look over the instrument revealed why the thing had caught his eye. The topmost string of the guitar was strung incorrectly. It didn't take long for him to see that what should've been a low E string was actually an A string. While the incorrect string had been tightened somewhat, it wasn't even close to being in tune with the rest of the instrument, which was very nearly in perfect tune.

Lawrence came up as he was picking at the instrument.

"Going to chase a music career?" she asked pointing at the guitar.

"I'm fairly certain I've found what strangled our farmer," Conners said, and explained the issue with the instrument to Lawrence.

She nodded in agreement with his findings, only then mentioning off-handed, "Do you play guitar? Only I wouldn't have thought to look for that."

Conners was slightly thrown by this question, because he didn't play guitar. He'd never so much as touched one… or had he? He hadn't done any special research on the instrument since escaping the hospital, and definitely couldn't play one or recognize the proper strings… only he had. He certainly didn't remember touching one, but what if he used to play one? The information was in his brain from somewhere.

Cautiously, he tried to place his fingers in what would be the proper position for a chord, though he had no idea what position that ought to be. Yet his fingers knew. They placed themselves and without even strumming the note flew to Conners' mind.

A minor

"Maybe," he said, more to himself than Lawrence.

He put the instrument back where it belonged and shook himself slightly to get his brain back on task. Still, in the back of his mind, the question lingered... how could he play the guitar without knowing it? The idea made his head hurt. Staggering slightly, he reeled back with his left hand and slapped himself across the face, jolting him out of his musings into the present moment forcefully.

"Whoa!" Lawrence exclaimed, taking a step back from him. "What was that about?"

"Sorry," he said, slightly embarrassed. "I sort of forgot you were there. It's a habit from my time with Bill. When my mind gets stuck on something, I sort of have to jump-start it a little."

"Right," she said, hesitantly. "Just... don't do that in front of anyone else, all right? It's already hard enough convincing people you're not completely nuts."

"Fair enough. Let's go talk to the sons. The guitar string being the murder weapon shoots them right to the top of the suspect list I think."

"I agree."

They head down the staircase together. Conners sat across from the two brothers. Had it not been for their matching eyes, Conners might've thought they weren't related at all. Lars wore the same rough clothing as the dead farmer. His hands and arms were scarred and sported callouses, and his face and hands were tanned by the sun. Lucas by contrast was thin and wore a decent suit and thin glasses, with clean, office-worker hands.

Lawrence waved to Luke, who followed her somewhere where he could be questioned separately. Privately, Conners thought this was a mistake. It was a long-standing practice of police not to question suspects in the same room to keep emotions in check and more easily pit one against the other. However, when it came to family there was plenty of emotional discourse they could've used, especially when the brothers were as different as Lars and Luke. Still, he knew he had to watch himself if he wanted to keep working on cases with her, and he did. So he kept silent about it.

"Hello," Conners said to the larger son. "I am Detective Michael J. Conners. I hope you don't mind answering a few questions for me."

"Lars Carter," said the boy, shaking Conners' hand quickly before nodding that he should sit.

"So Lars," said Conners, throwing his feet up over the armrest of the chair as he sat down. "Why do you think your brother killed your father?"

"Luke was always the black sheep," said Lars, looking Conners in the eye. "Father and me always tended the land and saw to the animals together. Luke weren't never one for all that. I was always to take care of the farm, not Luke. I think Luke hated father for it."

Father, Conners noted. *Always 'father,' not 'pop' or 'dad.' Uncommon for a farmhand.*

"And what was so different about Luke?" asked Conners, noting Lars' steady tone and hands. "Why wasn't he ever interested in the farm work?"

"He always were a pussy," said Lars, and the right corner of his lips twitched upward for a moment.

Contempt, Conners noted mentally.

"He'd carry three bales of hay into the barn and need a breather. He got a letter to go to the city for a college, and he sign up that same night. He barely ever come home after that. Maybe twice a year or so. Last time he stops by, he and father get into it. Father says he's an ungrateful bastard and all that. I think that set him off. Next day, father turns up dead. Can't see as how it was really suicide."

Conners nodded and stood up, stretching slightly.

"Well Lars," he said. "I'm quite in agreement that your father did not commit suicide. We found a second mark beneath the rope, typical of strangulation."

Lars flashed his contempt again for a split-second, and Conners turned to follow after Lawrence.

"I'll need to question your brother," he said, not looking at Lars. "But I'm confident we'll have this wrapped up very quickly."

"Thanks detective."

Conners smiled softly to himself and went to the bedroom where Lawrence was questioning Luke. The door was closed and a police officer was standing outside the door. Conners raised his hand to knock on the door. At first the officer moved to stop him. However, he seemed to think better of it and Conners rapped his knuckles on the door sharply.

A moment later, the door opened about a foot and Lawrence's head poked out from the room. For a moment she stood there, merely staring at him. When Conners didn't speak she sighed.

"What do you need?" she asked, impatiently.

"You know, I had a dream like this once," Conners said, rubbing his facial hair softly.

"Asshole," she hissed. "I'm kind of in the middle of something here."

"Luke is innocent," Conners said. "Lars is brimming with contempt all over the place, uses distancing language, and his right hand at least has a fresh cut on the inside of it. I felt it as I shook his hand."

"You're sure?"

"Like ninety-five percent sure," Conners said. "I mean, I could talk to Luke to be completely sure, but then my whole conclusion becomes way less impressive. Although I'm going to make one last really cool deduction if you'll indulge me."

"I've been indulging you since we met," Lawrence sighed. "Why would I stop now?"

"Ask Luke how his dad felt about his efforts in college and what the farmer had to sell to send him. If the answer is 'nothing' I'll rescind my accusation."

Lawrence stayed put for a moment, then went back into the bedroom, reappearing a few seconds later with a defeated expression.

"He says the dad nearly went bankrupt and had to sell his crops and livestock at a much lower price to pay what parts of his tuition the scholarship didn't cover."

"I know," said Conners, smiling. "But I do so love it when I'm proven right."

"All right," she said, letting out a long sigh again. "Miller, go read Lars his rights and cuff him. I'll talk to Luke. Conners... insufferable attitude aside, good job on this."

Conners winked, popping a Jolly Rancher into his mouth.

"Thanks for the party invite. I'm always down to be your plus one."

Chapter XIII: Delivery

Still riding the high of having successfully collared a killer alongside Lawrence, Conners was practically skipping as he turned the key in his mailbox. He reached into the depths of the little box and pulled out only two thin envelopes; neither of which seemed important at a glance. As he started to head up the stairs to his room, the landlord—a large, kindly man by the name of Benny Kullen—waved to Conners to get his attention. As Conners paused, Benny adjusted his small, round spectacles.

"Hey there, Mister Conners," he said, smiling jovially. "I was hoping to catch you."

"Benny," said Conners, smiling kindly at the man.

Conners liked Benny. He was a genuinely kind person and a much better landlord than many of the others in the area. At first, Conners had feared complications. But once Benny had learned Conners was a private detective, and that he worked closely with Bill, Benny had become extremely accommodating. He was pleased that Conners wouldn't likely be a problem tenant.

"You got a delivery today. Looked important, and they said you'd signed for it to be delivered. So I had them drop it off in your room. I hope you don't mind. Only I didn't want it to be in the hall where they might be in the way or get stolen."

"I appreciate the thought Benny," said Conners, still thinking over his most recent case. "If you don't mind, I'm going to go take care of that now."

"Of course," said the large man, wiping his glasses off with a cloth in his shirt pocket. "If you need anything else, give me a ring."

"Will do," called back Conners, already at the top of the flight of stairs.

Conners opened the door to his apartment and was instantly taken aback. His apartment was fairly small, even by Chicago's standards. It totaled only three-hundred and fifty square feet. Still, it was space enough for what he needed, and given how little time he actually spent relaxing at home, he really hadn't seen the need for a bigger area.

The center of his studio apartment had an opening about ten feet by seven feet. During the day it allowed easy access to the kitchen, sitting area, and bathroom; and during the night he would pull his mattress down from the wall and sleep on it for the evening.

However, the opening was now occupied by a small mound of boxes, all taped closed and piled up to his waist.

When Benny had mentioned *a* delivery, he'd expected a small package or a file box at most. He hadn't expected what seemed to be the contents of a storage shed.

He sighed and went to the first box and pulled out his pocket knife. He made quick work of the packaging and pulled out a very old and worn policeman's belt that had a holster attached to it. For a long moment, he sat in stunned silence. Then, deciding to check the holster, he felt his heart skip a beat.

Inside the holster was a .44 magnum revolver that Conners recognized in an instant. This had been Bill's revolver. He'd seen it at the old man's hip too many times not to realize what it was. How had it survived the fire? Thinking back, he recalled that the pistol had been on Bill when he'd died, though it hadn't been fired.

Why wouldn't he have tried to go for the gun if he were shot? he asked himself.

Because I knew it was going to happen, Bill's voice answered in his mind. *I knew it was going to happen and I didn't stop it.*

Conners shook himself to avoid falling into the rabbit hole of possibilities around Bill's death, and pulled the weapon out to examine it. It was a beautiful revolver, shining like a star and bore an engraving along the bull barrel.

Sherry

"You would name a gun, old man," Conners said softly, smiling to himself.

The box also contained a half-dozen boxes of ammo for the revolver and couple of speed loaders to boot. Conners smiled and placed the belt and extra ammo in a drawer of his dresser before pulling his old Glock off his hip. He emptied it and placed it in the drawer too. He'd had the gun for a long time now, and it still reminded him of Bill. However, it felt more appropriate to use Bill's revolver. Conners knew he still owed the old man everything that he had become, and in that it felt right to wear Bill's weapon of choice.

Struck by a sudden urge, Conners gingerly pulled out the letter Bill had left him. He opened it as carefully as if it were made of dust, and reread the note. He wasn't sure how long he sat reading Bill's final words over and over again, cherishing the feel of the old man that still existed in his distinctive handwriting. It surprised him a little when several drops hit the wooden floors. Concerned that his ceiling may have a leak, Conners glanced upwards, but saw nothing that indicated damage overhead. Then he realized he was crying.

The motion surprised him and he reached up, examining the tears as if they were a foreign substance.

"I've gone soft," he said aloud. "I'm crying over a death I had nothing to do with that happened a week ago."

He placed the note on his kitchen counter and collapsed onto his couch, running his fingers through his hair. He was cracking up, crying nearly as much as he had when he'd shot the boy in the alleyway. This was ridiculous—insulting even. He was a supercomputer of a brain. He solved puzzles to help set things right. There was no room in that for emotional ties and weakness.

Yet still he wept, unable to stop the tears. He missed Bill, and Conners knew he would've given anything to have the old man walk through his door at that moment, grinning softly. Conners never would've been one to guess that he'd weep like a child over the death of someone he'd only known a little over a year.

"What's happening to me? What's wrong with me?"

You're only human kid, he heard Bill's voice in his head. *Why shouldn't you be sad at a death?*

"I was never... like this!" Conners growled, pacing around his apartment and kicking the coffee table hard enough to stub his toe.

Angrily hopping up and down on one foot he hissed at the offending piece of furniture, briefly contemplating the idea of chucking it off the roof to shatter it. As the pain in his toe and the sudden destructive impulse died down, Conners went to the boxes again and began to search through the remainder of his inheritance.

There were dozens of files on closed and open cases, as well as several legal papers, not least of which detailed the signing of the business and deed Bill's office over to him. Conners hadn't been back to the office since the fire. While he told himself it was because there was nothing there for him, he knew that it was really because he didn't want to be within a mile of the place if he could help it.

Still, it seemed an insult to just leave the building empty. Yet, in the same breath Conners knew he wasn't ready to work out of the building either. Perhaps he could repair the outer work of the building for now, leaving the inside hollow until he knew what he wanted to do with it. Shaking himself, he continued through the possessions.

There were a great number of books, which made Conners lament his lack of a shelf for them as he resorted to arranging them on top of his dresser. Merely reading the spines of the volumes gave him a little jolt of excitement, as they mostly covered police tactics and criminal history. The odd outlier was a cookbook that boasted several easy recipes. This volume was the only one that was brand new and had a sticky note taped to the front of it.

Learn to eat something that's not purchased from a truck or made in a microwave.

Conners smirked softly and placed the cookbook on his kitchen counter, already mentally noting his fridge likely contained none of what would be needed to utilize the book.

Finally there was a long, thin box that Conners was perplexed by. He picked it up and while it wasn't all that heavy, it had a decent amount of heft behind it. Conners carefully opened it and found a long, African Blackwood cane with a silver head and tip detailing it. Conners weighed it in his hands, and was surprised by how heavy it was. Canes were typically fairly light so as not to be an extra weight to their users. After examining it for a moment, Conners smiled softly.

Putting his hand atop the cane's head and pulling softly, he revealed a thin blade, three-and-a-half feet long, sharp, and securely attached to the head. The sight of the object made him think of Bill once more. Swordsticks were pretty decent weapons, quicker than a pocket knife, and had several times the reach.

He gave the sword an experimental swing and found he liked the weight and balance of the weapon. He gave it a final flourish and sheathed the blade. Conners carefully broke down the cardboard boxes and placed them by the door so he could recycle them later, and then looked over the pile of objects Bill had left him. Tears were still in his eyes and he shook himself, setting the cane against the desk while he sat down and began to pour over a few of Bill's unsolved cases.

Despite his best attempts, he couldn't focus on the work and ended up giving up two hours into a thoroughly unproductive evening. Instead, Conners opted to go through the mail he'd dismissed upon walking in.

The first was a bit of junk mail, declaring he was pre-approved for some card or other, which he tore up before even reading properly. The second was a public notice of a new restaurant opening in the area. This Conners set it upon his countertop, making a mental note to check the place out sometime if Bill's cookbook didn't end up working out.

Finally surrendering to the whims of the day, he pulled out his laptop and decided to check his e-mail in the hopes that someone would've had the decency to commit a crime that the police hadn't jumped on just yet. At first, there was nothing more than spam, but buried in the increasing amount of crap in his inbox, there was a piece of mail from a personal address. Excited, Conners clicked on it and sat back to examine the e-mail.

To: Knighthawk Investigations

My name is Rick Louis. I was informed by a friend of mine that you are a reliable private investigation company. I work at Kingston Inc. and need your help badly. The police are trying but they won't take anything I say seriously, neither will my boss. A number of my co-workers are being murdered. If you can, I would really like to sit down and talk to you about this case. I can't afford to pay you much, but someone needs to look into this.

Rick Louis.

Conners smiled down at the electronic letter and quickly typed a reply. Then he set about quickly cleaning his apartment. Not that there was all that much to clean. It really only involved him finishing some dishes, sweeping up a bit, and taking the cardboard boxes to the bin out back. However, by the time he'd finished, he received the reply and saw that Louis would be able to come within a few hours. Conners hastily replied, confirming the meeting and spent the time quickly pacing around the apartment and ignoring the television which was determinedly displaying some boring reality show.

As his little digital clock turned to show that it was nearly seven in the evening, there was a knock at his door. Conners straightened up and quickly finger-brushed his hair into at least a poor semblance of order, and opened the door slowly.

Chapter XIV: Five-Star Murder

Conners leaned back in his armchair, examining Rick Louis with a practiced eye while the light snow and fog that had come with February misted up his singular window. The haze obscured the street below and made the city seem oddly deserted, as if the only people in all of Chicago were Conners and his client. Louis was a large man, just under six feet, with very pale skin and a clean-shaven head. His goatee was full and lended a professional air to his appearance. Despite his nervousness and desperation, it was clear Louis was not a common laborer by any standard.

His shoes were high-class, custom-made, polished to a shine, and likely cost over five hundred dollars. He sat slumped over in a way that came from professional stress and irritation instead of casual living. The Kenneth Cole Reaction white shirt was clean and pressed. His tie was a soft purple silk no one working a physical job could've desired or afforded. Lastly, he was a slightly rotund man who didn't seem used to walking more than a few blocks on foot.

Conners pressed his fingertips together as Louis dabbed at his head with a handkerchief.

"Well detective," he said, casting a curious eye around Conners' apartment for the dozenth or so time. "Several of my co-workers have been killed recently, and the police think it's tied to the company."

"And you don't," said Conners, absently. "Why's that? You work for one of the largest companies in the city."

Even as Conners asked the question, the work Kingston flashed through his mind, making his brain throb angrily.

"Yes sir."

Conners had done a bit of digging on James Kingston during his downtime. Sadly, it hadn't turned up anything all that interesting. James Kingston had once been the C.E.O. of Kingston Inc. He'd apparently come up in the company back when it was Wilson Inc, and had eventually made partner and then taken over once Wilson had passed away. There were a few odd situations that Conners was suspicious of—such as the suicide of Kingston's co-worker Jacob Miles or the moment in late 2005 when he'd handed the entire company over to his wife, apparently to pursue his philanthropic interests. But nothing criminal had ever been linked to Kingston officially.

Still, every time Conners thought of Kingston's name, his head throbbed and everything in him tensed up, but he could never say what it was that caused that. It was like trying to hold cupped water in his hands. He might get a glimpse of something for a moment, but it would never last and he'd soon be back to square one. He wished Bill were still alive… for so many reasons.

"So why shouldn't the murders be related to… whatever it is you're doing there?" Conners asked Louis. "I mean, everyone's always ready to strike out at the big guys, aren't they? Besides, who knows *what* your lot get up to?"

Louis seemed a little confused by his accusation. Conners saw his mouth drop open for a half-second in surprise and mentally cursed. If there really *was* anything strongly illegal going on at Kingston Inc, Louis wasn't a direct part of it.

"Well sir, I think it's related to the hotel we stayed at," said Louis, scratching at his left bicep nervously. "The co-workers of mine who are being murdered all stayed there with me."

"I see," said Conners, standing and pacing around what open space there was in the middle of his tiny apartment. "Why not go to the police with this? Why come to me?"

Louis opened his mouth to explain, but no words would come out. Instead he reached across his body with his left hand and gripped his left bicep for a long moment and Conners nodded to himself. It was a classic defensive pose and given the man's position in a popular company, Conners took a pretty good shot in the dark.

"So, is it a drug problem?"

The man's eyes widened in fear and he searched Conners' face worriedly. Conners smirked softly.

"How perfectly predictable and boring. All right then, I suppose I could open my schedule. But you're asking me to cover up a lot and look into a murderer."

"I'll pay your price," said Louis, much softer than he had been when he'd first entered.

"You'll pay triple my usual rate," said Conners, throwing his coat over his shoulders, and stuffing a few essentials into his pockets.

"T-triple?!"

"Or you can try your luck with the police. I can even give you a reference."

Louis glowered, but Conners already could see the defeat in his eyes.

"Fine. But you'll make this top priority!"

"Done," said Conners, already heading out the door towards the street.

I'll have to remember to actually come up with a standard rate before I close this one, he thought nonchalantly while hailing a cab down.

Soon a yellow cab slid to a stop in front of him and Conners clambered into the back seat.

"The InterContinental, please," he said to a driver wearing an old, grey cap.

Never known you to push for money, kid, Conners heard Bill's voice fill his ears.

Conners opened his mouth to reply, then noted the cab driver and reached into his pocket, unearthing his cellphone and pressing it to his ear.

"Normally I suppose I wouldn't," he said, not caring if it didn't make sense to open up a conversation that way. "But that guy's a selfish prick. No concern or remorse for his partners being killed. His singular concern is his own neck. So if it's worth that much to him, I'm gonna charge him for it."

And you're sure it has nothing to do with the fact that he works for Kingston?

Even in his own head, the name made his brain throb painfully.

"Yes!" he growled angrily. "I'm perfectly sure. Besides, been a while since I had a client I feel comfortable taking money from and as cheap as my rent is, I'll still need to pay it somehow. That farmer case helps a little, but police consultant doesn't pay as well as I'd hoped. I didn't think they were going to pay me by the hour."

The police station *had* granted him a consultation check. They counted his work as four hours after considering the drive time, casework, and his typed report afterward. All this resulted in a glorious forty-six dollars. Sure, he'd known he wouldn't make much, but he'd hoped for a dent in his rent.

Lawrence pointed out if you get regular work from them, they'll pay you regularly. Over four hundred a week isn't too shabby.

This was also true. Being that'd he'd never been directly hired by the station before, his pay had been on the lowest end that was offered, but there was the chance that if he were a regular consultant he could get paid a weekly, or even monthly rate by the city. It would've been a good pay raise, but he also wasn't sure what would be required from him if he were officially on payroll from the city. Would he be forced to take cases he'd rather leave? Or would he still be free to take the ones that were truly interesting?

"Yeah... Well, until those eggs hatch, let's not count them."

He put the phone away, and whether it was due to his mental ending of the conversation or because his mental voice of Bill had no further retort, there was no response.

After a short enough trip, the cabbie pulled up to the curb in front of the hotel, and his first glance at the place took him aback. The outside was polished to a golden-like sheen and boasted three revolving doors and double door just to either side. The words *Inter-Continental* were emblazoned above the doors and the windows could've been one-way mirrors.

Conners tossed the driver a few bills and climbed out of the car, staring in awe at the building. He'd never stepped foot in a hotel like this. Oh sure, plenty of cheap motels and places that could've been hosting roach concerts, but never a place that looked like it catered to the one percent.

As he walked inside, he felt his jaw physically drop. This hotel was extravagance to the point that is was almost insulting. The lobby was a huge circular room with blood red walls and marble pillars, making him feel as if he'd stepped into an ancient roman structure. There was a grand curved staircase leading up to the next floor where several meeting rooms lay. Some could've only fit a half-dozen, while others would've seated fifty. The floor was comprised of several small ceramic pieces placed together in an intricate and confusing pattern. Every fiber of his brain screamed at him to try and solve the puzzle it presented.

There was a small, circular table in the middle of the open room that had a base composed of what Conners assumed were supposed to be three bronze sphinxes standing back-to-back. Upon the table was a cast-iron bowl full of red roses. Conners couldn't help but appreciate the connection between the lobby and all the recently-spilled blood of the guests. He managed to turn his head to the right were there was a concierge in an ironed white shirt and red tie, with a golden plaque inscribed with his title on the wall.

Anymore red and you could miss a murder in here, thought Conners, dully.

He tried to get the concierge's attention but the man held up a finger and pressed a phone a little harder against his ear. It took a lot of Conners' focus to not press the button on the receiver to end the call, but he didn't want things to start off hostile. However, after over ten minutes, he found himself growing annoyed. Right as he was about to ask for someone else, the man hung up and looked at Conners with an annoyed expression.

"Good afternoon!" said the concierge. "And how can we help you today?"

Conners looked around, feigning confusion.

"Who's *we?*" he asked, looking around the concierge as if he might have the ability to unearth several more employees. "I only see you."

The man grinned in a way that suggested he was enduring physical pain due to their interaction.

"Just a figure of speech sir. Are you checking in with us today?"

Conners almost doubled down on the man's use of plurals again, but decided to spare him the headache.

"Actually I was hired by a former guest of yours, Rick Louis. I am Detective Micheal J. Conners here to investigate an increasing series of murders of a group of individuals from Kingston Incorporated who all stayed here a couple weeks ago."

Conners showed the man his identification and badge. Of course, it wouldn't have held up to scrutiny, but to the common man's casual glance, a private detective's badge and homicide detective badge were similar enough.

"Oh," said the man, his face immediately displaying regret at his attitude to someone he thought was a cop. "Well detective, let me see here."

He began typing rapidly on the computer and Conners cast a glance over the man's posture. He seemed nervous, but didn't display any guilt or remorse. Instead it just seemed more likely he wasn't used to dealing with a murder investigation.

"It looks like they were registered in one of our penthouse suites, sir," said the man after a moment. "Do you need to examine the room?"

"No," Conners said after a brief pause. "I will need the name of the employee responsible for cleaning the room though."

Searching the room could take ages and likely wouldn't turn up anything useful. Even if there *had* been anything interesting, it would've been cleaned up by the staff once the room was vacant. There *was* a decent chance the person who cleaned the room had either found or overheard something if it was connected to the murders. Also, he wanted to check on the employee themself. If anyone had reason to hate a group of people who trashed a hotel room, it would be the person who had to clean up after them the next morning.

"Of course sir. One moment please."

The man typed in more information on the computer and then began printing something out. Meanwhile he reached for the telephone.

"And do you have a number I may call to confirm your involvement, detective?"

Conners grinned softly and gave the man the number of the homicide station and Lawrence's extension, which he'd committed to memory after the Lars case. Conners let his mind wonder over what he had so far, little as it might've been, and after a couple minutes the concierge came back to him with the paper and an angry sneer.

"Here you are *private detective*. The police sergeant was quite clear as to your title."

Conners pocketed the paper and glared at the man.

"I would've thought you were smart enough not to piss off the man who clearly has at least some connection with the local PD. You may want to call your boss and inform him that your penthouse suites are about to be considered crime scenes. Of course, I would love to limit it to just the one, but since you didn't tell me which one and are a complete tool, I suppose we'll just have to close them all down."

"No wait!" said the man, his anger replaced by panic. "There's really no need to…"

"Have a great day," Conners said and spun on his heel to exit the building.

Of course, he had no actual intention to try and get the rooms declared as crime scenes. As willing as he might be to go toe-to-toe with an egotist, the rest of the staff didn't deserve it and there really was next to nothing to gain by searching the rooms.

Another cab ride to a far more rundown district of the city brought Conners to the listed apartment of Harry Cordon. The apartments here reminded Conners of his own: cheap and cramped. The carpets here were stained and peeling up in the corners. The wallpaper was torn and faded. Still, it was nearly affordable housing, so nearly every unit was filled by singles or new couples just starting out.

Conners walked down the halls and stopped at the door with *18* marked on it. Almost subconsciously, he reached into his coat pocket and unearthed the little key with the same number taped to it. He'd had the key ever since escaping from the hospital, but had yet to find any person or door that would accept it as a match.

Slowly, he approached the door and pressed the key against the lock. It slid in the first quarter-inch or so and his heart leapt into his throat. He pushed a little harder… but the key went no further in. Conners tried jiggling it, but to no avail. However, a moment later there was a sound of the door unlatching and the knob turned of its own accord before the door flew open.

"What're you doin'?" asked a man who appeared to be in his early thirties.

Conners looked at the man, feigning shock and surprise before looking down the hall, as if he had made a mistake.

"Sorry," Conners slurred, adopting a drunken tone. "Wrong door."

The man rolled his eyes.

"Right," he said, warily. "Be careful. Scared the shit outta me."

The man slammed the door in Conners' face, and Conners shrugged, pocketing his key again before continuing his trek down the hall. This time he stopped at number *24* and knocked twice. The door opened after a slight pause and a young man with brown hair and a weak mustache opened the door, looking half-asleep.

"Harry?" asked Conners, looking into the young man's eyes.

"Yeah?" asked the youth, in a groggy voice indicating Conners had woken him from a deep sleep.

"I'm Detective Michael Conners. I wanted to talk to you about a room you cleaned at the hotel a couple weeks ago."

"Oh," said Harry, his face breaking into relief. "Right then. Come in."

Conners did as he said and Harry led him to a tiny table. Conners sat down while Harry filled two glasses with ice and water before joining him. Conners took a long sip from the glass before pulling out his phone and tapping the record function on it and setting it in the middle of the table.

"So Harry," he said, double-checking the printed piece of paper. "You were responsible for cleaning up the penthouse that Kingston group stayed in on January 22nd?"

"Um, yeah," said Harry, glancing down at the phone.

"Tell me about it."

"Well… what do you want to know? Pretty standard stuff. We make sure the rooms are vacuumed, change the sheets, spray down the windows and tabletops: all that type of stuff."

"Anything unusual about this group, or the room?"

"Um… not really."

The pause caught Conners attention. Normally he would've attributed it to the presumed tiredness. However, when Conners had asked about the room, Harry had perked up and given just a bit more attention to the question.

"There was nothing abnormal at all? You just cleaned it and it was just like normal?"

"Yeah, totally," said Harry, breaking eye contact and crossing his arms.

Conners leaned forward.

"Look kid," he said, adopting a tone Bill had used when he was done playing with people. "I want to keep this simple; I do. But you're starting to cause me problems and if I have to dig through every inch of your life until I get something, I will. You'll find I can be just the biggest pain in the ass when I'm irritated. So, tell me what happened while you still can and I might be able to leave you alone."

Harry sighed and Conners saw the defeat in him. After a long moment, Harry pulled out a pack of cigarettes and lit one up, taking a long pull on it before he finally responded.

"Look," he said, leaning forward and speaking softer, as if people might've had their ears pressed to the paper-thin walls. "I wasn't actually in that day. I stayed out to get in a bet at the track. It was a sure thing kinda hookup. I agreed to place a bet for myself and a buddy who works with me if he could cover my rooms. He agreed, and punched in for me. So yeah, on the file, I cleaned the room, but I never actually went in."

Conners ran a hand down his face and groaned.

"Skipping forward because there's only so much stupid I'm prepared to handle right now, who was this buddy of yours and where is he?"

"Chris Hartford," said Harry. "I don't know for sure where he is. He stopped coming in and I've stopped by his house, but he never answered the door. I'm not sure if he was home or not. It has me a bit freaked out. I mean, Chris liked to bitch about work all the time, but he's never just gone dark like this."

Conners almost wanted to slap the kid, but resisted the impulse.

"Give me his address. I think your buddy has just become a really dangerous person. Do yourself a few favors. Quit gambling, quit lying to your employer, and maybe pay attention when someone is really angry and then vanishes for a while. Seriously."

Conners snatched up the phone and dialed Lawrence's cellphone.

"Hey there Conners," said Lawrence. *"Got a call about you earlier. Something about impersonating a police detective."*

"I did no such thing, and have no clue what you're talking about," Conners said, exiting the building. "Got you a present though."

"Aw, and its not even my birthday for another seven-and-a-half months."

"Well it may be early, but the murderers are in season, you know? If you can get your boys to keep a lookout for this kid, he should be involved in the murder of a few executives from Kingston's company. I'll give you a hand if you need, but it should be straightforward."

He gave her Hartford's address and description before pocketing his phone and hailing a cab to bring him back to his apartment. While he waited, he placed a cigarette in his mouth and smoked while he tried to alleviate the pounding in his head. Once he was inside the cab, he pulled a small notepad out and began drafting up a rate to triple for Louis.

Chapter XV: Diamond in the Rough

Conners groaned and lazily flipped through the songs on his stereo with one hand. He'd been spread out on his coffee table for the past two hours. Unfortunately for his racing brain, he was completely without any stimulating work since the case at the InterContinental Hotel, and the satisfaction from that had barely lasted the rest of the day.

Oh sure, he'd had a few cases since then. But they were barely worth the effort of solving them. One marriage affair, two stolen cars, and a store manager who had wanted him to look into an employee who was stealing headphones and other simple electronics. Boring, double boring, and put-wooden-splints-under-the-fingernails levels of boring.

Of course, he had little choice but to take the jobs or else go back to living in abandoned houses, and now that he had found a purpose it was impossible to go back to what he'd been after the hospital. More than once he'd considered starting the process of rebuilding the office and moving into Knighthawk Investigations permanently, but he'd never managed to convince himself to actually do it thus far.

Right now the office was an empty, two-floor place totaling around six hundred square feet. Truly, a place of luxury. So far he hadn't done anything more than work up the courage to merely pass by the building. It felt odd to be afraid of a building he owned. Conners didn't know *what* he expected would happen if he set foot in the place he knew so well. Perhaps he expected Bill's ghost to rise and punish him for his failures.

He still heard the old man's voice on most of his cases. He'd half-heartedly researched it on the Internet, but nothing that came attached to hallucinations was good. Still, he wasn't particularly worried about it, because he knew his own mind and felt secure in the fact that he was *not* insane or losing touch with reality. There was just a tiny piece of his mind that was utilizing the voice of the man who had taught him all he knew. There was nothing wrong with that. If Conners were really honest with himself, he didn't *want* to lose that part of his mind. It would be like letting go of Bill… and the old man deserved so much more than Conners could give.

Rolling off the table, Conners flipped on the television and snatched up a tennis ball from his desk, tossing it so that it could bounce off the wall and rebound from the floor back towards him.

The clash of noise from the stereo and television made a horrible sound that he allowed himself to get lost in, even as his neighbor banged on the wall in aggravation. He tossed the ball again as the lady on the news talked about a barbecue place. Aside from making a mental note to try the place out someday, Conners scowled softly.

"Come on," he muttered, tossing the ball again.

The next story was about a car crash with an intoxicated driver. It could've been something but the police hadn't had an issue with it. Conners tossed the ball again, harder. The car crash gave way to a new policy the mayor was considering. Again, he hit the wall.

The same neighbor angrily pounded back three times. Conners smiled softly and waited a second before chucking the ball as hard as he could at the wall. It ricocheted and rocketed around the room, smashing one of his few drinking glasses and he swore softly. Moments later Conners heard someone knock on his door with the force of an angry rhino.

Conners opened the door and looked questioningly at the man beyond it. He was a large being, weighing over two-hundred-and-fifty pounds. He didn't so much have a bald spot as a small horseshoe of black hair remaining around his head. His face bore the stubble that came from a few days of not shaving, and he smelled as if he'd also neglected to bathe during that time. He wore a pair of cargo shorts with sandals, and an open bowling shirt over a gray wife-beater.

This man was Barry Tallow, and he'd been a right thorn in Conner's heel since he'd moved in. Barry had no job, unless one considered professional complaining a job, in which case Barry was a workaholic. While Conners was out and working on a case, things were great between them. However, when Conners was actually *in* his apartment, any noise he made caused Barry to throw a temper tantrum. Once Conners was properly aware of this, he decided to alter his behavior, and began *intentionally* making noise that would be audible in Barry's apartment.

So when Barry began speaking, it wasn't so much talking as it was shouting.

"What the hell are you doing?!" he bellowed. "Always making a huge fucking racket and banging things against the wall like a freak! Some of us like peace and quiet!"

Conners smirked at him.

"So sorry about that, Barry friend. It's only that your mother decided to come over and I suppose my bed is just a touch too close to the wall so it keeps banging against it."

"Oh you think you're clever! You're not half as smart as you think you are, you punk!"

"Still twice as smart as you," Conners said, winking at Barry.

"What's that?!" asked Barry, taking two steps forward, actually into Conners' apartment. "What did you just say?"

"Hey, hey," said Conners softly, as if talking down an angry horse. "It's all right big fella… No one expects you to understand anything we say. So really, you're already exceeding expectations!"

Barry let out a shout and swung at him, but Conners had seen the blow coming and calmly ducked out of the way, pulling up the cane Bill had left him. Not that he was going to cause any serious injury to Barry, but the man had long-earned a swift smack or two across the shins.

Barry snarled and moved forward again, but Conners swung with his off-hand. Barry was big but knew how to dodge at least one blow. So he leaned back out of Conners' reach, but the detective spun on his heel and allowed the momentum to spin him round in a circle and brought the cane across both of the large man's shins. Barry hissed and fell back into the hallway, landing on his rear-end.

As this happened Conners heard the story on the news switch over again.

"And in other news, wealthy stock trader and community activist Harry Wilson was robbed last night."

Conners turned his attention to the television eagerly while Barry rubbed his bruised shins.

"While Harry and his wife, Lucille, were out at dinner, their Chicago home was broken into and robbed. The thieves took a number of treasures from the home; most noticeably a large gem known as Piceno's Diamond. The diamond was purchased at auction by Mr. Wilson three months ago. While the diamond was insured for half its cost, Mr. Wilson is offering fifty-thousand dollars to anyone who is able to recover the diamond."

Conners was already belting *Sherry* in place and filling his pockets with small tools, Jolly Ranchers, and cigarettes. He quickly walked out of his place and locked the door behind him, stepping over Barry, who was still moaning.

"Later bud," Conners said, leaping down the flight of stairs and hitting the landing with a solid *thud*.

He practically skipped out the door before hailing a cab down, and gave the driver the address of Harry Wilson. The driver looked at Conners a little askance, given that he was heading from a hole in the wall to a far more upscale part of town, but in the end the cabbie decided not to question it. They moved quickly enough through the morning throng of traffic and Conners felt himself getting excited and the adrenaline began to pump through his veins.

It had been entirely too long since he'd managed to land something good. He sincerely hoped this case would present a challenge for him. The cabbie eventually pulled up near a large, white home with three stories and huge tall windows, which meant that the ceiling was likely twelve feet tall instead of the standard nine.

Conners walked up the white stone steps and rang the doorbell by the elaborate glass door. A moment later a beautiful woman with blonde hair opened up. She was made up like a movie star on the red carpet, with expensive jewelry hanging from her ears and adorning her fingers.

"Hello?" she asked as a way of greeting.

Conners smiled and waved cheerily.

"Detective Michael J. Conners, ma'am. I'm here to find your missing diamond."

"O-oh? So you're from the police department?"

"No," he explained. "I'm a private detective, though I have been a consultant for the police when they are out of their depths."

"Oh," she said, a little brighter. "Come in. I'm Lucille Wilson. My husband is in the study. I'll just have to let him know you're here."

Conners followed her into the house and was taken aback by the elaborate decor. The walls in the entranceway bore no art, but had simple carved boxes he supposed were to dictate class and elegance. To him, they just seemed a little goofy. To his left there was a small bronze statue of a naked man posing as if he were competing for the title of Mr. Universe.

She led him to a large sitting room with four blue armchairs surrounding a round table. He took a seat and kicked up his feet on the table, glancing about the room. There was a huge, ornate fireplace that was nearly large enough for him to lay down in, and two huge mirrors with gold trim opposing one another on the walls, making the room appear even larger than it already was. Two tall windows showed the bare tree limbs outside, which had yet to come into bloom.

"I'll return shortly," she said, sounding more like a secretary than a wife.

Then Lucille turned and left him to his own devices, which meant he quickly unwrapped a Jolly Rancher and popped the candy into his mouth. As he enjoyed the cherry-flavored treat, he couldn't help but examine his reflection in the mirror. If the scene in the mirror were a painting, his figure would've had to have been added in later by an entirely different artist. He was horribly out-of-place. The thought made him smile.

After a few minutes, Mrs. Wilson returned and smiled brightly at him.

"If you will follow me detective, my husband can see you now."

Conners nodded softly and stood up, stretching slightly. She continued to lead him through a house that was far more extravagant than it was practical. Each hallway and room seemed intimidating, and Conners immediately missed his shoebox apartment with dirty floors and peeling wallpaper.

When they finally stopped outside the door to one of the far-too-many-rooms, Lucille knocked softly.

"Come in," said a voice behind the door, and she opened the door for Conners.

Conners walked in to see a man in his late forties with a pair of thin spectacles and a retreating hairline. He was fairly thin and wore a blue silk shirt above an expensive pair of slacks. Conners felt a small sense of pride that—despite his obvious wealth and expensive clothing—ultimately, Mr. Wilson left less of an impression than Conners himself did.

"Detective," said Mr. Wilson, smiling softly. "Please come in."

Conners walked fully into the room and was immediately enveloped in a rich, red atmosphere. There were bookshelves along one wall with thick volumes that looked to be unopened, and a large desk with meticulously placed items atop it. Conners always was interested in the correspondence between someone's work space and their behavior and attitudes. This level of obsessive order suggested someone who was a planner to a fault. Plans could be useful, but adaptation and improvisation could never be tossed aside.

"What brings you to my home today?"

"I'm here to find your missing diamond, Mr. Wilson."

"Oh? Well I'm glad to have another person assisting in the search. Anything I can do to assist you?"

"Search? No, searching takes ages. I'm just going to find the diamond. That's far quicker and my time is finite."

Mr. Wilson let out a soft chuckle, which Conners noted. Any man who was willing to make light of someone who was trying to help them find a lost valuable was someone who raised a red flag for him. That sent a desire through him and Conners decided to act impulsively.

"Actually I'm only here to make you a bet, as it were."

"I'm sorry? I don't understand."

"I bet you that I can have your diamond back in this house before noon tomorrow."

Mr. Wilson's eyes went wide, but he forced his face back into composure quickly.

"Well... that is a mighty claim. If you are able to do this, what would you ask?"

"Double the reward."

There was a long moment of silence. Conners could tell that Mr. Wilson was expecting him to amend his statement or laugh and claim to be joking, but he didn't. Now, Wilson actually laughed aloud.

"All right, Detective Conners. However, if you fail to get my diamond back before noon tomorrow... I want you to agree to run background checks and dig into the laundry of anyone I ask for the next three months free of charge, yes?"

"Deal," said Conners, shaking the man's hand and smiling. "Well, I've got work to do."

"Don't you want to know about the break-in?"

Conners turned away and began walking towards the exit.

"Of course not, the break-in is by far the least interesting part of this whole ordeal. I know a diamond cutter I intend to have a quick word with."

This was a lie. Oh sure, Conners did know a few cutters and fences that could move stolen merchandise, but none that were anywhere near this part of town. Something as valuable as this diamond would've been very hot, and unlike the lower parts of the city, a couple of hoods breaking into an upscale mansion would raise alarms.

What really concerned him though, was Harry Wilson's dismissive attitude towards his stolen property. Granted, he certainly looked as if he wouldn't be hurting monetarily, but even so, people who lost expensive or sentimental things were usually either angry or depressed. The only people who were happy to be robbed were people who had insurance, which suggested motive. Means and opportunity were also a given, and so Conners knew his first suspect was the very man who was so confident that Conners couldn't find the thing.

However, Conners doubted it would be in the house. That would be dangerous, even stupid, regardless of how large his place was. No, more likely he wanted to hide it somewhere nearby that wouldn't be thoroughly searched. That ruled out most public businesses. Banks, restaurants, and stores all saw too much foot traffic and cleanings to ensure that it wouldn't be discovered. Instead, it was more likely that there was a place nearby the was often empty with few visitors.

Conners hailed down a cab and after the man pulled up, he climbed into the back seat.

"Where to sir?" asked the cabbie in a thick accent.

"Where's the nearest construction site, preferably one that's been there for a while without actually seeing work."

"Oh yeah, I know the place," said the cabbie, smiling brightly, which caused Conners to smile in turn.

No one but no one knew the state of the city better than a cab driver. They saw the streets every single day and knew the constant construction sites because they had to be driven around when possible. Sure enough, the cab driver drove him twelve blocks to an empty lot that had recently lain gravel, but clearly was suffering some building issues, as the foundation had not yet been lain, despite being marked.

Conners tossed the cabbie the money and thanked him before climbing out of the cab and immediately doing some research on his smartphone. Wilson did *not* own the site, but it was well-known that the developers and the construction crew were having a long-standing debate and the land had basically sat in limbo for the past couple weeks. Debates like this could go for months, over a year if they were particularly stubborn. It was the perfect hiding place if you knew what was happening. Besides, even if the job *did* continue, it would be simple enough to come by at night and retrieve the gem and find a new place to stash it until the search died down.

Admittedly, it took Conners longer than he would've liked to find the correct spot, but after a fair chunk of false starts, he found one recently disturbed spot and begin digging through the area and luckily, he unearthed a glittering diamond hidden beneath the rock.

"Heh, talk about the tree hidden in a forest," he said softly.

Then he felt his phone *buzz* in his pocket and he saw Lawrence's name on the display.

"This is Clearly a Better Detective Than You Agency. What crime can we solve for you today?"

"Oh well since you're asking, apparently there have been a few calls about some weirdo in a long, black coat digging around in a construction site that's been blocked off for a few weeks. Don't suppose you'd know anything about that?"

"No idea what you're talking about," he said, smiling at her exasperation. "However, if I *were* digging up a recently missing diamond that was reported in the news, it might be worth mentioning that I've been on this for all of a few hours."

"You're not serious?"

"I am, and getting a decent payday for it too. Oh, but you might want to have a squad car come over because you'll need to arrest Harry Wilson for attempted insurance fraud."

"Why do I feel that you get into way more trouble than you're worth?"

"And here I thought I was jazzing up your life."

"As much as I'm sure I'll regret this, you might be jazzing it up on a more consistent basis. If you really did *find the diamond, first*

off I want pictures. Secondly, my lieutenant wants a word with you if you're not busy on Wednesday."

"What'd I do now?"

"It's not a punishment. Just… can you come by then?"

"I suppose… and you swear I'm not being arrested?"

"I swear that I currently have no reason to arrest you… aside from trespassing on a construction site."

"Close enough. Well, sure. Send over a squad car and text me when you have a meeting time."

Conners hung up the phone and carefully placed the diamond in his coat pocket before heading back towards the street. It ultimately hadn't been a bad day. He got to collect a nice check and the police would get to collect a bad guy.

He'd had less productive Saturdays.

Chapter XVI: Lieutenant

Conners looked down at at his selected outfit for the afternoon's meeting with the precinct's lieutenant. He'd wore nothing that he was uncomfortable in, but had at least taken care to make sure that his t-shirt had no holes and that his shoes were clean. Conners had never spoken with the lieutenant before, though he had spied him through the glass windows that led into his office when the blinds weren't drawn.

The lieutenant was a beefy, dark-skinned man with a large mustache and when he spoke his voice tended to have a low-end rumble. It was almost as if the man had a built-in subwoofer. Lawrence had more than once hinted that he was someone who preferred to have rules followed to the letter, and had been heavily against using Conners as a consultant in the first place. It was only due to his high rate of success that the lieutenant hadn't frozen Conners out.

What you so nervous about, kid? asked Bill's voice in his mind.

I just want to do well, he thought back. *I want this guy to like me so that I can solve more cases, and do more good.*

Can't solve cases without a big brother looking over your shoulder?

It's not like that, Conners fought angrily. *This could give me first access to cases. Just imagine how nice it'll be to avoid all the legal trouble.*

Oh, so you're trying to get in with the cop to avoid *red tape. Good luck, kid.*

The voice stung. Bill's voice had never been disapproving like that. Sure, it had been joking, even slighting at times, but never disappointed. Conners shook himself violently. Bill's voice was just a figment of his overactive mind. So there was nothing to feel disapproval over. Right? What did it matter that Bill had left the cops to go start his own agency? Times were different now. Besides, it wasn't like Conners could just strike out on his own and be entirely his own agent.

This was a good thing: so he told himself, even if he had to repeat it a few times in his head.

Conners walked through the front doors of the station and saw Officer Miller actually enjoying a doughnut. Unable to resist the chance to be a pain in the ass, he swung by the patrolman.

"So is this a perk of the job or is it actually down in the rulebook to be a stereotype?"

"Conners," said Miller, and he rolled his eyes exaggeratedly. "I just needed a hit of something sweet if I have to deal with you today."

Conners couldn't help but laugh. He couldn't say he liked Miller as much as Lawrence, but at least the officer wasn't boring. He waved farewell as Lawrence descended the stairs and smiled at him.

"Hey there," she said brightly.

She seemed pretty happy to see him, and Conners winked at her as she waved.

"Miss me, Lawrence?"

"Nah, anytime you're around you instantly remind me what an asshole you are."

"And yet, somehow you enjoy spending time with me."

She chuckled softly.

"Somehow. How you feeling?"

"Bored," he lied. "I mean, unless your lieutenant has been murdered or received a threatening e-mail, I really don't know why I'm here."

"You're here," she said, after sipping from a coffee cup. "Because you are actually pretty good at casework and we want the chance to work with you more."

"And by 'we' you mean…"

"Ok. I mean *I* want the chance to work with you more. So, I put in a request and the lieutenant always vets people in this situation. He wants to meet you."

"These all sound like things for *you*. What am I getting out of all of this?"

"Cases, mostly. Besides, this will be good for you: help you move up and all that."

"And bury me under a mountain of paperwork."

"It's not like that. The lieutenant's a good man."

"Can't be," said Conners, more playfully than anything. "He's a cop."

"Oh?" she asked, and he saw her raise and eyebrow behind her aviators. "Cops are bad people now?"

"Plenty are… but I'm really not sure about this one chick."

She swatted him on the shoulder and he defensively held up his arms. This made her laugh a little, and because she found it funny, he did too.

A strange thought struck him at that moment: Lawrence was his friend. It was a word he hadn't really had a strong use for before. Oh sure, he'd been close to Bill, but Bill was a teacher—even a father to an extent. Bill was the one who had taught him and brought him along, but Lawrence was the one he laughed with and spent time with. Sure, so far that had all been work, but there was no reason he could see that it *had* to be work.

"Dinner," he said suddenly and she shook her head, taken aback. "What?"

"I go in, behave myself for a bit, and we grab a bite to eat together. Nothing formal or fancy, just a moment to pick each other's brain when we're not standing around a body."

"Can you behave for a couple minutes?"

"I don't know," he said, in mock-seriousness. "I've never tried before. I can only promise to try. What do you say?"

She studied him for a long moment, and he could tell she was fighting something deeper in herself, something that he suspected had nothing to do with him personally. Rather it was a part of herself that had been built up over years and did not want to come down in a hurry. Well, he was certainly not someone who could call fault in that area.

"Fine, but I pick the place. I've seen your apartment, and I don't trust you to know a half-decent restaurant."

Conners dramatically reeled back, clutching at his chest.

"You wound me, dear lass!"

"And I'm already regretting this decision."

"Do I have to wear a dress and heels for this place?"

"Didn't anyone ever tell you not to make a threat you aren't prepared to keep?" she asked, smirking slightly.

Conners smiled and followed her through the glass double doors past the receptionist towards the back of the building, where a set of twin staircases led to the homicide detective offices in the 14th precinct. Lawrence led the way in and she was greeted half-heartedly by a few of her fellow detectives.

"Got your lapdog with you today?" one man with greying hair asked her, indicating Conners.

"Woof," said Conners, sardonically. "Hope you don't expect me to hump your leg. At least I'm housebroken."

"Lieutenant wants a word with him," said Lawrence, trying to hold her smile back at Conners' behavior.

"Your golden boy finally get himself in trouble?" asked the detective.

"Nah," said Conners, crossing his arms. "He just wants to offer me your job, and figured it would be really awkward to do it out here. You know: people will talk and all that? Best just to put together a press conference saying that you're leaving to pursue your own interests. Looks better on an application and all that."

A woman sitting at a nearby desk chuckled at that.

"Careful Jones," she said, smiling brightly. "Her doggie can bite!"

A few short bursts of laughter came out around the office. Conners made a small leap onto a nearby chair and gave a deep bow, which led to the room smiling back a little more. Despite the fact that he didn't really trust any of these people, he couldn't deny they wouldn't be so horrible to be around… at least sparingly.

Lawrence led him to the back of the room where there was a smaller office that was properly walled off and had a glass door with the words *Mark Guston: Police Lieutenant* emblazoned on it in golden letters. Lawrence rapped her knuckles on the glass twice and the man behind the desk looked up and nodded, gesturing for them to come in with his left hand while holding a phone to his ear with the right.

Conners' mind began making notes of its own accord.
- *Left-handed: holds the phone with his right, takes down notes with his left. Hip holster on his left side.*
- *Still uses a revolver as his department-issued handgun: old-fashioned. Stubborn. Set in his ways.*

Conners tried to determine the model of the gun, but in the holster it was difficult to tell. He thought it was likely a Smith and Wesson, but the model could've been a .581, a .586, or even a .681. Still, it made him wish he'd brought *Sherry* with him, however unwise it would've been to bring a loaded magnum into a police station.

Lawrence entered the office first as the lieutenant hung up the phone, and Conners got a good look around the office. There were no family pictures or telling personal possessions. In fact, the only two items on the wall that definitely belonged to Guston were his own uniformed picture, and a plaque declaring him active lieutenant of the 14th precinct.

"Hey Lieutenant," said Lawrence, sitting in one of the chairs across from the desk. "This is Michael Conners, the P.I. I've had assist me on the Sillow and Carter murders. He also basically gift-wrapped us Hartford and the Wilson Insurance cases."

"Impressive resume," said Guston. "Four high-profile cases, and from what I can tell, you don't brag about it to the public."

Guston spoke with a low timber in his voice and Conners could tell that the man was used to intimidating people merely by conversation.

Tough luck bud, thought Conners. *I was* trained *by someone who was scarier than you any day of the year.*

"I'm not interested in crowd-pleasing and sucking up to city officials. I leave that to the experts."

Lawrence instantly stiffened, and he could tell that had they not been in front of her lieutenant she likely would've kicked him.

"She said you were mouthy," said Guston, giving no indication of annoyance or enjoyment.

"She was being kind. I'm a two-bit prick," Conners swung around the chair and collapsed into it, kicking his feet up onto the man's desk. "I am unpleasant, unpredictable, and I make a mockery out of almost everything."

"So I can see," said the lieutenant. "Why should I allow you to work alongside one of my very best detectives if you are so very impossible to like?"

"Impossible to like?" he repeated, looking over at Lawrence. "I didn't say I was impossible to like. Am I impossible to like?"

"It's certainly easy to be irritated with you," hissed Lawrence through gritted teeth.

"Sorry," he said, grinning brightly. "I'm bored."

"I am regretting so many things."

"And you actually *bribed* me to be here is the weird part."

Lawrence put her head in her hands and Conners turned his attention to the lieutenant.

"As for why you should allow me to work with Lawrence, it's pretty straight-forward. I'm expertly trained and damn good at closing cases. Besides, you already know I'm not interested in personal glory. So it's not like I'm going to be stealing thunder or anything, and if what I do isn't useful, I don't get paid. So there's no inclination for me to waste anyone's time."

"I see, tell me about your 'expert training' then."

So Conners launched into his time with Bill. He didn't go over everything Bill had taught him, rather explained the multitude of cases that they had helped close, especially those that the police hadn't been able to crack. To his credit, Guston kept silent and just listened to what he said and didn't interrupt or make any sounds of disbelief. In fact, Conners almost felt like he was explaining his casework to a computer more than an actual person.

"I have to admit, your history is impressive," said Guston. "However, I'm concerned about your ability to work with others."

"I work well with Lawrence," Conners responded. "Why not just stick me with her? I guess her partner doesn't like me, though: Detective whatshisname?"

"Higgins. He was transferred to another station."

"Oh? What'd he do?"

"It's not like that," said Guston. "He wanted to move his family and we agreed that Lawrence was ready to take lead in cases."

"Did he harass someone? No. He stole something, didn't he?"

"He didn't do anything!" said Guston, emoting for perhaps the first time in the conversation.

"…Well now I'm all interested."

"Point being that, yes, you *could* perhaps serve with Lawrence. How would you feel about that, Sergeant?"

"Despite this meeting, sir, Conners is a great caseworker and I can't deny that we do work well together. I'd like to have him with me."

"Well then, I say we give him a shot. We'll have to get you through your classes, of course, but if you're as smart as you claim it shouldn't take longer than a couple weeks."

"Whoa, wait now. Training for what? I'm already a huge brain on legs."

They both stared at him.

"What exactly do you think you're here for?" asked Guston.

"To be allowed to be a sort of goto consultant on future cases."

Guston laughed, which actually frightened Conners as he wasn't sure the stoic man could do such a thing.

"Conners, we don't *have* goto consultants. In fact, it's been a long time since we've had a consultant at all. No, we don't use consultants. We use detectives."

"Wait... you want me to be a police detective?"

"You'd be on a trial period for a few months, until you truly earn your rank, but if you continue to deliver work like you have then yes, we would make it official. Then you would have all the casework you could ever want."

Conners felt himself go slightly cold. He hadn't expected to be officially joining the police force. His mind began to split the pros and cons of this possibility of its own accord.

- *More casework, but that also means boring and tedious cases.*
- *More resources, but that means more reports and explaining everything I do.*
- *More chances to help people, but that comes with protocol and rules outside of my own.*
- *I get to work with Lawrence...*

He couldn't find a con to meet that. So, with a heavy heart he nodded and the lieutenant began to have an officer bring in paperwork upon paperwork.

Well... there you go, kid. You get to be a police detective just like you originally planned to. Hope it's worth it.

Conners had never felt so stabbed by the mental words of Bill. Half in anger, half in resignation, Conners began to sign the paperwork and give them his information. He would have to go through some physical tests and learn police protocol and take a detective's exam, but it would hardly be anything he couldn't work out in his sleep.

He was going to be an actual police detective. It was just what he'd once wanted. So why did it now feel so hollow and empty?

Chapter XVII: When you Bleed Blue

Conners groaned and pulled at the tie around his neck. This had become a nervous habit of his and he did it subconsciously several dozen times a day. He honestly couldn't help it. The singular tie that he owned was a simple, grey piece of fabric and was the closest thing to a comfortable tie he'd been able to locate. That didn't help the annoying sensation that the tie was both a physical and mental leash for him to be yanked around by.

"Stop fidgeting," said Lawrence, as he pranced around by accident.

"Why exactly don't *you* have to wear a tie? *This* is sexism."

"At least we get to keep our choice in footwear. Lots of departments enforce full suits, so take your freedom where you can get it."

Conners growled and tugged at the tie again. He hated the tie. He hated the department-issued semi-automatic at his waist. He hated wearing button-up shirts. He hated having to wait hours or even a day for permission to do every little thing. He'd been officially employed by the department for all of a week, and had already entertained ideas of burning the building down a total of eighty-six times... not that he was counting or anything.

He missed the comfortable weight of *Sherry* on his hip. He missed his coat. He missed the cabbies who didn't give two shits for the rules of traffic. He missed taking cases that interested him regardless of protocol. He missed following the most direct route to a solution. He missed taking action as soon as an idea popped into his head. He missed a lot of things he hadn't realized he'd be giving up.

If there was any saving grace to the job, it was Lawrence. She at least made the job tolerable and he knew he would've walked out during his first day if it wasn't for her. At first the idea of more cases had seemed exciting, but it quickly became apparent how much of their work was simple legwork in which he could've practically turned his brain off.

There was no challenge in what they did most of the time. So far, the most interesting case they'd had was a dead body that had been found in the crawlspace of a house. The thrilling conclusion was that he'd become stuck near the house's ventilation and either starved or suffocated. Something which the autopsy would confirm... How Conners had managed to stay awake so far was beyond him.

"How do we get the good cases? Like, do I need to slip the lieutenant a twenty or something? Cause I'm losing my mind."

"We work what's assigned to us. Don't worry; it's Chicago. Something interesting is bound to hit us soon."

"Well, it certainly can't come too soon. I'm over this natural cause crap."

"Conners!" called the lieutenant. "You have a comment to share with the rest of us?"

Conners looked up at the lieutenant and had to take a long breath to avoid lashing out at him. From the moment he'd signed the forms, the lieutenant had made it clear who Conners worked for. The man's military-like love of the chain of command wouldn't allow him to tolerate anything less than total obedience. Naturally, Conners had replied to this demand with as much maturity as he possibly could.

"Only that your nose hair appears to be winning the battle of territorial control, sir. In fact, our intelligence suggests that it's taken over your entire upper lip, Lieutenant."

Several of the other detectives quickly tried to silence their laughter or hide their smiles behind their hands.

"That's funny Conners," said Guston, his tone low and irritated. "So funny that you should work overtime this weekend and crack me up some more."

"Would love to, sir. I just don't want to be the one to make the call to Mrs. Guston about how you're never home because you're spending all your free time with me."

"I'm not married, Conners."

"I know, sir. I was referring to your mother."

More chuckles and even a snort from Detective Homer, who sat behind him and Lawrence in briefings.

"Anyway, if we're all done with the one-man show that is Michael Conners, I have case assignments. Johnson and Homer: there's a shooting down on North California, one dead. And Lawrence, you and your comedy act have a death at Shedd Aquarium on South Lake Shore."

Lawrence took the file and left the room with Conners on her heels.

"You know you're making things worse for yourself by antagonizing him, don't you?" she said over her shoulder.

"Probably," Conners said, disinterestedly. "Please, please, please tell me it's something good. It's an aquarium. So... I don't know, strangled by an octopus?"

"Not exactly."

"What, he go swimming with the sharks?"

"Yes, actually. It was the shark trainer. Says here that what's left of him was discovered in their tank by the owner this morning."

"Oh..." said Conners, suddenly feeling very queasy.

Lawrence noticed his change of tone and stopped, turning to look at him.

"What's wrong? Two seconds ago you were yapping like a Yorkie. Now you suddenly turn all green gills on me."

Conners didn't know how to explain to her what he couldn't explain to himself. While he'd joked about the animals being involved, and *knew* the case was at an aquarium, he hadn't *actually* expected the case to involve the water this directly.

Conners had found that he had an issue with water for a while now. He wasn't sure exactly when it had started. Maybe it was something from his life before the hospital. Maybe it was living for months without heat or decent shelter when it was very cold and very wet. Whatever it was, water—especially large bodies of water—held a very real and very primal fear for him. He hated being too close to the river and even a heavy storm could make him reluctant to go outside.

"I mean... this one actually sounds pretty boring. Simple stuff. Why don't you go check it out and I'll see if there's a beat I can help out with?"

"You'd rather walk a beat than take a murder case? With sharks? Come on, what's with you?"

"Nothing's with me. I mean, if we split up we can do more work right? And it's not like we can't go over anything you find together later."

"Conners, you tell me why you don't want to go, or I swear I will handcuff you and walk you into the crime scene personally."

Conners sighed and looked at his shoes.

"I don't... like the water."

"I'm sorry?"

"I don't like large amounts of water. I just can't help but get distracted and I'm afraid I might fall in and I can't swim and who knows what is even *in* water. I mean, in the aquarium especially we know there's killer sharks and I'm not a fan of that and…"

"Conners!" said Lawrence, firmly enough to stop his rant. "It's gonna be fine. It's not like I'm gonna throw you in the water and the first cops on the scene already did a sweep. This is just a normal case."

Conners took a deep breath. Lawrence was right. If he allowed himself to see this as the case it was, then he could get through this… He just sincerely hoped that he wouldn't have to go into the water or near the creatures of death at any point.

They hoped into Lawrence's muscle car, and she navigated them through the slow flow of traffic through the city. After a little over half-an-hour of traffic, they pulled into the parking lot. Conners was mentally grateful that it was nearly empty, because by size alone it could've been at least a ten-minute hike to the front doors. They were greeted at the front door by Jake Miller.

"Hey Miller," said Lawrence. "What's the situation?"

"Hey Sergeant. The deceased is Garret Pallos. Owner says that Pallos was the shark trainer. This morning they found bits of him in the tank and his water suit torn to shreds in bloody water. So far, there's no evidence of foul play. Owner's inside, says he'll talk to you if it'll help."

"All right," said Lawrence. "We'll talk to him first."

She led him into the aquarium where a middle-aged man sat on the bench in a suit one size too small. Lawrence subtly pointed two fingers straight down. Early on, the two of them had developed a small collection of gestures to use between themselves in addition to the common gestures used by police and SWAT teams. This gesture was made so that he would take lead in the questioning without discussion that might tip a person of importance off.

They both altered their pace just slightly so that he took the front and reached the owner first.

"Hi sir," he said. "I'm Detective Michael Conners, and this is my partner, Jessica Lawrence. We're here to figure out what happened to your employee Garret Pallos."

"Right," said the owner, nodding slightly. "I'm Jonathan Vanderhill. I own the aquarium. If I can help you in any way, don't be afraid to ask."

"We appreciate that," he said, already growing bored of the conversation. "Got any ID: just to confirm?"

Truthfully, Conners didn't care about the man's identity. He wanted to see his wallet. Single men, married men, and fathers all had vastly different contents in their wallets. Vanderhill opened his and Conners saw a picture of a young, blonde girl who appeared to be in her late teens, several small bills, a few bank cards and his identification.

Conners then got a solid glance at the man's left hand while he was busy removing the license from the wallet. His ring finger didn't look as if it ever bore a wedding ring. So the man was a single father, running a fairly large business. That was interesting.

"Our officer tells us you were the one who found the remains of the employee?" asked Conners, pretending to pay attention to the man's license.

"Yes," said Vanderhill. "I came in at maybe 7:30 or so, and checked on the different stations, just to make sure everything's up to par, you know?"

"Of course," Conners said as he began to walk deeper into the aquarium, already uneasy due to the excessive amounts of water.

He noticed a sign on the wall that read: *UNDERWATER BEAUTY COMES IN ALL COLORS… see them up close.*

Yeah, not for a double in my salary, Conners thought, giving an involuntary shudder.

"When I arrived at that station with our Black Tipped Reef Sharks I saw… what had happened to Mr. Pallos. Then I called the police. It's not a pretty sight, detective."

Conners said nothing, merely followed the man past a large central tank and off to the right side of the building.

"Any clue what would've caused the sharks to attack?" asked Lawrence, after waiting for Conners to speak for a little while.

"Unfortunately I have had a thought. I don't like to admit it, but he had a bad habit of taunting several of the fish—the sharks especially. I always told him off when I caught it, but he apparently wanted to see if it was possible to start a proper feeding frenzy."

"A what?" asked Conners, more afraid than curious.

"Oh… sometimes if sharks are kept in high enough quantities together, when fed they can go into a sort of rage and attack anything near them. It's actually very rare. We always took care to prevent something like that from happening by making sure they were fed regularly and we didn't include especially violent breeds. Feeding frenzies are far more common amongst the more predatory breeds like the Great Whites. Typically, Black Tipped Reef sharks will work well with one another."

"Do you think a feeding frenzy could've cause this?" asked Lawrence, leaning forward.

"It's possible I suppose, but our sharks have always been fairly docile, and their breed are considered relatively safe to swim amongst."

"Yeah," said Conners, dismissively. "And every dog owner swears their dog has never bitten anyone, yet repairmen across the city have to keep going to the hospital for dog bites."

The owner had no real answer to that. He led them through the aquarium and into an elevator that brought them to another level of the place. Conners had to do his best to focus his breathing to try and deny the impression the water was going to come crashing in on them. If that were to happen, it's not as if the walls of the elevator would do any good to stop the hundreds of thousands of gallons from killing them due to the sheer force alone. And that was nothing compared to the horrible feeling of drowning in an elevator, trapped and unable to escape. Sure, there was a small emergency hatch in the ceiling, but what good would that do? Then, he would only be trapped in an elevator shaft, and still drowning.

Wham!

He hissed as he felt Lawrence kick him in the back of the shin, not hard enough to bruise, but enough to snap him out of his spiraling thoughts. He silently pointed his ring and pinkie fingers at the ground that they used to symbolize an affirmation, hoping it would keep her from kicking him again.

The doors opened the reveal what a bright red and yellow sign deemed the Wild Reef Exhibit. They walked up on a relatively small tank that came up to around waist height. Thankfully they didn't stop at it, and Conners managed to keep himself from shivering as they passed whatever dirty, slimy thing lived in the tank.

"We're currently about twenty-five feet beneath street level," said Vanderhill, as if that thought wasn't extremely terrifying. "Our Black Tipped Reef Sharks are usually kept towards the back of the exhibit."

The next area echoed deep sea diving. Even the walls were made to look like blown up bits of reef and coral and gave him the unpleasant feeling of being a tiny sea grub just hoping to avoid death by shark or some equally horrifying creature. They soon passed under an archway and Conners nearly backpedaled out of instinct alone as he noticed several fish swirling directly over his head, looking as if they were trying to create a hurricane.

Nearby was what Vanderhill referred to as "mid-sized" predators. Conners spotted several large-teethed barracudas and nearly turned to leave then and there. However, Lawrence kept him moving forward. They passed by several more exhibits and he did his best not to look at the tanks. He still nearly threw up as they passed what seemed to be a black tank with small fairy lights that turned out to be what were called Flashlight Fish.

After far too long, they reached a colossal-sized tank filled with a great many different fish, several of them sharks. Conners consciously kept several feet back from the edge of the glass, uncomfortably aware that this would not do a damn thing if the glass were to break. What didn't help his fear of the sharks was the easily visible sight of a half-eaten diver in the middle of the exhibit, floating like some grotesque display.

"How did he get in there?" asked Lawrence, puzzled.

"There's an employee entrance back there," said Vanderhill pointing to a door that blended well with the decorated walls. "It's how they enter to treat and feed the fish, and clean the tanks. There's also a locker room back there where they change their gear."

"Is it surrounded by more fish tanks?" asked Conners, keeping a nervous watch on a nearby shark that seemed to be studying them.

Vanderhill shook his head slowly and Conners practically power-walked to the door. The locker room was, mercifully, not surrounded by visible fish and sharks. In fact, it reminded Conners a little of the locker room at a gym, with a few rows of lockers, showers, and sinks located nearby. Conners immediately head to the locker that was designated as Pallos' and opened it, searching through the belongings.

At first there was little of interest, merely some clothing, a few cleaning products that smelled even worse than body oder, and a small fiction novel. The inner door had a few pictures taped to it, which Conners examined carefully. One was a picture of presumably Pallos and two of friends holding up a fish on the edge of large boat. That was a little odd. Why would someone who worked with fish want to pull them from the ocean? After all, many people who worked with animals famously had trouble eating meat afterwards. This was like a farmer who visited a butchery in his spare time.

What proved far more useful was the picture of a young woman who looked to be a freshmen in college, sitting on a bench with Pallos' arm around her. At first, Conners thought nothing of it. It was a picture of a man and his girlfriend. Not a big deal. However, what fascinated him was Vanderhill's reaction to the photo. His fists and jaw were clenched tight and his knuckles were turning white. It was classic anger, but why should a picture of young couple cause the owner anger? After a second glance Conners realized the girl in the picture was the same girl Vanderhill kept in his wallet, grown by about a decade.

"Who is this girl?" asked Conners, pointing at her.

Vanderhill swallowed.

"My daughter, Juliet."

"They dated?"

"For a while. They broke up about six months ago."

Conners waited but Vanderhill offered no more information.

"You didn't approve of their relationship?" asked Lawrence.

"I don't like the idea of her dating anyone that I have to do business with… it can make things messy."

"But there was more to it than that," said Conners, moving slightly as the crime scene photographer moved past them, taking pictures. "Seeing them together makes you genuinely angry."

"He… could be hurtful to her. He had anger issues and sometimes he would be… rough with her. I kept saying she should leave him."

"That's not all," said Lawrence moving forward. "You weren't disappointed or worried, you were pissed at him. I can't imagine you just sat by the side doing nothing while your daughter was being hit."

"When she was ready, we filed a police report," said Vanderhill, gritting his teeth again. "But nothing came of it. Not enough evidence to do anything… apparently."

Conners felt the bite of the system hit him like a blow to the chest. The unfortunate reality was that quite a few claims of abuse and stalking were dismissed and not taken seriously due to the overwhelming number of cases that came in each week. It was a pathetic excuse and it never sat well with him.

"So you went to talk to him?"

Vanderhill hung his head and Conners saw the man appear utterly defeated. This had been weighing him down for hours and he knew there was no easy way out. So, he began talking in earnest. He began crying softly and collapsed onto a bench.

"He hit her again, and I knew it wasn't going to stop. The cops already proved they weren't going to do a damn thing. So I went to him. It turned… violent. I hit him and broke his nose, and I'm not sorry about that. He deserved far worse than that. However, he had been getting ready to go into the tanks… I couldn't have guessed his nose would start bleeding… or that he'd fall *just* wrong into the damn tanks. The sharks had been waiting to be fed and so when he fell in… they did what they knew to do."

"I swear I didn't mean for it to happen, I just wanted to scare him a little. I didn't want my daughter to be hurt anymore. I didn't… I never wanted…"

Conners ran a hand over his face. He knew what the right thing was, and what his job demanded he do. The problem was these two demands appeared completely detached from and opposed to one another. Jonathan had been defending his daughter, and even then he'd only really caused harm because the police had failed to do their job. What decent man wouldn't have defended his daughter from a beater?

However, he was a police detective. Regardless of the reason behind it, Vanderhill had killed a man. Besides, they could always talk to the judge and try and get him a reduced sentence. Conners reached for his handcuffs and pulled them out. Vanderhill knew what was about to happen.

"Jonathan Vanderhill," he began, and then stopped.

For the first time since becoming a cop, he heard Bill's voice echo in his ears again.

Do the right thing, kid.

This arrest, however legal—however demanded, was *not* right. Conners knew he would've done the exact same thing in Jonathan's place, and he would've been right to do it. He knew that this was going to cause issues for him and Lawrence, but that didn't matter. After all, he was the lead on the case and it would be his report at the end of the day. He sighed, and placed the handcuffs back in their holster, and Lawrence looked at him, neither accusing or forgiving, only watching.

"Thank you for your assistance in helping us with this case," Conners said, so disconnected he almost didn't catch the words as he said them. "Clearly, your employee was injured and fell into the tank while trying to instigate a feeding frenzy among the sharks. I'm sorry this happened, and wish you the best of luck in dealing with the new nightmare. However from what I see, no one here is at fault for what happened, legally speaking. I don't know how the insurance companies will see it. But as far as the police are concerned, this was a case of someone neglecting the rules of the company and endangering their own life until it was tragically lost. Thanks again."

Conners shook Jonathan's hand at the same time he heard the door to the locker room open behind them. The one thing that comforted him more than his knowledge or the act was the soft approval he could feel coming from Bill. In fact, Conners felt it was the first time he'd done the right thing since signing the papers to become a detective. Conners turned towards the door and his heart jumped as he saw Guston approaching them, along with two officers in tow.

"Hey lieutenant," said Lawrence, looking curiously at the man. "What are you doing here?"

"I wanted to see how you and Conners were getting along, sergeant, but it appears you've just closed the case. Congratulations. Go on boys."

At his word the two officers pulled out a set of handcuffs and moved towards Vanderhill.

"What the hell?" demanded Conners. "Lieutenant, what is this?"

"*This* is the system at work, Conners!" snarled the Lieutenant, jabbing him with a finger. "Now, I'm willing to overlook that little moment of compassion you just had in there, but your overtime's gone for the week, and if you *ever* try to pull something like this again, I will have your ass off the force so fast your head will spin. Understood, detective?"

Conners looked at the man, and felt a rage building up in his chest. The lieutenant had no moral right to do that—none at all. Jonathan had been defending his daughter where the force had failed. *They* were the morally dark ones. Instead, Conners had made a call and it had instantly been unmade. The one thing he'd felt even a little ok about had just been snatched away from him. Then it was as if the world split into three factions for him.

There were the criminals, those who killed and stole and cheated. Then there were the police, who might want to do good, but where shackled by the system, who cared nothing for the moral position of a man. Then… there was who Bill had been. There was only one sensible course of action.

"Perfectly clear, sir," Conners said, yanking the issued gun and badge off his belt. "It's clear you don't give a damn about doing the right thing, and would happily burn a decent man if it meant you covering your own ass. So you can take this and choke on it, you bureaucratic, puffed-up, empty-minded, morally bankrupt asshole!"

He slammed the badge and gun into the man's hands, then as an afterthought threw the tie at him as well. Then he turned to Lawrence.

"I'm sorry," he said so that only she could hear him.

"Me too," she said quietly. "But I don't blame you. It was great having you for a partner."

"I wish you'd come with me."

He saw the hesitation in her eyes, and for a moment he thought she would. However, a moment later, the logic took her and he knew her answer before she said it.

"I wish I could. But I can't do it like you can. Still, I'm a sergeant and I can bring you in the good cases as I like. But, probably better if we go our own ways for a bit, right?"

Conners smirked and winked at her.

"Don't spend your whole shift daydreaming about me now."

She rolled her eyes and embraced him briefly before Conners turned and began to walk away. He noticed several of the employees were filming him on their phones eagerly. He shrugged. It wasn't as if he hadn't already resigned and blown up rather spectacularly. He walked up to Vanderhill, who seemed twice as defeated as when he had confessed his crime to Conners only minutes ago.

"I'm truly sorry for this," he said. "I promise I'll speak to the judge: even testify on your behalf if it'll help."

"It's a shame this city just lost a decent cop," said Vanderhill, just loud enough for them to hear.

Conners nodded and walked back towards the elevator, already going over a plan of action in his head. This wasn't the end… now was the time for things to really begin.

Chapter XVIII: Back in Black

As the September morning sun began to warm up the city after a slightly cool evening, Conners took a long sip of his coffee, smiling at his brand new office. After quitting the police department, Conners' life had taken a strange shift. When he'd returned to private detective work, he'd found a small amount of fame. Apparently a fair number of employees had captured his full fight with the lieutenant and his resignation. At least one had posted it on a few video sharing sites and it quickly gained a lot of popularity. Soon after, that video was—of course—taken down by the department's legal team, but a few eager viewers had stored it already and had the video back up within a few hours.

The end result was that Conners became something of a local celebrity. Sure, he didn't have people wanting his autograph or wanting to meet him or anything. Still, once it got out that the man who'd quit the force for a morally wrong arrest was doing private detective work, he'd found his case load flowed in quickly. It had been only around four months since he'd quit, but he'd had to rent a proper office space only a week into his resumed work. Even then, he'd already decided that the rented office was only temporary. He wanted to get Bill's old place up and running again. The place was a little on the small side. Still, it was enough space for him to convert the second floor into a living area and the bottom level into an office.

The only issue he had with the place was that the single bathroom was built downstairs. This he'd done as a courtesy to his clients, and during the day it wasn't a huge problem. However, if he woke in the middle of the night needing to pee, it meant an uncomfortable hike downstairs with a full bladder. Overall though, he was thrilled about his new place.

The desk had two huge filing cabinets next to it, and while he'd already nearly filled one of the drawers with case files, he knew the others would follow in the coming years. He'd also spent money on a good desk and office chair for himself. Most of his furniture was new, especially in the kitchen. He hadn't cared much about the kitchen though, and bought whatever seemed affordable and functional. He did make sure to stock his fridge with enough ingredients to try some of the simpler recipes from Bill cookbook. However, in his living quarters he had picked two items and spent a little extra. The first was a stereo system that had speakers hooked up throughout the building so he could work to music wherever he was, and the second was a new, comfortable mattress. He'd hoped to put in a fireplace like the one Bill had used, but the budget was beginning to stretch thin and he had to make the call against it.

He'd never been one to really care for the extravagant or expensive things of the world, but he had to admit that there was something to be said for a few comforts. While he was not as callous or desperate as his time spent in the streets, he hadn't forgotten what it was like to be without much of the basics.

Conners also refused to allow his newfound success turn him into a businessman. When a client was well-off, or wanted something boring and basic, like a background check, he would charge them based on his time and expenses. Just as often his clients were desperate and out of hope. In these cases, he'd refuse to take their money and tried to do what Bill would've called "the right thing."

He'd set Bill's urn on his dresser, and it helped him get his mindset right in the morning. To his pleasure, he found that returning to private work and doing things in this way had also caused the mental consciousness of Bill to reappear, and it would often guide him along while he worked and especially when he struggled with something morally. It helped Conners along, even if he couldn't deny that hearing his dead mentor's voice probably wasn't the healthiest thing in the world.

This is going to be a fun day, isn't it kid? asked Bill's voice. *First time working with the cops since your blow up.*

"I'm working with Lawrence more than the cops," he responded aloud. "Besides, this is more about the casework."

You could just admit you want to see her again, kid. She's a good one.

Conners shrugged, but already knew that it was true. He *did* miss Lawrence, and for more than just the casework. He missed her manner of joking around and found himself almost wishing she would chastise him for the Mexican food truck he frequented. Still, he could at least take some solace in the fact that he would get to see her briefly today.

Apparently the police had gotten a heads-up that an escaped convict from Missouri was heading to Chicago to try and get lost before disappearing into another part of the country properly. Most every precinct had men out looking for him in case he made an appearance, and the local news had covered the escape. The good news in all this was that Lawrence had been green-lit for what resources she determined were required to assist, and in this case that included Conners.

Out of respect for her job, he'd kept his nose out of police affairs since he'd left. Getting too involved would've put her in a bad spot. She would've become the cop who had the explosive P.I. as her partner, and it would seem she was pulling strings to do him a favor if she brought him in too often. With something like this though, no one would likely call her out on using a consultant.

Conners slid *Sherry* into his holster, placed two sets of handcuffs on his belt, snatched up Bill's old cane, and put on his long overcoat, smiling at the feeling of relaxation and comfort it brought him. His wardrobe consisted mostly of jeans and t-shirts, and he had no reason to change that. Due to feeling they were tainted, he'd burned what button-up shirts he'd owned as a cop. He walked down the stairs, and glanced at the files on his desk that were still waiting to be solved. It was going to be a busy week, no mistake.

The thought made him smile brightly.

Conners almost skipped as his feet hit the street. Smiling at the pleasure his life had given him, he gave a cab driver the instructions to the 14th precinct. The driver made quick work of the path and twelve minutes later, Conners found himself jogging into the precinct, waving his credentials to the receiving desk cop.

"Sorry," he said, grinning. "Off to help catch a killer!"

"You don't have to look so thrilled to be here, Conners."

"Nope! I don't have to make a point of gloating when I show you up either, but it's just *so* much fun!"

He jogged to the briefing room and was greeted by the immediate mix of reactions from about two-dozen officers.

"Hello, hello!" he said, waving like a movie star walking down the red carpet. "Yes it's so nice to be here. I enjoy many of your local features! I enjoy your cases."

"This is Michael Conners," said Lawrence, trying to hold back a smile at his antics. "A police consultant who is going to assist us on this case. Don't worry if he's an ass; it's not personal."

If the gathered officers, detectives, or marshals had objections or questions, they kept them to themselves.

"All right, you all have your assignments. Let's go!"

The team broke up and Conners went to Lawrence, and she embraced him quickly.

"I missed you," she whispered to him.

"I missed you too. I mean, I've eaten so much crappy food lately and my stomach has a mad case of the revenge rumbles right now."

That did make her laugh a little.

"Somehow I have no trouble believing that. Anyway, let me go over this quickly. Our guy's name is Terry Ryan. He escaped from St. Louis County Jail, and they think he arrived in town a couple hours ago, but he'll need some place to rest and change. We've got people at the train stations, docks, and the airport, but he might choose to lay low for a while. It's a big city after all."

"Oh, well we need to have this guy back in cuffs for his name alone."

"His name?"

"Yeah, Terry Ryan? Dude has two first names. You have to pick one."

"View must be lovely from the glass house of yours, Conners."

He winked at her as he popped a Jolly Rancher into his mouth, largely because he was now free to do so.

"He's not going anywhere quickly. He'll have to stay here a few days at the very least, and likely a few weeks."

"How are you so sure?"

"He can't move easily or in the open, even if he did find a hiding place. Plus file says he was born and raised in Bowling Green. That's a country town, not a metropolitan city. I doubt our man can even board the L-train smoothly. Forget trying to look like he knows where he's going in cabs and the like. Plus, it's not like he had access to a smartphone and computer in prison. Even if he did have a drop-off outside of the jail, he won't be able to smoothly look up where he wants to go. He's *got* to spend time in the city, figuring things out."

"You seem to have really thought this out," said Lawrence.

"I know, I know," he said. "I'm a big, sexy brain on legs, but we have a job to do sergeant. Stop flirting so much. I'm just not that kind of woman."

She rolled her eyes at him, but he could tell she enjoyed his joke. That came as a relief to him, because he certainly didn't want to go over the *real* reason he knew what it was like to be scared and lost in the city with no idea of how to get around in it. He'd never gone into the details of his life before Bill with her. He didn't think he could bare the judgement he'd face if he did.

"So what's he most likely to do?" Conners asked, half to himself, half to Lawrence. "If you were lost in a new city and needed to lie low for a bit?"

"Well it's not like he can go out and check into a motel right now. Even some of the seedier places could be looking out for him after the news report. We should check through his old contacts and see if any of them could've gotten him some place in the city."

Or he could just get an illegal ID, said Bill in Conner's head. *Plenty of people in prison would know people in that line of work. St. Louis and Chicago aren't all* that *far apart and it's unlikely he picked it at random.*

"That's a good start," said Conners. "I want to hit up a few contacts and see if he might've picked up a street ID. If he *is* planning to stick around it'd be good for him to have one regardless."

Conners quickly ran through a list of people he knew from his time with Hunter's gang. He knew it wouldn't be an exhaustive list, but it was a starting point. If none of those on his list had seen Ryan, perhaps they would know someone who had. Conners nodded softly to himself and began to jog out into the street when Lawrence called out to him.

"Conners! Look, Ryan's dangerous. So be careful, ok?"

Conners flashed her a smile and winked.

"Hey, it's me."

"Yeah," she said, so quietly he almost missed it. "That's why I'm worried."

He hailed down a cab and gave the driver instructions to the area of town where one of his old contacts like to lurk. These day the contact was going by Melborn, but everyone just called him Mel. Conners suspected that it was somehow connected to his actual legal name, but he'd used so many through the years it was impossible to be sure. It was Mel who had made Conners his fake papers before he'd met Bill, and while Conners had kept his distance since then, he hoped that their past business would still count for something.

"Hey Mel?" Conners called out, walking into a small space behind an apartment building. "You working?"

Mel didn't respond quickly, but that wasn't unusual. Back when Conners had gotten his fake ID, Mel had made him wait half-an-hour before he'd responded. This time it was closer to twenty minutes. Eventually, one of the windows slid open half-way and Conners saw a heavily dirt-stained man standing behind his makeshift counter looking at him with a weary eye. Mel's eyes slowly focused and he smiled, showing two missing teeth.

"Conners," he said. "Good to see ya, lad. Was wondering when I'd be running into you again. Figured you'd find trouble soon enough. Your kind always do. So, what do you need?"

"Information," said Conners, pulling up Ryan's picture on his phone. "This is an escaped con from St. Louis. You make anything for him?"

Mel leaned forward, smiling slightly.

"Can't say as I have. I'd heard you'd turned streets on us. Have to say I'm pleased."

"Not a cop," said Conners. "Private work, or I'd be arresting you instead of paying you, wouldn't I? Why would that make you glad though?"

"Oh, because otherwise I'd have felt a little guilty."

Wham!

Conners felt something slam into the left side of his face so hard, it knocked him to the side and sent him sprawling on all fours. Before he could focus himself properly, he looked up to see a huge man charging him. Conners took a second to release a breath and his adrenaline kicked in.

The man charging him was very tall, even taller than Conners was—and he stood at six feet and two inches. On top of that, the man was heavily muscle-bound; the white t-shirt he wore seemed to be straining with he effort of keeping his muscles contained. His face bore several scars and Conners had no doubt his body was just as disfigured. He wore black jeans, a worn leather coat, and a flat cap. All-in-all his clothing might not be out of place, but he still cut an impressive figure. As best Conners could see, the man bore no weapons, but also didn't appear to need them.

With what time his mind could give him, Conners reached for *Sherry* and raised it as quickly as he could. Before he could've aimed the weapon, he knew it was already too late. This large man moved far quicker than Conners had given him credit for. The scarred man gave a long swipe with his left hand and knocked *Sherry* from Conners' grip.

Time sped up again as Conners spun on his feet readying his grip on the cane. He didn't release the blade just yet, preferring to keep what cards he still held secret. The man made no move to go for the gun, but cracked his knuckles and scowled at him.

"Hi there," said Conners, holding the cane in front of him as if it were a broadsword. "My name is Michael Conners and I suppose you're wondering…"

The man did not let him finish and charged. Reacting instinctively, Conners swung hard with the cane, and his blow connected with the man's left shoulder. While the hit was solid, the man didn't give any reaction at all, as if he hadn't noticed the attack. He wrapped his huge arms around Conners' waist and tackled him, sending them both to the ground.

Conners felt the concrete ground dig at him as he brought the handle down on the man's back as hard as he could repeatedly.

"You! Are! Very! Rude!" he yelled, striking between each word.

Finally with that last strike, the man grunted and rolled away from Conners, who sprung to his feet and charged. The man assumed a defensive pose, but left his legs spread too wide. Conners waited until the last second and let the adrenaline take over him again.

He used his momentum to go into a long slide right between the scarred man's spread legs. The classic move at this point would been to hit his foe in the crotch, but the would require some very fine aim and might end up causing him more trouble if he couldn't release from the attack before he kept sliding. So instead Conners unsheathed a small portion of the blade within the cane and used it to cut deep into the man's calf. This blow landed well and as Conners came up on the other side of his opponent, he heard the man hiss and curse quietly in what he took to be Russian.

"That was a dirty trick," said the scarred man, his voice heavily accented.

"Welcome to competition in America. Mind telling me why you're attempting to make me into your afternoon workout?"

"Not part of my job," said the man, and Conners felt fairly sure he was either Russian or Serbian.

He's been hired to kill you, said Bill's voice. *Can't be that many people who want to kill you with access to assassins.*

Yeah. I'm normally so well liked. I've left Richards alone for too long anyway. Ten-to-one he works for her.

"I'd still at least like a name to call you by. It's ok; I know it likely won't be your real name."

The man seemed to consider him for a moment, then smirked slightly.

"Alexander."

"As in 'the Great' or 'Pávlovich?'"

Alexander smiled at him again.

"You *do* like to talk. Time for talking is over."

And he rushed again and Conners quickly removed the blade from the cane, readying himself. Alexander made to bat the blade away as he'd done with *Sherry* but Conners was expecting it. He ducked down beneath the blow, and stabbed out with his weapon. It entered Alexander's other leg at the shin and poked clean out the other side. Conners yanked the blade back out, twisting it as violently as he could to cause more damage. It worked, and Alexander collapsed.

Conners backed away, panting heavily. Their fight hadn't been going long, but it *had* been demanding and he could feel his muscles protesting the wear and tear they'd been through during the battle. Alexander wasn't out, but he was wounded, and that was enough for a very brief breather.

"Whatever you're being paid," he gasped. "It's not worth your life. Work with me and you can still come out of this alive."

Alexander forced himself to his feet, despite the pooling blood leaking from his right leg.

"I was not hired to make a deal with you. If you don't kill me, then she will."

She, said Bill's voice in his head. *Pretty well confirms it, kid. Unless you think Lawrence or Wilson's wife wanted to take you out.*

I have to agree.

"Right. Well, she wants me dead, she can come try it herself then."

Alexander rushed him again, limping slightly from his wound and Conners managed to side-step him fairly easily, dragging the blade along his opponent's thigh. This time, Alexander collapsed fully and seemed unable to rise. Conners cuffed Alexander by placing a knee in the small of his back to hold him down. Finally, he retrieved *Sherry* and kept it pointed at the man while he reached for his phone.

"Hey Conners," said Lawrence, sounding smug. *"Guess who found a jailmate of Ryan's with an old apartment in Chicago?"*

"That's great," Conners said, smiling softly even as he grunted from pain.

He gingerly touched his ribs and figured Alexander had either bruised or fractured them when he attacked.

"You sound hurt," she said, suddenly concerned. *"Are you all right?"*

"Mostly yeah. I'll need an ambulance and a squad car when you can, though. I'm not seriously hurt, but I think I've got some bruised ribs and I'll need to be checked out for internal bleeding. Ran into a... Russian assassin, I think? He's mostly subdued but sooner would be better."

"I'll have someone sent to you now. Where are you?"

"Thanks Lawrence," he said, leaning against the brick wall. "Knew I could count on you."

He texted her his location. Almost out of habit, he half-heartedly glanced towards the window, but wasn't surprised to see that Mel was long gone, and there was little doubt the word about his true allegiances would be out on the street soon. He'd have to be careful.

Chapter XIX: By Day and Night

Conners shook himself slightly, and glanced down at the check he'd recently been paid by the precinct for his help in assisting with the capture a small gang of burglars. He was actually getting paid at a decent rate. Still, Conners could tell that Guston hated him for the outburst during his resignation. The police lieutenant refused to come out of his office when Conners was around. He wouldn't acknowledge Conners and would often draw the blinds if he were in the bullpen.

It had been just over two years since he'd quit the police force, but Guston still detested him. The rest of the homicide squad at least were split into those who found him obnoxious and those who appreciated his work. Lawrence, of course, was still the only one who regularly worked with him. Conners found he preferred his relationship with the lieutenant this way. Instead of being forced to fall in line, the best way to get paid was to help their arrest numbers in crimes the police either didn't have the time or wits to solve. Guston might be stubborn, but he was smart enough to know that Conners was a valuable asset to his precinct.

Lawrence and he got to spend loads of time together too. While some of the force had originally suspected her of giving him preferential treatment (which to a degree, he supposed she did) they also couldn't deny his abilities or his successful closure rate. He'd also received an official document as a thanks from the chief of the metropolitan police, which Conners had proudly flaunted for a time before setting it next to Bill's urn on his dresser.

As the summer wind blew, Conners took a moment to enjoy the breeze as it cooled and relaxed him. Due to the weather that day, he'd abandoned his coat and simply worn his jeans and a t-shirt which proudly displayed the words *Silence is Golden. Duct Tape is Silver.* Lawrence had rolled her eyes at this, but he could read behind the annoyance in her eyes, and knew she liked having him around.

"What do you think?" asked Conners, as he looked over at the sergeant. She was sporting a white button-up shirt he'd not seen her wear before.

"How about we get some *proper* Mexican food?"

"Great," he said, smiling. "I don't know if the truck I like is open right now but—"

"I will seriously kick you. There's a restaurant nearby I like. It actually reminds me of my mom's cooking: real authentic stuff, like the kind she used to make growing up."

Conners cocked his head slightly.

"Guess I never really asked," he said, feeling a little guilty as he recalled the pictures he'd seen in her apartment. "Is your mother Mexican?"

"Half," she said, climbing into her wine-red car. "But she grew up in Mexico until she was nearly sixteen. Then, her dad got her citizenship and moved with her to America. Her mom never got to move out of Mexico, but they kept in touch and visited every couple of years until she passed away."

"Wow," Conners said, taking a moment to respond. "I'm a bit surprised you knew all that. Still, seemed like your relationship with your mom's good."

"It is. I mean, she worries too much. And I think she's asked me a thousand times this year alone when I'm going to settle down and have kids, but she cares about us. I think she's a little closer to Janice because of Mikey though. He's cute, but a *real* handful. The moment he started crawling I wished she could put him on a leash or something."

Conners laughed.

"You know, I hear they have those now? Blue leashes you just hook to the kids or whatever?"

Lawrence shook her head, laughing.

"Those exist purely to be laughed at. I mean, I *want* my nephew to be kept ahold of, but those are just… no."

Conners laughed with her again and when it died down, she turned right at a stoplight and glanced over at him.

"What about you then?"

"What about me what? I mean, I'm flattered if you're asking me for kids, but I'm not putting leashes on them."

"I meant your parents, you ass."

Conners frowned. He was scanning through his head for some convincing lie, but as he did, he heard Bill's voice protest.

If you want this to work, kid, you can't just lie to her. Besides, she trusts you, doesn't she?

Her background isn't highly illegal, though.

Respect the one friend you've really got, Conners.

"Honestly? No idea."

"What does that mean?"

"I have no idea who or where my folks are. I don't know if they're alive or not, or what they did for a living."

"What? Were you adopted? Foster kid or something?"

"No idea on that either. Honestly I have no clue what my life was like until February 21st, four years ago. I woke up in a hospital with amnesia and no ID or anything."

"No one knew you were there?" asked Lawrence, her voice suddenly as curious as it was concerned.

"No idea," he said, sounding like a broken record. "Left before I found out. Hospitals scare the crap out of me. I don't know what they meant to do with me, but the idea of truly being in the system without knowing who I was scared me. So I left."

And so he explained his life up until meeting Bill. Of course, he skipped his murder of a young child. Friend or not, he doubted she would be willing to forgive that particular act. It wasn't like he'd forgiven it, and he had been the one who understood it better than anyone else likely could. Lawrence for her part was a very good audience. She listened and asked questions without really interrupting, and let him talk for long periods of time when he wanted.

He wrapped up with Bill's death and let the moment hang there for a long while. Lawrence seemed to be chewing on everything he'd said, but he wished he knew what she was thinking. While he'd left out the shooting, he'd still admitted to an awful lot of crime and morally dark decisions. However, when she spoke, her words were compassionate and caring.

"I'm sorry. Things have been hard for you, and I didn't know how much Bill meant to you. I promise that we *have* been digging into the woman you told me about, but she is frustratingly clean. I get why you wanted to go after her so much. Bill sounds like he was a good man."

"He was the best. He taught me most of what I know and was…" Conners began, before mumbling. "…like a father to me in ways… I guess."

It was the first time he'd ever admitted the feeling aloud, and couldn't help but feel like a child. Lawrence placed a hand on his shoulder.

"It's ok to care for people, you know? I'm sure Bill cared about you just like you care for him. For my part, I care about you too."

Conners smiled and hastily wiped his eyes while Lawrence had the grace to pretend not to notice.

"Care about you too. Now, let's grab some food I'm sure I'll instantly regret."

Lawrence nodded and led him into the restaurant and Conners had to carefully consider the menu several times over before he felt confident enough to order anything. They had seven different listings under quesadilla. Conners knew of only one: a quesadilla. The restaurant boasted several different types, all of which broken into subsections based on what you wanted the main filling to be. Finally, he found one that offered that he understood to be either steak, chicken, or peppers, and chose the steak.

He found himself slightly frustrated when fifteen minutes later he received a tortilla with one side soaked to a greasy mess and filled with steak, cheese, peppers, and onions. Resigned to his choice, Conners merely scrapped off the majority of the peppers and onions and tried to eat his collection of odd components. Lawrence at least seemed to genuinely enjoy the chimichanga she'd ordered, along with the salsa and chips. Conners found that he didn't much care for the authentic Mexican food. He was good with the deep-fried American substitute, but the genuine article was a whole other affair. Still, he enjoyed the time Lawrence spent with him and because he enjoyed his time with her, it became a positive experience.

When they walked out the restaurant after their meal, Lawrence embraced him for a second. He found that he'd really come to enjoy the contact. It was as if in that brief embrace there was a gesture of friendship that neither of them had the words for. There was nothing romantic or sexual in the gesture, just an expression of trust and understanding that connected them at a deeper level than talking could.

"You want a lift back to your place?" she asked, pulling out her keys.

Conners gave an overly dramatic flourish and held his hand to his chest.

"Detective!" he said, exaggerating the word. "I appreciate you treating me well as a true gentlemen should, but I am *not* that kind of girl! How *scandalous*!"

She rolled her eyes again.

"Take care, Conners."

"Catch you later, Lawrence!"

Conners strolled down the sidewalk, swinging Bill's cane from side-to-side. He liked to have the cane with him, especially on days when it would've been a pain to openly carry *Sherry*. The city had gun laws that made anyone who even legally owned a firearm a suspect, let alone anyone who actually wore the thing openly. But sword canes were hardly as popular, even if a younger man with a cane seemed a bit odd.

He walked a few blocks, letting the wind blow past him and smiled again.

"The Windy City indeed," he said and pulled out his phone to call a cab.

In the busier parts of the city, it was a simple enough matter to hail one down, but out towards the suburbs it was a bit of a different game. Still, it was a simple enough matter to call a dispatch, and he wanted to have some time to relax and let his mind unwind without talking much.

As the cabbie slowed to a stop, Conners noticed that the driver seemed to be eyeing him particularly hard. Instinctually, he tightened his grip on the cane. Nevertheless, he climbed into the back of the cab and gave the address of his office. As the cabbie took off, he looked at Conners again in the rear-view mirror.

"Hey," said the driver suddenly. "Not for nothin' but uh... ain't you that private eye? The one who helps out the cops all the time?"

Conners mentally took note of the best way to either fight or duck out of the cab if he had to.

"I might be," he said slowly. "What of it?"

"Oh no!" said the cabbie, his face showing embarrassment. "I was just wondering if I might run into you. So, I took your call myself. My name's Joe, I run the cab depot you called."

"That so?" asked Conners, still suspicious.

"I'm not explainin' this well. See, ya helped my brother about a year and a half ago. It was Christmas and he bought my niece a new car... well, not *new* but new to her."

Conners tried to think back to the case the cabbie mentioned. That would've been just a few months after he was attacked by Alexander. It wasn't hard to recall the basics of the case, and his mind brought them up as if reading from the physical file. Christmas day of 2011 a red convertible had been stolen from a driveway. The police had put the word out, but Conners had been the one who had thought to check a few chop shops and junkyards to make sure the thing wasn't being scrapped. All-in-all it had been a simple enough case, nothing that particularly challenged him. Still, it had been more fun than sitting in an empty apartment watching the television all day.

"Oh… Well if I said anything rude or insensitive, you should know I'm always like that. It was nothing personal."

"No, no," said Joe, who seemed slightly distressed at the way this conversation was panning out. "Nothin' like that. I just wanted to thank you."

"Thank… I'm sorry?"

"My brother was losing his mind, and the cops all seemed to accept that the thing was gone. An hour later you and that detective friend of yours roll up and toss us the keys like a Hallmark movie or somethin'. My sister-in-law actually called it a Christmas miracle, jokingly of course."

"Oh," said Conners, a bit thrown off.

He'd never really been thanked by a client or their relative like this. Granted, most of the time, he was either arresting someone or solving a murder. It was rare the families or clients were truly happy, and the police usually took the spotlight. He'd been fine with that arrangement too, it meant he could operate with a little anonymity. Being known by someone he'd never met was an odd feeling.

"Well, hope your niece enjoys her car," Conners said, without any clue of *what* he was supposed to say to the man's thanks.

"Oh, she does. She still tells that story to friends sometimes. Anyway, I asked around a bit about you, and it seems like you help people out a lot. A half-dozen of my guys seemed to know who you were. I even saw that clip of you shouting at the police lieutenant."

"I like to help people sometimes, and I enjoy annoying the lieutenant all the time," said Conners, smiling at his own joke as Joe pulled up to the curb in front of his office.

Conners reached into his pocket to fish for some bills, but Joe waved his hand to reject the money.

"Nah, your money's no good to me. You do some good for people. Having you around lifts people's spirits and whatnot. You need a ride, you call me, and I'll make sure you get where you need to go. No charge."

Conners froze, sensing a trick or trap.

"Why would you do that?" he asked, cautiously.

"Detective, you recall what you charged my brother for your work?"

He tried to think back. The family had hardly been well-off, but he didn't recall what he might've asked for in terms of expenses. The few high-profile cases he'd solved were covering his bills until he was regularly paid by the police again.

"I... not really."

"Not a dime. You just helped him out and told him he didn't have to pay you. So, if you're riding with my guys, you pay exactly what my family had to pay you."

Conners felt a strange mixture of relief and gratitude. Joe seemed genuinely interested in helping him out in whatever way he could, and he couldn't deny that having some free ferrying around the city could be helpful. Several cases required a lot of travel and Lawrence wasn't often free to drive him around if they weren't working together.

"You're sure?" he asked, not wanting to take advantage of a spontaneous offer. "I do keep fairly busy."

"Good," said Joe. "The busier you are, the more you're helpin' folks. I've been waiting a while to meet you, detective. I'm sure."

Conners nodded and clasped Joe's hand.

"Then, I'm happy to accept your offer, Joe. And please, call me Conners."

"Conners it is."

He smiled and Conners returned the expression before he exited the cab and walked into his office. He had to admit that free travel from a depot was not something he'd have foreseen, but it was a huge perk, and cabs were often even quicker at getting through the city than a cop car could be. Conners saved the number for Joe's cab depot in his phone before heading upstairs to rest.

He put his cane up against the dresser and collapsed into his bed, face-first. He took a deep sniff of the freshly laundered pillowcase, relishing in the clean scent. After a long moment, he rolled over to look at the dresser which held Bill's urn and his thanks from the chief of police. It was odd that the two items were completely different in almost every way. The certificate was an official recognition of his abilities and efforts awarded to him by a highly decorated official, and it meant very little to Conners all things considered. The urn was simple and outwardly held no value. Yet it was something Conners appreciated far more than the certificate, and the thing that made him try to be better.

Even after all this time, he still couldn't say what it was about Bill that had changed things for him. When had the old man gone from a teacher to a life guide? What about him had caused his voice to become Conners' moral guide?

Conners rolled back over onto this stomach and after a few moments, fell asleep still fully clothed.

His dreams were far from relaxing, though. He dreamt that he was in an alleyway, a pistol very unlike *Sherry* in his hands. He could not force himself to move. His body was not under his own control, and he was paralyzed inside of his own mind. He was left helpless to do anything but watch as the scene played out before him.

The pistol was pointed squarely at a young boy, who Conners had no name for, but the blonde hair and blue eyes were instantly familiar to him. Despite screaming inside of his own head, Conners watched in horror as he shot the boy in the chest. Three people stood nearby, just watching: Joe, Lawrence, and Bill. Joe spoke first, his eyes wide in confusion and pain.

"I thought you helped people!" he screamed, and the words hit Conners as if they were a sledgehammer.

Lawrence had disgust and hatred etched in every line of her face as she looked at him. The look said more than she could've with words. The disgust was a knife in his heart, making him weep internally, still unable to move.

Finally Bill walked two steps forward and looked Conners in the eyes.

"I thought you could be better," he said, his voice low and filled to the brim with disappointment and pain.

Conners awoke in a cold sweat, and flailed so hard that he actually fell out of the bed and hit the floor hard. It took him a full ten seconds to realize where he was and what was going on. It was another four before he realized he was crying, and dehydrated. He stood up slowly, his legs and hands shaking so bad he nearly fell over again. He forced himself to move cautiously to the kitchen.

Conners filled a glass with water from his sink, and felt himself whispering over and over, "I'm sorry…. I'm so, so sorry."

He apologized to everyone except himself. He was the only one who didn't deserve one.

Chapter XX: About the Classics

Conners exhaled and threw another dart at a dartboard he'd put up a few months ago. He was a little fuzzy on exactly why he'd thought it was a good idea to buy the darts and board, because so far the board had fewer holes in it than the surrounding drywall did. Still, it did allow him to kill some time between cases. Somehow, the end of the year had brought the city's desire to provide him with difficult cases to dead crawl.

That Saturday was fairly warm, considering they were only ten days out from Christmas, and the city had been decorated with several wreaths. Millennium Park was boasting its free ice skating season and Daley Plaza was sporting that year's gigantic lit-up Christmas tree. Though it was a decent way away from his office, Conners had stopped by the plaza a few times that year to look at the giant tree. There was something strangely impressive and captivating about the display. It also helped that the attraction allowed him to share a connection with people he usually lacked. It helped him feel slightly more human.

Christmas had never meant much to him as a holiday, but he couldn't deny the appeal it gave the city overall. People were marginally nicer and most of the streets were lined in decorative lights and bows. It made his own Christmas ritual a little more fun.

Most national holidays if he didn't have any casework or paperwork to demand his attention, Conners made a habit of traveling around the city, trying to find the illusive lock that would fit his key from the hospital. It was largely a nonsensical habit, as it would've been nearly impossible to actually find the lock by randomly testing ever number 18 he could find. The far more practical benefit was it familiarized him with the ins and outs of the city. He didn't know what he expected to find even if he could find the corresponding lock, assuming it hadn't been changed. The key could've belonged to an apartment, a storage unit, a mailbox, or something else entirely; and it was entirely possible that none of them would hold anything meaningful for him now.

Still, he wanted to know what it belonged to.

His past three Christmas days had been spent on his own. However, Lawrence had invited him to spend that year's Christmas with her family and he had to admit that he had no idea exactly *what* was expected of him or how he should respond to it. Still, the offer had touched him. The idea that Lawrence liked and trusted him enough to include him in a family holiday meant a lot, even if he couldn't articulate why that was.

He'd spent a while going over ideas of what to buy her family as gifts. Lawrence had been easy enough, given how close they were. He'd gotten ahold of a nice wool coat in her size, because she had repeatedly mentioned that her jacket was both a bit thinner than she'd liked and more than a few years old. After a moment of consideration, he'd bought a matching coat for Janice.

Her mother had been far more difficult. After a lot of consideration, he had at least managed something more thoughtful for the latin woman. He'd remembered the pictures that had hung around Lawrence's apartment and gotten a framed photo of himself and Lawrence from his days as a cop, short-lived as they were.

The entire experience made him seriously question the whole gift-given tradition. At that moment, the front door of his office opened and Conners heard the bell ring. Thrilled at the prospect of a case, he rolled over his bannister and moved quickly down the stairs.

Standing about ten feet from the base of the stairs was a man in a very fine suit, and Conners spied an expensive wristwatch and custom-made shoes.

"Hello," Conners said. "Please tell me you need to hire a private detective!"

The man smiled brightly, reminding Conners a little of a politician. He reached out and clasped Conners' hand firmly.

"Well, that is exactly why I'm here, my boy! Paul Boston. Are you Mr. Michael Conners?"

"Detective Michael J. Conners," Conners said, bowing in a mocking way that appeared to go completely over Boston's head. "At your service."

"Excellent! Excellent!" exclaimed Boston, clapping his hands together merrily. "I was so *hoping* I could find you. I seem to have found myself in a spot of trouble with the local police and need someone to help clear me before the issue goes to trial. While I am certainly not guilty, it would be rather annoying for me if this whole ordeal came out publicly. I've been informed you're a rather reliable detective, and you know how to be discreet."

"Well, *discreet* is a bit out of my wheelhouse," said Conners, smirking. "But I can keep a lid on things for a little bit, depending on what exactly it is you need quiet. So, what exactly is it you're being accused of? Some illegal business deal or something?"

"Oh no," said Boston, as Conners flopped into his seat and began typing. "I have lawyers for any accusation like that. No, no. I'm afraid my wife died a couple nights ago."

Conners froze. This man spoke so casually about his wife's passing that Conners almost thought he'd misheard.

"I'm sorry?"

"Yes," said Boston, his tone more wistful than sorrowful. "She was a wonderful partner. Can't say as I've seen her like elsewhere. Her passing was most unfortunate."

Most unfortunate? This was his wife?!

Conners resumed typing up some notes while his mind tried to accept what he was being told.

"I see, and the police think you had a hand in your wife's death?"

"Quite so," said Boston. "I arranged bail this morning until such time as my court date, but it would be more prevalent for me if the real killer were revealed before all this were made public. That's where I intend to hire you, my boy. Are you available?"

"I am..." said Conners slowly. "But I should warn you, if you are attempting to trick me or use my investigation as a means to clear you when you're actually guilty, you'd be better off leaving now. I dig into assigned cases and turn up the truth. So if you're merely hoping to use your hiring me as a type of alibi..."

"Not at all!" said Boston, seeming genuine. "I chose you precisely *because* you're so thorough. I need someone who can really get to the bottom of what's going on."

Conners rubbed his chin thoughtfully.

He could *still be trying to trick me,* he thought. *Might think he's smarter than me and just wanted an all clear from me.*

So what if he is trying something? Bill's voice responded in his head. *You afraid that he's right? If he's guilty: nail him up. If not: clear the case.*

"All right," said Conners, standing up and sliding *Sherry* onto his hip. "Give me your address and I'll be there shortly. I'll need to explore and understand what your home life is normally like, but I'll get to the bottom of it. Of course, you'll have to pay twice my going rate as well. After all, you are having me work during the holidays."

"Of course!" said Boston, still cheery, as if this was nothing that bothered him. "I was actually a little surprised to find you don't have a full firm set up. With your name my boy, you could have the firm of the century! I'm headed back to the home now; so you can ride with me if you prefer."

Conners ignored the comment on his business and followed Boston outside where a sleek, black car awaited them. A man in a black chauffeur's suit stood waiting, and opened the back door as they exited the office.

"Excellent," said Paul, climbing in and moving over for Conners. "We'll be heading back to the manor, Edward."

This was so absurd that Conners chuckled softly.

"What? Couldn't spring for the limo?"

He'd meant it as a joke, but Boston seemed to take the question seriously.

"Of course," he said, still as bright as if he'd just won a bet. "But it's just not practical in the city, especially when it's so busy. Besides, the Lincoln is nearly as comfortable."

Conners shook his head. He was working for someone who *actually* owned a limo. He had half a mind to refuse Boston's money and get out of the car then and there, but the horribly open maw of his empty caseload kept him in the vehicle. As much a rich prick as Boston may be, an annoying case was better than no case.

All the way into the suburban neighborhoods Boston rattled off the pros of Conners turning his business into a full firm with employees and business contacts. Conners had to admit, Boston was a decent salesman, but he didn't even like to work with others, let alone have them work for him. So he let his mind begin to form possible answers to the question of what had happened to the man's wife, although that was hard as he had no real evidence as of yet.

When they pulled up to Boston's manor, Conners did a double-take. This was far larger than any home he'd ever seen, and every inch of it shouted old money. He managed to clear his head and close his mouth in time to exit the car relatively composed. He walked up to the front door where a man stood in a fitted black suit with coattails. He was just under five and a half feet, and had close cut black hair that had begun to retreat just an inch or so up his scalp.

Conners smirked slightly as the man bowed low before him.

"Greetings my fine sire," he said, repeating the gesture. "And whom mightn't I have the pleasure of addressing?"

The man didn't respond to Conners' mockery at all, but instead replied in a deep voice tinted with a slight German accent.

"My name is Stephan Wagner. I am the butler and caretaker for the Boston family. May I take your coat, detective?"

His hands were covered by fine, white gloves. They were already halfway to Conners' coat when the detective held up his own hand defensively.

"It's Conners, and I'll keep the coat, actually. I don't expect I'll be here long."

"Detective Conners," said Wagner, solemnly as he opened the door and took Boston's coat. "If you should require anything of me, please do not be afraid to ask."

"You serve the Boston family?" asked Conners, as he walked into a grand entrance hall that echoed slightly with his steps.

"Indeed Detective. I have served Master Paul, Lady Bethany, and Master Ryan since I first immigrated to the country in 1983."

Ryan? he thought to himself.

Their child most likely, he heard Bill say.

"Nearly twenty years then?"

"Yes sir."

"And how is it having the power of two rich people lorded over you all your life?"

Conners expected he might see resentment or anger at his quip, but Wagner's face betrayed nothing. In fact, the man's face was so flat that it was slightly disturbing. Many people had a standing expression that conveyed emotion. However, Wagner's face was… neutral, as if he were merely a sculpture of a human being.

"The Bostons have been very good employers."

Paul walked into the building and the butler quickly stored Boston's jacket in a closet near the front door. Conners carefully walked forward, peering into room after room. He saw into an elaborate kitchen that sparkled to a shine as if it were cleaned by gnomes every morning. There was a fairly large reading room with several comfortable armchairs and several bookshelves full of such exciting titles as *Chicago: A City History*. Not a single book had a cracked spine, but he wasn't sure if that was due to overcare or underuse.

"Where did your wife die?" Conners asked, curtly to Paul.

He was almost frustrated when the man betrayed only a second of emotion, and gestured grandly towards the staircase.

"Upstairs. Second door on the right, detective. Shall I have Stephan bring you some tea? Stephan! Prepare the detective some tea."

"I'm good," said Conners dismissively.

"Coffee it is then," said Boston, still smiling cheerily.

Conners climbed the stairs, and entered the bedroom as it had been indicated to him. It was a grand room with carpet that seemed to be made of a finer fiber than anything Conners owned. Cautiously, the detective lowered himself and began to creep along the floor like an enormous spider approaching its prey.

As his examination took him to the area between the bed and the nightstand he noticed a vent cover just under the leg of the bed. What left him curious was the small scrape mark that the headboard of the bed had made against the wall.

What do we think? Conners queried in his head. *Can't imagine that's just a coincidence.*

The universe is rarely so lazy as to provide happenstance, responded Bill's voice.

Conners grabbed the bed by the frame and pushed, managing to move it the couple of inches required to free the vent cover from the bed leg, and removed it. He unearthed a latex glove from one of his many pockets and carefully reached into the vent covering, and felt something solid and cylindrical. Slowly, he pulled up the object up and found he was holding a drinking glass that still held a couple drops of moisture.

Without a word, Conners placed the glass into a plastic bag and put it into one of the deeper pockets of his coat, mentally making a note to get the glass to Lawrence so the forensics team could run a check for poisons or paralytics.

Confident that he'd found an important piece to the puzzle, Conners head into the hall, quickly running through the facts. As he was about to descend the stairs again, he glanced down the other side of the hallway and saw one of the doors was cracked open. What stuck out to him wasn't the cracked door, but rather the mess evident from the sliver of a room visible beyond it.

This chaotic interior stood in stark contrast to the rest of the house, which was pristine almost to the point of offensive. Curiosity overruling his sense of caution, Conners moved towards the room and heard heavy metal coming from within the room. He was surprised when he opened what appeared to be the epitome of an angsty dream. The room was lit entirely by blacklights and a dozen or so band posters littered the wall. The bed *might've* had sheets on it, but they were buried beneath a dragon's hoard of laundry that had begun to smell. The entire room reeked of weed, despite the efforts of a small fan in the window, pumping the inner air outside.

It wasn't until what Conners had taken for a tasteless decoration stirred that he realized he wasn't alone in the room. There was a boy Conners took to be in his late teens reclined in a black beanbag chair with a freshly rolled joint in his mouth. His hair was long and unkempt, falling to his shoulders, and he had the scratchy unshaven shadow that was all the beard the boy could likely grow at his age. His clothes were old and torn, though they seemed to be that way due to design instead of heavy use.

Conners glanced down at the boy, who was either too stoned or too apathetic to care about a total stranger appearing in his living quarters.

"Ryan?" asked Conners, making an educated guess.

"Sup?" asked Ryan, coughing several times as he did so.

Conners was even more disturbed meeting Ryan than he had been when he met Paul. The entire family had a strange sort of emotional despondence that was disturbing—boarding on psychopathic. Conners sat on the bed and looked at Ryan. Then he decided to hit the issue harder than he normally would've.

"Heard your mom kicked it."

"Yeah," said Ryan, taking another pull on the joint. "It's a shame. She was a decent woman."

"You don't seem all that grieved about it."

"I'm not," said Ryan, looking at the ceiling. "Mom always wanted us to feel things more deeply, but it just wasn't how that worked... not for dad and me anyway."

"You don't feel anything?"

"Of course I feel stuff," said Ryan, as casually as if Conners had asked about his hairstyle. "I just don't do the whole 'overwhelmed with emotion' thing. I mean, I don't know that I've ever actually cried... It sucks what happened to mom, but crying isn't gonna undo it. So, why waste the time?"

And I thought I was an emotionally cold bastard.

"Right," said Conners, thrown. "Well, I was hoping you might be able to help me find out what happened a bit."

For the first time, Ryan sat up a little straighter.

"Sure."

"Did your mom commonly take a glass of water with her at night?"

"Often enough," said Ryan. "Actually, she'd have Stephan bring it to her. She liked to have a glass most nights. Never thought much of it to be honest."

"Right," said Conners, still distinctly uncomfortable. "Thanks."

He stood and pulled out his cell phone to call Victor, a friend of his from the Immigration Office.

Conners had met Victor years ago, back when he was first applying for his own legitimate citizenship papers. He hadn't thought much of the man then, but Victor proved helpful on a few cases, and Conners made sure to keep in touch with the man and keep their relationship in good standing. Victor answered the phone on the second ring.

"Hello?" he answered in a bored voice.

"Hey there Vic," Conners said, smirking. "I was wondering if you guys were still open during the holidays."

"Conners!" Victor's voice brightened immediately. *"What a day for you to call! I am bored out of my mind right now. There's nothing fun going on!"*

"Well then, I'm just the man you need. Need you to run a name for me. I'm after something on an immigrant from '83. Name's Stephan Wagner; he's the Boston family's butler now."

"Let me see," said Victor, typing furiously. *"Oh, yes... says here he immigrated to the country legally in April of '83. He came here with his wife, and their unborn child. Aw... says she didn't get approved. That's too bad."*

"Really?" asked Conners, interested. "When did she get to immigrate?"

"She didn't. Never got cleared to enter. Probably found another way to come here at a guess."

"Really? All right. Thanks Victor. let's grab a drink later this week."

"Happy to."

Conners hung up and as he turned, saw Stephan standing by the door, his face grim. From his expression alone, Conners could tell the man had no intention of denying the murder he'd committed. Conners pulled out his handcuffs and the German didn't argue or attempt to resist. Rather, he simply turned around and accepted the arrest without complaint or comment. Conners read Stephen his rights and Boston came down the stairs as he was finishing.

"I had wondered," Paul Boston said calmly, as Conners finished tightening the cuffs. "But I always thought… Why kill my wife Stephan?"

"You always promised to help my wife," said Stephan, his voice distant and bitter. "Yet, we lost our child and she killed herself while waiting for you to fulfill that promise. You took my wife from me, and I have taken yours from you."

Conners pushed Stephan towards the gate while dialing the local station, and let his mind wonder over the case. Instead of being relieved for the case during a long period of stagnation, he instead felt anger and frustration. He was angry at the Bostons for their lack of caring or compassion and angry with Stephan for his vengeance.

The world's a dark place at times, kid.

Yeah… but knowing that doesn't make it easier to deal with.

Conners began to smoke while his mind ran around. He couldn't help but think of himself when he'd first found Bill. Could he have been like the Bostons: cold and calculating: able to understand but only superficially appreciate emotions and the ties that bound the world? It was not the first time Conners realized just how different he had become, but it planted a small seed in him. He had no idea if it was the seed of hope or helplessness, but it was rooted so deeply that he knew he'd never be able to dig it out… even if he'd wanted to.

Chapter XXI: Prey

Conners tapped Bill's cane against the concrete twice as he walked down the street and did his best to ignore the freezing cold. He'd just finished the slightly annoying process of depositing his check from the Boston case into the ATM, given that the bank wouldn't be open until the following day. He couldn't help but still feel disturbed by the case. He probably could've put it off but he was already out and about, and given his tendency to get distracted he didn't want to forget about the check.

He had thought that the idea of solving the murder would help his aching mind. He'd been right in his arrest, of course... but instead of helping him, the casework had only caused him to feel uneasy and given him a creeping sense of dread that had no logical source. It gave him a weary feeling, not unlike the tension in a horror movie right before the monster appears onscreen for the first time.

More than once, he'd argued with seeing a doctor or therapist, but always quickly discarded the idea. The truth was he feared what might become of him if he let anyone else into his brain like that. After all the work he'd done over the past four years, he was reluctant to let it all be undone by someone who would want to "fix" him. Besides, he was still trying to get comfortable with the idea of who he was; how could he let some white-coat mess with that?

Still, he couldn't deny the increasing feeling that he *would* need to do something. It wasn't like he had really taken a moment to get things right since he'd become a murderer. It wasn't exactly a world-shattering realization. After all, he still had nightmares involving a blonde-haired child with blue eyes from time-to-time, and it wasn't exactly difficult to see what he was stressed or guilty about.

Keep pressing on, kid, Bill said in his head. *You're not gonna earn absolution by wallowing in your own pains.*

Conners nodded softly and put in a pair of earbuds connected to his phone. He hit the shuffle button on his music before popping a Jolly Rancher into his mouth and marching down the street, spinning Bill's cane like it was a baton. If he hadn't been distracted by his own existential crisis, he might've been more bothered by the sound of a car door slamming behind him. As it was, it wasn't until a rough pair of hands grabbed him by the shoulder that his body registered the danger.

Conners spun on his heel, using the cane like a bat and struck one of his assailants across the head with it. He started to draw the steel blade from within the cane body, but saw the flash of a gun just as the second man clearly came into view. Instinctually, Conners changed his movement to reach for *Sherry,* but stopped when he saw he'd never reach his own gun in time. Surrendering to the pair, he held up his hands. The first man he'd hit slowly got back to his feet.

"Told her he'd be a pain about it," the man mumbled, as he searched Conners and took the cane, his phone, and *Sherry* from him.

"I'm gonna want those back," Conners said. "If they're scratched or dented it'll be worse for you."

"Shut up," said the second man, hitting him squarely in the stomach, causing him to double over in pain. "You're lucky the boss likes ya. I'd have ya shot and forget ya, but she wants sommit from ya."

The man gestured with the pistol for Conners to move toward the street. Conners turned and looked around. He spotted a sleek, black van which was still running. a small cloud of exhaust spewed from the tailpipe. Conners mentally ran his mind across what remained in his pockets. Nothing there would serve as much as of a weapon. After struggling to think of an alternative, he was forced to admit his best option was to play things out for a bit.

He entered the van and saw instantly that the inside had been custom designed to be more like a luxury car or limo. Two sets of seats faced one another with a wall separating the driver from the passengers. There was a slim figure already sitting in the opposing seat, who Conners took to be the leader of the goons who had just nabbed him.

He tried to peer through the darkness inside the van, but the figure wore a fedora tilted downward so he couldn't see their face, though he felt confident that the person was female. The suit they wore indicated a womanly figure and it was custom fitted: like something he would've expected Boston to wear.

"Hello Michael dear," said the woman softly.

Conners instantly knew he was right about the figure's gender, even if her voice was somewhat lower than other women's voices might be. He had the sneaking suspicion he'd heard it before, but couldn't quite place it.

"Aren't you happy to see me again?" she asked, and suddenly it *clicked* for him.

He should've suspected this had been an act of hers from the start. As the goons who had attacked him sat next to him, the van started to move. Conners suspected this was pre-established, because he couldn't deduce any way that the driver had been given additional instructions.

"Not exactly happy to see you're still free," he said to Richards.

He still couldn't make out her face, but he would've sworn she had smiled at him.

"Come now. You're not still upset over William, are you? What's past is past. Surely, we can move forward now… in the name of business?"

"B-business?" he asked, more taken aback than angry.

"Of course," said Richards, her voice carrying upward as she formed the words. "I wish to hire you."

Conners let the words hang in the air for a second, expecting some sort of punchline to the joke. When none came, he heard Bill's voice in his mind.

You're letting her *dictate the terms and permissions of the meeting, take back some control.*

"I take it you're not hiring me to find someone who can kill you? Though, if you are, I'll be sure to double their payment."

"Cute," Richards said, smirking again. "There's some recent evidence that has come to light at the 14th police precinct. It would be rather annoying if this evidence were to reach the courtroom. I need someone to make a certain blood-stained sweater disappear before testing is completed on it."

"And, why would I *ever* consider doing something that will wind up with me being arrested? I've not been arrested for at least four years now, and I would really like to keep that streak going."

"It's a minor issue, and I'm prepared to pay you six figures."

Conners opened his mouth to tell her exactly *where* she could stick her six figures, but Bill stopped him again.

Think this through for a moment, kid. Despite your digging, you've got nothing on her. This would be your chance to help dig a nice hole for her to fall into.

You're right, Conners conceded. *But this will be risky. Lawrence isn't going to like the idea of killing an investigation.*

Think this through, kid. Be smart: calculating. Richards is the one who picked this game. You just have to win: no matter what.

No matter what, he agreed.

"Well I can't say you don't have my attention," said Conners. "I'll need the name of the man involved and a rough estimate of the date it would've been logged. You get me those and I'll make sure your man's kept on the right side of the bars."

Richards smiled again.

"I *thought* we might reach a reasonable agreement."

She began to scribble on a piece of paper in a notebook which she tore out and handed to him. Shortly afterwards, the van stopped a block away from his office.

"Now, hand the detective his belongings," she said to the man on his right.

The man did so, and the moment *Sherry* was securely in his grasp Conners felt a desire tied to his very being nearly overwhelm him. It took every bit of his willpower not to remove the revolver from its holster and gun down Richards and her two accomplices.

Follow your head Conners, not your heart, he chastised himself.

He exited the van and walked quickly to his office. Even though he knew there was little reason to do so at that point, he slammed the door closed and triple-checked that the heavy-duty lock was secure. It was stupid… Richards likely wouldn't double-cross him, and if she *did* decide to kill him, a lock wasn't going to keep her out.

Conners head up to the second floor of his office and shut the curtains completely before he head to his kitchen table and cleared it with a sweep of his arm. The napkin holder and his chipped salt and pepper shakers clattered to the ground, but he ignored the mess. He pulled out a large sketch pad and quickly lay out three pages, and pulled out a large 18-inch ruler. After a few minutes he had a good approximation of the three rooms of the police station he was concerned with: the entrance area, the homicide bullpen, and the evidence room.

He quickly considered the defenses he would have to overcome.

The police force wasn't much of a concern; he wasn't going to brute force his way to the evidence lockup. This had to be a stealth mission, not a smash and grab. The issue was actually getting ahold of the sweater without his name being attached to the robbery. If he were still a detective with the CPD, he could've signed it out himself, replaced it with an identical sweater, and even pointed out something was wrong once it was safe. Sure, an investigation would've been launched, but it would've ended up going nowhere. However, that easier line of trickery was no longer open to him.

This was going to be tricky…

Still, there was a point when the materials had to be pulled for forensic testing. The best chances he had were to either swap the evidence before it was tested, or to swap the results. He considered both options. The former was preferable because it required the least amount of follow-up. If he swapped the sweater ahead of time, there would be no results he would have to worry about.

Good, he heard Bill's voice say. *We have an avenue to pursue when Richards asks. Now we have to consider what we're going to do with her.*

"What's the best way to entrap her?" he asked aloud, considering his options.

It was as if a fast-forwarded film played before his eyes, playing out the scenario. Following through on the swap would enable him the chance to get in Richards' good books, and allow him to catch a bigger glance at her plans which *might* lead to a solid arrest and imprisonment.

The idea that everything only *might* lead to the desired conclusion didn't sit well with him.

He wiped the screen clear and considered his next option. He *could* use the pretense of the evidence clearing to draw out Richards, and kill her himself. That would be a more final result, but there were complications. For one thing, Richards was clever and likely wouldn't allow herself to be lured into too dangerous a situation, regardless of how completely he planned out his move. Secondly, even if he did pull everything off he would always run the risk of being arrested for her death. He wanted to avoid jail if at all possible. There was a *chance* he could fool CSI, but if Lawrence was put on his case he doubted he could get away completely clean. Besides, they'd very likely bring him in on a case where Richards was either missing or found dead, and he didn't like the idea of lying to Lawrence's face repeatedly on a case that he would *have* to bomb intentionally.

He wiped the screen clear again and considered *another* idea. He could always bring Lawrence in and officiate the operation. Richards was a big fish, and the chance to bring her down would look really good on both of their records with the station. That idea appealed to him, but it came with a massive question that Bill posed.

Do you trust her?

"With my life," Conners said without hesitation.

What about with my justice?

To that Conners had no answer. He believed when push came to shove, Lawrence would follow the law. She believed him about Richards, but she wasn't willing to do *whatever* it took to get Richards, and the killer was too clever to leave much to chance. However unfortunate the case with the sweater might be for Richards, he doubted it would be enough to imprison her all on its own. It might put down one of her men, but it was unlikely they would flip on her.

"Option one," he said aloud, pacing back and forth at a furious pace. "Result: Richards *might* end up with serious a sentence, and I have to work *around* the police. Option two: Result: Richards is dead. I have to betray the police and dance an incredibly thin line. Option three: Richards' fate is uncertain: likely a free woman, but my relationship with the police is intact."

What you wanna do, kid?

"The first option seems the best compromise," he said. "The second is more assured, but more difficult and leads to future problems. The first is less extreme and if pulled off successfully will not arouse suspicion. The biggest danger is the possibility that it will lead to nothing useful. Still, I think it our best option."

All right, you have an overarching plan, and a basic plan to begin that path. Follow it through.

"It's going to be too difficult to actually obtain the sweater while it's in police possession. Best to nab it during the transfer to forensics."

Good. So, what's the next step?

"I need to get a decoy sweater. Easy enough to call Richards and get a description and purchase a replacement. I'll have to use cash; no reason to leave a paper trail in case someone *does* get curious. Then, best to take the place of either the delivery man or an officer and make the swap manually. The window is tight, but doable."

So, who are you going to portray: the delivery man or the officer?

"Officer is easier to get a uniform and I'm more acquainted with the layout of the station. Besides, an extra cop could likely go unnoticed. An extra delivery man will be difficult to hide. So, I'll need a uniform. Not hard, and I can order a custom badge online. It wouldn't stand up to scrutiny, but if I'm studied that closely we'll have other issues. I'll have to disguise myself a little too so none of the homicide squad recognize me. Not too difficult: dying my hair and a little make-up should assist the uniform into being enough of a distinction. I'll have to use one of my prepaid cards for the badge, and get it delivered elsewhere, but that's not impossible."

Good. Entrance and exit plan?

"Exit is easy enough, there's a bathroom on the entrance floor with a small skylight window. I can squeeze out that way. I'll have to enter through the side entrance. There's a keycard entry. Easy enough to fake a card. From there I should be able to talk my way in by feigning a glitch in the electronics."

Plan's complete, said Bill's voice. *And you're sure this is the best plan?*

"...This is the plan I'm going with."

Best start practicing and preparing.

Conners nodded and pulled out his laptop, setting about the designing of his badge. Once he felt confident in the design, he ordered a set of police blues from an online retailer, and charged everything a prepaid debit card. He'd made it a habit to occasionally purchase a card like this with cash in case he needed to order something online that couldn't be easily traced back to him. This was going to be unpleasant and he likely wouldn't sleep well for a long time, but he refused to leave Richards' fate to the chance of a system that had failed before. The Vanderhill situation flashed through his mind.

And Lawrence... well what she didn't know couldn't hurt her, right?

Chapter XXII: Lessons

Conners shook despite his determination not to be noticed. He brushed his new blonde bangs nervously out of his eyes, tucking them into his policeman's cap. He had the replacement sweater neatly tucked in-between his undershirt and the standard issue navy blue shirt all the officers wore. Luckily, he was able to wear a windbreaker over the shirt without any suspicious glances due to the chilly weather.

He'd nervously touched the edge of his fake entrance card a dozen-odd times in the past hour.

You need to relax, he heard Bill say. *You're going to give yourself away by being suspicious, not by any part of your disguise.*

Conners forced himself to breathe and began to try and recall all the elements on the periodic table, a habit he'd picked up to force himself to relax while studying polygraphs.

Hydrogen, helium, lithium, beryllium, baron, carbon, nitrogen, and on and on he went until he reached *lead*, where realized he was calm and breathing normally. He checked the street corner and saw the large truck moving amongst the traffic like some extremely boxy slug.

Time to act. Just get through this and we're one step closer to justice.

Just as he was preparing to move, he felt a rough hand grab him from behind and *slam* him into a brick wall. He coughed violently as all the air in his lungs was forcefully knocked out of him. He reached forward to fend off his attacker and was stunned to see none other than Lawrence standing there, her left hand pinning him to the building and a furious flame in her eyes.

"Hey *bud*," she said, practically spitting the word. "How are things going?"

"H-hey," he said, stuttering despite himself. "What… what are you doing here?"

"Oh well, get this: I actually *work* here. See, *I* have a reason to be here. I also have reason to be really curious when Miller comes and informs me there's an order placed for a badge that *looks* suspiciously like a policeman's badge. Apparently it's by someone who isn't actually authorized to issue them. Now, normally this means someone's impersonating an officer of the law, which is sort of a serious crime. Normally, this means we lock up someone, and go on with our day. *But* when I recognized the address as a favorite drop-off of yours, I decided that *surely* my friend would never do something so stupid as to impersonate an officer of the law, and that I needed to look into this. So Conners, why are *you* here?"

Conners felt his blood run cold. How could he have made such a simple mistake? He couldn't believe he'd been this dumb. And to be found like this was the worst of it. His realization did nothing to ease the twisting, writhing guilt that had been building up in him over the past week.

"Lawrence, please listen. I'm really, really sorry but…"

"I am about two seconds from tossing you in a cell, and letting the courts handle you. I don't know *what* you were planning to do, but if you don't tell me the truth right now, I'll make *sure* to testify against you as much as I can. There's only one thing saving you right now, which is that I can't believe even you would do this for *no* reason. You mock, you belittle, but you never crossed us, at least not in a way that betrayed a moral compass. So, why now?"

"It's… Richards."

"Yeah, we've talked about her."

So, Conners explained. He explained being forced into her van and what she'd asked of him. If it had been *any* other cop, he might've embellished, lied, and exaggerated his plight. However, Lawrence's anger with him was already more than he could handle, and he didn't have the heart to try and deceive her again.

"So I decided to try and entrap her, but I needed to earn her trust first."

"Why didn't you come to me? This normally isn't *that* far outside of something we might plan. The difference is that any undercover move like this *needs* to be on the books—planned way in advance!"

"I didn't trust you would put catching Richards above the system," he said, and she froze. After a long moment, he continued. "I *couldn't* let her get away. We've faced a lot of people, but no one like her. I *couldn't—can't* let her beat this. If I rely on the system and she wins, there's no follow-up. You've got *nothing* on her after almost three years. You told me to be patient: to do the right thing. Three years and we've got nothing! She *killed* Bill. We catch murderers, but not her. I just… I can't keep waiting when no one else seems to care that she's walking free."

Lawrence pulled back, releasing her hold on him. Conners breathed deeply, and suddenly felt something hit him on his left cheek. It was hard enough to knock him off his feet. He could taste blood from the contact the inside of his cheek made with his teeth. As he slowly sat up, he realized she'd punched him—really hard.

"*I* care, and yes, I admit, it's been frustratingly slow. You work cases for a day, or a few at the most, and normally you know who it is. It's just a matter of the legal system after that and it's rare you get called into court. I *understand* you're frustrated and you want results. But you went behind my back, behind *all* our backs. You became a criminal and broke I can't even explain how many laws doing what you did, but impersonating a policeman for a start, plus planning to steal evidence in an ongoing investigation."

"You're right," he said, wincing as he touched his cheek. "I can't make any excuses for it. You really *should* arrest me. I won't fight back or escape."

She stood above him, and he saw her anger and fury mix with understanding, and he could see that she was working something out furiously in her mind. He said nothing. He'd already done more than enough damage. Whatever she decided to do—however bad it might be—he'd earned it. He'd followed his logic and Bill's instructions, but abandoned the moral side of things that Bill had tried to enforce on him.

Eventually, Lawrence sighed.

"Here's what's going to happen: I'm going to go upstairs and file a request with the lieutenant I'm going to make sure he understands your concerns and why it's important to catch her. I'm going to explain I want this to be quiet, because I'm concerned about a possible plant in our department, which actually *is* true. *If* he agrees to make this legit, and *if* we decide to involve you, you're going to tell Richards you destroyed that evidence while we plant a fake result in the file. You're going to explain this to her on a cellphone that *we* can track."

"You're going to help me?" he asked in disbelief.

He'd been fully prepared to give a full confession. It would've ended with a nasty prison sentence, if not life in prison once he tacked on the child's murder. But he was prepared to pay for his sins when his time came. So he'd planned to hold nothing back.

"Against the entirety of my better judgement? Yes. But I want to be clear: *everything* you do from here on out is part of our investigation. From here on out, I hear about *every* move you even think about making. I don't want you leaving your apartment if Richards is involved unless I say so."

Conners nodded, unable to look her in the eye.

"I'm so angry with you right now, I can't even think straight. You never should've been so stupid as to actually follow through with this. Now, you need to get out of here before I hit you again. I can't *believe* you right now."

That stung far worse than he thought it would. Lawrence may have been working on the other side of legal enforcement from him, but there had also been trust between them. In one foul move, he'd ruined that, and the full weight of his desire and greed crashed down on him.

"I'm sorry," he said, and meant it.

"Just… just go away, Conners. I can't deal with you right now. Dye your hair back when you get home. You look like an idiot."

That bit might've given him hope for their friendship if it had been said with less contempt. He watched helplessly as the delivery man head inside to receive the evidence he was supposed to capture. At this point, he knew there was nothing more for it. He watched as Lawrence turned her back on him, and he felt the sting of his action flare up anew.

Bill would've been ashamed of him.

He walked back home, letting the chilly wind bat at him as he reflected on all he'd done and been planning to do. How *could* he have sided against Lawrence? She was his best friend, and seen him through so much. He was forced to admit that in his desire for revenge, he'd betrayed everything he'd really learned. He was more like the robotic jerk he'd been before meeting Bill.

This isn't what I taught you, kid.

Yeah, Conners thought furiously. *Now you remind me of that! Where were you when I was making this stupid plan?!*

He was forced to admit something he'd been trying to avoid really making peace with. Bill's voice, however much it might sound like him, wasn't really Bill. Conners had allowed the voice to twist into something it wasn't supposed to be. It had moved from his moral support to a mental tool. He'd dishonored Bill's memory in more ways than one recently.

He reached his office a few minutes later and let himself drift through actions as if he were on auto-pilot. He trashed the uniform, badge, and false sweater. Then, he grabbed the dark dye and head to the sink to dye his hair back to something nearer its true color. Finally, he realized how incredibly exhausted he was, and he collapsed into his bed.

He had no idea how many hours he lay there. He didn't know how long it took him to really think or feel anything. He let his mind cast over his time with Bill. The more he thought about the old man, the more a crazy idea began to bounce around in his thoughts. It was very, very far from anything he would've come up with himself, but Conners thought it was exactly the type of thing Bill would've come up with when he was alive. So, Conners ended up doing something he never thought he could do in his life… and he prayed.

He didn't kneel down or clasp his hands. He merely lay there and spoke softly to the ceiling.

"Hey… God; I don't really know how to do this. I don't actually believe in you, I think. But, there are two people in my life that are smarter than I am, and they both believe you exist. Besides, not like following my own brilliance did me so much good. I know I messed things up pretty good and I don't deserve it, but I need a favor. If you could… let Lawrence and I stay friends. I screwed things up today. I swear, I'll try and live by the morals Bill taught me. I don't know how this works, but I know I'm better because of her friendship. Just please leave me that."

If there was an answer, he couldn't hear it. He lay there for a while longer. Despite his stillness, he never drifted off to sleep. Consequently, he heard it clearly when the door downstairs opened and closed, and a pair of feet in heavy boots ascended his stairway. The bedroom door opened slowly and he heard Lawrence walk in. Without a word, she sat on the end of his bed, and he sat up. He pulled his knees to his chest and wrapped his arms around them, not looking at her. He waited, knowing better than to speak or make a joke. Eventually she broke the silence between them.

"I understand *why* you did it," she said, softly. "I know what Bill meant to you, and I suppose I should've worked harder to show you that you could trust me with something like this. But if this is going to work, I need to know I'm not working *against* you. I'm not looking to be a mom; I can't look over you *and* work this case. If that's the way it's going to be, this is as far as we go… You understand? I consider you my friend, Conners. But if we're going to be at odds, I'm done."

Conners nodded softly before speaking.

"I understand."

She turned to him and held out an open hand.

"If you ever do something like this again, I'll bring you in myself. Now, can I trust you?"

Conners looked up at her, into her wild green eyes, and saw the sincerity and the hurt that rested there, and the guilt in his gut twisted painfully. He knew he would never be able to do that to her again. He held her gaze solidly, and grasped her hand.

"I promise."

She nodded and stood.

"Good, because our next step is going to be a lot easier with you as a player."

She walked into the kitchen and Conners followed her. She pulled down the only two mugs he owned and began making hot chocolate. She knew her way around his apartment almost as well as he did.

"Operation's approved. Just a few people in the precinct are in on it. There's myself and the lieutenant, of course. Officer Miller and Narvaez are also up to speed. Anything suspected to be related to Richards will come to one of us, and *then* you'll be looped in. We're running point on this. We've got a phone that we can record messages and conversations on. If Richards asks, you thought it was a good idea to buy a burner phone in cash."

"That actually *would* be a good idea."

Lawrence glanced at him and raised an eyebrow.

"I mean if I were working for her, I actually *would* do that. So it's a good explanation."

"That's what I figured too," she said, placing one of the cups before him and sipping the drink from her own mug. "We should be able to link the case to her, provided there's any useful DNA on the sweater, which I'm assuming there is since she's so worried about it. But we'll have a fake file put together claiming that there was no usable forensic evidence. If we do have a plant in the precinct—which I suspect we might—she'll be thrown off the trail."

"Makes sense," he said. "So we'll have the phone conversation, some physical evidence, and my testimony against her. Anything else?"

"We'll need an attorney willing to prosecute. That's actually going to be harder than it would normally be. Richards is public figure who helps the area with charities and group work. We'll need a decent legal team to even get a proper trial."

Conners cast his mind around a bit, when a thought struck him.

"I might know someone who could help with that. I just finished working on that Boston case. If Richards were taken out of play, that would likely open up good business opportunities for him. He might be willing to lend us the use of his legal team for something like that. They managed to keep everything at bay when he was suspected of killing his wife."

"That's actually not a bad idea," said Lawrence, tapping her leg thoughtfully. "Boston certainly can afford to do a legal tango with her, and his team would be better than us just using the D.A. That's a decent start, but being involved in a murder is going to be difficult to pin on her. After all, whatever henchmen actually pulled the trigger is likely to claim solo involvement. Your testimony will help, but it's hard to get a jury to convict a woman, especially if she plays off their emotions or claims she was a victim."

Conners scowled and thought again. Eventually he thought of Joe, and the beginning of an idea came to him.

"What if involvement in a murder and coverup wasn't her *only* charge?"

"What do you have in mind?"

"As a warning: this travels into the not exactly legal side of things. I know a cabbie who runs a depot. If I could convince him it would be good for the city to testify to a racketeering ring, we could add that to her list of charges. She might be able to talk her way out of involvement in a murder if it's just my testimony, but if we add an upstanding business owner claiming theft and threats, it might sway a jury. Right?"

Lawrence considered his words.

"You're sure this cabbie would testify to help you out?"

"Not just me," he explained. "If I convince him it's good for the city, I think he'd jump at the chance to help. He raved over that whole deal with Vanderhill. I reckon he'd be happy to help lock away someone as dangerous as Richards."

"A racketeering charge is serious stuff, but I don't know how I feel about lying to put her away."

Conners almost tried to persuade her, but felt Bill's voice spring up.

Need to leave this to her, kid. We've done enough damage. Let her make the choice, and respect it, whatever it is.

Eventually, Lawrence spoke again.

"Talk to your guy, and Boston, and we'll see how everything lines up. If they're both willing… we'll move forward on the racketeering charge."

Conners let out a long sigh.

"Thanks."

She smiled softly at him, and while it didn't bear the warmth of her usual grin, it was far better than the anger and pain she'd worn the rest of the day.

"Thanks for being honest."

They stayed around the table and continued to talk out everything that had happened, and what their plans for the future were. A lot of mending would need to be done, but the door was open for him to fix things… if only just a small crack. He knew he'd do all he could to fix things between them, no matter what it ended up costing him. His friendship with her was important, even more important than arresting Richards.

And so, there was a chance for him to become something better. That was what Lawrence wanted of him, and exactly what Bill would've wanted.

Chapter XXIII: Strike

Conners smiled slightly as he glanced up at the midday sun, still hidden behind several clouds. The end of May was resting solidly in the low seventies and Conners wore most of his usual attire, only switching out his trench coat for a black blazer. He reached into his pockets—lamenting the smaller amount of pocket space his change in clothing offered—and unearthed a racquetball which he bounced off the wall of the courthouse. He allowed his mind to wonder while his hands were kept busy.

Today was arguably the most important day of his career. He had been subpoenaed to testify against Richards during her trial. All things considered, his part in the trial was fairly straight-forward. He only have to testify that he had met with Richards, she'd admitted to killing Bill, and she'd tried to hire him to steal police evidence… Well, all that and somehow avoid ending up in contempt of court, if at all possible.

They'd agreed it was best to kick the trial off with his testimony, given his connection to Richards and his tendency to grow bored of court proceedings. The faster they were able to formulate a picture of who Richards was for the jury, the harder the defense would have to work to dispel it. Between Boston's legal team and Joe's agreement to testify to Richards' racketeering, they stood a decent chance of winning the case, but Conners knew he wouldn't take anything as read until the verdict was given.

"Conners!" called Lawrence from the entranceway to the courthouse. "We're starting. You ready?"

"Ready as I can be," he said, sticking the ball back into his pocket.

Lawrence smiled softly at him and embraced him for a half-second before stepping back.

"Together," she said, looking him in the eye.

"Together," he agreed.

Their relationship had taken a large hit from his attempt to rob the station, but they'd worked closely together over Richards' case since then. Slowly, chances for him to earn Lawrence's trust back were showing themsleves. After a few months, the work could be punctuated by jokes and other conversation, and the awkwardness had begun to ebb away, replaced by the earnest care and respect they bore for one another.

He'd kept to his word too and tried as much as possible to rely on Bill's teachings. He never kept Lawrence out of anything he was doing. If she was curious about a case or something he was digging into, he laid it out for her and concealed nothing. It was a courtesy he didn't allow any other officer or detective, and she had yet to betray his trust.

Conners pushed the doors to the courtroom open a couple minutes before the defense finished their opening statement. Then, the D.A.—Joseph Green—stood and cleared his throat slightly.

"The prosecution calls Michael Conners to the stand, your honor."

Conners stood and strolled up to the stand, where the bailiff stood as Conners held up his hand.

"Do you swear to tell the truth, the whole truth, and nothing but the truth?"

Conners glanced at the jury. Two were watching him with interest, but many of the others had their eyes unfocused or glazed over. That was bad; it was too early to lose the jury.

Do what you do best, kid. Be a sideshow. Make them laugh, but make them listen.

"Not possible," said Conners, smirking.

"I beg your pardon?" asked the judge: a woman in her early sixties by the name of Julia Harris.

"Well, no one can tell the whole truth without exception, your honor," he explained, and mentally smiled as the jury perked up slightly. "The truth is subjective, such as we all see it. However hard we try to prevent it, it is interpreted through our own experiences."

The judge held back a smile that could've been either amusement or irritation. It was difficult to tell from his angle.

"How about, 'do you swear to be honest to the best of your ability?'"

"That'll work. I do... Well that's awkward because now I feel like I'm supposed to kiss someone."

"Mr. Conners..." said the judge, warningly.

"Sorry, just being open and honest, your honor," he said, as he threw himself into the chair and kicked his feet up over the armrest.

The jury chuckled slightly at this, and a few of the spectators joined in. Richards glared at him from her position at the defendant's table. He had to resist the urge to wink at her. Goading the defendant wouldn't score points with the judge or jury, and he'd only just gotten their full attention.

Reign it in, just a hair. Keep control, but don't go too far.

"Mr. Conners," said Green. "Would you please state your full name and occupation for the jury?"

"Private Detective, Michael J. Conners."

"And how would you describe your experience as a private detective?"

Conners glanced at the jury again. They were beginning to fade out.

"Oh it's been crazy," he said, smiling. "I have to clean up so many messes we considered changing my title to maid, but I don't think I could pull off the skirt... Pay might be better though."

More smiles. Now the jury was focused entirely on his testimony.

"Could you explain some of your work in a professional capacity?" asked Green, trying to hold back his own irritation.

"Of course. I take on several cases that go unsolved by Chicago's finest, and regularly assist them on cases that require some extra brainwork or legwork."

"How many cases would you say you've assisted the Chicago Police Department in?"

"I've been directly listed as a consultant over sixty times, and for a week in May of 2010, I was a homicide detective with the fourteenth precinct. However, it was quickly evident I worked best when left to my own devices and when I could choose my cases for myself."

"And in your professional opinion, what do you provide that the homicide detectives of the fourteenth precinct cannot do?"

"I'm incredibly quick at putting together a crime scene, and have a number of resources and contacts that allow me to follow evidence in a case quicker and to a more thorough end than what the cops can manage on their own."

"Detective," said the judge, holding up her hand. "Are you suggesting you are more capable of solving a crime single-handed than the homicide squad is with all the resources of the city behind them?"

"No, your honor; my record suggests that. I just like to solve puzzles."

More laughter from some of the spectators.

"Detective, are you acquainted with the defendant: Mrs. Kelsey Richards?"

"Tricky question actually," said Conners. "We met twice, about fifteen minutes in total. She killed my boss and her ex-husband, William Scott."

"And why are you under the impression she murdered him?"

"If you're asking as to motive: because Bill was her ex-husband, and was one of the only people I imagine stood up to her properly. If you're asking as to how I'm certain it was her: she admitted that she killed him to my face. She left a note in his shirt pocket for me to find labeling her office address. I ventured there and she gloated about the murder to my face."

This caused the courtroom to fall silent, while Richards radiated murderous intent, even as she pretended to cry into her hands at his accusation.

"Objection!" called out Richard's lawyer: a man with grey hair with the surname Rodney. "Narrative, your honor."

Narrative? he thought, amused. *Haven't heard that one before.*

It was a rarer objection, usually used when a witness was going on too long in an answer and attempting to control the flow of the questioning.

"Sustained. The jury is instructed to disregard any statements after the motive."

Truth be told, it was the right call for the judge to make. Conners knew it didn't matter though. The official record might not reflect what he'd said, but the jury heard him, and it would be impossible for them to unhear it.

"So you feel quite assured of her guilt in this matter?"

"Objection," called out Richards' lawyer again. "Leading the witness."

"Sustained," said Judge Harris. "Prosecutor, please rephrase the question."

"How assured are you of her guilt, in your professional opinion?"

"Entirely," said Conners, staring at her. "I have no doubts or questions in my mind regarding Richards' guilt in this matter. She has displayed multiple symptoms that indicate a complete lack of any empathy or understanding of another human being's feelings, indicating a form of psychopathy."

"And your second meeting with Mrs. Richards: this was on the 16th of December, correct?"

"Yes, although I would object to the term 'meeting.' She had a man point a gun in my face and force me into a van."

"And why did she want to speak with you so desperately?"

"She attempted to hire me to steal police evidence that implicated one of her men in a murder."

"And did you agree do steal that evidence?"

"Yes," said Conners, leaving only a half-second of silence before continuing. "But I instead revealed her request to Homicide Sergeant Jessica Lawrence, and we agreed to catch her on a traced phone call."

"I would ask the jury to examine the transcript which was presented into evidence."

There was a long pause while the jury read through and passed around a transcript of the conversation between himself and Richards that the police had taped. They also had access to the tape itself, but Richards' lawyer had objected to it being played in the courtroom aloud as it would damage Richards' reputation.

"So what, in your professional assessment are the defendants crimes, Detective?"

"At least one count of premeditated murder, at least one account of hiring a man to commit murder, and attempting to steal evidence and shut down an investigation. There are surely a great many others, but as far as my own personal experience is involved in the charges brought forth today, that's all I can testify to."

"Very well," said Green before turning to Richard's lawyer. "No further questions at this time, your honor."

"Your witness," said Judge Harris to Rodney.

"Detective," said Richards' lawyer, making Conners skin crawl unpleasantly. "You have levied heavy insults and accusations against my client today."

"Not unduly," said Conners, nodding.

"Yet, by your own admission, you have spoken to the defendant a total of two times, totaling less than twenty minutes?"

"We weren't exactly having a huggy moment. She *had* just killed someone I cared deeply about prior to our first meeting and had a gun on me during the second."

"Yet you have suggested Mrs. Richards: a woman who heads several community outreach programs, and who donates regularly to charities, is a psychopath, and a killer?"

"Shockingly," said Conners, leaning forward. "Psychopaths are actually rather capable liars. It has something to do with that complete lack of empathy I mentioned."

"And you feel confident enough to swear by this diagnosis, despite a lack of *any* medical or therapeutic training or schooling, after knowing her the length of a single meal together?"

"Hardly," said Conners, smirking. "I knew she was a psychopath after about thirty seconds, the following time was just me being held against my will."

"So you admit you had a preconceived notion as to my client's mindset and behavior after knowing her for half-a-minute?"

"I do."

"So, in your professional opinion, is it viable for anyone to understand another human being after so short a time?"

"Some people—like murderers—manage to make an opinion far quicker than others. Per example: you are incredibly condescending."

The judge had to quickly cover her mouth at this, and she was far from the only one. Half the courtroom was stifling a laugh or disguising a chuckle as a cough.

The lawyer scowled, and Conners saw the frustration build up in his eyes, before he begrudgingly admitted defeat.

"No further questions," said Rodney, heading back to the table to review his notes.

"We'd like to thank and excuse Detective Michael Conners," said Boston's lawyer before checking his own notepad. "The prosecution would like to call one Sergeant Jessica Lawrence, of the Chicago Police Department, please."

And like that, it was over. Conners was escorted from the stand and walked towards the entrance. As he passed the defendant's table, he would've sworn Richards bared her teeth at him for a flash of a second, but he ignored her. He couldn't give into her games or show aggression that might cause the jury to lean in her favor. He passed Lawrence, who had begun to head towards the stand.

"Good luck," he whispered, winking.

"Thanks," she said, smiling softly at him.

Conners couldn't help but feel just a little happier at her smile. It was like a soft assurance; regardless of the stuff they had to face, they could do it if they did so together. Somehow, his lone wolf attitude from a few years ago now appeared laughably quaint, if not downright delusional. The idea of fighting Richards, or indeed of just continuing his detective work without having Lawrence to turn to as a friend and partner seemed dark and depressing. He had no idea how he could've met two people he would actually come to rely on so much. He'd met people he truly loved.

He hailed a cab back to his apartment. On the way, he allowed himself a moment on Twitter and saw that the court case was rapidly shared and talked about. Even a few news articles had covered his testimony, brief as it might've been and most of the coverage suggested that his record meant something. He put his phone away, and let his mind cast over the two people who meant so much to him, even with one of them passed from the world.

Bill and Lawrence... they were family to him. He knew the word wasn't exactly right. But it was the only one he could find. He knew—without question or hesitation—that if Lawrence needed him, he would help her regardless of the task or challenge. He would've done the same for Bill, and in a small way he had. He hadn't saved Bill's life, but he had helped catch the old man's killer, assuming the jury convicted her.

Perhaps with that realization accepted, he would finally be able to sleep without having repeated nightmares about a young blonde child. With that hopeful idea in his mind, Conners lay his head down on his pillow, and prepared to have a peaceful afternoon nap.

He had no such luck. Once more nightmares filled his sleeping hours and a young blonde child demanded answers Conners couldn't provide. So the boy assaulted him in his dreams, and demanded an answer while he attacked Conners, as if unaware of the bleeding bullet hole in the center of his head.

"Conners!"

He was awoken by someone shouting his name and sat bolt upright, and only then realized his shirt was damp and his hair was matted to his forehead. He also felt unpleasantly cold, as if a winter wind had just overtaken him. Shivering, he swung his legs over the bed and looked at the entrance of his bedroom to see Lawrence standing there with a pizza box in her hands.

"You ok?" she asked, the concern evident on her face.

"Yeah," he lied. "Just some bad dreams. Not a huge deal. What's up?"

"The trial let out about half-an-hour ago."

"Oh?" asked Conners, slapping himself quickly several times to help wake up. "What's the verdict?"

"Guilty, on all counts," she said, smiling softly. "Took the jury all of ten minutes to reach a decision. Honestly, I'm surprised it took even that long."

"Must've been a line for the toilet," Conners said, smiling. "What's with the food?"

"Surprisingly, it's hard to find a cake right now. So, figured a deep dish was close enough."

"Of course," he said, as they moved to the kitchen. "And why exactly are we enjoying a cheese, pepperoni, and sausage cake?"

"To celebrate," she said, as if it should've been obvious. "Look, Richards was a big bag, and more than that... she hurt you. I know how much closure matters."

He nodded and opened up his fridge, pulling out two beers, tossing one to Lawrence and sitting across from her at his small kitchen table.

"Lawrence," he said as he popped the cap off of the bottle. "Thank you for everything, seriously. I know I don't always make things easy for you, but this *was* important to me, and you helped me. That means a lot."

"Hey," she said, taking a bite out of her slice of pizza. "You're my friend. Besides, Richards made my skin crawl."

He chuckled softly at that, and reached for a slice of pizza himself. They spent the rest of the evening joking and making fun of people from the office, telling stories from cases, and enjoying an old police show that was playing on the TV.

Human connection, he thought. *This is what we live for... I get it. This is nice.*

Part II: The Watcher

Chapter XXIV: Sex, Drugs, and Murder

Conners groaned and looked up at the ceiling for the umpteenth time that hour. His eyes were automatically pulled towards the fan as it made its way round and round. It was just slow enough that it could still be tracked by the human eye, though doing so for too long would make him feel slightly dizzy.

"You know Michael," said his therapist, leaning back in her chair. "This really is designed to help you, but I can't begin to help you with your struggles if you don't tell me what it *is* you're struggling with."

"Actually," said Conners, placing a piece of gum in his mouth casually. He desperately wanted to smoke, but she didn't allow it in the office. "You're helping plenty. I'm here practically under duress, because a friend of mine is being a little... overly concerned."

Petra Gardner: his new therapist didn't seem at all discouraged at his dismissal of her services, but instead scribbled something on her notepad and looked up at him, as if he were a mildly interesting painting in a museum.

"And what is it that your friend is so concerned about?"

"Nothing of consequence," Conners said, chewing the gum and fiddling with his cane. "We got the woman who killed my old boss convicted, and my friend is worried that I'm unhinged by the whole thing."

To her credit, Petra didn't show surprise or disbelief, but merely nodded and scribbled on her pad.

"You said this woman killed your old boss?"

"Right," said Conners, tracing a crack in the ceiling with his finger. "Well he was her ex-husband, but to me, he was just my boss."

"And why does your friend think you're so 'unhinged'—to use your word?"

Conners shrugged. After all, the blunt truth either wouldn't be understood, or wouldn't be believed. So there really wasn't any reason to bother trying to cover it up.

"Multiple reasons, I suppose. I readily put myself in danger, I challenge authority and order when I'm bored, I have trouble sleeping, and I talk to an imaginary version of my boss in my head when I'm trying to problem-solve."

Petra nodded again.

"Let's talk about your trouble sleeping," she said, turning the page over.

"Really?" asked Conners, and he looked over at her with surprise. "That's the thing that most interests you out of that whole list?"

"It's a good place to start."

Conners held up a hand, and listened closely, more grateful than he'd ever been to catch the sound of police sirens wailing a block or two over.

"Actually," said Conners, crossing over to the window and opening it quickly. "I'm getting a call. Gotta take this. You know how it is. Catch you later and you can send your incredibly inflated bill to my office."

"Mr. Conners!" Petra protested, and she stood up as he stepped out onto the ledge.

"Detective Michael J. Conners," he corrected her before holding an imaginary phone to his ear. "Hello? Crime scene? Why yes I'll be right over!"

And with that he threw himself from the second-story window, landing and rolling onto the sidewalk before he took off at a sprint. He allowed the adrenaline of a new case to flood his system as he exhaled and his world slowed.

The sirens are up ahead on your left, came Bill's voice.

That's North Hampden... and they're slowing down now. Crime scene must be nearby.

He took a brief second to triangulate the rough location of where the crime scene should likely be and barreled between two buildings. He hopped the chain fence separating the lots and sprinted towards the crowd gathering on the opposite side of the street. He beat the approaching car by about a minute and smiled to himself.

"Hello there!" he said, cheerily to the patrolmen, who he didn't recognize. "What lovely excuse have you just provided me with?"

"What? Who are you supposed to be?"

"Wow," said Conners, feigning an introspective look. "That's deep. Like who are we all supposed to be, man? I mean I feel like I'm supposed to be the person who's looking into whatever you've got going on. And you're the person who's supposed to let me do that, but that's like so far out."

"Are you high?"

"Don't deal with drugs," said Conners, winking. "After all, that'll kill ya. Look kid, I consult for the fourteenth precinct all the time. I needed a reason to be not where I was. So just let me look at whatever it is, please."

"Oh, *you're* Conners. We were warned you might be a problem."

"Well, they *do* know me so well. So if you could fetch my pipe and funny hat, I'll Sherlock all over this and be home before dinner."

The patrolmen spoke into his radio for a moment, and Conners heard the lieutenant's weary voice reply within a couple seconds, allowing him in. He assumed an exaggerated look of pleading.

"Fine," said the patrolman. "It's all above my pay-grade to deal with anyway."

He lifted the police tape and Conners slid under it, and took a moment to appreciate the crisp look of an uncontaminated crime scene. There was almost as much beauty as there was horror in the fresh sight of a murder. He knew that it was a murder before he'd even crossed the line. He could *sense* it more than smell or see it. It was like a prickling in the back of his brain.

As Conners examined the scene before him, the familiar rush of adrenaline flooded his system, and he took a look around the place that lasted an eternity, but took only a second. There was a woman lying on the ground. Between the blood pooling around her, her pale face, and the fact that her chest wasn't moving, her death wasn't a difficult conclusion to reach.

He spied bruises on her bare arms and one that was just beginning to purple around her remaining eye: she'd been attacked and beaten violently. Her lack of modesty and clothing suggested she was a hooker, which wasn't especially surprising given the area. There was a clear bullet-wound where her left eye ought to be. There were also powder burns clearly visible around the eye socket.

She was shot at close range, came Bill's voice.

Agreed. That suggests?

Revenge as a motive.

He continued his search and saw the murder weapon lying a little way away: partly hidden behind a leg of the nearby dumpster.

Hidden, but not well.

We were expected to find it. That suggests?

Intent to implicate the owner.

Agreed. If weapon still has the serial number, owner is cleared.

Conners slipped a plastic bag over his hand and reached for the gun, and saw that the serial number was still clearly printed along the barrel of the weapon. He mentally took a snapshot of it for future reference and quickly let his mind identify the weapon.

HK forty-five. This would be an impressive piece for a street thug.

More likely a personal weapon.

Conners nodded and checked the magazine, and saw that only a single shot had been fired from the weapon, assuming it wasn't loaded with one in the chamber. It was only then he could clearly hear the footsteps behind him. He finished bagging the gun and turned, with a bright smile on his face. He didn't recognize either homicide detective.

"Detectives!" he said brightly, bowing as sarcastically as possible. "So good to have some dead weight around. You'll want this. Say you found it, if you like; it's not useful anyway."

"What? Who is this?" asked one of the detectives.

"Michael Conners," said the other. "He's a right pain that Lawrence usually deals with, but apparently he's figured out how to get away from her."

"Don't tell mom," said Conners.

He tossed the gun to the second detective and ducked out of the scene, and reached into his pocket for his phone.

~*~

Three hours later, Conners pushed his way into the police station, his cuffed bounty in front of him. As he entered, a few of the nearby cops glanced at him. Luckily, most of those who didn't know him from his time working *for* the department knew him as the private investigator who helped bring down Kelsey Richards and occasionally worked with Lawrence.

Conners nodded to the desk officer: Daniel Harper and he pressed the release button for the door.

"Have fun," said Harper.

"Don't I always?"

He made his way down to the interrogation rooms where to his exuberant joy he found the lieutenant standing on the other side of the one-way mirror looking into the room.

"Howdy lieutenant," said Conners, as he put on a comically broad western accent. "Pardon meh interruptin' but I do believe yer looking for this here fella."

"As if today hadn't given me enough headaches. What is this, Conners?"

"*This* is the man who killed your hooker on Hampton: Bruce Luna. Say hi Bruce!" Conners shook Bruce forcefully, but the man didn't speak. "Aw... he's a little shy 'round strangers."

The lieutenant grimaced and ran a hand down his face.

"We've already got the killer. The gun you recovered was registered to John Snatcher, and we already cleared Luna earlier. He had no gunshot residue on his hand. We already interviewed him."

"Ah, but *I* noticed something you lot didn't: as is so often the case in our relationship. You see, Mister Luna here, is *left*-handed. So when you tested his *right* hand for residue, it came up negative. I'm guessing Snatcher is also negative or you'd be waving that in my face?"

The lieutenant growled as a response.

"The other problem is that Brucie-boy is wearing long sleeves today."

"So? It's like fifty outside."

"True. So it *could* be to block out the cold... or..." Conners said as he reached down and yanked Luna's left sleeve up his arm past the elbow. "He could want to cover up this quickly spreading rash."

The lieutenant looked nonplused. "And what am I supposed to make of a rash?"

Conners rolled his eyes.

"I honestly thought the dead hooker would be enough, but let me put it this way. If I were to show you where the rash starts, he'd have to drop his pants."

It *clicked* then.

"He has syphilis... from the hooker."

Luna grimaced and spoke softly, but still loud enough for them to hear.

"I want my lawyer."

"So when our unfortunate friend here realized what he had, he decided to right what he viewed as a sexual wrong. Given how hard it can be to get a gun in Chicago, he just borrows his old roommate's piece. In the future: penicillin is a thing, man."

The lieutenant groaned and pointed to the nearest empty interrogation room.

"You can keep him in there until we can test him; and if you're wrong, *you* can be the one who spends your entire Sunday trying to convince him not to sue you."

Conners smirked and winked at the lieutenant.

"And when—if you could be so kind as to indicate—have I been wrong lately?"

"You are the reason cops drink."

Conners smiled and led Luna into the interrogation room before closing the door and practically skipping up to the homicide bullpen. Lawrence was bent over her desk as she typed up a case report. Conners smiled softly as he saw her foot tap in time to a song she must've been subconsciously listening to in her mind.

He walked up to her twirling his cane somewhat like a baton before he sat on the edge of her desk. She barely glanced up at him and focused on her report. He smirked down at her and flipped the cane up onto his shoulder where it sat, balanced.

"Stripper gram?" he asked, catching the shadow of a smile at the corners of her lips.

"I wasn't aware you ever asked for permission before making a mockery of yourself."

"Is this just the office's day to try and throw shade or something?"

"Oh when it comes to you Conners, we make it a bi-weekly event."

He smiled and winked at her.

"In all seriousness, you look like you could use a break. You take lunch yet?"

Lawrence let out a long sigh before looking at her watch. She then stood, put on her tan jacket, and stretched slightly.

"I suppose I can go on break. After all, I haven't hit up that Mexican place in a bit."

"Or," said Conners, hoping to avoid a repeat performance of her chosen restaurant. "We could grab some nice Italian food… or even find a hole-in-the-wall."

He saw her shoulder shake just a little as she giggled at his desire to change the destination.

"I'm messing with you, you absolute nutcase," she said as they walked into the parking garage

He rolled his eyes playfully.

"Very funny. You know how ridiculous it actually is to own a watch, right? I mean, your phone can actually tell the time and isn't an uncomfortable thing around your wrist all day."

"Oh well you would know all about comfort," she said as she opened her car door and climbed inside. "Not all of us get to work in chucks and a t-shirt."

As they pulled out of the parking lot into Chicago's traffic flow, Conners felt his pocket *buzz,* indicating a text. Mildly curious, he pulled it out and read the alert on his screen. The alert had no number attached to it, but read as blocked. His curiosity now peaked, Conners swiped the message open.

Most impressive, detective. I expected nothing else from the man talented enough to defeat Kelsey Richards. I do think you and I will have lots of fun together.

- The Watcher

Conners sat staring at the message for several seconds, trying to decide if this was a mistake, a joke, or a threat. After almost half-a-minute he locked the phone and put it back in his pocket. He'd have to get ahold of a few of his tech-savvy contacts and see if the message could be traced to a number or cell tower. He'd also have to check his place for bugs and see if The Watcher came up in any of his criminal research.

There was no point focusing too much on the text until he had more to work with, but he kept it in the back of his mind, and his brain worked and spun like a top while Lawrence drove.

"You all right?" she asked, noting his silence.

"Yeah," he responded, snapping out of his musings. "Just thinking of some stuff that I need to handle. I'll let you know if it's anything to worry about."

"I'll hold you to that," she said, and sped down the road.

Chapter XXV: A Good Impression

Conners groaned as he looked across his desk at Jerry: his tech wizard. Jerry had long brown hair that was pulled back into a ponytail, and a trimmed goatee that caused him to look like the result of cross-breeding a rock star and an I.T. specialist. Normally, Jerry was able to help Conners whenever a technical problem heeded an investigation. Jerry had hacked laptops and sim cards for him. So he was Conners' first thought when he'd gotten the mysterious text. However, when it came to trying to trace this text, Jerry was coming up completely empty.

"I'm gonna want my money back," he said to the twenty-two-year-old.

"Look man," said Jerry, sliding his laptop back into his carry bag. "You asked me to run back the text to see if it was possible to get a tower or a number. I found where the signal pinged from."

"I asked you to give me something to help figure out who sent this, and yet I sit with no phone number and a half-dozen towers that somehow bounced the signal around. Apparently they could be anywhere along the eastern seaboard."

"And that's all there is to find."

Conners grumbled and wrote Jerry the check for his work as he felt his cellphone *buzz* again. Almost expecting another text from The Watcher he pulled it out. But it wasn't the mystery being, rather it was a text from Lawrence.

Had a mobster turn himself in for racketeering, but I get a funny feeling from it. Mind giving me a hand on this one?

Conners smiled despite himself. He knew he was even happier to see Lawrence than he was to help solve the case. Not that the casework couldn't be fun as well, but he hadn't had much of a chance to hang out with Lawrence in almost a month.

If you miss me so much, you could always just stop by the office. I'll stop by soon as I'm done talking to an annoyance.

Her response came a few seconds later.

You know, they say talking to yourself is the first sign of madness.

He chuckled as he slid the phone back into his pocket and leaned back in his chair, letting his mind empty and clear of The Watcher. When he felt confident he could absorb new information without bias, he reached the phone and dialed Joe's number.

"Ah, my very favorite customer," came Joe's voice through the earpiece. *"I'll have a cab to you in less than a minute."*

"Joe, you're a beautiful human being."

"Don't tell me things I know."

Conners hung up and rose from the desk. He found it strange that he had relationships and had even grown close to multiple people over the past few years. How could it be he had set out with the goal of equalizing his influence in the world and instead made friends? Lawrence and Joe both helped him in casework, but they were also a force in his personal life and people he looked forward to seeing. Even Lieutenant Guston—for all their differences in beliefs—had something of a relationship with Conners. Even a few of the patrolmen like Jake Miller had become friendly faces over the years.

A few moments later, one of Joe's cabbies pulled up to the front of the office and Conners climbed in the back of the car, giving the address of the police precinct as he did so. The cabbie nodded and smiled brightly as the car took off. Joe had made sure his drivers were compensated to ferry Conners around, which had apparently made him something of a popular fare. Personally, he was just relieved to be able to travel quickly without having to worry about the hit to his wallet. Granted, his payment from Richards meant he certainly wouldn't be hurting for cash anytime soon. He'd even considered renovating the office again, but couldn't help but enjoy the slightly rustic charm it currently held.

They moved swiftly through the traffic and were at the station within only a few minutes. As he opened the door the cabbie spoke out.

"Hey, if it's not a big deal, mind if I get a picture for my kid? He's a bit of a fan of yours."

Conners was slightly thrown but recovered quickly enough and shook hands with the cab driver while the man took a selfie with his phone.

"Hope your kid can geek about it a bit," Conners said, grinning.

"Oh, he'll be a regular pain about it, no doubt."

Conners nodded good-naturedly as he head in the large, glass double-doors of the 14th precinct, still trying to come to grips with the idea of being something of a local celebrity. It wasn't quite the first time that he'd been approached by someone for a picture, but it still slightly baffled him. He really wasn't someone who was publicly known as an altruist or even a kind person. Yet, people still considered him… what? Some sort of vigilante? Was he perhaps a hero out of the comic books? Or was he closer to a side-show attraction: someone so incompatible and broken that nothing in the current world could understand or accept what he really was? And that was before knowing his greatest shames.

Conners shook himself violently. More than once he'd fallen into the trap of over-analyzing both himself and his place in the world only to end up horribly rattled and more than a little disturbed by what he'd let his mind wonder into. It was dangerous to get too far inside his own head. It was like a black hole: a place of such depravity and focus that he could lose himself there for hours at a time. Only last week, he'd sat down to reflect and consider only to look up at the clock and realize that it had been several hours since he'd moved.

The desk officer greeted him with a perfunctory nod, and Conners grinned slightly and slid past the desk, almost gliding down the stairs to the station's interrogation rooms. He saw Lawrence before he had even taken a full count of the officers surrounding her. Including her, there were nearly twenty detectives staring through the one-way mirror.

Conners fell into place alongside Lawrence, and couldn't help but catch a slight whiff of her shampoo that reminded him vaguely of chestnuts. It was a comforting smell—something that brought to mind the image of a warm fire on a cold, rainy day. Aware of the unfortunate lack of focus he held, Conners deliberately stubbed his toe on the wall. It didn't hurt much, just enough to help snap him back to attention.

The man on the other side of the glass wore a suit that was a size or two too large for him, and bunched awkwardly at the pits and stomach. His hair was pulled back by product, but was almost too stiff and harsh to be an expensive hold. This man was a budget-built mobster, at best. The best confirmation of this though, was the man's shoes. They were nice-looking, but they were costume compared to what most of the real kingpins wore. Most mob bosses wore expensive, genuine leather shoes, or even had a set custom made. Their suits usually held a more tailored look, and while not all the bosses wore ties, it was customary to at least bare a silk pocket square or nice jewelry. An expensive watch or gold and diamond ring often served as a display of wealth amongst competing mobsters. Suburban housewives could learn a thing or two from criminal showboating.

What held far more interest for him was that the man's hands were completely wrong for a leader's. Even from this distance, Conners could see the scars and marks custom of a laborer. This man likely worked as some sort of enforcer, or even a grunt for his capo. There was no way any self-respecting mob boss would have hands like this man's. Then Conners noted the grunt's left pinkie. There was a sizable bit missing at the end, and the cut was too clean to have been caused by a bite or accident. No. It was a surgical, deliberate cut… a ritual to serve as an apology and a declaration of loyalty. It was an old Japanese and Sicilian custom amongst mafia forces, and Conners could only think of one mob boss who held to so ancient a practice in the area.

"So, Ray Vinci's guy is taking the fall for his rackets then? Or I should say for the rackets you're close to closing down."

The detectives all turned to look at him.

"How you work that out?" asked Officer Miller, standing on Lawrence's other side.

"Ray and I are secret lovers," said Conners, smiling broadly. "He's a decent cuddle, but a big pillow-talker."

"Oh yeah, he a top or bottom?" replied Miller.

"Careful. It's learning."

Lawrence sighed, but without even looking in her direction, he could hear the smile she wore. The thought of it made him smile too, and so he explained what he'd seen in the man pretending to be a mafia leader.

"We haven't heard anything from Vinci recently," said Lawrence. "He works for the Genovese Family, right?"

A man Conners didn't recognize spoke up.

"Right, though we aren't sure how deeply they run in Chicago. We've got some rumors that they've been aiming to hit Kingston Inc. but nothing concrete right now."

Kingston…

Kingston…

There it was again—that name, and it rang like a church bell in his head echoing and growing louder and louder with each repeat.

Kingston…

Kingston...

Conners ground his teeth and instinctively threw his hands up over his ears, but as the noise came from inside his own head, it did no good. Then all at once, the voice stopped and a new voice took its place. Unlike the strange, muddled sound of the Kingston name, this voice was clear and distinctive.

"Shame you'll miss that birthday, kid."

That sentence overcame his mind, and caused his essence to reverberate as if his skeleton were a ringing gong. It took him several seconds to come to himself, but when he did, he realized that his phone was *buzzing* in his pocket.

As disturbed as he was curious, Conners pulled out his phone and saw a text on his alert screen.

Well done, detective. I'd recommend trying Anthony's Diner on S. Indiana Ave. Wonderful Panettone.

- The Watcher

Conners stared, caught between shock and indignation. Once he managed to regain control of his faculties, he checked the number, but again it was blocked. Scowling, Conners turned quickly, examining as many of the people in the room as he could. There was *no way* that The Watcher could know what he'd just done without having ears in the room.

One of these men was a snitch, but it was impossible to tell who. The case was too wide-spread. There were detectives from homicide, vice, organized crime, and other offices besides. There were too many bodies—too many unknown variables.

Casually as he could, he leaned over to Lawrence and whispered in her ear, "Watch what you say, someone here is spying."

Lawrence didn't give any indication that she knew anything was wrong. She was good at throwing up her defenses when the need called.

She leaned back and whispered so quietly he almost missed it, "I'll give you what time I can. Run with it."

He stretched slowly and walked back up the way he'd come in.

"Well as much as I'd love to sit here and be congratulated again—Why yes I *did* do a marvelous job—I'm afraid I've got far more important places to be. But if any of you want me to do you jobs for you, feel free to stop by my office, or more realistically just leave it with my secretary."

He pointed at Lawrence with both of his index fingers and she gave a one-fingered salute in response. He waited until he was completely out of the station before getting another cab to drive him back to his place. He opened the door before the cab had even fully stopped and warned the driver to wait.

Quick as he could, Conners went to his dresser and dressed in a pair of grey slacks and a black, silk shirt. Finally, he replaced his converse with a decent pair of dress shoes and finger-combed his hair into a semblance of order. Lastly, he opened another drawer and slid on two gold rings and a thin, golden chain. Truthfully the pieces were nothing special, but gangsters had a long-standing thing about jewelry.

He rushed back out, already missing the familiar weight of *Sherry* on his hip, and Bill's cane in his hand. He quickly looked up the actual address of Anthony's Diner and relayed the location to the cabbie. Then he leaned back in the seat, and carefully considered what approach he wanted to take. Mobsters weren't exactly known for their patience and leniency.

The place they pulled up to reeked of Italian inspiration. Conners saw that the tables and chairs were made from a fine, rich wood with red covers and detailing. Even from outside he could make out eight separate wine stands, and each was at least as tall as he was; and that was before he could make out the richly-stocked bar.

The clients in the building were mostly couples, with a few smaller families dotted throughout. Conners had an uncomfortable feeling even a simple chicken dish would cost twice what most other places would've charged. What held far more interest for him was the doorman who was clearly armed and dressed in a dark suit.

Conners walked up and nodded at him, feigning a self-importance that bordered on true arrogance.

"You have a reservation?" asked the doorman.

"Nah," said Conners, with just the hint of an accent. "I'm 'ere to try out the Panettone. Was recommended by a friend up north."

The man eyed him up and down for a long moment. After a considerable pause, the gorilla of a man spoke slowly, as if each word took a great effort to form.

"One moment," the man said and made a short call on his cell phone. "Hands on the wall."

Conners did as he was asked and the man quickly frisked him. Without even meaning to, Conners noted three separate places he could've hidden a weapon if he'd needed one.

"All right," said the man when he'd finished. "Follow me."

Conners let the man lead him into the back of the establishment, past the restroom doors into the kitchen. None of the cooks or staff gave them a second glance as the man opened a door Conners took to be a cellar, and was surprised to see that a small dining area had been set up.

Real old-school mob style, he heard Bill say.

Too right. We'll have to be careful.

Stay vigilant, kid.

The doorman led Conners past a small handful of patrons, and the difference from the crowd upstairs was staggering. Many wore expensive clothing, often made of silk. There was only a single woman that Conners could see, and every patron bore the unmistakable air of danger.

At the table at the end was a lone man in a fine, beige suit. He wore a dark shirt and yellow tie, and his hair was slicked back with product. Yet there was more beyond his fine facade. His eyes had heavy bags beneath them that spoke to weeks of long nights and restlessness. The slight tremor in his left hand spoke to stress and panic. The gun under his left arm and the knife inside his right sock spoke to a desire for safety—something no mob leader could have.

The doorman looked to the man, who nodded once.

"Leave us," said the man before he turned to Conners. "Michael Conners? Ray Vinci. Pleasure to meet you. You here to arrest me?"

"Course not," said Conners, and he slid into the seat across from Ray. "I'd prefer to leave without a new hole in my head."

Ray laughed, which briefly displayed a mouthful of chewed meat.

"Good one, kid," he said, and Conners felt his skin crawl unpleasantly at the use of the word. "They told me you can be a smartass. So, what's so important you had to interrupt my lunch?"

"Only that the police know about the man you sent to take the fall for you."

That stopped Ray for a second.

"And how would they know about something like that?"

Conners watched as Ray slowly reached for the holster under his left arm.

"Your man turned on you to run a deal. He's already signed a statement and plans to testify in court."

"I see," said Ray, with one hand still hidden beneath his jacket. "And why would a snitch like you tell me this?"

"That's a bit hurtful," said Conners. "I'm not out to help the cops. I'm out to help me. You can't imagine the money and business I got out of that whole deal with Richards. But I like to back the winning side, and in this case… I think that's you."

"Smart boy, but what's in it for you?"

"Oh simple enough," said Conners, smiling. "I figure I keep an ear out, and keep your head clear, you might be willing to send a little something my way."

Slowly, Ray released the pistol and smiled at him.

"Always comes down to brass, don't it? Fair enough kid, you give me a chance to deal with our would-be snitch, I'll pay you four figures. Consider it an advance on our partnership."

"Done deal," said Conners, smiling. "I'll make sure there's a shift change at eight tonight, you get a couple uniforms, no one will ask too many questions. Holding cells are on the lower level."

Vinci smiled and reached below the table into a black bag, which he opened and pulled out a small stack of bills. He slid these over the table to Conners, who pocketed the cash and stood.

"Pleasure doin' business with you, Ray. See ya 'round."

"Later kid."

Conners smiled and walked away from the place. He waited until he was two blocks away before sending Lawrence a text, letting her know to be ready to catch Vinci in an attempted murder. It was standard practice. After all, snitches got stitches.

Later that evening, as Conners was pouring over his inbox, he felt his phone *buzz* and pulled it out to read Lawrence's text.

Vinci's under arrest. Thanks for the help. Check's heading your way for your consultation. Dinner?

He grinned brightly and sent back his reply.

Chapter XXVI: Brothers in Blood

Conners sat at his desk, and idly examined the client sitting across from him. He was a little, round man with round glasses, dark hair and a plump face shiny with sweat. He wore a dark green suit that was a size too small for him, and tight around the pits of his arms, leaving his chest just slightly over-exposed. He wore no ring on his wedding finger and there were bags under his eyes from lack of sleep. The man's name was John Barns.

Barns had found his way into Conners' office in the late hours of the afternoon. He had been dazed and confused, and could only ask for a detective.

Conners had sat him down and Barns had taken a long drink of water before mentioning his brother had been killed in the night.

"So Mr. Barns, how did your brother die, and how can I help?"

"Well," said John slowly. "I'm not exactly sure what happened. His wife says she found him this morning, and that he'd been choked in the night."

He means strangled, Conners heard Bill interrupt. *You don't choke another person except by serving them too large a cut of steak. His brother was strangled.*

Not the central information to take away there, Conners replied in his mind.

Recently, Bill's observations had become far more frequent. Instead of being helpful, sometimes he would note things Conners had already noticed or would talk while Conners was still processing them. It was actually more common for Conners to hear Bill's voice in his head than it was his own.

"His wife *found* him?"

"Well, I mean, she realized he was dead. She slept by him in the night and says she remembers him coming to bed, and woke in the morning to find him dead. I live with the two of them since I lost my job. I used to be an account manager for a computer parts company, but after the recession... I was part of the downsize, and I've been staying with them ever since."

"I understand, please continue."

"Right. Well, once she told me about that, I called the police straight away. They came out and asked us a couple dozen questions and then took my brother to a coroner. Later, they told us he was choked to death."

He said the wife realized he was choked to death earlier.
Conners decided not to mention Bill's observation aloud.
Let's see what else we can dig up first.

"Well my brother and I had a bit of a fight recently. He was angry that I was staying there for so long and he and Martha fought. I felt guilty they were fighting 'cause of me and tried to talk to Frank about it. I don't really know who started it, but we ended up fighting on the front lawn. A few of the neighbors heard it and called the cops. No one ended up seriously hurt or anything. I decided to not try again, but they fought about it a few more times... at least from what I could hear."

"I see," said Conners, as he pressed his hands together and placed the tips of his fingers just below his lips in thought. "And when was the fight with your brother: when the police were called?"

John's eyes flicked to the lower left as he tried to remember. After a short pause, he answered.

"About two weeks ago."

"And did you hear your brother ever argue with his wife before that night?"

This time John's gaze was steady and he did not look away.

"Once or twice a week they'd really get into it. They'd fight about some little thing or other. I was just the most recent source of argument."

Liar, said Bill.

Conners didn't actually care when the fight had happened. He just needed to force John to remember something. Of course, he would have Lawrence check on the report, just to be sure John hadn't been lying about that too. When John hadn't needed to focus on the alleged arguments he hadn't looked away at all. He was lying about their history of fighting. Conners shook himself slightly, hoping to clear Bill's voice from his ears a little.

"I see," he said, standing and moving over to his filing cabinet. "Let me get your address and you can leave. I'll likely be by a bit later, but I'll sort this out."

"Thank you so much!" said Barns. "I don't know how to thank you for this."

Conners said nothing but waited until Barns had left the office and closed the door behind him before moving. He pulled his phone out and dialed Joe's number to request a cab before sending a text to Lawrence.

Should be handing you a killer before 7.

Her reply sent a soft wave of pleasure through him and made him smile genuinely.

Is it nice starting work after lunch? I'm off at nine tonight if you want to have dinner at my place.

He quickly typed and sent his reply before gearing up for his newest case.

Late night dinner? Hope you're not trying to get me in bed, sergeant. Look forward to seeing you then.

Once Conners had thoroughly handled his flirtation and transportation responsibilities, he threw on his overcoat and pushed his hair back to its usual style before heading out the door and grabbing Bill's cane. He highly doubted he would come across any real trouble, but since carrying *Sherry* too often in the city could cause long and annoying conversations with cops, Bill's cane was a decent backup if he didn't suspect a shootout.

Joe's cabbie was a tall woman with blonde hair named Monika. She had driven him around a few times before. Conners had been a little wary of her at first. She had a few tattoos and an air that spoke to a stint in prison. While he'd resisted the urge to do a background check on her, it had taken some time until he was comfortable with being driven by her. Still, she'd had ample chance to refuse to drive him or harm him in some way, and never taken advantage of it. Plus, she seemed to approve of his actions as a detective.

Monika dropped him off at the curb in front of a modest two-story building with clean, white siding and a blue-shingled roof. He walked up, examining the yard as he did so. It was relatively well-cared for, but showed a couple bare patches and bore no garden or flowers to speak of.

Unlikely they use a lawn care service.

Conners walked up to the front door, which was a vibrant green, and knocked three times in rapid succession. After a long pause, the door unlatched and opened. A woman in her early forties with brown hair looked him up and down. Conners took advantage of the moment, and allowed his brain to dissect her.

- *No makeup and her hair is undone: genuine grief or shock…*

- *Lack of makeup speaks to no recent bruising or injuries: not a physically abusive marriage.*
- *Engagement ring is polished but the wedding ring is left dirty and smudged: struggling marriage.*
- *Nails are short and untreated: Neither vain, nor a materialist... money troubles unlikely to serve as a motive for murder.*
- *Her eyes are ringed red and puffy: crying heavily.*

"Y-yes?" asked the woman, her voice crackling slightly.

"Martha Barns?"

She nodded, still looking confused.

John didn't talk to her about hiring you. He's acting independently.

"Sorry to bother you ma'am. I'm Detective Michael J. Conners: a private investigator of some repute. Your brother-in-law came to me earlier; asked me to look into your husband's death. Is it all right if I come in?"

He saw his words register in her mind, and could read the mixture of shock, anxiety, and the slight touch of relief that came over her face. After a long moment, she stepped away from the door and pulled it open fully so he could walk in. He casually entered the house, examining the place as he did so.

At a quick glance, it reminded him a little of Lawrence's apartment, with several personal touches and photos. It was clearly a place where a family lived and spent time together. While the couch and chairs they owned were certainly nicer than the worn-out piece that adorned his place, they also showed signs of regular use and accustomed placement. A laptop and half-empty water glass adorned an end table, and a pair of reading glasses sat beside two different remotes on an armrest.

The first floor was mostly an open design, in which both the kitchen and living room were clearly visible from the dining table.

"Can I get you water... or coffee?" asked Martha, and her voice grew so soft towards the end he could barely catch her words.

"A coffee would be great, actually," Conners said.

Truth be told, he didn't care one way or the other about the coffee, but he understood better than most the desire to keep busy after emotional trauma. While she pulled down a mug from a cupboard, Conners took a closer look at the photos around the living room. Most showed Martha and Frank together, sometimes alone, sometimes with other friends or couples. There were three exceptions to that pairing. One frame held a picture of Martha with a couple Conners took to be her mother and father. Another was a photo of Frank and John standing in a side hug and smiling for the photographer. Lastly, there was one of John giving a toast or speech at Frank and Martha's wedding.

This final photo captured his attention, and Conners took a long look at it. He couldn't quite place it, but there was something about this photo that bothered him. It was like a soft flow of wind in his ear: persistent but difficult to pinpoint.

Martha returned a few moments later and handed him a mug full of steaming coffee. He noted with mild displeasure she'd added cream to it. He always took his coffee black. It was far from the important thing at the moment; so he stomached the drink and asked her a few quick questions to back up John's story. Conners quickly finished both his first line of questioning and the coffee, before he stood up slowly.

"Would you mind if I take a look around your home? The more I see, the quicker I can draw a conclusion and get both myself and the police out of your way."

She nodded softly and her gaze quickly unfocused as she was absorbed by her own thoughts.

Conners moved quickly and quietly up the stairs, letting the carpet make him silent as a church mouse. There were four rooms upstairs: three to the left and one to the right. Of the three on his left, one was clearly a bathroom. Moving forward a little, Conners saw the second door contained a small office, and the third a bedroom. This bedroom almost certainly belonged to John. The bed was only a full, which would make it difficult for Martha and Frank to sleep together, and the decorations suggested themselves to belong to a single man. There was an aged computer on a small desk near a photo album with an office chair that was missing a wheel.

Conners spent a while looking through John's room. He found the man owned only a couple suits and shirts, likely due to his being out-of-work. The photo album near the computer was an album of Frank and Martha's wedding, which contained several photos—including the picture that had bothered him downstairs. Again, the strange whistling filled his head as he stared at it.

Why does this picture bother me?
Look at it harder, kid. Trust your gut.

Conners did as Bill instructed and peered harder at the photo, and after a long moment, he realized what it was: John's expression as he stared at Frank was completely wrong. Sure, he was smiling at him and toasting him with the glass, but the eyes were wrong. For one thing, there was no crinkling at the corners of his eyes, as there was in a true smile. His eyebrows were lowered and drawn together. Conners struggled to place the emotion for a moment, and then covered the smile up with his index finger. The moment he did, the emotion on John's face was clear: anger.

Why would he be glaring daggers at his brother on his wedding day?

Jealousy, suggested Bill. *His brother is getting married and he's being left out.*

Conners nodded to himself and carefully put the photo album back. He spent more time looking around the room, but the biggest piece of information he uncovered was that John was a serial masturbator. At that revelation, Conners felt instant relief he didn't shake hands with the man.

After gaining what he could from the room, Conners retreated to head back into the hallway and took a quick glance inside the office. The office had obviously belonged to Frank. There were several touches that indicated it was as much a workspace as it was a place of leisure. A small box sat to the side of the computer, which Conners checked only to find a few ounces of weed and some papers, and to the left of the desk was a laptop bag which had a few stray folders sticking out of it. Conners poked around the room for a while, but found little else of interest.

Finally, he walked inside the last doorway, which contained the master bedroom. This room was certainly cleaner than John's bedroom had been. The floors were recently vacuumed and the nicknacks on the dresser were neatly arranged so as to be ascetically pleasing. While the bed was unmade, the sheets had been laundered within the past couple days.

Conners dropped to the floor and moving along like a bizarre earthworm, checked the room for any evidence that might've gone unnoticed by the cops. The only major note he found was a tear in the bedding on Frank's side of the bed. Conners examined the mattress beneath the sheets and felt where it had started to give due to years of use. Frank did not sleep on his side, which meant he either slept on his stomach, or more likely his back.

Conners took a few steps back, and reached into one of his many pockets. After a moment, he put his earbuds in and selected a playlist on his phone, playing the music loud enough that the world around him was completely drowned out. Once he had desensitized himself to all else but his thoughts, Conners mentally placed two ethereal versions of Frank and Martha into the bed where Frank had been discovered.

Conners began to pace through the room, and his vision was so real to him he could no longer see the room as it currently was, only as it had been when Frank was murdered.

"Let's see the facts," he whispered under his breath, only able to feel the vibrations of his vocal cords. "Positioning of the victim?"

Bill's voice answered quickly.

Discovered dead next to his wife in the morning.

"Suspects?"

Wife and brother.

"One-by-one then. Wife: motives?"

Unhappy marriage; likely a bit of life insurance too.

"Means?"

Strangulation; not impossible for a woman her size, but unlikely.

"Opportunity?"

Ample, but obvious.

"Brother: motive?"

Hatred, possible resentment. Possibly punishment for the wife.

"Means?"

Strangulation: far more likely to have come from the brother.

"Opportunity?"

Not as easy as the wife, but far from unlikely.

Conners nodded to himself.

"John resented Frank because of Martha. Maybe he wanted her, maybe he just wanted someone of his own. Either way he planned to frame her for his brother's murder, and to use me to do it too. Too bad I'm at least a little decent at my job. He's gonna have a hard time becoming a criminal mastermind if this is his best."

Probably saved Martha's life, kid. That's the good in this.

Conners shrugged to himself and put his earbuds away before dialing Lawrence's number. After he explained what he'd uncovered at the house, she put out a notice for John's arrest.

"Patrol teams are on the lookout and we'll have someone stay with the wife," said Lawrence. *"Either we'll find him on the street or get him once he comes home. Nice catch, Conners."*

"Well, I always did think I'd make a good fisher of men," he said, chuckling a little at his joke. As he paused, a strange thought struck him, and acting on impulse, he spoke again. "Hey Lawrence, you still want me over tonight?"

"Yeah," she said. *"Why? Something up?"*

"No, everything's good. I just… I wanted to know if maybe you could go over some points of Christianity with me. You seem to make some sense of it all, and I… trust you."

There was a short pause before she spoke, and her voice cracked just a slight amount, and he could tell he'd caught her off-guard with his request. That was more than fair. After all, he'd caught himself off-guard.

"Oh… yeah. I mean, sure. I'll talk through what I can; not that I know it all, of course."

"Thanks," he said, smiling. "See you around nine-twenty or so."

He hung up the phone and placed it back in his coat pocket, before he prepared to explain what he'd discovered to Martha.

What was that about, kid? You asking to learn about God?

"Absolutely no idea," he whispered, honestly.

Chapter XXVII: Dishonorable Discharge

"I *swear* you are one of the most annoying human beings I've ever met," said Lawrence, trying and failing to hide her smile.

Conners winked at her and looked gratefully at the blazing fire warming her apartment as they sat next to one another on the couch. It was easily one of the coldest days Conners could remember having experienced. Despite it being ten in the morning, it was sixteen below zero, and he didn't even want to guess what the wind chill might be. His office (while highly personalized) wasn't really built to deal with that level of cold. Luckily Lawrence had offered her guest room to him for a few days. He was certainly luckier than many of the citizens of the city. Many were having power and heating issues due to the insane weather, and several even had frostbite or had to fight off hypothermia.

More as a coping mechanism than anything else, Lawrence and Conners had taken to their habit of joking and teasing one another. Between the disruptions in public transportation and overflowing shelters, it was easy to feel overwhelmed. As such, Conners was happy he had Lawrence to keep him company or he would've been at risk of losing his sanity. Rather, he'd be in danger of losing *more* of his sanity.

"One of?" he repeated, feigning a scandalized expression. "I'll have you know I'm the favorite for the heavyweight annoyance worldwide championship."

"And *that's* why no one else in our department wants to talk to you for more than two minutes."

"Two minutes? That's a decent amount of time. I must be slipping."

Lawrence wrapped her blanket a little tighter around herself as Conners went to make a couple of cups of hot chocolate using the kettle that was whistling insistently. Lawrence had a thing about hot chocolate; whether it was a trigger from her childhood, or a calming connection to Christmas she always wanted hot chocolate when it was a cold or stressful day. As he walked back over to the couch, he was mentally thankful for the warmth of the mugs in his hands as it brought more feeling back into his fingers.

"Thanks," she said as he handed her one of the cups.

"Welcome," he said, tossing another log in the fireplace, slightly let down when he noticed the dwindling pile of remaining firewood.

For a while they sat together, watching a digital copy of Lawrence's favorite sitcom as the cable had gone out in the night. Conners was forcibly reminded a passage Lawrence had gone over with him as they read the Bible together.

There are "friends" who destroy each other, but a real friend sticks closer than a brother.

It was simple, and something that practically seemed quaint by current standards. However, it was no less true for its age. Lawrence had been there for some of the worst parts of his life. She'd been there through Bill's death, his attempted robbery of the station, and Richards' trial. No matter what had happened, she hadn't abandoned him even when he'd deserved it.

She's a good one.

How often had he heard Bill say that? Honestly he'd lost count a long time ago, and yet it was still true. She was his only close friend, but he couldn't have asked for a better one.

~*~

A couple hours later, Lawrence's phone went off. She took it out quickly and glanced at the screen.

"It's the lieutenant," she said, though Conners wasn't sure if she was talking to him or herself.

She answered and listened intently for several seconds. Conners glanced curiously at her, and saw a flash of worry on her face, which slowly turned to a grim determination the longer he watched.

"Copy that. I'll be there as soon as I can."

She hung up and leapt from the couch. Without a word of notice she reached for her gloves, boots, and heavy-duty coat.

"What's wrong?" asked Conners, already putting on his own coat and gloves.

"Shooting is going down a little way downtown."

"A shooting? Surely, that's SWAT, right? Why are you getting called in?"

"SWAT's still mobilizing, the cold has everyone filling in all over the place. Plus, this guy's got an automatic rifle. So, anyone nearby who can keep things held down until they're ready is being called in."

Conners nodded. It was true the weather had the police stretched thin. The patrolmen had been working doubles for several days now, and even homicide was often called to assist. Lawrence was already well into overtime hours, but kept doing whatever was asked of her. He had to admire her tenacity even while he worried for her health.

For the most part, he had been outside of the police's efforts. Instead, Conners focused what resources he had on the homeless population through his street contacts and the few people like Joe who wanted to help those trying to do some good. He already felt the first pangs of guilt at the thought of sitting in a warm apartment while Lawrence went off to deal with an active shooter.

"So, what's our plan?"

"What?" she asked, looking at him for the first time since the call. "You don't think you're coming?"

"Either I come with you, or I run there in the freezing cold," he said, grimly.

He could see the desire to reject him in her eyes, but also saw the resignation quickly settle in. They'd been friends for far too long for her to think she could really stop him.

"Fine, but don't get in the way, all right?"

"Course," he said, already making plans in his mind's eye.

The journey was slower than he'd have hoped. Lawrence's car wouldn't start; the cold had completely drained the battery. So they'd needed a pickup from a nearby patrol vehicle. With small spark of relief, he saw it was Officer Miller who was sent to collect them. During the drive, Miller and Lawrence discussed the case, and Conners was forced to ride in the back. He didn't find that he minded much. He let his ears take in their conversation while his brain automatically considered the area of the shooter's house.

"The shooter is an Afghanistan veteran," said Miller. "We don't have a definite make on the gun yet, but we suspect it's an AK. It's been impossible to coordinate anything because he has a scanner. Took a few failed approaches to figure that out. Between the cold and radio silence, we're having huge trouble getting anything put together. People keep nearly passing out from the cold, but we've got a couple warming stations put together now. He's got two hostages held last we could tell, but everyone else in the building was evacuated."

"Any casualties?"

"A few civilians were hit. One dead, and three injured. Already on their way to the closest functional hospital. The injured civilians *should* be fine, but we haven't heard anything back yet. The hospital's jammed up and public transports suffering massively. So we're on our own for now. One of ours caught a shot to the shoulder, but it's clean in and out and he's bandaged up now."

"How many of ours on the scene?"

"We've got seven active uniforms including myself and the lieutenant. We've got a total of three shotguns and one M4 rifle."

Lawrence swore softly. It was a bleak prospect. Still, Conners felt something pressing at the side of his mind. It took him an extra minute before he finally realized what it was.

There's a sewer system that runs right up that street, he heard Bill's voice. *You could crawl right past the parameter without the shooter ever seeing you.*

He chewed on that idea for a long moment. Lawrence wouldn't like it. She would shout and argue about it, but he didn't consider hiding it from her. He could still remember her fury when he'd nearly stolen police evidence for Richards. They reached the nearest cross street and Miller pulled over and switched the siren off while leaving his flashing lights on.

Lawrence stopped and turned around to look at Conners.

"You ready?" she asked, and he knew she was giving him the chance to back out.

"Already got a plan."

She smiled and threw her hood up before opening the door. Conners secured his hat and scarf before joining her. The split-second the door opened he felt the torrent of freezing air crash over him, which instantly sent his body shivering and teeth chattering no matter how hard he tried to stop it. For a moment he doubled over and his legs refused to move. Even breathing was painful. Summoning up his strength, Conners forced himself to walk. He forced himself to focus step-by-step while his brain began to calculate the nearest entrance to the sewer.

"So tell me," Lawrence called over her shoulder, shivering herself. "What's this great plan of yours?"

"W-well," he began, pulling his coat tighter around himself. "The good news is it's warmer than it is up here."

"The bad news?"

"It likely involves being shot at and will break protocol."

She seemed to consider his words for a long moment, then nodded.

"Explain."

So he launched into the nearby sewer tunnels and how they led right by the veteran's home. He let his brain focus on the evolving plan rather than the freezing cold around him. It wasn't easy to do; every intake of breath physically hurt his chest and he could feel his fingers and toes going numb. To her credit, Lawrence didn't interrupt him or get irritated. She listened patiently, and let him finish laying out what he'd been working on.

"Lieutenant won't like it," she said eventually. "But if you can convince him to clear it, I'll join you."

He paused for just a second.

"You're going to complain about the sewer the whole time, aren't you?"

"Oh absolutely. You're paying for new boots and the cost of cleaning my clothes, but it isn't a bad idea."

He rolled his eyes—a wasted effort as she couldn't see it. After nearly seven minutes of a hike in the arctic wastes, they came up to a small tent Conners could see had several space heaters inside. He walked in and was welcomed into the huddle of officers without question and they allowed the feeling to return to their extremities.

"Conners!" he heard the lieutenant bark with far less than his usual spite. He'd never *really* forgiven Conners for quitting the force in the way that he had, but he didn't actively try and keep him out of the station anymore. "What are you here for?"

"T-thought with the cold, m-maybe you would finally be willing to snuggle with me," he joked, his voice still shaking. "I think I know a way to bring our shooter in without charging the door."

The lieutenant shook his head angrily.

"Absolutely not, we've notified SWAT and they're mobilizing now. You'll just get in the way at this point."

"How far out?"

"What?"

"How far out is SWAT?"

The lieutenant grimaced.

"We don't know for sure, since we've been on radio silence for a while, but at least an hour last we heard."

"You really want to sit in the freezing cold for an hour while that guy keeps taking pot-shots at anyone he can see?"

The lieutenant paused, and Conners could see the mounting conflict behind his eyes. His dislike of breaking the rules was clashing against the desire for action and results.

"Run your thoughts by me."

He did and he could see the ugly look on the lieutenant's face grow more and more stern.

"It's too unknown," said the lieutenant. "We'd get past the street just fine, but there's no way of knowing where a good entry point is or what kind of protection he's got inside. He could have a bomb ready to blow in there."

"In which case, best to get him before he can set anything else up! We've got the place as evacuated as it's going to get, right?!"

An officer nodded.

"Just the shooter and two hostages," he said.

"So, the sooner we move the better. If we wait, he'll kill the hostages or escape and I want this guy off the street."

For a moment, Conners saw a strange look in the lieutenant's eyes. It was as if the older man were seeing a friend from decades ago, and discovered that they hadn't aged a day.

"What… what would we need?" asked the lieutenant.

"Lawrence and I can knock this out ourselves," he said, lowering his voice slightly as Guston seemed to be giving in a little. "Though a shotgun wouldn't go amiss."

The lieutenant hovered for a moment that seemed to last an hour. Finally, he turned to an officer and barked at him to give Lawrence his shotgun.

"You've got four shots," said the lieutenant to Lawrence. "If you can safely bring him in alive: great, but if he's going to shoot you or your boy, drop him."

Lawrence nodded.

"Copy that sir."

"Lawrence," said Guston, suddenly sounding far softer than he had. "I won't order you to do this. This will be dangerous. It's your choice."

"It's the right call," she said. "Conners is an ass, but he's got a good brain in there somewhere."

"Right here guys."

"All right," he said. "We'll make sure he keeps the focus on us, but ammo's low. So don't count on too much time."

They nodded in unison and Conners led the way to the nearest manhole he'd spotted. It took the pair of them a while to pry the cover loose, as it was nearly frozen in place and was heavy enough to cause issues besides. After a couple minutes, persistence won out and they both climbed into the sewer tunnels. Conners immediately felt a strange combination of relief and disgust. The disgust was, of course, due to the smell and sights around them. The relief came from the sudden warmth the tunnels provided. They were still very cold, but compared to what the streets had been like, it was like sitting beside a cozy campfire.

"Whoo," said Lawrence as she let out a breath. "At least it's a little better down here. I'll admit, you've had worse plans than this."

"Well, plan's not over yet," said Conners, clicking a flashlight on and pulling out *Sherry*.

Beside him, Lawrence switched on the tactical flashlight on the shotgun.

"How far is it?" asked Lawrence.

"If I'm right, it should be about a thousand or so feet ahead. Then we'll have to hope there's another cover near the building."

Lawrence went notably quiet for a second.

"And if you're wrong, or there's not a cover?"

"Then you should know you are a far better friend than I deserve," he said softly.

She didn't speak, but he saw her stand a little straighter and grow more resolute.

They crept forward, often startling rats and bugs that had also sought refuge from the cold. Luckily, nothing unexpected approached them, and only fifty or so feet from the shooter's building, they saw another ladder leading up. Lawrence took point, using the mouth of the sewer to peek out onto the street.

"Nothing much," she hissed down to him. "I believe we're on the south side of the building, opposite the nearest barricade. A couple windows this direction, but they're too far for me to see if he's looking this way."

"Here," said Conners, digging through his pockets and unearthing a monocular.

"You always carry this around?" she asked.

"Often, yes. Just see if you can make anything out."

She peered through the scope for a few minutes.

"Nothing that I can see. If he is watching he's keeping perfectly still. The blinds are down but slanted. So I can see just a little into the house. Best possible conditions for him to be looking out."

"Well, you're in charge here," he said. "We moving up or going back?"

"Let's move up on my mark," she whispered, and began inching the cover off carefully. After a few moments, during which his feet and hands began to numb again, she said, "Ok, are you ready?"

"Ready."

"Go!"

They sprang up and ran for the nearest cover, a parked pickup truck that was only a good twenty-foot dash from the nearest window. No bullets flew at them and Conners let out a breath he didn't realize he'd taken. After a few more seconds, he chanced a glance with the monocular. He didn't see any movement and motioned to Lawrence to move.

The pair ran forward as quickly as they could without making too much noise and pressed their backs up against the brick wall near a window. Lawrence pulled the shotgun back to smash the window in, but Conners held up his hand to stop her. If they smashed the window in, the shooter would know *exactly* where they were. They needed a diversion.

"Twelve seconds," he mouthed to her before running around to the east side of the building, counting off in his head.

As he reached the last second, he pointed up with *Sherry* and fired a volley of shots through the nearest window, doing his best to angle the shots down so it would look as if they'd been fired from a rooftop. The moment he finished, he ducked back around the other side of the building. A second later, a small burst of bullets answered his shots, hitting the wall of a building across the street. Conners could tell that the shooter had made a quick guess as to his location as much as anything else.

He slunk back to Lawrence and saw her sitting by the smashed window, grinning at him to show her appreciation. One after another, they climbed into the window and snuck up to the door like a pair of vipers. Lawrence pressed her back up against the door and pulled out her can of mace.

"What's that?" he whispered so soft she almost didn't hear him.

"Count to three then call out 'flashbang' so he can hear," she whispered back.

He smiled and nodded.

Lawrence mouthed her count off and tossed the can in. Conners called out loudly enough so anyone in the room would hear them. Lawrence dove in after he gave the false call. When Conners didn't hear a shot, he dove in too, holding *Sherry* out just in case. The shooter was an aging man with thick brown hair and a beard the reached almost to his stomach. He wore a white t-shirt and a pair of jeans that were tucked into black combat boots.

In that millisecond Conners' mind slowed everything down. He could see Lawrence's ploy had paid off. The veteran had his eyes screwed up tight and his left hand was held up to shield them from the flash that he expected. His right hand held an AK-47, and Lawrence was already in full sprint for the man.

As time crept forward, Conners saw the recognition that came across the man's face and he started to raise the rifle. Out of fear and instinct, Conners raised his revolver and fired off a shot, hitting the man in his left leg. A second later, Lawrence tackled him to the ground and wrestled the gun away from him before pinning him face-down with her knee while she reached behind her for her handcuffs.

"Nice move," she said over her shoulder. "Clear the house while I search him."

"Copy that," he said, smiling.

After a few minutes, he'd recovered the remaining hostages and Lawrence was able to march their shooter right out the front door. He nodded and relaxed just a bit.

Nicely done, kid.

Chapter XXVIII: Homecoming

Conners groaned and turned about in his reading chair, lamenting the size of his tiny office for the first time, as it meant he had no space for a couch. He had been incredibly bored for the past two days. Somehow (and Conners wasn't sure that it was not some intentional form of punishment from the criminal class of Chicago) the city's rate of interesting or difficult crimes had sunk to nearly nothing.

Even though he already knew perfectly well what was in it, Conners forced himself to go downstairs and check the state of his inbox. He moved down the stairs slowly, savoring the chance at movement. The lower floor was just as deserted as it had been the last twelve times he'd checked it, and Conners briefly considered if he should get a dog.

I'm not quite sure my demand for companionship outweighs my distaste for picking up dog poop, he thought, chuckling a little at his own joke.

He reached the small tray and picked up the few pieces of paper that lay in it.

- *Suspected insurance scandal... yawn.*
- *Infidelity case... I'd sooner take a spoon to my eye.*
- *Stolen jewelry... probably pawned nearby... Well, it's either that or count my ceiling tiles again.*

He yawned widely and moved towards his back door, not bothering with *Sherry,* though he did take the cane. As he head out of his office, Conners peeked up at the cloudy sky. The sun for all its power and size couldn't penetrate the blanket of grey smog. He couldn't tell if that observation was encouraging or dismal.

At least it's warm, he thought dully.

His journey through the surrounding streets and alleys took no thought on his part. His feet automatically navigated their way past shops, homes, cars, and other pedestrians, all just as uninterested in him as he was in their movements. Truth be told, Conners had little real hope of finding the exact pawn shop that would've been used. Chicago was a huge city, and there were plenty of places to pawn jewelry and unwanted wares. On top of that, it wasn't unlikely the thieves had decided against pawning it at a shop at all, and instead used a fence. Or it was possible the jewelry had never been stolen in the first place, and the owner was merely claiming it had been.

None of the possibilities really interested him all that much. He *might* enjoy shutting down a fence, depending on who it was and what they usually moved, but there wasn't really enough information to track down anyone who might move relatively commonplace jewelry. Famous jewels and art pieces were possible to track, but no one really cared enough about a simple ruby necklace to care where it was from or where it was going.

The first four shops Conners hit up all came up empty. As he entered the fifth, he put on the same facade he'd used at the previous four places: that of a young man hoping to buy his girlfriend a necklace just like the one her grandmother had owned. The tiny man behind the counter had thinning brown hair and a pair of aviator sunglasses on his slightly pasty face. He wore a white t-shirt and a pair of black cargo pants that entirely failed to hide his slightly pudgy stomach. As Conners entered the building fully, he saw the man's eyebrows raise up just above the rim of his sunglasses.

Surprised, said Bill. *Think he recognizes you, kid.*

Conners mentally ran his brain through a list of any known criminals that fit the man's description. Nothing came back to him, not that he had expected it really would. Most likely, the man had seen Conners on the news or in the papers. That wasn't such a big deal.

"Morning," said the man, even though it was closer to evening at that point.

The man quickly busied himself his phone as he typed in a text. All the same, there was a slight flush around the man's neck.

He seem nervous to you?

Well he's a pawn shop owner. Quite possibly not everything in here is totally above the table. He's got reason to be a bit nervous when a detective checks up on him.

It was certainly possible the man was engaged in some sort of illegal activity. This part of the city was mostly full of low-income families or ex-convicts. It wasn't all that far from where Conners had first decided to lay low after escaping the hospital. Unbidden, an image of a young blonde boy with a bullet hole in his head flashed before Conners' eyes.

He shook himself slightly to clear the vision, and refocused himself on the shopkeeper.

"Yo," he said, with just a slight gruff edge to his voice. Here, it actually would've been *more* suspicious to speak brightly to someone. "You sell much jewelry here? Hoping to buy my girl sommit she's wantin'."

The man nodded and jabbed a thumb over to a display case. Conners walked over and feigned an interest in the pieces; it was obvious none of the pieces in the case were the ones he was after. For a while, he stood in front of the case, scratching at his chin. When what felt like an appropriate minute had passed, he straightened.

"These aren't bad," he said, dismissively. "I'm actually lookin' for sommit like this."

He showed the man the picture of the missing ruby necklace. He saw the same micro-expression flash across the shopkeeper's face as when he had first entered the shop.

Surprised again. He knows that necklace.

"Nah," said the owner, though his voice had gone up just slightly. "Don't know it."

For just a split-second, the man's eyes flicked below the counter, where doubtless he kept some treasures he didn't want easily accessible. If Conners hadn't been quite this close, he could've easily missed the glance from behind the man's sunglasses.

"Damn shame," said Conners, already eyeing a way to sneak back into the shop once it closed.

As Conners turned to walk out of the shop, he had to step back as three figures walked in. Conners felt the blood drain from his face as he recognized Hunter, trailed by two thugs with pistols at their waistlines. Behind them, Conners could hear the shopkeep hastily unlock and leave through the back door.

Hunter looked different from when Conners had last seen him. Granted, more than five years was a long time for someone to change; he was proof of that himself. Hunter was in better shape than he had been: his arms lined with muscles and clearly defined veins. His shirt was some designer brand Conners had vaguely heard of, but never taken much interest in. Hunter's wrists, fingers, and neckline glittered with several pieces of expensive jewelry.

Conners couldn't see a weapon on Hunter, but his pants legs were wide enough to hide a knife or pistol without difficulty. His grip tightened on Bill's cane and his mind slowed down the world for a second, allowing him to identify points of attack and escape as he might need them. The two men were large. That was problematic for melee combat, but Conners suspected they were going to rely on their guns if a fight broke out... *when* the fight broke out.

My advantages:
- *I'm faster than the three of them are likely to be.*
- *Hunter holds enough of a grudge to corner me after all these years: suggests rage.*

Their advantages:
- *They outnumber me.*
- *They have guns.*

With a sweeping glance, Conners noted the glass cases around them that would serve as points for damage. Unfortunately nothing in the shop would serve as a great weapon. There was an acoustic guitar hanging above the jewelry display, but that wasn't going to do the job. He took a deep breath and approached Hunter.

"Hunter," he said cheerily, as if greeting an old schoolmate. "Been a while."

"How you doin' Michael?" asked Hunter, his voice crawling sickeningly through the air like a snake. "Hear ya got some name now, huh?"

"Bit," said Conners as the two thugs moved a couple steps closer. "Don't suppose you're here to catch up though."

"Nah," said Hunter smiling brightly. "I keep some people 'round here. Thought maybe you'd show up. Took you long time, boy."

"Yeah. Well you know how it is. Business calls and all that. I see you've been doing well in the meantime."

"I do it up some now."

Conners let the cheer and whimsy drop out of his voice as he replied, "Really ready to throw that away over our past?"

"You stole from me," said Hunter. "So now you gonna pay me back."

"Sorry," said Conners as he planted his left foot solidly. "Forgot my checkbook."

And on that word he spun on the ball of his foot, kicking out high with the other leg. His kick moved right past the arm of the nearest thug as he'd been reaching for the gun, and connected with the man's chin. The man stumbled a little, dazed from Conners' kick. Conners spun behind him, using the larger man as a shield while the other thug fired off two rounds. The first missed by inches, and the second caught the first gangster in the chest as Conners took cover behind him.

Pushing the man forward like a living barrier, Conners rushed the shooter and pushed him on top of the attacker as another gunshot rang out. He didn't see where the shot went, but he didn't feel any pain. It must've missed him. With a mighty heave both men were sent toppling into the sales counter, shattering it into pieces. Conners got his mind to take a snapshot of the contents beneath where the counter had been.

There was a single safe, and there was a simple lock on the front which would be easy enough to pick… assuming he lived to try.

As the shooter collapsed under his former ally, Conners reached down and pulled out the gun that was still in the first man's waistline and fired at the second gangster. His shots hit the man dead center, killing him instantly. Conners moved the gun over and put a bullet in the back of the head of the first thug, and turned to look at Hunter. The gun in his hand was a 9mm Luger. The magazine held twelve shots, but they'd likely had an extra in the chamber as neither had retracted the chamber before attacking.

That meant the gun held ten more shots: more than enough for him to use it against Hunter. However, Hunter was far quicker than he had been in Conners' gang days, and was already on top of him. Conners saw the flash of a machete and ducked under Hunter's swipe, hitting him in the side of the leg with the cane. If he'd had the blade drawn or had better leverage on the attack, he might've dropped Hunter. As it was, the hit didn't slow the man and he slammed the handle of the weapon down on Conners' spine. Pain jumped through him and Conners dropped to the floor. He tried to raise the gun but Hunter stomped on his right hand and Conners heard the bone *snap*.

Conners let out an angry snarl and dropped the gun involuntarily. Rolling away from Hunter, Conners pushed himself up with his good hand and stared at him. Being down his primarily hand was going to complicate matters, but not so much that he was done for… yet.

"You've gotten faster," Conners gasped, hoping Hunter would talk for a second so he could catch his breath.

"Yeah, I forgot how slippery you were."

"Well, you know how it is. Someone tries to shoot you and all those instincts come right back."

"Good. I'd hate ta think I beat ya once you was old and broken."

Hunter moved forward, but more cautiously this time. Conners brought the cane up and used his mouth to grip the sheath and pulled the blade free with his good hand. Conners knew in his prime, he'd win this duel without breaking a sweat. But he was out of practice, and hadn't focused much effort to dueling with his off-hand. That wasn't to say he'd never done it, or that he'd forgotten his lessons.

He slid his feet shoulder-length apart in an L-shape and bent his knees slightly, with his left side facing his opponent. Hunter glanced at this stance quizzically, but then seemed to consider it not worth troubling himself over and slashed out.

Clang.

Their weapons met in mid-air with a resounding ring. Hunter backed away and held his blade out in front of him for defense. Even at this distance Conners could see the flash of pure anger on his face. He forced himself to relax and analyze his opponent's swing in his mind. Hunter was swinging the machete more like a baseball bat, but Conners was pleased his own lack of practice hadn't left him defenseless.

Small movements, kid, said Bill. *Remember: fencing is a dance, and he's going in freestyle.*

That was true; Hunter's style displayed no real training or discipline. Already Conners' brain began forming a strategy, and he began to needle Hunter mentally.

"Thought you would've learned how to actually fight," he said, smirking. "Or where you busy sitting on your thumbs all these years?"

Hunter let out a yell and charged at Conners like a bull. Conners used Hunter's momentum against him, spinning and circling around the man's attack. As he spun, Conners slammed the hilt of his blade into the small of Hunter's back. The attack sent the larger man stumbling and Conners leapt at him, landing a solid kick in the man's lower spine. The gangster slammed against the wall hard enough to leave some of the wood splintered before he turned and glared at Conners.

The man's upper lip was split, his nose was bleeding heavily, and it looked crooked, as if it had broken when he hit the wall.

Conners didn't waste any time and dropped back into his stance. Hunter seemed to be practicing a calming ritual, but Conners could see a vein pulsing in his neck.

"What? Did that hurt? You want me to get a couch so you can sit down and tell me how you really feel?"

"Shut up!" Hunter snarled.

"Naw, seriously. If I knew we were gonna play happy slaps, I'd have sent a child in my place."

"SHUT UP!" he roared and charged again.

This time Hunter led with his weapon and Conners managed to parry the swing before quickly stabbing out with his blade. The attack wasn't perfect. He'd been aiming at Hunter's shoulder, but hit the man's bicep instead. Still, it was a solid hit and he began bleeding from the puncture.

"Oh noes," said Conners, exaggeratedly. "You gots a boo-boo! Want I should kiss it better?"

"Oh," said Hunter, drawing out the word menacingly. "I'm going to enjoy skinning you alive, boy!"

"Yeah, yeah. You're not even the dozenth person to make that threat. Take a number, you two-bit hustler."

Hunter charged, swinging wildly. Conners backstepped and timed the attacks.

One...

Two...

Three...

After the third swing, he suddenly changed directions and lunged, extending his arm to skewer Hunter. The larger man twisted and nearly managed to avoid the blow. Nearly. A solid line of blood began to spill from behind the new hole in his shirt. Hunter fell back and collapsed on the ground, dropping the machete. Conners calmly walked over and picked up the pistol Hunter had made him drop. He pointed it at the man who had been hunting him for years. His hand was steady and his aim was true. Hunter's eyes went wide, and Conners saw a mixture of fear and excitement come across Hunter's face.

"Ya gonna do it?" he asked. "You just shoot me down like that?"

Conners paused and considered it. He *shouldn't* do it, but what if that was the right answer to this problem? Hunter was obviously capable and driven. He would come back if Conners didn't stop him. For a second his finger tightened on the trigger, and then he paused.

Lawrence and Bill appeared before him. He could see them as easily as Hunter himself. He could see the pained look on both of their faces and instantly knew he couldn't do it. To kill a man he could've spared would shame both Bill and Lawrence. With a sigh, he reached back and tossed the gun to the side.

Hunter laughed.

"I knew you was always weak. You better be prepared to look over your shoulder, boy! When I get out, I'm gonna come back at you!"

"No you won't," said Conners, as he pulled out his phone.

First he called Lawrence, and explained the attack. She asked a few quick questions and told him that she was on her way.

"Make sure you bring an ambulance," Conners said. "The lead gangster's alive, but he's got himself rather badly injured."

"What's wrong with him?"

"He's got a puncture wound in his stomach, a cut on his right bicep, a broken nose, and appears to have broken a leg," Conners said calmly and hung up.

Hunter's eyes went wide again and Conners reached for a toolbox and pried the lid open. After a quick moment he unearth a hammer and chisel.

"I'm not going to kill you," Conners said. "But you aren't going to ever fully recover from this either."

Quick as a flash, he placed the chisel down on the knee of Hunter's right leg and slammed the hammer down on it. Blood and screams flew through the air, but Conners didn't hesitate and struck twice more: not enough to go completely through the leg, but more than enough to split the bone.

Exhausted, and utterly spent, he dragged himself to the safe he'd spotted while Hunter screamed and cursed him repeatedly. Two quick strikes with the hammer, and Conners managed to bust the lock on the safe. He opened the safe's cover and unearthed several things the shopkeep had wanted to keep private, including a decent sum of cash and the missing ruby necklace. He smiled and collapsed against the wall, listening as the sirens grew closer and closer.

Despite his utter exhaustion and weariness, Conners felt his pocket *buzz* and he reached for his phone. There was a new text message on it.

Interesting solution, detective. I hope you continue to prove interesting. I'd hate to get bored with you.
- The Watcher

Chapter XXIX: Care

Conners groaned as Lawrence pounded on his office door again. It had been a little over a month since he'd fought with Hunter, and his sleep had been dismal ever since. As it was, he hadn't slept properly for four straight days, and wasn't getting more than a couple hours rest when he *was* able to pass out. His nightmare about the child he'd killed had grown exponentially worse, and he was suffering from the attacks on his brain.

He'd had a persistent headache for the past three weeks, and he'd been taking ibuprofen like it was candy to try and manage his aching head. In desperation he'd switched his phone off and shut himself up in his office to try and get some form of rest.

It hadn't been working.

He knew sooner or later Lawrence would come check on him, and he'd been determined to avoid talking to her about what had happened.

He'd filled out his report and been questioned extensively by homicide detectives, and in the end was released when it was agreed he had only killed the two thugs out of self defense. For whatever reason, Hunter hadn't contradicted anything Conners had said. He hadn't mentioned the child to the detectives. He hadn't even brought up that he knew Conners in the past, instead inventing a tale about seeing Conners on the news and wanting to increase his reputation. What had bothered Conners was the suggestions of fear and paranoia Hunter was displaying. Nothing during their fight had suggested such traits.

Then one full day after his report was filed, he'd received another text.

You're welcome, detective.

- The Watcher

Conners had fretted about this for a few days—wondered what level of influence and power The Watcher had to scare Hunter into keeping his past a secret. Why would The Watcher even *want* to keep it a secret? It surely wasn't an altruistic desire on the shadowy figure's part. Of course none of these texts had come with a number he could reply to or track... not that he hadn't tried.

Then had come the headaches and the nightmares. Strangely, his head pain wasn't in his temples or forehead, like when he got the flu. Instead it was the back of his head that hurt. A few times—after he'd gone several nights without sleeping—he could've sworn his head was bleeding. In these times he could've sworn there was a voice whispering to him.

This isn't anything personal, kid.

While the attachment of "kid" had almost reminded him of Bill, the voice was entirely different. It had malice and disgust attached to it, and reminded Conners unpleasantly of a growling panther.

Lawrence knocked again and Conners rolled off his bed angrily. It wasn't like he'd been getting any sleep anyway. He moved almost blind through his little office and down the stairs, and gripped the door with his left hand, because his right still had the cast on it. Conners threw the door open and almost screamed at her.

"WHAT?!"

Surprise and a slight amount of hurt showed on his best friend's face and Conners instantly felt a harsh stab of guilt in his chest.

"What do you want?" he asked, much softer.

"Can I come in?" she asked, much gentler than she usually spoke to him, which only served to amplify his guilt.

"Course."

He stepped back and led the way upstairs to the kitchen, switching on the lights as he did so. Half out of apology and half out of habit, Conners began making hot chocolate for the pair of them. While the water heated up, he went to his bedroom and threw a shirt on. It had been too long since he'd done laundry, but the smell wasn't too strong.

"You've been out a while," she said. "I've been trying to resist the urge to check on you for a couple weeks now. Well that, and I've missed you."

"You *have* been checking on me," said Conners.

She's not going to get that, kid, said Bill, who currently was appearing as an apparition sitting in Conners' reading chair. *She wasn't really there for it.*

"*Shut up!*" Conners snapped, and flung the spoon he'd been using to stir the hot chocolate at Bill.

It clattered uselessly against the wall two inches to Bill's left, and the old man grimaced sadly.

"Sorry!" said Lawrence, more taken aback than frightened.

"No!" he said quickly and apologetically. "Not you. I've been hallucinating a lot recently, and it gets… annoying."

"You're hallucinating?" she repeated, and Conners could hear the way her voice automatically slipped into the detective clarifying a statement.

"Yeah. That's what I meant when I said you checked in."

"You've been hallucinating *me*?"

Conners frowned and sat down across from her at his little table.

"Not like I chose to," he said, then shrugged. "At least not consciously. I don't know. Guess I've been missing you, too."

She walked over to his side of the table and knelt to slide her arms around him. Without being aware of asking his body to do so, he returned her embrace. They stayed like that for a while, and he enjoyed the feeling of her hug. After a long moment she spoke.

"I think you need a shower," she said softly, and he knew she was trying to make him feel better.

It *did* make him earnestly chuckle. It was perhaps the first time he'd smiled in a few weeks.

"Well, you know, mid-life crisis and all that."

"You're *not* middle-aged."

"Do we actually *know* that? I mean, I *think* I'm twenty-eight or so, but I could be one of those infuriating people who never age. Isn't Gwen Stefani in her mid-forties now? She still looks young."

"Well if you have a Hollywood doctor on call to turn half your face into plastic, then we need to have a very long conversation."

He smiled again.

"All right. I'm going to get cleaned up."

"If you don't come out in twenty, I'm going to come in after you," she said, before the implications of her own statement fully hit her.

"Tempt me with a good time," he muttered, just loud enough for her to hear.

He took a quick shower, moving more methodically than anything else. Amazingly, cleaning himself up *did* help lift the dark cloud over his mind a little, although he was still completely exhausted and his head still hurt. He dressed just as methodically before heading back up into the kitchen.

"One Michael J. Conners, cleaned and returned in nearly working order," he said, filling a glass with ice and water.

Lawrence did appear to brighten a little at this.

"Speaking of working order," she said. "I was wondering if you might be interested in a case? Either that or we could go out and do something together."

"Very subtle there, sergeant. If I didn't know better I'd say you were trying to get me out of my lovely little hovel here."

"Conners," she said, seriousness returning to her voice. "You've been in here for over a month. You *have* to get out."

"Fine, but I don't want any casework right now. Let's just go to a show or something. There's something going on in town right now, right?"

"Ok, it's nothing all that interesting anyway," she said, putting the file into her bag.

Conners stared at it for a long second. A big part of him wanted to take the file. In a way, a case sounded like exactly what he needed. It *would* get him out of the apartment, which is what Lawrence alleged to want for him. However he also knew he wasn't fully stable, and diving back into the familiar might be the hair trigger that broke his brain. He remembered all too well his obsession with tracking Bill's killer, where it had led, and the impossible strain it had placed on his relationship with Lawrence. Above even his own health, that was the thing he least wanted to put at risk.

"So," he said, casting around his mind for something to do. "What should we do? What do tourists do in the city?"

"We could visit the aquarium," she said with a smirk.

"Oh ha ha," he said, laying the sarcasm on thick.

"Actually," she said, growing suddenly serious. "I think I do know something you would like, and I doubt it's something you've ever done… Well, not since your accident anyway."

She half-guided, half-pulled him from the chair. She led him downstairs and out the front door to where her wine-red muscle car sat. Conners would've sworn even the car itself seemed giddy with anticipation.

"Mind telling me where we're going?" he asked as Lawrence peeled off into the busy streets.

"Not at all."

"But you're not going to."

"Nope."

"Sometimes I think you're just using me as stress-relief for your job."

"Probably."

He looked out the window and tried to work out where they might be headed, but he only saw she was driving deeper into the city, instead of towards the outskirts. After a long moment, he spoke again.

"Technically, I think this is kidnapping."

"What?" she said, with feigned indignation. "This isn't kidnapping: you're not a child. If anything, this is abduction."

"And you're completely comfortable with the idea of a homicide sergeant breaking the law?"

"Bending it, just a little. If I weren't made comfortable with that in mild amounts then you and I wouldn't be working together and my life would be considerably worse."

He felt his face get slightly warmer at her comment and went back to staring out of the window. The day was bright and sunny, and kids and adults alike where enjoying the weather. Plenty of people were jogging or walking, letting the rays of the sun wash over them as if they were at the beach instead of in the middle of a concrete jungle. That thought sent a weird shiver through him.

When he'd thought of the beach, he'd actually pictured it in his head. That alone wasn't so unusual. After all, Conners pictured almost everything that crossed his mind as a visual component. It was how he was. What made him stop was the realization that in his vision, the waves had moved and crashed against the sand, causing foam and spray. He had no idea where he'd gotten that vision from. He'd never seen more than a picture of the ocean, and he'd never even left the state…

Or had he? Was this a memory of his past coming back at him?

I could actually be from another city altogether.

He couldn't fully understand why that should matter to him, only that it would bother him greatly. There was a sense of togetherness, of belonging, in his being a native to Chicago. Sure as Conners, he'd had spent his entire life here, but *he* might not have been in the city even most of his life. The sudden weight of his unknown past sank in on him. He could've been born and raised in San Diego for all he really knew. Or he could've even been a foreigner, although his natural grasp of English and lack of an accent made that unlikely, but not impossible.

I really have no idea who I was. I think I know who I am, but doesn't it matter where I came from?

It's never bothered you much before, said Bill in his ears. *Why would it bug you now?*

Shouldn't it? I mean, maybe it shouldn't. Why does my head hurt so much every time I think about this type of stuff?

His head certainly was pounding, almost like someone had taken a mallet to the back of his skull, and the bone was struggling to try and knit itself together. He mentally growled at his own struggle and concerns, pushing them down into the depths of the back of his mind.

I don't care, he thought. *Whoever… whatever I was, it's not who I am now. I'm Michael J. Conners: private detective, personal protege of William Scott, best friend of Jessica Lawrence, and…*

And what?

A murderer.

That hadn't been Bill's voice. It was the same voice he heard every time his head began to hurt too badly. He *still* hadn't been able to place the owner of the voice, but he *knew* he'd heard it before. He knew it in the same way he knew it was dangerous to delve into his own past too quickly.

"We're here," said Lawrence, snapping him out of his musings as if she'd dumped a bucket of cold water on him.

He looked around and slowly realized where she'd brought him. The enormous monolith that was The Willis Tower glittered before him in the midday sun. He'd studied up on it briefly when he'd first began working with Bill as part of his research into many of the most notable landmarks in Chicago. Back then, it had actually been called The Sears Tower, but they'd changed the name the following year for some reason he'd never bothered to find out. However, he'd never really given it much thought beyond what he'd read.

"What are we doing here?"

"You're going to see the city in a whole new way," she said, her face glowing like a child on Christmas morning.

He followed her inside and after a brief interaction with a secretary they joined a small group of people in one of sixteen double-decker elevators. Conners mentally shrugged as Lawrence led him in. He'd been to the top of a few large buildings before and honestly couldn't imagine what would make this view special, but it was worth humoring Lawrence. So he settled in for the long climb of the elevator to whatever floor they were going to.

What he had *not* prepared for was to be rocketed in the air at what he later discovered to be nearly twenty miles an hour. Out of reflex he latched onto the nearby handrail, knowing even as he did so it was beyond useless to hope it would help. He glared daggers at Lawrence as they plummeted upwards, surely about to smash into the ceiling and meet an untimely death and found her grinning and laughing, as if they were riding a roller coaster. He could even feel the pressure in the elevator changing, as if they were attempting to escape the atmosphere along with the building.

Then, the elevator slowed came to a stop, and the group began to exit, chatting animatedly about how exciting the ride up had been. Conners took several long seconds to remember how his legs worked. Luckily, Lawrence was there to help him move forward and she didn't mock him for his found fear of the elevator.

"Sorry," she said, smiling despite herself. "I should've warned you the elevator's pretty quick. I've been here a few times."

"*Pretty quick?!*" he hissed, angrily. "And you have any reason why I shouldn't try and chuck you out one of these windows?"

"Aside from the fact that they're shatterproof and you would lament not having me around? Yes. Follow me."

She led him to one of the windows and Conners was shocked to see the building jutted outward into something akin to a glass box, with a clear floor that dangled over the street below. At Lawrence's prodding, he stepped out onto the glass flooring and looked over the city he knew so well.

He was completely lost for words. He knew the layout of the city, and even had a good mental picture of much of it from a map view. He knew the distance between certain streets, side-streets, and alleyways. He knew the location of many of the one-way streets and traffic lights which would allow him to intercept a fleeing car if need be. However, none of that actually prepared him to *see* the city from the top of The Willis Tower.

The world below almost didn't appear to have people in it at all. It was almost like looking at a colony of ants, except the ants had built skyscrapers and a skyline that was one of the most beautiful in the world. He could clearly see the surrounding lakes and even beyond the outskirts of the city. Directly beneath his feet he could make out the ant-like beings who were going about their daily lives as if nothing was happening above their heads. Exactly as a fish had no concept of what it was like on land, those people had no idea what it was like to see the world as a bird did.

It was truly beautiful.

He spent so much of his life on the ground that he'd never stopped to think of the massive city as a real city. He'd pictured it as a hotbed of crime and targets. He saw it the same way a soldier saw a city in a foreign country: as a place full of dangers and threats. He'd never seen it... like *this*. He was vaguely aware of Lawrence walking up beside him as she wrapped herself around his left arm.

"Forgive me?" she whispered so only he could hear.

Unable to speak, Conners only nodded dimly. He never was sure how long they stood there. Time didn't seen to exist while they stood upon the precipice of the world, admiring the combined works of man and nature. Eventually they stepped back onto what seemed to be far more solid ground and began the descent to the main floor. Whether it was because they were descending or because he knew to except it this time, the rocketing speed of the elevator didn't bother him *quite* as much as it had on the way up.

They moved smoothly back towards Lawrence's car and after they climbed in, Conners turned to Lawrence.

"Thanks for... that," he said, a bit sheepishly. "I really did enjoy it, all things considered."

"Anytime," she said, smiling at him. "You're my best friend, Conners. I've got your back: shootout or mental stress."

"Yeah. Same to you," he said, returning her smile. "Whatever you need, I've got you."

"I know," she said, her thanks apparent in her eyes. "Oh, let me move this."

She reached for the bag by his leg, and he saw the file of the case she'd offered earlier poking out the top of the bag. Try as he might, he couldn't deny the appeal that now lay in that file. Lawrence nonchalantly moved it to the backseat and didn't so much as glance at him. He wasn't fooled.

"Don't," he said warningly.

"Don't what?"

"Don't try and make me take that case."

"I'm not."

"Yes, you are. You think you know me well enough that you can hold up a case, and then take it away because you think I'm an inpatient child who has to see whatever toy it is I'm not allowed to play with."

"Aren't you?"

"…Please give me the file."

She smirked and pulled her satchel back up and pulled out the file.

Chapter XXX: Pull Around to the First Widow

Conners mentally ran over the latest details of the file Lawrence had handed him as they pulled up to a fashionable two-story home. The recently-widowed Sandy Everette was a forty-three-year-old woman with dirty blonde hair and a face treated to defy age. Her husband of twenty years had been poisoned and while she was temporarily out on bail, another detective in the homicide department felt sure of her guilt.

"What makes you think she's innocent?" asked Conners, glancing at Lawrence.

"Who says I think she's innocent?"

"You *never* bring me along to close a sure thing unless you think it's *not* a sure thing."

"Fair enough," she said. "Honestly, based on the evidence we have she's guilty, but… I can't explain it. I just feel something's off here."

Conners laughed, thinking of something Bill had once said to explain this type of sixth sense.

I know it in my knower.

It had been—and still was one of the most ridiculous things Conners had ever heard the old man say. But as time went on, he started to understand more and more of what Bill had meant when he said it. Often without logic, without a reasoning, or without even following common sense, some people could sense another's guilt or innocence. It was frequently referred to by cops as a gut feeling, but Conners had come to prefer Bill's phrasing, insane as it sounded.

"All right," he said. "Let's see what we can find."

They walked down the outer path and along a garden filled to the brim with all different types of flowers and bushes. Conners briefly looked through them, but none appeared to be poisonous unless swallowed in absurdly high quantities. There were far more potent plants that were far easier to get ahold of, and even then it would be pretty stupid to keep the plant right by her front door if she *were* guilty. Then again, criminals often did stupid things.

Lawrence knocked on the door and after a pause and the scraping of the latch, it opened.

"Mrs. Everette?" asked Lawrence. "I'm Jessica Lawrence: a homicide detective with the fourteenth precinct. This is my consultant, Michael Conners."

Conners waved at the mentioned of his name and examined the woman closely.

Her hair was in a slight disarray, as if she'd tried and failed to keep it in a semblance of order and reason. She wore no make-up, and her eyes were red and puffy.

Genuine grief. Good sign. But not a determinate indicator of innocence.

"Haven't you accused me enough?" she hissed, clearly angry at another visit from the police. "I'll call my lawyer about this!"

"Ma'am," said Conners softly, holding up his hands. "The sergeant and I are here because we believe there's reason to doubt your guilt. If there's evidence that can cast reasonable suspicion on another person, then we'll find it."

Sandy didn't relax; her body was tense and poised like a frightened cat. But her eyes did flash a spark of hope. After a pause, she stepped back and fully opened the door, inviting them inside.

"Sorry," she said softly. "It's been hard enough dealing with Patrick's death without this investigation."

"I can't imagine," said Conners, though truth be told he'd seen this exact sort of thing plenty of times. Many homicides *were* committed by an angry spouse. "Can we go over the facts from your case?"

"Of course."

Conners glanced at Lawrence as they sat on a couch next to one another. Across what was likely an absurdly-expensive coffee table, Mrs. Everette sat in an armchair to face them properly. It carried the experience of polite society about it. Lawrence pointed straight down with two fingers, indicating she wanted him to take the lead. Conners nodded and pulled out his own notes.

"The coroner stated your husband was poisoned during a meal you two shared?"

"Dinner last night," she said.

"All right, and was this a home-cooked meal, or did you order out?"

"We ordered it from Bacchanalia: that Italian place in town."

Conners scribbled the name down.

"A frequent choice for you two?"

"Yes," she said, slightly curious. "It's my favorite place."

"And did you place the order or your husband?"

"I did. He was just getting off from work. So I wanted to take care of dinner for us."

"And about what time was this?"

"Just before six, I think."

Conners nodded, and finished writing down what he needed.

"Well, Mrs. Everette, we're going to take a careful look into this. For now, I'd advise you to try and relax as best you can and get your affairs in order for your husband's funeral."

She nodded as tears slid down her cheeks. Conners felt an impulse to comfort her but did what he could to shake it off. Caring and compassion were not his strong suits. He was a thinker, a puzzle-solver, and a joker. He certainly wasn't a caretaker.

You're not as cold as you pretend to be. You're not who you were six years ago.

No, Conners agreed. *My goatee is fuller and I can't burn fat quite as fast now.*

You know what I mean, kid.

And he did. He had changed. He had impulses to help people. He wanted to make things better. At some point (and try as he might he couldn't pinpoint it) the idea of evening his scales had faded away. His work had become about helping people with what skills he had. He wasn't a politician or judge. He was a detective, and he put those skills to use helping those around him. Sure, he liked the interesting cases, but it didn't stop the fact that he really was hoping to help people by solving them.

His internal debate lasted about half-a-second. He moved as if someone else were in control of his body and he were merely a prisoner of his own flesh. He watched as he sat next to the recently widowed woman and put his hand on her shoulder before he squeezed it softly, but not in an invasive or intrusive manor.

For her part, Sandy neither pushed the hand away nor reacted to his touch. After a couple of seconds, Conners seemed to regain control of his facilities and withdrew. Lawrence watched him with wide eyes but didn't speak until they were both seated in her car.

"So…"

"Don't," he said solidly, not expanding on the word.

"It was just… unexpected."

He didn't respond, more disturbed by his own actions than she was. Eventually Lawrence drove into the street. Her phone directed them to the Italian restaurant Mrs. Everette had mentioned. While they pulled into the parking lot of the little beige and green restaurant, Conners allowed the excitement of the chase to flood his system. As he inhaled, the seconds around him slowed and his brain began to process all the information around him like a computer.

The outdoor patio was packed, each chair hosting someone who was eating some type of dish that was sure to be overpriced and underwhelming. Without even being aware of what he was doing, he took note of all the people that were outside.

- *Total number: thirty-two*
- *Five families, totaling twenty-one in number.*
- *Four couples.*
- *Three solos.*

Lawrence led the way this time as they entered the restaurant. A moment later, Conners was grateful that she did, because in his hyper-alert state the obnoxiously-decorated interior was nothing short of an assault on his heightened senses.

Every square foot of the wood-paneled walls had some type of picture or framed photo, frequently worded in Italian: which Conners would've bet not even the owners could've spoken fluently. Each of the dozen-odd tables were decorated with cheap red and white checkered cloth and the high ceiling showed the underside of the slanted steel roof.

"Wow this place is astonishingly ugly," he muttered to Lawrence. "I take back any insult I have ever levied at your apartment."

"What's wrong with my apartment?"

"Compared to this place? Not a single thing. Geez, did grandma save everything from the old country when they opened this place?"

"We're not here to be interior decorators, Conners."

"There are actually drug dens that look better than this."

"Speaking from experience?"

She moved forward and he followed until they came face-to-face with a young woman with dark hair that was pulled back into a tight ponytail. She wore very little makeup and a white, buttoned shirt with a bowtie and vest. The ensemble was enough to make him snicker inwardly. Any uniform with bowties and vests seemed stuffy and pretentious, but at something as casual as a family-style restaurant they were downright laughable. It was like watching a zookeeper come out in a three-piece suit. An idle glance at her name tag revealed that her name was Grace.

"Hi," said Grace cheerily, a false smile plastered on her face. "Just the two of you today?"

"I'm Police Detective Lawrence," said Lawrence, holding up her badge. "And this is my colleague, Michael Conners."

Conners waved noncommittally as the hostess' smile vanished from her face.

"Oh, sorry officers. How can I help?"

"We'll need to speak with your manager, and the owner if they're here today."

"Right, one moment ma'am."

"*Ma'am?*" he mouthed at Lawrence pointedly.

Without looking, she aimed a kick at him. He managed to dodge it and chuckled to himself. A moment later a bald, shiny man in a black polo and round glasses came up to the stand. Trailing him was a woman with dark hair and a slightly wrinkled face who looked more like she were expecting to be invited to a female empowerment seminar than a restaurant. Her jacket was form-fitting and could've been pulled straight from the eighties for the prominent shoulder pads it bore. Conners took it that this woman was the owner and immediately focused his attention on the manager. Owners who didn't work in their own establishments were often the last people to understand what was going on under the roof they'd paid for.

"Hello folks," said the man, offering his hand. "I'm Frankie: the general manager here, and this is Jeanne: our owner. How can we help you this morning?"

"We need to talk somewhere privately," said Lawrence, eyeing a few customers nearby.

"Of course," said Jeanne and Conners almost missed her words as he was distracted by the thick eye shadow she'd applied. "We can speak in my office."

He and Lawrence followed the pair to a set of swinging doors that went through the kitchens. Men and women were shouting at one another desperately trying to cook and prepare the food that needed to go out while maintaining some type of standards. Still Conners spotted at least five practices that made him want to gag, and he immediately crossed the place off of his ever-dwindling list of acceptable restaurants.

When they reached the back of the kitchen, Frankie opened the door and revealed a tiny office that had a table, four chairs, an aging computer, and a safe squeezed into it. The place made his first apartment seem spacious. Frankie and Jeanne took the two far seats and Conners couldn't help but notice the united front they presented to himself and Lawrence. It was similar to the practices of police when they were questioning a suspect.

He ran his index finger along his left eyebrow to signal Lawrence that they were likely to protect each other and she flexed her right hand to acknowledge his gesture. He clasped his hands in front of him to ask if she wanted lead, but she held two fingers straight down. He nodded and they sat down.

"Thanks for agreeing to meet with us," said Lawrence to help the pair relax a little. "We're here on behalf of Sandy Everette."

Conners watched closely, but saw no flash of recognition on either of their faces. That was hardly surprising though. Restaurants were like convenience stores in that they saw too many people and paid too little attention to remember most customers from one another especially by name alone.

"Her husband Patrick was poisoned by eating food at your restaurant last night," he said.

"You mean he got food poisoning," said Frankie, almost automatically.

"Yes," Conners said sarcastically. "Two *homicide* detectives are talking to you about a horrible case of food poisoning. No. Patrick Everette was poisoned by someone adding Atropa Belladonna to his meal. You may have heard of it as Deadly Nightshade. It's a very sweet-tasting berry that can easily kill someone, even in relatively small quantities."

"Oh," said Jeanne as a combination of horror and understanding crossed her face.

"Now don't get me wrong," said Conners as he held up a finger and continued. "I'm sure you've given quite a few of your patrons food poisoning. Between the frankly disgusting case of cross-contamination I witnessed on our way in here and the frozen burgers you're trying to pass off as freshly prepared, I'm sure you've poisoned a great many people. However, today we're really just interested in finding out who *intentionally* killed a customer. So if you'd be so kind as to get us a list and the contact details for the crew working here last night, then I'll be kind enough to forget call up a restaurant inspector and have them shut this place down."

"Of course!" said Frankie, as he hastily typed figures into his computer while Jeanne just looked at her clasped hands.

"Thank you," said Lawrence when Frankie handed her a printed list a few moments later. "How many of the kitchen crew from this list are on-staff today?"

Frankie considered the list for a moment.

"The head chef is here, as well as Lewis and Carleen. They should all be in the kitchen now."

"And what about the host that was working that night?" Conners asked.

"Why the host?" asked Lawrence. "The kitchen crew would've prepped everything."

"It was a to-go order, so the host is the one who physically *handed* her the food. They're the last point of contact and the one who would've seen who Mrs. Everette was."

Frankie peered back over the list and considered for a moment.

"That would've been Max. He's been here a few years. Never really been very impressive, truth be told. But he's off today. So I'd imagine he'll be resting at home."

"Right. Well, we'll deal with your kitchen trio now and track down the others afterwards. In the meantime, clean up your kitchen before you kill *another* customer."

He stood and Lawrence followed him as they crossed back into the kitchen.

"Meat or potatoes?" he asked, as soon as they were out of earshot of the manager and owner.

"I *really* hope you're not asking me about food after you went all Gordon Ramsay in there."

"I meant do you want the kitchen boys or the wayward host? If you don't care, I'll take Max."

"You just want the least amount of work."

"Fifty bucks says I get our guy."

She raised an eyebrow at him.

"You're going to give me ten-to-one odds on catching our murderer?"

"You know I like to beat the odds."

She smiled and shook his hand.

"Good luck."

He took off before she'd even finished the sentence and flew out the front doors, already ringing Joe's number.

Max Turner's place was one of many in a tiny, dirty group of buildings called the Howling Wolf Apartments. Conners approached the building, double-checking the number from his phone. Max supposedly lived in number twenty-two. The place was dingy, cheap, and couldn't have been up to code. It was only slightly nicer than some of the section-eight housing in the southern part of the city.

For some reason, his head was pounding as if his brain was trying to escape his skull. He searched himself and found a couple of wayward aspirin pills in one of his pockets. Swallowing the medicine, Conners shook himself and moved forward. He couldn't shake the feeling the place was haunted or someone was watching him.

Well, he heard Bill's voice say. *Likely that Watcher is watching you right now. Still never could solve that texting thing he does.*

One case at a time, Conners responded.

Conners entered the building and looked around at the aging interior that reminded him of many of the shabby apartments the immigrants of the 1940s had found when they arrived in New York. There was an exposed water heater and connected pipes off to his right. Even from this distance the thing whistled and hummed in such a way that left him slightly worried it might blow up. The wooden desk had aged so much it was practically molding and several of the walls showed signs of water damage.

"They must pay any of the tenants who agree to stay here," he muttered.

Conners rang the bell at the front desk but there was no response. So he glanced at the stairs before he started to head up them. They were as decrepit as the rest of the place and poorly carpeted. Tentatively, he placed a foot on the bottom-most step and it let out a squeal as if it were a living creature. All the same, it held solidly. Confidence only sightly restored, Conners moved up and came upon the first set of rooms. They were all labeled as being in the teens though. So he ignored them and head up to the top floor.

The first door on his right showed the rusty number 22. Conners steeled himself and knocked twice on the door.

"Mr. Turner? I'm Detective Michael Conners. Wanted to talk to you real quick."

"One sec," Turner said before the sound of rapid packing reached Conners' ears.

"Stupid choice," said Conners and he took a step back before kicking the door hard at the point where the mechanism latched.

The handle and latch came loose, but the chain held solid and kept the door from opening fully. Inpatient, Conners drew *Sherry* and shot the chain before pushing the door open. Turner stood frozen at a window that was clearly refusing to open for him, packed bag at his feet.

"Going somewhere Turner?" asked Conners, already knowing the boy wouldn't be able to answer. The guilt on Turner's face was confirmation enough for him. "I'm placing you under arrest for the murder of Patrick Everette."

Chapter XXXI: Whomsoever Believes

Conners shuddered and pulled his coat tighter around his body. A high of twenty-eight degrees, a fair dusting of snow, and no real sunlight meant most people in the Chicago streets were freezing. Most of the public buildings were full of a mixture of homeless and tourists. Part of him found this humorous. Two completely opposite types of people inhabited the same place due to the same basic desire: get warm.

He made his way slowly to the precinct in the hopes for a new case. Of course, he would've normally taken a ride with Lawrence or one of Joe's cabbies. However, due to a certain misplaced bet with Lawrence on the hockey game last night, he was forced to walk in the cold. He'd spent much of the morning going over the game in his mind to find his blunder. He'd be sure even the score when he got he chance.

As he crossed an intersection with a small throng of people, a hot-headed driver leaned on his horn. The sound was so commonplace in the city that it might as well have been a gust of wind. He knew most places in the country weren't so noisy or unique as Chicago was. Only two days ago he and a number of people unfortunate enough to be on the L-train had been subjected to an accordion player that was only tangentially familiar with his instrument. He wouldn't have given it up for the finest living in the world.

Without the aid of a car or something to distract himself with, it seemed to take ages to reach the precinct. When he finally *did* cross the threshold of the glass double doors, he took a moment to bask in the warmth of the heating system basting him with a warm wave of air. It reminded him forcibly of when he had passed out at Lawrence's apartment last week. The cold had been strong then too, and she was lucky enough to have a washer and dryer. So she'd warmed his sheets and comforter for him before they'd gone to bed. He'd stubbornly refused to admit how incredibly comfortable and relaxing it felt to fall asleep wrapped in warm sheets.

"Oh, that's better than sex," he muttered, and he rubbed his arms and chest to try and warm himself up.

"How would you know?" asked Lawrence, as she smiled brightly at him.

"Well I don't *know* exactly but I've been told that a bagel and a corndog can do a very special hug…"

"We're three seconds in, and I already regret my choice."

"Conners," said a voice to his right and Conners spun on the ball of his foot to see the lieutenant standing there with a grimace that suggested he'd stepped in dog crap.

The lieutenant might have allowed Conners to take cases with Lawrence again, but it would take a lot more than a few wins in the department's corner to soften Guston's heart. The brick wall he'd built by quitting publicly meant Guston would sooner have Conners ostracized than involved. Conners had a sneaking suspicion Lawrence had convinced the lieutenant he was a better tool when he was allowed to do as he wished.

"Hey lieutenant," he said cheerily, as if they were old friends. "How's the coffee this morning? It's freezing out there!"

The lieutenant only scowled in response.

"Well," Conners said as he turned to Lawrence. "Do you have a nice case that might help me forget the fact I've likely lost a few toes?"

"Maybe you shouldn't bet against me on hockey games."

"I still maintain the Blues are a stronger team this year."

"Conners, I grew up watching hockey. I'll watch the Blackhawks anytime."

"Good. Now I know what to get you for your birthday."

"I'll hold you to that. Montreal's playing them tomorrow night."

He considered the team for a moment.

"Yeah I'll take Montreal in that."

"Now I have to find something even more fun to take from you. In the meantime, I think I have something you and I can check out. There's been a hanging in a church."

"Interesting. Isn't killing yourself against one of those commandment things?"

"Gets better," she said, and snatched up her keys and the coat he'd given her for Christmas. "The man who hung himself was the priest."

Conners couldn't help himself and grinned brightly at the prospect of an interesting case. He moved to the garage with Lawrence. After she teased a bit that she should have him walk, she agreed to drive him.

"Besides, I couldn't stand to hear you complain just because you were late to the scene and we got all the good evidence first."

"I figured you would've wanted the head start."

Half-an-hour later they pulled up in front of an ornate, though not particularly large building. Conners couldn't help his excitement and felt a small burst of adrenaline as he opened the door, which meant that for him the action took minutes instead of a few seconds.

Nevertheless, Conners eventually got past the officers at the entrance and upon his first step into the sanctuary, he saw the body. It still swayed back and forth slowly. The man had thick, dark hair that went just past the tops of his ears and was very heavy. The rope tied round the priest's neck cut so deeply into the flesh Conners almost couldn't see it anymore, but there was little else that could be causing the fat of the man's neck to push inward like it was.

The man's wallet was placed next to a police marker. It was extremely old and made out of a faded, brown leather that would've been popular among men in the early nineties. A quick flip through the wallet revealed the man was named Ray Fulton, and he had been sixty-four years old.

Unbidden, a snatch of a song by *The Beatles* came to his mind.
Will you still need me?
Will you still feed me?
When I'm sixty-four.

He shook his head hard to try and clear it. What was strange was his left hand began forming chords in time with the chorus without him commanding his hand to do so. This disturbed him all the more.

I could've heard the song anywhere, but why am I playing guitar along to this song? I don't play guitar! How do I even know that I'm supposed to be playing guitar right now?

He slammed his left hand against a pew to force it to stop breaking the laws of logic and both the song and his air-playing stopped.

The next thing that caught his attention was the message scrawled on the east wall in a fine script.

My brethren, let not many of you become teachers, knowing we shall receive a stricter judgement.

"James," said Conners softly.

"Sorry?" asked Lawrence.

"The verse on the wall. It's James, right? I remember us reading it. Well, a different version, but same verse."

"Oh," she said, looking over at the wall for the first time. "Yeah. James chapter three. Not a great leap to see the connection."

"Guess not," said Conners, looking around for an access to the wooden rafters that were barely visible from their position. "They already search the place?"

"Ran a basic sweep," said Lawrence. "Nothing out of the ordinary; definitely murder though. His neck's snapped but a fall from that height wouldn't do it."

"Yeah. I need a ladder to see where the rope's tied. The knot or marks might help tell us something."

Lawrence used her radio to call for a ladder and after a couple minutes of awkward fumbling and placement, they got the large ladder in place. Conners smoothly swung up as if he were a spider until he reached the top. Even at the peak of the ladder, he couldn't reach the rafters except with the tips of his fingers. He crouched slightly to test the strength of the ladder. It swayed worryingly for a second, and the officers at the base tightened their grip on the metal. When it didn't give, he leapt from it and got his left hand and right arm solidly around one of the beams of wood. The ladder tipped back for a second, but the base was spread far too wide to allow it to fall over in the direction he'd pushed against. Far below him he heard Lawrence gasp.

"Be careful!" she shouted up at him.

"Been cooped up too long," he said, smiling at her. "I'm like one of those chickens they keep in the too-small cages. If I can't stretch my legs and get out every once in a while I get crazy."

"No argument here," she muttered, even while her soft tone carried up to him.

Conners crept forward and focused on his balance. The detective moved slowly amongst the beams just like an extremely large cat, balanced on all fours. Once he maneuvered his way over to the top of the noose, he carefully examined the wood and rope. The rope had begun to fray and have several splinters sticking out of it, and the wood bore marks that were not under the placement of the noose.

Failed hangings, said Bill. *Someone attacked the priest elsewhere and dragged him here.*

They attached the noose before hoisting him up with the rafters, Conners responded.

Murder, and since the logical action would be to hang the rope first, there's an emotional attachment here.

The message speaks to a deep-seated sense of betrayal or justice. Most likely perp is someone who has known him for years. Speaks to family. Likely either a brother or son, given the priest's natural size advantage over most women.

Conners looked back towards the ladder and suddenly realized he had no clear way to head back down. The easiest solution was to slide down the rope. However, there was a… swaying issue with that plan.

"I think we could cut the body down now," he said to Lawrence.

Lawrence seemed to consider what he'd said for a second before smirking.

"No. I think we need to preserve the crime scene. It would be wrong to disturb it until we're sure there's no evidence left."

"Ok, we both know I *will* attempt to jump back down that ladder if I have to."

After another few moments of making him sweat it out, she obliged and she and an officer removed the body from the rope and moved it away so he could slide down the rope and drop to the floor safely. Conners bent over the body with Lawrence, but something slightly surprising stuck out to him.

"We locate a next-of-kin?" asked Conners.

"Yeah," said Lawrence flipping through the file. "Name's Ray North, a baptist preacher in the suburbs."

Wouldn't be the first time a preacher killed someone, and it speaks to religious motive, said Bill.

No. It also wouldn't be the first time a son killed his father.

"He's a preacher too?"

"Yeah. That might explain the finger painting."

"That's what I thought. Let's hit up his church first, eh?"

"You take the church, I'll try the house."

"You gonna make me walk there?"

She smirked slightly.

"Wanna make a bet?"

Conners, for once, chose to remain silent.

As they drove to Ray North's church, the atmosphere lightened slightly. No matter how used to it they got, the fact was crime scenes could put a serious damper on any situation, even if it was a scene for someone who had no living family or was a scumbag. Still, there were moments when they could enjoy each other's company and he cherished them as dearly as he did his memories of Bill, even if they were very different.

They moved steadily if slowly through the traffic of the city. They shared jokes and sang along with whatever ridiculous song the radio dragged up, even if neither of them knew most of the words. What surprised him slightly was Lawrence was a fairly talented singer. He couldn't carry a tune in a bucket.

Strangely though, he did have an ability to understand the music. He understood how to keep the time of a song and could even place certain techniques some of the players used, most often with the guitar. This bothered him and cause his brain to itch unpleasantly. The more and more he let himself be distracted with knowledge he shouldn't have, the worse that itch got, and there was no way to scratch it. He tried to push the thoughts away except *that* made the itching even worse.

So he did his best to find a happy middle ground and kept the realizations in the back of his mind while focusing on the time he was spending with Lawrence. After an hour of slowly navigating through the city they left the shadows of the skyscrapers and entered into the trees and spread buildings of the suburbs. With the slight dusting of the snow, it reminded Conners forcibly of some of the cheesy Christmas movies from the sixties Lawrence made him watch.

Finally, they pulled up to North's church and any reminder of Christmas was driven from his mind as he stared at the building. It was hard to pin down exactly what it was that made the place feel so sinister. It was smartly built and painted, and wouldn't have looked out of place in a small town of about five-thousand people. Opposing that was a feeling of darkness and gloom that made the alleged holiness ring hallow and false, even to him.

Mustering up his courage, Conners opened the car door and instantly felt the buffering of wind and snow.

"Well, see you soon," he said and winked at Lawrence.

"Be careful," she whispered just loud enough for him to hear.

"Always am, aren't I?"

He stepped out and shut her door as he wrapped his coat tighter around himself. Even the short walk to the front door of the church felt like a small hike and his nose and tips of his ears quickly grew numb from the cold. He reached the front of the imposing building and banged on the double doors with a closed fist.

There was no answer…

He slammed it again, and again no answer…

With resignation, Conners quickly removed his gloves and plunged his left hand into his coat pocket to unearth his lock-pick set. He muttered angrily under his breath, inserted one of the picks and a wretch into the lock, and then cursed when he realized he'd chosen the wrong pick. After a couple minutes and a slight fear that his fingers might go numb, Conners got the doors unlocked. He pushed them open and saw the surprisingly warm and dimly-lit interior.

The moment he crossed the threshold the feeling of foreboding and menace that had bothered him doubled in force. He felt as if he'd been slapped across the face. After a moment of recovery, Conners looked about the place. There were no overhead lights. Instead actual candles had been placed along the walls, slowly burning away.

Seems more like a cult than a church, he wondered and couldn't have said if it were Bill's voice or his own that voiced the thought.

Then he heard a loud, authoritative voice ring out and it seemed to be echoing from all around.

"You came here with a police detective. Yet you are not police."

Conners let himself fall into the easy cockiness he so often relied upon.

"Nah, they call me when they need someone to catch crazies like you, Ray. Why don't you come on out and make my job a little easier?"

"Indeed, all who desire to live a godly life in Christ Jesus will be persecuted."

Now Conners grinned in earnest because he recognized the verse. Lawrence had discussed it in detail with him during one of their study sessions.

"Second Timothy," said Conners. "Your desires are less my concern than the hanging of your father. What would your God say about that? I believe there's something in rule six about no murder."

"I will smite them with pestilence, and disinherit them, and will make of thee a greater nation and mightier than they."

This time Conners could not place the verse, though it sounded familiar. While he could not place the verse he did hear something alongside the voice. A very slight *buzz* of static.

Hidden speakers, he heard Bill say. *Explains the omni-directional voice.*

Conners took a deep breath and led by intuition more than reason, head into the sanctuary. Like the entryway, it was lit primarily by candles. A couple overhead lights shone with an angry, red hue. They did little to help the visibility. Conners swallowed and tried to push his fear down so he would not be frozen in place as he had been with Yusuf.

Carefully, he inched forward and had to squint to see in the near-darkness. His brain began to itch unpleasantly again. He could've sworn there were other voices in the room, though none was distinct enough to be definitive. Suddenly, Conners decided to try something for the second time in his life. It defied all logic, only that it seemed the type of thing Lawrence would do. So he prayed. He didn't speak but thought his words and tried to project them, as if he hoped someone had an antenna that might pick up wayward thoughts.

Hey God... Listen, Lawrence says you would protect people from evil beings sometimes. Your Bible is full of that. So if you still do that sort of thing, I could really use some protection. After all, I am taking out one of your enemies. How about it?

If there was an answer, he didn't hear it. Frustrated, Conners hissed and returned to his search. He drew *Sherry* and slowly head up towards the front stage, towards the pulpit. As he passed a row of pews, he checked for Ray. First he checked left, then right. Then again, left then right. And again.

As he checked his left on the fourth pew from the front there was a flash of movement behind him. He spun as quick as he could, but too slow to avoid the large man slipping a wire around his neck. At once the garrote was pulled tight and Conners' mind slowed everything down to a snail's pace for him.

Ok, he heard Bill's voice. *You've got at least seven seconds of consciousness before you're in trouble. What are your options?*

Go for the feet. Provided he's put his back into the strangulation, it would pull me closer to the feet. If they're out of reach I might be able to get a shot into his foot or ankle if I'm lucky.

He tried to stamp down on Ray's feet but couldn't find purchase or aim *Sherry* well enough to get a shot off. He twisted and turned as best he could but only succeeded in making a shallow cut along the wire at his throat.

Three seconds gone, said Bill. *What next?*

I don't know! It's getting hard to think straight.

Focus kid. If he's pulled his feet back from you, where does that place his nose?

A flash of their comparative stances flew through his mind's eye. If Ray had pulled his feet back it would almost certainly place his nose near the back of Conners' head, unless he was even taller than Conners was at six feet, two inches. So, Conners pulled his head forward and slammed the back of his head into Ray's nose, performing a sort of backwards headbutt.

This time he connected hard, and his vision flashed black for a split-second. The wire around his neck went slack, and Conners spun and thrust *Sherry* out at the man.

"Ray North, you are under…"

But Ray didn't seem to care about the weapon and he flew at Conners, arms outstretched. Reacting on instinct, Conners pulled the trigger twice, and *Sherry* rang out.

Bang! Bang!

Ray flopped to the floor, two holes in his stomach and Conners pulled out his phone to dial an ambulance.

~*~

As the EMTs were busy checking his vitals and getting Ray rushed to a hospital, Conners glanced up at the newly-activated lights above him.

Well, he thought, and wasn't sure what to expect in response. *Did you protect me here, or did you fail because I was attacked? Why don't you give me a sign if you're there? You liked to use signs in the Bible. Why not now?*

He waited a couple seconds. Nothing much happened except the EMT kept performing tests. As Conners was following the light at the end of a pen with his eyes, a lightbulb above them *popped* and went out. The EMT jumped slightly.

Great, he thought, dully. *For Moses and the jews you could make a pillar of fire and rain mana down from the heavens. For me, you pop a lightbulb. I think your powers are diminished, great creator of the universe.*

Chapter XXXII: Sealed and Buried

Conners stood on the other side of the interrogation room's one-way mirror, and studied the scene intently as Lawrence questioned their suspect, Gerald Brown. Brown was a man with olive skin and cold, grey eyes. He had dark hair that was slicked back and pulled away from his temples. He was perpetually calm, as if an explosion could go off behind him and it wouldn't bother him in the slightest. He displayed complete and total control over his emotions. He never got angry or frightened and was impossible to read.

This was actually the reason Conners had been consulted, but even he was having trouble reading the man. He could break a second down so that it felt like a full minute and still couldn't clearly read the man's face. He'd had a few (and only a few) moments when he'd actually picked up a small speck of emotional expression from Brown. Sadly, none of those moments had led to anything helpful.

Brown was guilty of the kidnapping and murder of at least two young women, and was suspected of stealing a third. Catherine Calloway had been missing for about six weeks, and had vanished about ten blocks away from Brown's home. While the D.A. was willing to bring the case to jury if they had to, they both knew Brown was able to manipulate people well enough that any evidence they had might not lead to a conviction. So pressure was on to either collect more evidence or get a confession. So far the first option was quickly striking out and the second seemed impossible. Resigned to the situation they were in, the lieutenant had finally agreed to allow Conners onto the team, but so far he hadn't been able to help much.

"Why don't you tell me about Rebecca Hill?" asked Lawrence, and she placed a picture in front of Brown.

Conners knew the picture without having to see it again. It was the photo of a young college student with shoulder-length blonde hair and deep brown eyes. She had been wearing a white button-up beneath a pink sweater. Her left cheek had a dimple from her smile in the picture. Rebecca had been found dead and buried about a mile from a small hunting shack Brown had rented about a week after she'd gone missing. That had been two years ago.

"Who?" Brown asked, dully.

Yet even as he asked it, there was a slight twitch at the edge of the lips.

"Pride," said Conners and felt like a broken record. "He knows we can't definitively tie him to this, and he's proud of what he's done."

"If you don't have anything new to say, then for once in your life shut the hell up!" hissed the lieutenant.

It was true that Conners had said something similar on the previous picture. It had been of Hilda Lane: a coffee shop barista who had gone missing almost four years ago. She'd shown up dead in a small lake Brown frequently passed on his way into the city. It was the first time the grey-eyed man had appeared on the detective's suspect list, because several people knew him as a regular at the coffee shop, especially if Lane was on-shift there.

How long did you plan their deaths? Conners pondered. *When you went and ordered whatever stupid drink you used to keep cover, did you already have her picked out? Is that why you chose that shop in the first place, or was it just happenstance that the poor girl crossed your path?*

You're getting too emotional, kid. Keep a clear head.

Conners scoffed at that.

There was a time you would've been pleased to discover I have emotions.

There was a time I didn't exist inside your head either, kid.

Conners focused his attention on the room.

"So how do you suppose Rebecca wound up dismembered in the woods, not twenty feet from where you rented a cabin?" asked Lawrence as she placed a couple crime scene photos before him.

Conners saw a small touch of color in the man's hands, which were still handcuffed to the table.

"Arousal," mumbled Conners, disgusted by the reaction.

"Sick bastard," growled one of the officers as he clenched his fist.

Conners couldn't help but share the sentiment.

"I don't know how she got there, detective. If I were to guess, perhaps she rented the place after myself and met with a very unfortunate accident."

"So she vanishes without a word and rents a cabin before being surgically sliced by a bear? I doubt it. Why don't I share a different story? I think Rebeca crosses paths with a stranger on the college campus. Sure she's cautious, but he's such a nice guy. Surely there's no danger in grabbing a cup of coffee with him. The coffee date goes great and he offers her a ride home. Except they never make it home."

Conners saw the slightest twitch of Brown's mouth and his mind set the pace of the world into a crawl so he could analyze it more carefully. It was a slight pursing of the lips and an applied tension from beneath.

"Anger," Conners muttered, thinking aloud. "Why would he be angry?"

"Because she's right," answered an officer whose name Conners could not place.

"No. He's proud of what he did to those girls. He relishes in being right and in being clever. Why would he be angry about that?"

Because she's wrong, but he doesn't know she's intentionally wrong. She's goading him by implying he got lucky in crossing the girl's path.

"So you meant to let things go on," said Lawrence. "Play a little cat and mouse, perhaps. Only something happened. Maybe she got angry, maybe you did, and you have to kill her. But you're sloppy—impulsive even. You have a dead body and nowhere to put it. And while it will take a while, people will notice a beautiful young girl like that is missing."

A vein jumped out on Brown's neck before he forced it down, but no one besides Conners seemed to notice.

"Good job, Lawrence," he muttered so softly that the sound didn't even reach his own ears.

At that moment Conners' phone *buzzed*. Smoothly, so as not to draw attention he pulled it out and glanced at the incoming text message. The attached signature and the blocked number sent a pang through him.

Cement.
- The Watcher.

"Cement?" he muttered, but no one near him acknowledged the word.

What's the significance of concrete?
Why else does he message you during a case, kid?
You think Brown used concrete to bury the girl?
Watcher does, apparently. Not like it could hurt anything.

"Now normally someone might make it look like an overdose. She's still fresh enough that alcohol wouldn't be widely questioned, but you got reckless and killed her in the wrong way."

"I don't know what you're talking about," said Brown, smoothly. "This is a really long, boring story with no proof behind it."

Conners quickly pulled out his phone and texted Lawrence.

Push him on the location. Keep implying he was lucky. Bring up concrete.

Lawrence read the message about a minute later, then snapped her phone shut before she briefly turned to the glass and winked at him to show she understood.

"You got lucky you remembered the woods nearby, and there wasn't a chance you could put her anywhere else. It's not like you had a hideaway stashed nearby."

"You're boring me, detective," said Brown, more force behind his words.

"Isn't it? I mean, you must've seen an ad on a billboard or something. What? You didn't have a basement you could bury her beneath, or you just too lazy to work with concrete?"

"I've worked with concrete plenty," said Brown solidly. "I used to work construction."

That was true enough. He'd spent summers in college on several sites. Those jobs had doubtless handed him several skills that would come in useful as a killer.

"But you didn't think of that, did you? You got so lucky!"

"I didn't kill that girl, but if I *had*," he said and his voice took on a sudden slant. "I would've known that it would be far too late to break up the concrete and reseal it before someone got suspicious. It takes a couple days at least for it to dry and nearly thirty days before it's finished being solid."

"Got it!" said Conners, excitedly.

"Got what?" asked the lieutenant, confused. "So it takes a few weeks for concrete to finish setting, so what?"

"So what?!" Conners almost shouted. "Brown grew angry when she mentioned he couldn't have put the girl in concrete. He knows he could do that if he'd wanted to, because he *has*. Maybe he's done it multiple times. He is a meticulous man. He'd want to watch until he was *sure* the concrete was set right if he buried Catherine. So, if we can pinpoint any time between when the girl went missing and now that he appeared to be somewhere slightly remote for a month or so, we can check there for concrete recently laid. I mean, it's not a solid thread but it's more than we've had."

Guston ran a hand along his mustache and growled slightly.

"It's flimsy at best, but we certainly don't have anything stronger right now. Miller, go through Brown's statements and follow up on anything that fits Conners' theory. You find anything, let me know."

Saluting quickly, the officer ran off to pull up Brown's credit card statements. Conners couldn't help but feel pleased it was Miller that had been assigned to help him. No one but no one was a replacement for Lawrence. Still, as far as uniformed officers went, Miller was one who had worked with him enough that he didn't cause problems. Plus he seemed to like what Conners did. There were plenty of cops who hated him and wouldn't work with him. Miller didn't have any such grudge.

Conners turned his attention back to the man locked in the cell. Nevertheless, in the back of his mind, he felt the uncomfortable niggling that came with the messages from The Watcher. There was no way he should've known Conners was watching the interrogation, unless he had someone inside the building.

If he *did* know where Brown had buried the girl, why not just say it outright?

Because you can't appear to have knowledge you shouldn't, said Bill. *He just points at the breadcrumbs of importance.*

So when is he going to try and push me into the oven? he thought, but got no response.

Lawrence stepped out of the room after another minute and Brown leaned back in his chair, as if he were growing bored, which was actually possible given his personality disorder.

"How you doing in there?" Conners whispered as they hugged one another quickly.

"I'm about a minute away from putting a hole in his head," she replied. "But I can hold back for a bit."

"Well you got us a lead in there," he said as they parted. "We're looking into his history for somewhere he might've buried Catherine and covered her with concrete discretely: most likely a disused building or a basement somewhere."

"Any solid ideas?"

"None yet, but Miller's checking credit card statements to see if he was hanging around an area long enough for the concrete to set. Then we can canvas the area for good locations."

"Well, if something does come up, be sure to let me know."

Conners walked to the nearby water cooler with her and filled two of the paper cups, giving her one and keeping the other for himself. The water was clean and cool, which helped relax the tension and irritation that had been growing steadily.

"I probably don't have to say it," Lawrence began, toss the cup into the recycling bin. "But thanks for helping us out on this one. Brown is a real grade-A creep and if we can put him away then at least a few women will be safer because of it."

"You didn't need to say it, but you're welcome. Besides it was this or follow up on another really annoying insurance fraud case."

"Oh, so we're actually doing you a favor?"

"I don't know I'd take it *that* far."

"No, no, we're always happy to help our little brother out."

"And at once I regret my decision."

She smiled softly and Conners returned it. They let that moment hang for a couple seconds. It wasn't awkward or difficult or painful. It was blissful: comfortable. It was peace, because it was a moment he shared with her. The moment came to an end, not because they broke it but because Officer Miller came speeding down the stairs.

"I've got something!" he said as he waved some papers over his head. "We've got something!"

Conners practically tripped over himself as he rushed to the officer and looked over the papers. Officer Miller pointed out the block of credit card receipts that he'd highlighted. Conners' mind slowed the second down for him and he examined the receipts.

They took place over the course of twenty-six days, which was perfectly within their ballpark. For a moment, he couldn't tell what was unique about the receipts. However when he examined the fast food and grocery purchases, he realized they lay north beyond the city limits. They were all near a small suburban area. It was the kind of place anyone would own a basement and no one would bat an eye at some slight noise from the neighbors.

"Why that area?" asked Conners.

"It makes since," defended Miller as several other officers joined them and began pouring over the papers themselves. "Perfect place to keep things secret and all that."

"No, I didn't ask why that *type* of area. I asked why *that* area. There's a dozen-odd places much closer that he could pick a house and bury a girl in. He picked *that* area. Any history there?"

"I was just getting to that," said Miller and he smiled like a kid on Christmas. "His mother had a house up in the area. Technically it went back to the bank two years ago, but it's never been sold. It's perfect for him."

Conners raised an eyebrow at the officer.

"Good work, kid," he said, accidentally reminding himself of Bill. "Right. Lieutenant, I'm on this."

Guston began to object but Lawrence cut across him.

"We *should* send him, not alone of course," said Lawrence. "This is great but there's no guarantee this is the right place. We can't afford to send a full team out without knowing we'll get something. We can only hold Brown for another ten hours before we have to officially charge or release him. If there's something there, Conners will find it and if not we'll need most of our forces here."

The lieutenant ran his fingers through his hair before he pointed at Miller.

"You take him up there. Conners, Miller runs point on this. You obey him like he's me, or I'll bury your ass under charges."

"Setting the bar low there, boss man. I don't listen to you all that much anyway. Let's go!"

Miller nodded and they moved to the garage to take one of the police cruisers. Conners' new appointee was not nearly as deft as Lawrence or one of Joe's men at shifting through the maddening traffic of Chicago, but with a bit of persistence and one or two illegal uses of the police lights, they managed well enough.

Soon they found the freeway and navigated up north and past the limits of the city to a weird mix of suburban and country life. While the houses were usually within five acres of one another, they were also far enough apart that a little breaking up and pouring of concrete would easily go unnoticed. At first, Conners thought it was strange the house would've been foreclosed on by the bank and not been fixed up or sold, but he came to realize this was something of a fashion out this far. At least two of the other houses on the street bore signs indicating both foreclosure and neglect.

After a bit of trial and error, they located the correct house. Conners volunteered to "check" the backdoor and picked it before Miller had a chance to check on him. As he got it open, he heard gunshots and flew into action. He drew *Sherry* and sprinted through the house. The front door was still closed, but Conners clearly got a glimpse of the source of the gunshot through the nearby window. He saw Miller lying on the ground just beyond the front porch. A man in a suit stood over him. Conners couldn't help breaking the image down.

The suit was grey, but slick and easily more expensive than most people's wardrobe. The man was white, but with spray-tanned skin: more ascetic than practical. He held a pistol in his hand but even with the time distortion, he was too far away for Conners to get a definite model. Conners lifted his revolver and prepared to take his shot when something collided with the back of his head.

Instinctually, he rolled with the hit and turned it into a summersault. The blow still pained him enough to make his vision go blurry and cause a small ringing in his ears. He groaned and shook himself. He blocked out the pain and focused on the foe in front of him. Still he couldn't help but hear a voice that sounded as if a third person were in the room.

Now, understand me John. This isn't anything against you as a person, but you just pissed me the fuck off!

Even as the voice faded, a fraction of Conners' mind latched onto the name John. He knew that name, even if he couldn't explain how he knew it. It could've been John Barns, John Snatcher, or any of the various Johns he met through his life as a detective, but that didn't *click* in the same way his brain was ringing.

The man before him raised the pole he'd struck Conners with and moved forward.

Not the time, kid!

Conners flicked up *Sherry* and deflected the blow. Quick as a flash he stamped on the man's foot and shot him in the leg. Normally, he tried to avoid causing permanent injury if he could, but Miller was down—possibly dead. His own life was in danger. He was not feeling patient. Another gunshot sounded outside and Conners glanced through the window. He saw the man in the suit running up to the door. Conners quickly flattened himself against the wall by the door. The man pulled out a key before he unlocked the door and flung it open.

Conners shot twice more, both shots landing in the suited man's chest. He reached down and put the man's gun in his waistband before cuffing the man he'd shot in the leg. Both bore signs indicating they were mobsters. He put that knowledge to the side and ran out to check on Miller. He'd been shot twice, once through the head.

"Damn it!" he hissed before whispering to the officer. "I'm sorry."

Conners already knew there was nothing he could do for the man at the moment. He only knew Miller had been a decent cop, and hadn't deserved to be shot down for trying to stop a serial killer. He radioed the station and updated them on what had happened. A squad was dispatched but Conners knew it would take a while before they got there.

As angry as he was about Miller's death, he knew the best thing he could do was check the basement. Practically on autopilot, he searched the garage and found an old sledgehammer covered in dust and grime from years of disuse. He made his way down to the basement and searched it before setting at the concrete with the hammer. By the time the dispatched team found him, Conners had broken through the recently-laid concrete and found Catherine Calloway's body. The Watcher's information had been good.

As he lay in his bed that night, he could feel the resounding mixture of anger and pain in his system that pushed away sleep. Even though he could've recited it from memory, he pulled out his phone and read and reread the message that appeared on his phone that evening.

You survived… I suppose I shouldn't be surprised. I'll see you soon, detective. I'm looking forward to it.

Chapter XXXIII: Babysitting

Conners sat bolt upright and rolled off his bed. He used the momentum to grab *Sherry* from his nightstand and pointed it into the darkness in wait for whatever attacker was after him. He waited twenty seconds and heard nothing. Cautiously, he grabbed a flashlight, a long one that could be used as a club if needed. He swept both his rooms and the office below thoroughly. Finally satisfied there was no one in the building with him aside from a rat in the office downstairs, he relaxed a little and turned on the lights in his kitchen before he collapsed into his singular armchair.

He'd only been asleep for a few hours before the nightmares had woken him up. He hadn't slept much since the Gerald Brown case. Miller's death had been like a splinter in his brain. A nagging itch had been attacking his mind ever since his fight. This itch combined with his guilt ensured he had grown short and irritable during his waking hours. Then the nightmares began and kept him awake. So there was no rest and no reprieve for him in the world of dreams. He hadn't slept more than three hours a day for the past two weeks.

Christmas had come and gone. He'd been invited to spend it with Lawrence and her family, but hadn't gone. He couldn't remember what excuse he'd given. He couldn't remember what day it was. He also couldn't remember if he'd eaten the previous day. He'd taken one of his pending cases that asked almost no brainwork of him and only required some basic legwork and scouting. Even at the time he knew Lawrence didn't believe him when he'd said he couldn't make it. She hadn't questioned him on it, and he knew it was to allow him time to cope.

His hands shook as he filled a glass with water from his sink and took it over to where he kept a small mortar and pestle. He tried to keep his brain from automatically adding up how much sleep he now owed himself. The knowledge would only frustrate him. He crushed several caffeine pills before he mixed the powder in with his water and downed the glass. It likely wasn't a healthy habit but it was far from the most destructive thing he'd ever done to himself.

Conners spent several hours trying and failing to read famous investigations from the stacks on his bookshelf, but his brain refused to focus on what he wanted. The sun had begun to peak over the furthest skyscrapers and bring a soft amber light into his building when his phone *buzzed*, throwing him out of his internal musings.

He stood and made another large glass of caffeine-laced water before he checked the text he'd just received. In the moment it took for his phone to unlock and show him the message, part of his mind threw up the idea that it might be another text from The Watcher. That idea terrified him and excited him. It was the thrill of the chase, the terror of danger, and the horror of the man's past crimes. Miller's dead body flashed through his mind's eye as the phone unlocked and he read the message.

It was from Lawrence.

Need you. My apartment. Quick as you can, please.

At once, he sprung up, his lethargy and exhaustion gone in the blink of an eye. Lawrence rarely requested him over text like that, and never with that type of urgency. He tore down the stairs and threw on his large overcoat, placing a pair of cuffs and *Sherry* on his belt before he made a call to Joe.

It was snowing lightly as he threw the door open, and a blast of chilly air hit him full in the face. He shuddered and not for the first time desperately wished his little apartment had a fireplace in it.

If I ever renovate this place again, he thought to himself. *That'll be the first thing on the blueprints.*

He reached one hand back inside to the coatrack and pulled a long scarf out. Desperate to block out the cold and wind, he folded it in half before he wrapped it around his neck, enjoying the sudden warmth this brought him. Joe's cabbie pulled up maybe two minutes later and Conners climbed in back to be sped off to Lawrence's apartment. Despite his better instinct, he checked and re-checked his phone to see if she'd texted him again. No more messages appeared, and he didn't know if that made him feel better or worse.

Thirty-two minutes after she'd texted him for help, they pulled up in front of her house. It was immediately apparent something was very wrong. There was a cop car as well as a crime scene unit van outside, and the officers were standing together talking with a third figure. Both his worry and his curiosity grew as he jogged up to the line. He waved at the nearest officer. She rolled her eyes as he approached. Despite his extremely high closure rate, his behavior hardly made him popular with most of the policemen. Miller hadn't displayed such hostility.

Stop it! he snapped at himself mentally.

As he approached, a civilian woman detached herself from the police.

His brain sent out an alert, almost as if it had received a text. This woman had the same slightly brown skin and auburn hair and even the same green eyes as his favorite sergeant. However, there was something different in the shape of the lips and the nose. She also wore a pressed suit that was very different from anything he'd ever seen Lawrence wear, even in court. This was her twin: Janice, who was so similar apparently most people confused the two, even after knowing them for years.

Conners could always tell the difference, but he did sometimes have to take a second glance at the face. He'd met her the first year he'd been invited over for Christmas, and had not been the biggest fan of Janice. She was kind enough but there was always a touch of dislike in the woman's eyes when she looked at him. Janice was a prosecuting attorney in Saint Louis, and apparently had a great dislike for Conners' tendency to bend the rules and laws as needed, and viewed him as more harmful to the system than helpful.

Only as she moved away from the two officers did Conners realize there was a fourth among them: Janice's son, Mikey. He was still an infant, and as far as Conners had pieced together there had never been a real father in the picture for the child. So he was often watched by his grandmother: Alejandra. Conners had taken a brief interest in the child, mostly curious if the intelligence and drive that Jessica and Janice shared contained a genetic trait that might be passed on to the child. The results were at best inconclusive. He appeared to have a good grasp of faces and voices. Even now he opened and closed his hand repeatedly at Conners in a gesture that was supposed to be a wave, but he displayed little skill in deduction or reasoning so far as Conners was able to detect.

"Ah," Janice said, as her eyes focused on him. "Conners. Good to see you."

Lair. You don't want me anywhere near here.

"You too. Got a text from your sister. What's going on?"

Her gaze fell and he saw that her eyes were slightly red from crying. He felt a small pang in his heart, which he quickly stifled.

"Jess and I were going to spend the afternoon together. So mom agreed to watch Mikey while we went out. When we came back… she was on the ground and there was blood everywhere," Janice let out a sob while her voice cracked, but she resumed a professional tone to finish. "She was dead for at least an hour before we returned and we'd been gone at least four hours in total. There's no signs of forced entry or of a struggle. Due to the marks on the kitchen floor, we suspect she had a slip or a seizure and her head hit the floor."

Conners reached forward and gently placed a hand on her shoulder. Mikey cooed softly, though whether it was a sympathetic sound or a vocalization of protest, Conners had no idea.

"Thank you for telling me. If I can help at all, don't be afraid to ask. I need to check on your sister."

Janice nodded.

"Be careful with her. She's still in a bit of shock, I think."

He nodded and moved past the police and into the apartment. The crime scene investigators and photographer were already looking through and marking everything of interest in the house. Lawrence sat on her couch with a blanket draped over her shoulders and stared blankly into the wall opposite her. She didn't even seem to register his presence until he sat next to her and placed a hand on her back.

"Oh!" she said, starting. "Conners. Thanks for coming. My... my mother..."

"I know," Conners said and waved his free hand. "Your sister explained. You want me to take a look?"

She nodded.

"I don't know if something hit her or what might've happened. The coroner said it was likely a stroke or seizure but I just... I need to be sure."

Conners rubbed her back softly, and tried to think of something that might reassure her without being calloused. He'd never so thoroughly regretted his lack of humanity as he did in that moment. Bill would've known what to say but he had no idea.

"I'll take care of this," was the best he could think of. "You should check on your sister."

That was an excuse and Lawrence probably knew it. Janice seemed slightly better-adjusted to the whole situation but the last thing either of them needed was for her to be in the house while he did his examination. There was a reason why officers and detectives didn't work on any investigations involving their own family members or close friends. Luckily, working as a private entity meant just *one* of his many perks was the opportunity to choose his own cases.

As Lawrence moved out of the house, Conners removed a pair of latex gloves from one of his many pockets and removed his coat. He walked up to where the older latin woman's body still lay on the kitchen tile, with blood pooling around the head.

"Careful there, boy wonder," said a detective Conners didn't recognize.

"Can't do anymore damage than your tornado of a team," Conners muttered as he slipped on his gloves. "Anytime you all want to get out of my way, it'd be a big help."

The detective appeared to be about to retort, but either thought better of it or else couldn't find a good response, because he turned around and left Conners alone. Conners tried to treat the investigation as if nothing was unusual or abnormal about the case. This was merely a death that had been discovered by family members and he needed to determine if it was a murder or natural causes. For a long moment, he managed it, until he reached Alejandra Lawrence's face.

The problem was that he couldn't *just* see the face of an aging latin woman who would've still been in relatively good health in spite of a large wound on the left side of her head. That was the factual side of things… The *other* side of him acknowledged this was a woman he'd sat across a table from at dinner. He'd given her Christmas presents and gotten them in return, even made horrible excuses to try and avoid eating whatever terrifying dish the woman had cooked and presented.

That memory hit him hard and he couldn't help the smile that broke out across his face. He could see their time together too clearly. It didn't help that the table they'd eaten at was literally feet away from him, and that he could see the couch where they'd sat to exchange presents. He could remember asking probing questions to Alejandra about her daughters, and remembered having to dodge them in return. She certainly could give as good as she got.

He shook himself and rubbed his face. He wasn't allowed to be the weak one right now. If Lawrence could keep it together enough to have him here, he would hold everything together for her. That was who he was. It was the only way he knew how to be. He wasn't a cold and infallible machine, but he was the one who always... always had to put things right.

Bang.

A small child lay bleeding in an alleyway with a bullet wound from the head.

He growled and shook his head hard.

Focus kid, dead body. What caused it?

Blunt force trauma to the left side of the brain. Cracked tiling at point of contact indicates high impact.

Which means?

This wasn't someone collapsing normally. She fell very quickly: possibly tripped or was pushed.

Where from?

Conners turned and examined the surrounding floor and space. Plenty of objects one might trip on lay in the main travel path: chair legs, kid's toys, a pair of Lawrence's boots, The problem was none of these appeared out of place or moved unduly. The chairs were all still pushed into the table and the boots were neatly placed next to one another. The toys *were* scattered haphazardly but it was impossible to distinguish use from chaos where children's toys were concerned, so that was of little help.

Straightening up, Conners groaned and stretched out his back.

I'm in... what? My later 20's and already I hurt, he thought as he tried to relieve some of the pain in his spine and shoulder blades. *Not that being shot and thrown like a ragdoll helps any of that, I suppose.*

At that moment something caught his gaze. He had bent backwards slightly and noticed Lawrence's sink had something resting in it. Normally, he didn't pay *that* much attention to people's sinks, as they so often contained either nothing or dirty dishes. Quickly, Conners swept over to the sink and glanced around before fishing out the foreign object. What he pulled out was a wooden block, a few inches in diameter with large, singular letters painted on each of the sides.

His first thought was Mikey easily could've thrown the block into the sink by accident, until a nasty secondary idea came to his mind. He took a moment to mentally stand Alejandra up and saw her position would've allowed an unobstructed line of sight to the highchair Mikey had been sitting in when the sisters had returned home. His stomach dropped out at he realized the likeliest answer was the child had thrown the block: either as a joke or in a moment of rage, and hit his grandmother in the head hard enough to either knock her off balance knock her out for a second... long enough for her to fall and for the block to go bouncing off the counter into the sink.

He started to redeposit the block when he realized something. The block hadn't had an evidence marker next to it. Even if someone had seen it, it wasn't considered to be anything related to the case. It would be a simple enough matter to tell the detective about it, or even ensure someone took a photo of it for the file, but he paused. If he shared his theory and he was right (which he was more often than not) what would it do to Mikey and to the Lawrence twins?

Another curious glance revealed most of the police team was busy examining the guest bedroom. No one else would know he'd found this. His desire for answers and a solved question battled against his care for his best friend and he knew it was never truly going to be a competition. With a deep sigh, Conners placed the block amongst its fellows and took his gloves off before putting his coat back on and preparing himself.

By the time he opened Lawrence's front door, his face was calm and his eyes betrayed no sign of his moment of humanity. He would be exactly what she needed at that moment: a comfort. It didn't matter if the comfort was founded on a lie. It was what he'd slowly been making himself into over the course of the past seven years: ever since the hospital.

"Hey," he said as he rejoined Janice and Jessica. "You two holding up?"

He couldn't help but give a double-take, because they were wearing the matching coats he'd given them for Christmas and even he was having a moment's trouble telling them apart.

"As well as we can," said the sergeant, as she looked *through* Conners instead of at him.

He pulled her into a hug and did his best to push aside the natural discomfort that came from the feeling of the sets of eyes that were on them as they embraced each other.

"Find anything?" she asked softly.

"Yeah," he said, and Janice's eyes snapped onto him. "It turns out it was a stroke. There wasn't anything either of you could've done to prevent it. For what it's worth, she must've passed quickly and without any pain."

Janice nodded and Jessica just clutched onto his coat. He didn't let go or try and escape her grip, but let her grieve the loss of one of the few people she loved and relied on. After a few moments, she released him and hugged Janice and Mikey, and Conners felt his phone *buzz*. Far angrier than he expected to be, Conners checked the phone and his heart froze in his chest.

Time to play, detective. Howling Wolf Apartments. Room 18.

Chapter XXIV: Room Eighteen

Conners didn't know how long he sat there, examining the phone in his hand. He couldn't have said when the twins retreated, most likely to start making arrangements for their mother's funeral. He didn't remember calling Joe or asking for the cabbie that pulled up and looked pointedly at him. He was only vaguely aware of the order he gave his body to climb into the back of the cab and give the cabbie the name of the apartments.

Howling Wolf

He'd been to those apartments before. He'd been chasing down Max Turner. He remembered them clearly enough. They were dirty, disgusting, and cheap. His head began hurting as he considered that. He knew they were cheap, but something in him also knew that they could be made livable with a good amount of effort. But it was important the landlord didn't see how nice you made the place because he'd up the rent for the unit. Not that it was much of a problem. The landlord almost never came down to the apartments.

I knew this place. I knew this place well, long before I tracked Turner down.

There was no way the number eighteen was an accident. The Watcher *knew*. He had to know Conners still had that key and he'd been searching for his past. He must've known Conners couldn't remember anything of his past and every time he got close, it made his head hurt. Everything about The Watcher made his head hurt. It hurt to remember Miller's death, even when he tried not to. It hurt to think of all the cases The Watcher had weighed in on. The Watcher had made him who he was almost as much as Richards and Bill had. It made him sick, and it made his head pound like a damn war drum.

Robbers.

The word popped into his head without connection or demand. It took him several seconds to shake off the thought because it was almost as if someone had hijacked his brain for a split-second. Yet the voice that had said the word was very much his own, even if it wasn't in a tone he usually used.

Robbers.

He sent the word through his mental database to see if it could return any results. He got back too much information: statistics and information on robberies and famous thefts over the past five years, cases he'd worked, cases from the police files and Bill's old work, tv reports and newspaper articles, and his own personal studies into the mindset of thieves. None of this stopped the horrible, painful itch in his brain that felt uncomfortably like a cockroach was chewing its way through the center of his frontal cortex. Angry and driven to extreme frustration he reeled back and slapped himself across the face, hard. It stung but somehow only made the pain in his mind worse. Nothing he could pull up answered that pain in his mind.

The cab traveled through the city streets, navigating the traffic with a deft skill that completely eluded Conners. He hadn't attempted to drive in a couple years and Lawrence had more than once threatened to arrest him if he piloted anything larger than a bicycle. He couldn't remember if he'd ever driven a car before being in the hospital. He couldn't recall if he had anything akin to a family either. He didn't know if he'd had a girlfriend or wife or even children.

His ignorance of his past had never particularly bothered him. He'd always been just as afraid of it as he was unaware of it. Yet now his head ached and it screamed at him to find his past, and that only got worse as he thought of the name of the apartment.

Howling Wolf

It was like a very annoyed wasp stung his brainstem everytime he repeated the name in his head. Unaware of what he was doing, Conners reached into one of his many pockets and produced the key with the number 18 taped to it. He always had this key on him, even when he wasn't wearing his coat.

Without command, his hand twisted to the left.

What are you doing, kid?

The answer came immediately, without thought or consideration.

Unlocking my door. I at least used to have a room there. I've only been here once, and yet I've been here many times—possibly lived here for years.

The cab came to a stop around twenty minutes later, and Conners looked outside the window at the shabby and run-down apartment building. It was exactly as he'd remembered it, and exactly what Watcher would want. Simply by the lights he could tell most of the rooms were empty. Only two were lit: the lobby and a room on the first floor. He knew it was room eighteen. Conners pressed on the floor of the cab with his cane in an attempt to prepare himself in case he had to deal with squatters, but he doubted it. The Watcher wouldn't want it that way.

He stepped out into the cold and turned his collar up against the wind and weather. The detective carefully approached the area as if it were hallowed ground.

Honestly, he thought to himself. *I've approached quite a lot of holy grounds with less reverence than this.*

He tried the door and after a bit of pushing and shaking, the old wood gave way and opened for him. The floor was linoleum, checkered black and white and bore a thin layer of dust. This was slightly odd. While the apartments certainly hadn't been filled when he'd arrested Turner, there had been other people living here. Now it was abandoned. A fresh set of footprints moved from the front door to the stairs. The same set of feet had eventually exited the building through the front door.

Someone else has been here recently, but not anyone who bothered to hide their presence.

Conners glanced around and his brain suddenly flared up as if it had been set aflame. The front desk was old, worn, and hadn't been painted since 2005. The flash made his head hurt again. There was no reason for him to know the year of the paint job exactly, but he *did* know it. He knew it as surely as he knew the day's date: January 4th, 2015.

He eyed the old water boiler in the corner. That water boiler was always problematic and he'd always been afraid it might explode. It was quickly apparent that even while the tenants had been cleared out, the heat and electricity were left on. They were old and in desperate need of repair, as the building made *clanks* and *clunks* of protest. The warmed air was musty and dirty. However, it was at least warm.

Conners followed the footsteps in the dust, and carefully head up to the next floor. While the stairs groaned in protest, they did not break or crack. As Conners reached the next floor, still following the footsteps, he saw the hallway was carpeted in a pale green color that would've been considered "dated" in the late nineties. Now it was beyond antique. The doors were all shut and testing numbers 15 and 16 Conners found them locked. Then he reached the door with a brass 18 hanging on it. The footsteps turned and went into the room, and a second set showed them leaving a little while later.

Conners let out a small breath he didn't realize he'd been holding in. The door was scratched near the handle, bearing a thick mark through the paint job.

From my eighteenth birthday.

Frustrated with himself, Conners scowled and inserted his key into the lock. It fit perfectly and he could hear the tumblers and pins as they slid into place. He slowly twisted the key to the left and jiggled the handle as he did so.

"Every third time or so it likes to stick," he muttered though he had absolutely no clue who it was he was explaining this to.

He pushed the door open and saw his old apartment. It wasn't an impressive sight by any means, yet it felt as much home to him as the Knighthawk office did. The whole place was fairly small, though it was larger than the apartment he'd started using while he worked for Bill. What quickly stood out was the whole place had been cleaned, thoroughly. There was no dust or cobwebs anywhere, and while there was clutter all around, it appeared to have been placed there intentionally by the tenant... by him.

The living room was covered with a simple, brown carpet and a number of papers and envelopes littered the floor. The corner had a coffee table with an old box television atop it. Both sat across from an armchair that he wouldn't have been able to give away if he'd been so inclined.

The wall had a cork board that was littered with notes and pictures, mostly of James Kingston, the ex-head of Kingston Inc. and mafia leader. A quick look at the notes reaffirmed his wife had come to run the publicly reputable company while Kingston handled the criminal enterprise. Conners moved past the kitchen, which was both noticeably cleaner and less-used than the living room, and entered the bedroom. It was just as disorganized and cluttered as the living room had been, with boxes and books piled all over the place.

There was an old desk with an even older computer sat atop it. Curiously, Conners turned it on and actually jumped back when the thing whirred to life. For a moment he felt the buzz and static of the monitor was attempting to actually suck him into it. Still, it did eventually power on and go through the start-up process. Unfortunately, it was password protected and after failing a few times, it threatened to lock him out, so he stopped and shut it off again.

There were no pictures in the room, save for the picture of a couple that sat just above the desk. Conners stared at the picture for several long seconds, willing his brain to tickle or burn, but it refused. With a sigh, Conners turned away from the picture and examined the rest of the room. There was a student's wardrobe in the corner that boasted even more books and few clothes— mostly t-shirts and cargo pants—and two coats: one light and one heavy. The coats were plain and nondescript, the type of thing he would only wear now if he were trying to blend in. The far end of the room had a twin bed on a boxspring with no frame. The sheets were tucked and folded by whoever had cleaned the place, but were also clearly old and well-used.

There was also an acoustic guitar in the corner, and a small box nearby had several picks and replacement strings as well as a good amount of sheet music.

I played guitar.

The thought reverberated through him and connected in a way that caused a satisfying scratch for that itch in his brain.

I played guitar. I slept here. I worked on this computer looking into the local crime lord.

Once more the cleansing feeling spread through his mind, as if his brain was relaxed in a spa. Conners bent and began to skim through the nearby notes and scribbled ideas that covered almost every piece of paper in sight.

I looked into local dealers and drug salesmen and apparently even reported a good number of them. I was a vigilante.

Again, the satisfying scratch, and with it there was a trickle of more. For the first time he truly started to remember.

I was exhausted more often than not. I was quiet, recluse, and kept out of the public flow as much as I could. I was socially anxious, hated talking to people, and preferred to live in the night.

He looked again at the clothes and saw a belt hidden at the back of the wardrobe. The belt was exactly what he'd already known was there. It bore a small collection of weapons, which included a baton and caltrops. Turning his attention to the bathroom, Conners located several first aid kits as well as the fishing line and surgical hooks he knew lie there.

I got hurt, and often had to heal superficial wounds to avoid suspicion. I was careful, but young and stupid. I got shot.

He placed a hand on his side where he'd always had some scar tissue, but no idea what had caused it.

I got shot by a heroine dealer when I was seventeen. He was a bad shot and it only scraped my side, but I learned how to do stitches. I bled in this bathtub, a lot. I worked a few different jobs, mostly security, things that would let me look over security systems to try and find weaknesses that lay there, so I could tell what criminals would try and do.

It felt like his entire brain were being bathed in a nice, warm bath.

I hid things… current casework, only I didn't call it that. I called it… my records. Where did I hide my records?

He moved quickly to the wardrobe and threw open the bottom drawer before pushing on the back of it. The end of the drawer shook when he pushed on it, revealing a false backing. Conners couldn't help but smile as he moved the panel, revealing a journal and several small notecards.

"At least this sounds like me," he said softly.

He pulled the journal out and began to pursue it, and it went into a detailed description of how his past self had tracked the movements of Kingston's men as they'd planned to rob a bank that had recently gotten a large shipment of small bills. He'd even made a note of the date of the robbery, but that was where the journal stopped. Conners couldn't remember what had happened, but given the context of the journal it wasn't the most difficult thing in the world to throw a decent guess at events.

He'd likely decided to go and stop the robbery himself, and been seriously injured at the scene, which would've caused his memory loss. It felt good to know this much about himself, but yet it was disheartening, because he still did not even know his own name.

Yes you do, said Bill. *Your name is Conners, regardless of what it might've once been.*

He wasn't exactly wrong. Whoever he had been wasn't the same as who he was now, even if there were a few similarities: the desire for a personalized form of justice for instance. He certainly could've discovered worse about himself. Suddenly, his brain sent an unpleasant niggle his way and he traveled back to the desk, picked up the picture of the couple, and examined it closer.

The woman looked to be in her early forties and had thick, black hair and grey eyes. She wore a bright smile for the camera and the ring glittering on her wedding finger indicated the relationship well enough. There was more to her face though. She had the same nose and lips as he did, and he could see something of his own ears in her picture. Her husband had Conners' blue eyes and strong jawline, and even the way he squinted reminded Conners of himself. Only he couldn't remember their names.

Still, he sat there and held a picture of his parents: people he'd always known and yet had never met. A tear appeared in his mind, like someone had split him. There was the (as of yet) unnamed him of the past, and there was Michael J. Conners: snarky detective of Chicago. These two men were at once entirely different and yet echoed one another. Both had a hunger for what they considered to be the right thing and were not shy about delivering their own version of that justice. Both were combat ready, and largely self-reliant.

However, his past self had been recluse and unsociable. Conners was loud and boisterous, even if much of it was just a show. His past self worked behind the scenes and relied on the police to actually arrest people and press the charges. Conners used the police to take on cases and spend time with Lawrence. His past self was estranged from everyone, including his own parents. Conners had made several friends, despite his efforts to the contrary. Something else struck him as he looked over the books that littered the shelves.

Conners carried the photo with him as he began to sort through the books until he found the one he'd been after. It was a well-worn bible with small golden letters in the corner that spelled out a name.

John Hatcher Black

He had been John Black... and John Black had been a Christian. This shook him thoroughly. Conners was an atheist. Rather, he was agnostic. He was at least unsure. Yet, John was a Christian and not just in name either. John had been adamant in his faith, regularly attending services and doing extensive research on his own. Peering around, Conners saw John had owned at least three bibles. The first he found was the King James Version, but he also owned a New Living Translation, and one in a copy of the original Greek.

I can read Greek? he thought, confused.

No, said Bill. *John could read Greek. You've barely seen enough to identify the language.*

Conners opened the bible and tried to read the lettering, but couldn't make heads or tails of any of it. Frustrated, he snapped it shut, and felt another twinge in the back of his brain.

Conners slowly turned the photo in his hands over to the backside. With shaking hands, he undid the latches on the back of the frame and slid the back of the photo out of place, where there sat a folded-over envelope.

The last letter I got from my parents.

John had cared a lot for this letter, enough to save it despite his anger with his parents. And John had been *angry* with them over… something. Why had he been so mad? He'd been mad enough to run off at the age of fifteen and get a G.E.D. before starting work and getting his own place. It wasn't horribly dissimilar from his life after escaping the hospital, although thankfully John had never gotten involved with dealing drugs and hadn't hurt a child.

Still, this letter had been important. Only, the letter wasn't there. The envelope was empty. Conners knew the letter was still somewhere, but it wasn't anywhere he could remember or access with his brain just then. Furious with his own brain he glanced at the front of the envelope where there was no clue as to the location of the letter, but there *was* a return address.

His parents' house: quite possibly his childhood home. Conners removed the envelope and picture and stuck both in his pocket before he turned and walked out of the room. There was plenty left to sort out in here, not least of all as to why The Watcher was wrapped up in all this, but at the moment, there was something even more important he had to do.

He pulled out his cell phone and dialed Joe's number.

Chapter XXXV: Parental Issues

Conners got out of the cab before he really looked carefully at the house it had brought him to. The house was a single story and had white siding while the windows had blue shutters. It was well-maintained. The lawn would be beautiful in the spring, and boasted a pathway that moved through the grass and alongside the small garden up to the front door. The address was emboldened on the mailbox in large, golden lettering that seemed vaguely familiar. Still, the side of him that was John gave up no memories of this place. He couldn't remember any afternoons spent with friends or his father. He couldn't see himself playing or running around the yard here.

He shivered in the cold and moved up the path, carving a set of footprints through the new snow as he walked carefully forward. Somehow, it felt as if he moved through a field of landmines instead of a carefully paved path.

"Conners?"

Tense as he already was, Conners leapt about a foot into the air and turned to see the Lawrence twins approaching him from her parked muscle car.

"What…" he began, thoroughly confused. "How did you find me?"

Jessica smiled softly, and he instantly wanted to kick himself for being curt with her hours after her mother had died.

"I saw you get into the cab, and Janice noticed how distracted you were. So, I called up Joe and asked him where his guy brought you and he gave me this address. What is this place?"

He paused for a moment, almost as if unsure of what to say, but then saw Lawrence's green eyes filled with trust, love, and a hope for the chance of an escape. He remembered Bill's death, and how desperate he'd been for the chance to do something: to keep moving. Besides, if there was anyone in the world he could talk to about this, it was her.

"I… I found my old apartment," he began.

Slowly, as if each word took a great effort, he explained everything to her. He showed her the text from The Watcher, told her about the Howling Wolf Apartments, described his old room in detail, and even went into the flashes he had gotten from his past life. Neither twin interrupted and both focused on him completely. Finally, he explained the photo and envelope he'd uncovered.

"This was the address on the envelope, and I... I need to see them."

Jessica nodded.

"Of course you do."

Conners examined her and decided on impulse that he was very glad she was here. She'd walked plenty of the hardest moments of his life with him. So, why shouldn't she be here for this one?

"Meet them with me?" he offered.

"Sorry?"

"Will you help explain everything to them with me? This is going to be plenty hard enough just on my own. I'd appreciate having you with me."

Janice awkwardly shuffled her feet before speaking up.

"I'd actually really like to go and grab a cup of coffee, Jess, if you want to stay. That way you and Conners can spend some time with them and I can get out of the cold at a shop or something."

"You sure?" Jessica asked, still full of worry.

"Of course," said Janice, nodding. "I can just grab a cab on the main road. It's not far."

The police sergeant nodded and turned to Conners, and took his hand.

Conners turned quickly to Janice and mouthed, "Thank you."

She smiled at him and nodded before she turned around and began the short trek to the main road to find a cab. He couldn't deny he would likely never be close with Janice like he was with her sister, but he *did* think she was a good person.

Moving as a pair, he and Lawrence finished the walk up the path to the little townhouse. He reached the door and rang the doorbell, now thoroughly nervous. What in the world did you say to a set of people who were probably your parents? What did you say to parents you hadn't seen for several years and couldn't remember? Conners felt the blood in his body rush to his biceps and thighs to prepare him to run or fight as needed. Next to him, Lawrence squeezed his hand for a second, and after he registered what she'd done, he reciprocated the gesture.

You're not going to run, Bill told him. *You need this, kid.*

Nevertheless as the doorknob turned, Conners felt himself try to turn and flee, but running was just as impossible as moving forward. So he sat there, frozen for what his brain turned into an eternity. The simple turn of the door handle took years for him to experience, all the while he sat in constant panic. The door eventually creeped open, and Conners looked unto the face of a couple in their fifties.

The man had a stern face and slightly crooked nose, and his eyes were a little more faded than they had been in the picture. He carried a cane and slouch that had not been present in the photograph. Conners suspected he was suffering from some type of nerve pain or damage, but it was unmistakably the same man. The woman beside him was even more recognizable than her husband. Her hair was still nearly the same shade and her jawline and nose were exactly as they had been.

For a long, long second no one spoke, but the man eventually broke the silence.

"John."

It was neither warm nor cold. It was a simple statement of fact, as if he were acknowledging the presence of a gust of wind. The woman bit her lip and looked as if she were on the cusp of tears.

"I… I don't… I shouldn't have come here," he said, and tried to turn away.

However, Lawrence had a firm grasp on his hand and she refused to let him move.

"You're ok," she muttered.

He took a deep breath and tried again.

"I'm… Could we come in, please? There's a lot I have to say and it will be easier if we could sit down."

The man nodded and stepped back, and as he did Conners got another flash from John. Vito: His father's name was Vito Carnell Black. He turned to his mother expectantly, and likewise he got the flash. Lydia: Lydia Nicole Black. Vito and Lydia were his parents, and he hadn't seen them for more than ten years. No wonder Vito was so stern and Lydia looked as if she were about to burst.

"Can I get you both anything?" she asked, her voice shaking. "Tea, water, hot chocolate?"

"Whiskey?" offered Vito.

"Hot chocolate for the both of us would be great, thank you," said Lawrence, still firmly gripping his hand.

Conners walked into his childhood home. The living room they entered had a deep brown carpet that bore small marks and stains from its years of use. They still had their Christmas tree out and propped up in a corner, along with several decorations throughout the house. He got a flash from John that involved them all decorating the house for a day or two every year. The tree in particular was a pain. It was one of those that had to be assembled and every year they'd struggled to try and put it together. Every year Vito swore they'd just buy an actual tree the following year.

The memory made him smile, but he could feel the part of him that was John grow equally angry at the memory, because Vito had done something. What was that? Why couldn't he remember the act, only the anger? No doubt John's anger and leaving had caused the rift in the family, but Conners couldn't remember what it was.

Vito led them into the kitchen through a large archway. The kitchen had blue-tiled floors and wood-paneled walls. Their equipment was decent—nicer than anything Conners owned at any rate. The simple oak table was surrounded by four chairs and had a laptop that was a few years old in the center of it. As far as Conners could tell, it was the only computer they had, and he hadn't spied an internet modem anywhere in the living room.

"Here you are dears," said Lydia, setting the drinks on the table. "I'm sorry honey, I didn't catch your name."

"Jessica Lawrence," Lawrence supplied, smiling softly. "I'm a close friend of your son's. I'm here to help explain where I can. He's... been through a lot."

"He's not the only one," said Vito, sitting across from Conners and Lawrence. "How do you want to start, son?"

The word hit Conners far harder than he thought it should've. He felt a combination of longing, loss, hope, love, anger, and betrayal all from that singular syllable. So, he took a deep breath and looked at Lawrence. She nodded. It was a simple gesture, but told him that she wouldn't abandon him here.

"Nearly seven years ago, I woke up in a hospital and couldn't remember a single detail of my life. Somehow I'd been hit hard enough to suffer total amnesia."

So he explained. He didn't leave anything out except his shooting of the child. *That* he was still too ashamed of to mention, even to his parents. But something strange happened as he thought of it. The part of him that was John Black grew furious at the thought of Conners' act of murder: far angrier than it was with Vito. So, had the old man betrayed some of John's sense of justice? It was possible.

He filed the thought away for later use and continued his story, explaining about Bill and becoming a private detective. He explained about Bill's murder and Kelsey Richards. He explained his friendship with Lawrence and even described a few of his cases. When he described his and Bill's work to shut down Yusuf's cult, Lydia put her hand to her mouth.

"He's worked with us a lot too," said Lawrence, when he paused to drink some of the hot chocolate. "Sort of became a goto consultant for our station, and was even a cop for a time."

Cop.

The word resinated with him: not with Conners, but with John. John was really angry at a cop... and then it clicked for him. Vito had been a cop, for quite a few years too. But he'd done something... betrayed the law in some way. Vito was dirty. He had trouble remembering exactly what it was they'd discovered. He and his father had been arguing over the moral code against the letter of the law.

Then Vito revealed he'd done something very bad. He'd been bought off by a mobster quite a few times to look the other way or mislead investigations. Vito had never stopped a murder investigation but had let several robberies and racketeering charges become lost in the cold case files. He'd taken bribes to mislead officers and his bosses. He'd accepted payment in exchange for "missing" a couple of high-profile collars. Vito had given plenty of excuses.

Do you have any clue how hard it is to raise a family on a cop's salary?

Corruption starts slow, son.

Plenty of cops do that sort of thing. If families were going to get paid for it, I was going to make sure ours was on the better end of things.

That was the part of Vito that made John so angry. He hadn't been able to make peace with it. While he'd never gone after Vito or turned him in, neither had John been able to live with the old man after learning what had paid for the house. John's sense of what was right had led to multiple arguments, which had created a huge wedge, and eventually left nothing but years of silence between them. If it hadn't been for his experience as Conners, he likely still would've felt the same.

However, he was *not* the same person he'd been more than a decade ago. He'd been through more than his fair share of moral conflicts and he'd killed a child. Conners knew he wasn't the best person to measure up moral shortcomings, but child murder must outweigh looking the other way on a mob's money schemes. There was a secondary aspect to it, too. Conners was trying to atone for his sins, instead of hiding behind excuses. He certainly wasn't innocent, but neither did he forgive his own sins.

Vito stood up slowly, using his cane for support.

"I need to go out and smoke for a minute," he said to Lydia. "Need to think about this."

"Vito!" she scolded him.

"No mom," said Conners, the word feeling foreign in this mouth. "It's all right. I need to get some fresh air for a second myself."

She stared at him for a long moment.

"And you'll be back?"

"Right afterwards. Promise."

She nodded and led Lawrence into the living room where the two of them sat and on the couch and began talking in hushed voices so that neither he nor Vito could overhear them. Conners followed his father outside and the pair of them huddled on the porch. In almost perfect unison, they simultaneously lit up a cigarette. He noted with amusement that they smoked the same brand.

"Wasn't sure we'd ever end up seeing you again," said Vito, somewhere between relief and an accusation. "We didn't part well."

"I remember," said Conners. "At least bits and pieces. I'm getting more and more recently. You were a dirty cop."

It was a statement of fact and not an accusation, and Vito didn't disgrace them by denying or defending it.

"I don't know if you recall, but we fought when you left. Argued about your leaving until it came to blows. You broke a mirror over my shoulder and I threw you over the porch here."

He jabbed at a spot of the railing with his cane. Conners tried to remember, and he got the flashes. A lot of shouting before John and seen red and lashed out with a punch, which had turned into a brief but furious fight between the two men.

"Mom screamed at us the whole time," Conners said, slowly. "And I landed in her rosebush. I was pulling out thorns the rest of the day."

He smiled slightly at that. It wasn't exactly funny, but there was so much darkness in all of this already that he didn't think he could bear to be angry or grim anymore. Vito smiled a little next to him and Conners could see the pain and exhaustion behind the smile. Vito was a stern and sometimes harsh man, but he did care. He missed his son likely just as much as his wife did. Conners suddenly felt a pang of guilt that he couldn't give them John Black back.

"I don't know what the next step is," said Vito, exhaling a puff of smoke.

"Doubt there's a *Reconnecting Your Family After One of You Has Amnesia for Dummies*. Look dad, I know you've done some bad stuff, but you're not alone in that and while I still disagree with what you did, I don't know that I have the right to punish you or mom for it. If you were still a detective I might force you to retire but as you already have… I don't know. It's not like you were embezzling millions or anything, but I don't like what you did."

"*Force* me to retire?" asked Vito, surprised. "Do you think you could've?"

Conners considered the question for a long moment.

"As John? Probably not, no. Now? Yeah, I think so. I've learned to be a much bigger pain in the ass now. Just ask Lawrence."

"I'm inclined to agree with that," said Vito, taking another drag on the cigarette. "Lawrence… You talk about her like a wife, and like a partner. But you don't wear a ring."

"We're not together… not romantically, but we're best friends and partners. She's been there for most of what I mentioned since Bill's death."

"Can't say I knew him personally, but I did hear about a William Scott. He liked to work active cases and homicides more than most private investigators did. Was supposed to be a right bastard too."

"He was," said Conners fondly.

"Good," said Vito. "You needed someone to show you how to have some backbone for what you do. I'm glad you didn't let the world steamroll you over. So, if you're not going to arrest me, what happens now? We disappear from each other's lives again?"

"No," said Conners. "I don't think that's best for any of us. I know we can't exactly pick up where we left off. There's a lot of pain there. But, I think we could try to do a day at a time."

They both puffed again and Vito nodded thoughtfully.

"I could do that."

"Good, then I'm going to had back inside because it is actually freezing out here and I do have a thing I'll have to handle this afternoon."

His thoughts turned to The Watcher, and what it was he could want from Conners. The Watcher had always been something of a double-edged sword, more than once proving helpful, but he certainly wasn't an altruist in Conners' life. He was at least responsible for Miller's murder. He wanted something... or was getting something in his having gone to the apartments, even if it was as simple as the pain Conners was now in. He'd always been afraid to know his family. The answers were both far better and darker than he'd hoped for.

"We *should* head back in," said Vito. "Who knows what your mother and your friend are getting into."

"Something extremely embarrassing, no doubt."

Conners led the way back in after they put out their cigarettes and tossed them in a nearby trash bin. As they entered, Lawrence grinned brightly at him.

"That look never means good things for me," he said, just loud enough for her to hear.

"You're fine," she said. "I was just going into some detail on how we met."

"You should know better than to treat a lady that way, John."

Conners winced and decided to bite back the retort that he obviously wouldn't remember being taught better.

"It's all right, Lydia. I've been teaching your boy, bit-by-bit."

Lydia stood up and embraced Conners. He involuntarily stiffened, his body reacting as if he were under attack. If she noticed his discomfort, his mother gave no sign. After a long second or two, she released him and both she and her husband sat down. Conners took one of the empty armchairs, examining the couple more out of habit than anything else. Lawrence stood and walked up to him.

"How are you?" she whispered.

"Well enough. The hard part's out of the way at any rate. Think we just need to iron some stuff out at this point. You want to go catch up with your sister?"

"Yeah, we still have things to work out about mom's funeral and everything."

"Of course... Lawrence? Thanks for being here. It meant a lot."

He stood and embraced her tightly, trying to let the gesture carry his appreciation for her in it.

"I've always got your back," she whispered.

"I know, and I've got yours."

They separated and she turned to say goodbye to his parents.

Chapter XXXVI: Purged by Flame

Not long after Lawrence left, Conners exited his parents' house. He was too exhausted to consider talking anymore. Somehow, the process of meeting his parents was both more rewarding and far worse than he'd hoped it would be. He still didn't know what to think about his father. Between the parts of him that upheld the law and the part of John that yearned for justice, he almost wanted to arrest the man. But the fact was he didn't have it in him to do it. At least Vito had retired. It wasn't as if he was going to continue being a threat to anyone.

Even in that, he could hear the justification: the excuse. But the fact was, he didn't have it in him to shut down that relationship again. It meant something to him to have a father, even if it was something he couldn't clearly define. It seemed an unusually cruel part of life to have to shut that relationship down again after only just rediscovering it. It had taken the majority of his time with them, but Vito had relaxed and warmed up a little. Now, the three of them had plans to have dinner in a few days, but Conners wanted to wrap up his business with The Watcher first.

He had originally decided to ride back to the Howling Wolf Apartments with Lawrence and Janice, but Lawrence's car was gone and she wasn't answering her cellphone. He mentally made a note to find a way to thank Joe for his service and ordered his fourth cab ride that day. His mind spun like a top as he watched the remaining rays of daylight vanish behind the towering skyscrapers that formed the city skyline. His entire life he'd lived in this city and it felt like he'd barely scratched the surface of all it had to offer him. Maybe it was impossible for one person to change anything for everyone, but he *was* changing everything for a few select people… Perhaps that could be enough.

When did I become some shitty philosopher?

As he mused he felt his phone vibrate in his pocket and felt a small surge of excitement. Letting his weariness and confusion fade away he answered the phone.

"Lawrence!" he said and let out a sigh or relief. "I was getting worried."

However, the voice that reached him from the other line didn't belong to Lawrence at all.

"Hello detective."

It was a low, slinking voice, and belonged to a man. John reared up in him and gave the voice a name instantly.

James Kingston.

All at once the memories of Kingston and The Watcher collided and Conners realized just who The Watcher was. It explained how he'd always known who Conners was. It explained his key advice in relation to mob activity. Kingston had been guiding him since he'd arrested Richards. John showed him flashes of an attack in a bank where Kingston had viciously beaten John down.

He put us in the hospital, Conners half-realized, half-remembered. *He tried to kill us, and thought he had succeeded until he saw us on the news. He wanted to kill us, but knew we would've made records about it. He had our wallet. So he knew our old address, but he couldn't find the books or hack the computer files. So he decided to show me where it was so I could show him. I did it too. I was so distracted by my damn parents that I left the notebook behind.*

I did everything he expected we would do.

Kingston's voice came through his earpiece again.

"Hope you weren't expecting to reach your friend. Afraid she's a bit tied up at the moment."

He heard muffled screaming and felt his blood run cold. Even without words to back it, he recognized Lawrence's pitch and tone. He was less than two blocks from the apartment but he already knew he wouldn't be able to run there any faster than the cabbie was driving. Anxious, he gripped the phone so hard he almost cracked the screen, urging the car to move faster so he could help Lawrence.

Kingston wasn't a man who took to idle kidnappings or threats. If he'd taken Lawrence he either meant to torment her or kill her. His only hope of extending her life was that Kingston might want to kill her in front of him. If he was right, it meant he might just have a chance…

"If you hurt her…" he began, but never got to finish his threat. *Bang!*

A gunshot from the other line killed the words in his mouth.

"Your apartment, John. Don't worry, you'll join your police girlfriend shortly."

Conners felt ice-cold, as if he'd been dropped in the lake. Lawrence surely wasn't dead. This was some trick: some coincidence. He didn't even know the woman Kingston had taken *was* Lawrence. Why wouldn't Lawrence answer her phone? She had been too present in his life to begin to imagine she might be gone.

Yet, the seconds dragged on, and he could find no other possible solution. Lawrence hadn't been answering his calls, then Kingston had called and made *sure* that Conners heard the screaming and the shot and the silence. He felt the dread and despair begin to ebb away as a pure rage engulfed him.

Kingston killed Lawrence.

He *killed* Lawrence.

There was no justice or reason in that. Kingston had killed her because she'd been his friend. It was exactly the type of thing John knew Kingston would do, and he could feel the old wounds on the back of his skull where Kingston had repeatedly bashed it on the marble floors of a bank several years ago. They burned almost as hot as his rage.

Conners forced himself to breathe—to think. It was the one tool he would have as an advantage. He couldn't undo what had been done to Lawrence, but he *could* end things. Lawrence would've said to arrest Kingston. She would've even helped do it herself if she could've, not that it would've mattered. Kingston had plenty of money, power, and legal defenses to stave off any criminal charges and clearly wasn't afraid of killing anyone who wouldn't be bought or intimidated. He was going to have to purge the earth of anything to do with Kingston.

Calmly, as if it were as simple as mentioning a need for some food, Conners asked the cabbie to bring him to the gas station on the corner of the same street as the Howling Wolf Apartments. The driver didn't appear to think twice about it, and Conners walked inside to the disinterested glance of a store clerk who had smoked a joint out back only minutes earlier.

Much larger fish to fry right now, kid, said Bill.

Conners nodded to himself before acting. Without betraying anything, he bought and filled two large gas canisters. He walked the distance from the gas station to the apartments, relishing in the freezing winds and letting them cool his hot blood. The part of him that was John recalled the water boiler on the ground floor, and gave him his plan. The front door was already ajar and as much as he wanted to kick it in, Conners forced himself to remain quiet, and slid into the apartments like a snake. Quiet as he could, he walked over to the water boiler and pulled the release tab on side. The water was steaming. The steam held possibilities, but the water itself was all he cared about.

As the water pooled and puddled on the floor, Conners removed his coat and hung it on a protruding nail by the front door. Then, as calmly as if he were actually a janitor, he opened a nearby supply closet and unearthed a dirty old mop. He poured the one of the gas cans out entirely and began to mix it with the water. The mixture smelled foul, but covered a large base of the old wooden floorboards. Then, Conners took the other can and soaked the front desk, his hanging coat, and the aging boiler in the gas. He would burn the devil to death tonight.

Purge it all with holy fire, he thought, grimly.

When he was satisfied with his work, Conners moved up the stairs to room eighteen. The door was slightly ajar, and Conners pushed it open. The room was almost just as it had been, but two figures were in the kitchen: one standing and one lying on the ground. He moved forward in deliberate and controlled steps. It was clear there was nothing to be done for Lawrence. Even from this distance he could see the shot to the back of her head and her cold, dead eyes.

He felt as if those eyes, even in death, were staring right at him. He couldn't look away, and the rational part of his mind left him. He knew in that moment if he lived to be over a hundred, he would never forget that stare. In what was several years for him, though only a couple seconds to the rest of the world, he managed to tear his gaze away from Lawrence's body.

The other figure was James Kingston, the ex-executive and mafia don. Kingston was only about five years older than Conners was, and wore an expensive, tailored suit with a blood-red coat. His brown eyes had deep bags under them and his hair was slicked back and tall. His body was slim but with a display of muscle that left no doubt he'd once been a much more intimidating figure. Conners turned his gaze back to Lawrence.

"I'm sorry," he whispered, even though he knew she couldn't hear him.

She'd deserved better. She'd deserved so much more. She'd been his best friend and the only person he'd really confided in, even more than Bill. She'd saved his life more times than he could've counted and he would've stopped the earth from spinning if she'd needed him to. Only he'd failed her. Why hadn't he made her stay at his parents? Why hadn't he left *with* her?

Focus! he heard Bill chastise him. *Pity and grief later, kid. Right now, we have an enemy.*

Conners nodded, turning to Kingston. Kingston for his part, was busy perusing John's old notebook with a calm air.

"Rather impressive research Mr. Black."

"I'm going to kill you," said Conners, firmly but without any harshness. "You're not leaving here alive."

That made Kingston look up and snap the notebook closed.

"All these years, and you're still no fun. Your friend was same way. She shouted and shouted about…"

Conners didn't let Kingston finish, and kicked out as high and hard as he could. The mafia leader hadn't been expecting the blow and it caught him on the chin. It sent him backward into the little table that lay there. Not giving him a chance to recover, Conners leapt forward and pulled up an ink pen that rested atop a piece of paper on the table. Kingston started to push him away and Conners stabbed the man in the armpit with his makeshift weapon. The pen broke in his hand, but it did puncture Kingston's clothing and body.

With a hiss like a feral cat, Kingston shoved Conners away and reached behind his back for a pistol. Quickly, Conners ducked into the living room and slid into the bedroom as Kingston loosed two bullets into the wall.

Bang! Bang!

"Come out and fight then!" shouted Kingston, chasing Conners into the bedroom.

In the brief extra second he had, Conners snatched up John's old acoustic guitar and swung it like a baseball bat as Kingston emerged. His first blow sent the gun skidding across the carpeted floor of his living room, and his second broke Kingston's nose. Conners smiled inwardly. All Kingston would smell now was the blood pouring from his nose, if even that much. There was no chance he would smell the gas Conners had poured downstairs. With a scream that expressed all his pent up loss and anger, Conners tackled Kingston, sending both of them flying down the stairs. Kingston grabbed Conners' right leg as they fell and twisted it hard enough to sprain it, but Conners didn't feel any bones break. Nevertheless it wouldn't support his weight anymore.

It didn't matter, they hit the ground floor and began wrestling furiously. Here, Kingston gained the upper hand, but Conners wasn't focused on causing damage. Instead, he did his best to soak every inch of Kingston's body in the gasoline and water that had puddled on the floor. Kingston was hardly a pushover and twice he hit Conners hard enough to give John flashbacks to the bank robbery he'd attempted to foil.

Focus!

He swung around Kingston and planted the killer's face into the gas, pushing down on the back of the man's head with his good leg. Kingston struggled for a good long second, and Conners almost thought he would be able to smother him to death then and there, but Kingston twisted and sent Conners rolling away. Using the momentum, Conners rolled towards his coat and stood up slowly, breathing heavily. It wasn't the worst fight he'd ever had, but this next part was going to hurt.

"You're not half bad, Black. At least this time you're giving me a proper fight. Glad to see you learned something after all."

"I told you. I'm going to kill you. I'm not an agent of justice tonight. Not after you killed Lawrence."

Kingston smirked.

"Well then, any last wishes before I kill you properly this time?"

"Just one," Conners said, and reached in the jacket, fishing for his lighter. "Burn in hell!"

He flicked the lighter, still in the coat and instantly the coat exploded in a rush of heat and light. He threw it at the desk as fast as he could, diving out of the door into the snowy street. Even so, he could feel the flames and heat coating his body. With what remained of his willpower, Conners rolled around in the snow, relying on the water as much as the smothering to put out the flames. The entire right half of his body burned so much he actually felt freezing cold.

It hurt so much he felt himself slowly drifting into unconsciousness. Before he completely blacked out, he was dimly aware of two things. The first was the night was full of strange lights flashing different colors, even if he couldn't place them at the moment. The second far more important fact was the entirety of the

Howling Wolf Apartments were aflame, and even in his pain Conners could hear Kingston screaming from inside.

Finally, Conners allowed his grief over Lawrence's death, his exhaustion from the battle, and the pain from his wounds overtake him. He allowed the blackness at the edge of his vision to bring in the welcoming void of unconsciousness.

Chapter XXXVII: The Man on the Bus

Darkness…

That was his first thought: everything was dark. He knew he existed, but couldn't remember who or what he was: only *that* he was. He wasn't in pain, or feeling anything outside of his body at the moment. Concentrating on his body he found it was familiar to him. It was a body he knew and had used for a very long time, he felt.

So, he thought to himself. *I am, and I am a physical being. Surely as a being I have something I am called. So what is it?*

He pondered on this for a very long moment. He wasn't entirely sure time existed here. He understood what time was, which meant he was at least from a place where it did. He thought harder on harder on his title, and eventually two came to him almost simultaneously.

One was John Hatcher Black: Christian, vigilante, security guard, musician, social recluse.

One was Michael J. Conners: private detective, a publicly liked figure, belittler of authority, murderer.

He had been all of these things, some moreso than others.

He saw snippets of their lives. He was the drug-dealers and street thieves John would eliminate. He saw the murderers and lawbreakers Conners put an end to. He saw John's self-righteousness turned arrogance. He saw Conners' murder of a child and later James Kingston. Neither being was perfect, and both were incomplete reflections of one another. He wasn't sure he liked either of them, and yet they had both been him.

With that thought, he felt something come into existence beneath him. In that same moment there was an orientation and a gravity to go with it. He saw rows of seats and an open isle in the middle along with several poles.

Bus, he thought to himself. *I am on a bus.*

He looked around curiously, but there was no driver and he couldn't make out anything through the windows that lined the bus. However, there were other passengers on the bus with him. No one was talking or doing much of anything, in fact. The passengers were varied and many. He realized the bus was a very, very long one. There was even a flight of stairs leading up to at least a second level.

We are all on this bus, he thought. *So where are we going?*

Curiously he turned to the elderly woman on his left. She had red curly hair that didn't pass her shoulders and glasses on her wrinkled face. She sat slightly hunched over and her hands were boney and slightly curved, as if used to gripping a walker.

"Hello," he said, his voice croaky and hallow, as if it hadn't been used for many years.

She didn't respond. In fact, she gave no indication whatsoever she had heard him. He felt slightly nervous, but tapped her on the shoulder. Again, she gave no reaction at all, and he even nudged her with his foot. There was no response.

"She's not talking to you," said a man standing across the isle from him. "Actually, she can't."

He turned his attention to the man and examined him. The man had the olive-colored skin of the middle-easterners, and wore white pants and a white button-up shirt. A dark, curly bush of hair encircled his head and a matching beard sat prominently on his chin. Yet, it was the eyes that were easily this man's most notable feature. They were vibrant green, and more full of life and beauty than any forest or gem could ever hope to be.

The man were staring at him as if he were the man's long-lost child, finally found after decades of being presumed dead. However, this man appeared hardly older than he was. The middle-eastern man was in his early thirties at the latest.

"Who are you?" he asked the man. "Why can you talk to me if she can't?"

"To answer the second," said the man, smiling softly. "It is because I am here to talk to you. She is here for the journey. I will have time to talk to her, but for now I am here for you. As far as the first: I am the man who is here to speak with you. I am more concerned about who you are."

He thought about this for a second and shrugged.

"I do not know. I should know, but I don't."

"Should you?" asked the man, kneeling to retrieve a white bowl and rag.

"I would think so."

Without asking, the man in white clothing reached for him, and took his left foot in his hand. He wanted to push the man away, but knew he shouldn't. The man washed his foot with the water and rag before washing his right. The ritual was practiced and gentle, as if it were being preformed for a child by a loving mother. Then, in the same way the green-eyed man washed his hands. When he finished, he placed the bowl back down and stood up to grab the pole again.

"Why did you do that?" he asked the man.

"Why did I?" the man asked, as if earnestly posing the question. "What reason did I have for that?"

"Well obviously my hands and feet were dirty," he said, staring into the bowl, which had become filled with dirt and grime he hadn't noticed he'd been carrying. "But you didn't have to do that for me."

"Didn't I?" he asked, suddenly serious. After a long second or two, the man sighed. "Everyone's hands and feet are dirty when they first meet me. So, I cleanse them of their dirt and of the earth they carry with them. They need to be cleaned and cleansed for where they're going."

"They're going somewhere very important," he said, not asking. "Am I going there, too?"

The man considered it very seriously for at least a minute before he spoke again.

"That depends on you. You have earned some rest, haven't you?"

He thought back over John's life and Conners' life.

"I don't know I agree," he said softly. "I didn't always do that well."

Now the man laughed, and while it was mirthful, it was not cruel. In fact, it reminded him of the chimes they would play at Christmas time.

"Now if that isn't the summary of mankind in a nutshell. Everyone falls short sometimes. I am more concerned with where you rose up. Tell me—and forget about Conners' desire for absolution and John's desire to overcome his father's sin—are you ready to rest?"

He considered it, and as he did, he looked closer at the man's hands. They were not especially remarkable hands. They bore the callouses of a construction worker, the marks of an experienced fisherman, and the slight tan of someone who spent most of their days outside. Yet, the most notable part was the mark in each of the palms. It was about an inch wide, and stood at the base of both of his thumbs. Without realizing he was even looking for it, he found a similar mark on the man's feet, just above the toes. The part of him that had been John's life almost screamed aloud, and he had a name for the man.

"Jesus."

The Son of God nodded, smiling lovingly.

"Tell me: do you think you are ready to rest?"

The question rang in him for less than a second before he responded, "Is there more for me to do?"

"That is what they put into you. John sought an evening of the scales, but knew my name. Conners sought justice, and was estranged to me. There is much work I have for you to do. Much of it will be hard, but much of it will also bring you joy. Yet, it is a choice to walk that path, and the choice must be yours. I cannot make it for you. So, I ask again: Are you ready to rest?"

"No... I am willing, but not ready—not so long as you have more I need to do."

Jesus smiled at him.

"And for that I am very proud of you. Just remember, even in the darkest valleys and loneliest nights I shall be with you and I love you."

Jesus reached up and tugged the rope to signal the bus to stop. Slowly, the rumbling bus came to a stop and the door at the front opened. Carefully, he stood and walked to the front of the bus, and saw it opened up into complete darkness. There was nothing to alleviate the utter black, no stars and no candle. He was at once extremely frightened and wanted nothing more than to remain firmly in his seat on the bus. Aside from that, he knew that The Son was with him and watching him. So, he took a deep breath and stepped off the bus into the darkness.

At once, he tumbled down and started to go into a free fall. There was a great deal of wind rushing past his head and his stomach dropped as he fell faster, and faster, and faster. He knew at some point soon he must hit terminal velocity, but he didn't. He simply started to move faster and faster until the wind made it impossible to even squint, not that there had been anything to look at anyway.

Blind, he began tumbling head over heel until he was spinning and plummeting with no understanding of where he was, what was happening, or where he was going. He had only one option which was a surrender himself to the movement and trust the fall wouldn't kill him... if he could even die. Then, something struck him.

Wham!

It was not dissimilar to being hit in the chest with a baseball bat and it sent a surge through his entire body. Strangely the feeling brought something to him he hadn't felt since before the bus: pain. His chest hurt. His right arm and leg hurt too, far worse than his chest did, as if someone had dunked half his body in acid. However, as he was both fascinated and horrified by the arrival of the pain, whatever it was hit him again.

Wham!

Angrily, he flailed around, hoping to hit whatever it was that struck him, but his fist and feet met nothing but air.

Wham!

His entire chest began to burn too, especially his heart. As he kicked out hard, he was hit again.

Wham!

Then there was a noise, and it took him a long second to understand what it was he was hearing.

Beep... Beep... Beep...

It was the sound of a heart monitor.

As that singular realization hit him, he felt the fall stop, as if he hit something, but he hadn't felt the impact. There was no crash and no new pain. As in response, the existing pain in his chest and right limbs did quadruple itself. He couldn't help but scream out in pain. It hurt so much worse than any pain he'd ever endured. He could hear people talking, but couldn't make sense of what was happening or what they were talking about. He only knew that moments later, even through the pain he started to get extremely drowsy, and his exhaustion overtook him and he feel into a dreamless sleep.

~*~

Bright...

That was his first thought as he tried to open his eyes: everything was really, really bright. It was like someone had turned the exposure up on his vision. He forced himself to blink several times, and slowly the giant white blur began to take form and shape around him. He was also aware he was lying down, even if he didn't quite know how. The pain he'd felt was still present, but it was now a much duller, aching kind of pain instead of the intense burning he'd felt as he fell. His left hand was also itching slightly. He tried to scratch it with his right arm, but couldn't move it.

Frustrated with this, he attempted to move his left hand to his right, but stopped when something pulled against it like a tether. Slowly turning his head, he saw there was a bandage on the back of his left hand with a clear tube leading to it.

An IV, he heard Bill say in his head. *You're in the hospital, kid.*

He nodded, even though he was really agreeing with his own observation, and looked over at his other side. His right arm and leg were wrapped in several bandages and hung, slightly suspended above the bed he lay in. He also felt and saw the slightly green hospital gown someone had dressed him in. Relaxing, he let his mind run a diagnostic on his physical condition.

- *Status: Alive, but injured.*
- *Brain function: Lowered, but increasing.*
- *Notable injuries: Right arm and leg suffering second-degree burns, but pain is dulled with morphine. Right leg is suffering at least two breaks and several lacerations.*
- *Extreme exhaustion.*

Well, he thought, dully. *Not the first time I've been in bad shape.*

Yeah, said another voice in his head. *Almost like I told you that you do stupid and risky things. You're an idiot.*

The voice brought a tear to his left eye, and he felt a strange combination of relief and grief at it.

Hey Lawrence.

Talking to yourself is the first sign of madness, Conners.

I'm talking to a version of my best friend and a father figure who live in my head as a method of grieving. I think we checked that madness box a long time ago.

"He's awake!" he heard a voice and brought himself back to the waking world. "John!"

He internally winced. He had no idea what to call himself any longer. He wasn't who he'd been when he was Conners, yet he grown far beyond John. Still, he knew the name was meant to refer to him. So he responded by glancing in the direction of the voice.

Lydia stood beside his bed in a styled shaw and what was likely a fashionable shirt; he honestly couldn't be sure. She carefully reached out and placed a hand on his right shoulder and he did his best to smile, but he could feel his mouth was lopsided and it probably looked more horrifying than comforting. He heard clambering and saw Vito moving as quickly as he could to get out of the chair he'd occupied and move up to his child's bedside.

"How are you, son?"

Son.

It felt great to hear that word, and yet it was also horrible, because it brought all his mixed feelings about Vito to the front of his mind.

You're hardly in a position to cast stones there, said Bill. *You've committed murder, kid.*

He winced at Bill's accusation, because there was no hiding from it. He was a murderer, five times over now. He shot a child because he'd wanted to deal drugs. He killed two of Hunter's men to save himself. He killed one of Kingston's men at the house because he was a cop-killer and it was the simplest solution. Finally, he'd burned Kingston to death because he'd shot Lawrence.

I'm a serial killer.

The thought chilled him and he began to wonder if dying wouldn't have been the more humane option. He remembered talking to a man who had washed his feet and hands. The man hadn't mentioned his sins. He hadn't accused or condemned him. He'd only spoken about his future and his task.

Here and now, he prayed mentally. *I repent of my sins. I do not deserve redemption or grace, but I will ask for it anyway. Give me my task Father, and I shall commit myself to it.*

He heard no reply, but felt a slight comfort that made the weight only a little easier to hold. He didn't mind the weight though, because it served as a reminder. He had to take all of his past to move forward. He couldn't be the arrogant fool that had been John, and he couldn't solely rely on the cold analysis Conners had tried to achieve. He needed Conners' skill and John's morality. He needed Conners' action and John's faith. He needed them both and was determined to have them.

"Hey dad," he hissed and his voice was hoarse and raspy. "I feel like I fell out of a bus and got set on fire."

Vito had tears in his eyes but turned away to hide them.

"The doctors have done their best to help you," he said, wiping his face with a cloth. "You've been in a coma for a few days… So, I don't know what you remember."

He couldn't help but chuckle at that.

"I remember everything," he said, and it was true.

For the first time there were no blank spots about John in his life as Conners. Sure he didn't have a perfect memory of every event he'd experienced, but there weren't glaring blank spots anymore such as he'd had for the past several years.

"Who found me?"

"Anonymous call to the police. Apparently they heard gunshots in the apartment and Lieutenant Guston dispatched a unit to find you and your friend. They... they never found her. Is she..."

"Dead," he said, his voice hallow and soft.

"Oh dear," said Lydia, hugging him as best she could. "I'm so sorry."

"I'll explain everything when I talk to the lieutenant," he said to his father. "I'm sure he'll want to annoy me with everything, if he doesn't arrest me."

"He's... I don't know him like you do, but he's concerned about you," said Vito. "Says he's held off any official statement regarding your condition. Some rumors were going around that you died, but there hasn't been any live report from the news yet."

Conners couldn't help but compare this hospital visit with his waking up from a coma. The two incidents were completely the same and yet as different as could be. He leaned back into his pillow and squeezed his mother's hand. He had no idea what he was supposed to do next, but knew it was important he do it.

Part III: Rebuild

Chapter XXXVIII: Broken

Eight…

He summoned his strength and pushed with his legs again.

Nine…

Again.

Ten!

He nearly collapsed and moved off the leg press. He half-limped, half-hopped to the wall so he could lean against it and take some of the weight off his bad leg. It had been more than six months since Lawrence had died and he'd blown Kingston to hell. Most of his injuries had healed well, and luckily it didn't seem like he'd suffered any brain damage… at least not in a way that limited his problem-solving or ability to do things for himself.

The psychological toll had yet to cash itself in fully. He wasn't sleeping much: sometimes going two or three days without even bothering to lay on the bed in his room. Even when he did black out, his dreams hardly left him rested. Not that his waking hours were much better. He constantly found himself seeing visions of Kingston, Lawrence, Bill, Richards, Hunter, and the blonde child. Sometimes he found he was crying or his right hand would tremble and it took all his focus and will to stop either event.

PTSD

That's what the therapist called it. He'd read up on the condition casually. It was a frequent enough issue for veterans and policemen. He vaguely understood it from his time as Conners. He'd never really thought about applying the term to himself. He'd been *mostly* functional as the detective, so he'd never sought to change things. Now, he was lucky to get through breakfast without at least one interruption. He'd been promised time would help heal him so long as he kept working at it.

His right arm had healed well enough, although it was hard for him to grip things firmly with that hand and he'd had to learn to write and shoot left-handed. The right side of his forehead still showed some burn marks, but it hadn't hurt for a while.

What hadn't healed properly was his leg. According to the doctors, the broken bones and burns had completely healed, but it still hurt all the time and it was almost impossible to walk long distances without using a cane. Part of his treatment was physical therapy, and supposedly it would help him gain most of his function back. Never before did he think that he would come to hate the words "exercise bike" but he'd come to have a passionate loathing for that particular machine and all it represented.

However, he was at least able to dress himself and get around in a limited way. One annoying thing was despite John's experiences, he couldn't drive anymore. For whatever reason he'd developed a block for cars during his time as Conners and his body and brain could no longer work together to react and drive safely.

He hadn't even tried to approach casework since Lawrence's death, though it wasn't like he hadn't had the opportunity for work. Maybe three times a month, the lieutenant approached him to badger him with some interesting or complicated case, and every time he turned the lieutenant away. He wasn't still completely comfortable thinking of himself as either Conners or John. So, he'd taken to responding to whichever one people called him, but Conners felt closer to home than John did. Luckily, his regular visitor list consisted of three people: the lieutenant, and both his parents.

Lydia and Vito had been firm and demanded he move back into their house until he was fully able to care for himself and he hadn't been in much of a position to refuse. The idea of walking up the stairs above his old office everyday filled him with dread. He'd paid a company to transfer some of his furniture from above the office to his old bedroom, and he spent most of his days either in the room or doing his therapy.

Vito and Lydia did their best to help him resume some type of life, and it meant different things for both of them. Lydia tried to take care of him by cooking and helping him keep things a little organized despite his protests. Vito on the other hand took to trying to stimulate Conners' mind. The two often played chess or other strategy-based games against one another. This was something Conners appreciated, but he couldn't help but notice the manipulation behind the gesture. Vito clearly still carried a mixture of guilt and worry over John's leaving the family and Conners' injuries.

Twice, Conners had tried to broach the subject with him, but Vito was even worse than he was at dealing with emotional issues. He would turn somewhat curt when the conversation came up. As such, Conners found himself both grateful for his parents and trying to limit his interaction with them to only so much every day. His first idea had been to try and take walks and reabsorb the city as he had when he was a detective, but his bad leg made it an impossibility.

For a while, he'd found a nice little park and enjoyed watching people as they jogged and walked. His brain had lost none of its skill in slowing down and dissecting people or events. It was fun to analyze the passersby. That had been forced to stop when he seen a man meeting with a woman for an affair and his instincts meant he nearly leapt up to stop them. Luckily, the immediate pain in his leg had reminded him of who he was and who he no longer was.

He still spoke to Lawrence and Bill in his mind, and when he was honest with himself he knew it was because he couldn't bear never hearing their voices again. In his own twisted way, he still had them with him.

It's a poor substitute, kid, Bill said.

And you know it's not healthy, Lawrence added. *You're refusing to process the truth. We're gone. We can't come back.*

Conners shook himself violently and took a long pull off his water bottle before he began his limp back to the locker room to shower and change into his street clothes. He enjoyed the process of a hot shower and when he could afford it, soaking his leg in a warm bath helped alleviate the pain. For a while, he'd entertained the idea of swimming. On his first venture, his leg had seized up and nearly trapped him under the water. It brought back the fears of water he'd held as Conners, and he promptly swore he'd never go swimming again.

After his difficult trek into the showers, he flipped the water on and undressed while he waited for it to warm up. While the water took the sweat and dirt off his body, he let his mind unwind, carrying the stress and pain of his adventures down the drain along with the stink of his rehabilitation.

You need to find a way to get back to normality.

That was what the therapist had told him: back to normality.

The problem was he couldn't get back to something he'd never had, and normality was an inherently flawed concept anyway. It was considered normal to work as both a cabbie and as a business executive, for example. However, it would be insane to consider those two jobs equal to one another. So either one was normal and one was not, or neither was and the concept was inherently broken.

How could he pursue something he'd never known and couldn't even conceive of, and what would it provide him?

Was "normal" working as a bank clerk forty hours a week? To what end? He'd end up bored beyond service or use before he collected his first paycheck. Was it "normal" to pursue a life of adrenaline? What job would allow him that? It wasn't like he had any desire to be a police detective again. As much as he might have the skill for it, he was afraid to resume private detective work, and he was both too old and injured to become a soldier.

Are you ready to rest?

He remembered the question. It circled around and around in his head when he stared out the window and when he awoke in a cold sweat with the remains of his nightmares still at the forefront of his brain.

Are you ready to rest?

He hissed angrily and punched the wall of the shower with his right hand but only succeeded in bruising his knuckles.

"How am I supposed to work when I cannot find the place to start and have no idea where it could end?"

Without any reprieve or answer, he reached for the bar of soap and continued to clean himself.

When he walked out of the gym twenty minutes later—leaning heavily on his cane—he checked his phone and realized he'd received several texts from the lieutenant. Without reading them, he deleted the conversation and blocked the lieutenant's cell number. If he wanted Conners to solve cases and be the department golden boy: he didn't care. If it was anything actually important: he knew where Conners lived.

A few minutes later, Vito pulled up and Conners slowly lowered himself into the passenger's side of the car. Without actually solving cases, Conners felt a deep reluctance to rely on Joe's offered cab service, even though the man had never expressed a reluctance to continue using his drivers for Conners' needs. Luckily, with Vito and Lydia both being retired, they were willing to ferry him around with the little traveling he did, and it let them talk a little.

Rebuilding his relationship with his parents was extremely difficult. Without the formation of the years that were his late teens, he had re-entered their lives a partial stranger, even after regaining his memories. Sure, there were a few times they could remember different instances of his childhood and laugh together, but for the most part, they were very different people. It reminded him of the extreme difficulty he'd had making and maintaining more than a few friendships. If he'd never known who they were, he would never have engaged much with Vito or Lydia unless they were clients or criminals.

Now, he was forced to try and find some common ground beyond a past that was merely half of his life: most of which he was too young to recall. He wondered if most adults had this much difficulty maintaining a relationship with their families. What could they talk about after they'd recounted what parts of the past weren't painful anymore, especially when they disagreed on much of their views of the world? Be it religion, justice, family, politics, or the future, Conners rarely agreed with Vito on much of anything. The old wounds were still too fresh to push them beyond an uncomfortable silence.

So when they talked, it was often about nothing substantial. Conners didn't voice his struggles and frustrations with his parents, and they pretended they didn't realize how much he was struggling. His entire life with them was surrounded by lies. They did truly love one another, but beyond that there was no real connection to each other. Vito would pretend the advice he gave was reasonable and just, and Conners pretended to at least consider the advice as plausible. His mother pretended they were a close-knit family who could present a Christmas card picture to the world, and he pretended she understood who he was.

It was so different from what he'd had with Bill and Lawrence. With them, they'd seen through whatever lies he'd put up, and weren't afraid to break what existed. It was that attitude that made the relationships so valuable. When he'd been a wreck over Bill's death, Lawrence had borderline abducted him and tried to make sure he didn't do anything stupid, even if it was ultimately unsuccessful.

He stopped there, because thinking of Lawrence was painful.

"How'd the workout go today?" asked Vito, as they merged into the main lane of the traffic.

"Pretty well," he said, which was at least only a half-lie. "Slow process and all that."

"Well just keep with it. I mean, you didn't learn guitar in an afternoon."

"Right, right," he said, searching for something that would help speed the conversation along. "I think mom mentioned she was going to cook ham tonight."

Vito sighed softly.

"Well, all I can say is damn it."

That made Conners smirk. Vito wasn't fond of Lydia's cooking. Personally, Conners appreciated her food, and it tasted better than most anything he could've put together himself, but Vito appreciated restaurants and grilled food more than most of what she cooked. More than once, he wondered if their relationship was better than it had been when he'd moved out or if they merely tried not to argue when he could hear them. As a young teenager he could hear them arguing a lot, and often over issues that seemed completely unimportant. Once he'd heard his father scream from the other end of the house about the type of sod they were going to use for the lawn of the house.

John had always been amazed their marriage lasted, but in the end something must've been there for the pair of them because even after all this time, they were still together. Personally, he didn't think of their marriage as a great example or indicator, but it wasn't like he had all that much to compare it to. Maybe they were just a typical couple. Maybe that was all relationships were and he shouldn't expect anything different from them.

This didn't sit well with him. If relationships within mankind was nothing more than a collection of comforting lies, there was no genuine connection in man. If you couldn't be honest with someone, how could you confront them in love? True relationships *should* have an effect on people. Lawrence and Bill had both affected him as he'd affected them.

Vito let the silence remain for the rest of their car ride and Conners didn't bother trying to break it. Personally, he was hoping to find an excuse to retire to his room for the evening without offending Lydia. Problematically, they pulled up onto the driveway and Conners noticed the lieutenant's personal car sitting on the curb. He felt his irritation spike up. This would be the third time this month Guston would try to push some case on him, and Conners' patience for the man was quickly running out. For all the arguments they'd had while he was a private detective, the lieutenant certainly had displayed a lot of trouble letting Conners go.

As soon a Vito stopped the car, Conners hopped out and pushed forward as fast as he could with his bad leg, fully prepared to start yelling at the lieutenant if that's what it took to make him leave. He opened the door and saw the man sitting in the leather armchair in full uniform. Lydia was on the couch, and even from this distance, Conners could see that she was on the verge of crying.

Scowling he limped forward and called out to the policeman.

"This is insulting!" he said, surprising himself with the volume behind his words. "You presumably could find your own ass for at least a few years before I turned up, even if you had to sit on your own thumbs to do it! If you can't manage now, retire and let some brain-damaged pigeon have a try at the job!"

"John!" Lydia hissed.

Without a sign he'd heard Conners' outburst, the lieutenant stood up and removed a file from inside of his coat. Conners couldn't help but note the file was slightly older and more worn than most of the files he'd handled in his time as a police detective. It wasn't so crumbled as to be years old, but was at least a few months in, and there was a mark along the top that indicated a level of confidentiality.

Curiously, Conners looked at the lieutenant's face and saw a grim determination that wasn't usually present, even when he was asking for Conners' input on a case. It was that look more than anything that made Conners limp forward and reach for the file.

"For the four months after you were hospitalized," Guston began. "We kept receiving tips and evidence linking members of Kingston's mafia family to open cases, and sometimes they'd even be handcuffed when we got there. Someone had tied them up and left them like a present. Honestly, they were effective enough that we weren't in a position to look a gift horse in the mouth."

Conners looked over several of the pictures and logged evidence in the file. Whoever it was taking out Kingston's men clearly wasn't afraid of danger, but still held a strong sense of justice and the system of the law. It was the type of stuff John might've done if he'd had friends in the police department before he'd been injured.

"So why come to me?"

"What do you mean?" asked Guston.

"Well either you're content with what they're doing, in which case: let them keep doing it. Or for some reason you want to stop and arrest them, in which case: find someone else. The benefit of not being in your employ was the ability to refuse cases."

"We would be willing to continue to look the other way," said the lieutenant, tugging at his collar. "But a couple months ago the tips and arrests stopped and I'm concerned something might have happened. If we find this vigilante, we'll likely have to put a stop to what they're doing, even if they're not in danger. However, if someone outside the law were able to determine who it was and if they were in danger… it might be worth going to someone who's not afraid to bend the rules to do the right thing. That's why I need you."

"I seem to recall you and I being at odds over my willingness to bend the rules…"

"I can't deny, as an employee you caused me no ends of headaches and I hated you… a lot. But, as a consultant… I can't deny you were effective, and you're able to move in places we were sometimes handicapped. It's the kind of thing Bill would've wanted you to handle."

"Don't!" Conners said warningly, and almost reached for *Sherry* before he remembered he didn't have it on him anymore. "You don't know the first thing about him."

"I don't?" asked Guston, raising an eyebrow. "Conners, William Scott was my partner back when we were both detectives. We had a case, not worth going into details on it. Point was he did the thing he felt was morally right and I did what the law demanded I do. He helped us close cases and we helped keep him out of too much trouble. Why do you think I was so willing to let you join us when Lawrence asked? Bill wrote me a letter all about you."

"You were his partner?"

He… had a good mind but was too glued to the letter of the law. We had a case where morality and legality butted heads; you'll find a few of those. I did what I felt was right, and he couldn't deal with it. We came to blows over it. Never spoke to me again. I quit within the week to start up private practice. Stilts took him under his wing after that.

Conners could replay Bill's words almost perfectly. He didn't realize Bill had been talking about Guston. He'd never thought to ask. So Guston had known about him long before Lawrence had set up their meeting. When Guston looked at Conners, he saw a reincarnated form of Bill. He saw the same skill and same stubbornness.

Suppose his outrage wasn't entirely unjustified, even if I'd do the same thing again in a heartbeat.

He took in a deep breath and considered the case placed before him. His instinct was to shout at Guston to get out, but something stopped him.

Are you ready to rest?

The one question held him back. It forced him to really consider what he was looking at and the chance that was lain at his feet. He started to consider what he wanted, but Vito spoke out first.

"John doesn't owe you anything," he said, firmly. "You don't have the balls to do the right thing. So you have the gall to ask him to do it? Fuck that."

"My boy got blown up working with you," said Lydia, with far more bite in her voice than Conners was used to hearing. "I don't want the next time I see him to be on a hospital bed."

Conners held up his hand to stop them.

"Guys, I appreciate your concern. Still the truth is, he's right. Whoever was doing this was putting an effective stranglehold on Kingston's men, and they could be in real danger. If they are in trouble, the police can't get involved in the right way until they have real evidence. The warrants and leads will take too long. I might not be able to literally run along the city as I used to, but I can at least move my brain from place-to-place well enough."

Vito and Lydia looked at him and then at each other, both flashing looks of worry and concern.

"You're sure on this?" asked Vito, placing his hand on Conners' shoulder.

"I'm sure."

Chapter XXXIX: Stomping Grounds

Conners stretched around the makeshift office that had been set up by the lieutenant. It was actually a cleaning supply closet a couple of officers had cleaned out for him. A small desk and laptop had been added, and over the course of a month-and-a-half he'd papered the walls with different crime scene photos and several maps of the city to try and find a central dwelling location for this wayward vigilante.

Whoever had been delivering Kingston's men to the police was very careful though—far more than most people he'd had to track down. They never seemed to dwell anywhere for very long, preferring to move from place to place every couple of days. Twice he'd found an abandoned building that seemed like it likely could've been a squatting place, but they clearly hadn't been there for some time.

Sighing, Conners took a long drink of the poor excuse for coffee the precinct provided. It was bitter and was flavored in a way he'd come to have a strong distaste for. Some people appreciated flavored coffees and syrups, like Lawrence. Conners had never been able to stomach the coffee she preferred, even if she did make wonderful hot chocolate.

Focus, he heard her tell him and he scowled at himself while he tried to clear his mind.

"Be helpful or go away!" he shouted and flung a coffee mug at her visage.

The mug passed straight through her and shattered against the wall. The pieces fell in a pile and he could've counted them in midair as his brain sent a burst of adrenaline through him when the shattering sound sent a jolt of panic through him. It took his rational mind several minutes to calm his frantic body.

He reached up with his left hand and idly tugged at the collar of the borrowed police uniform he wore while he worked from the precinct. The uniform had been his idea. While he didn't have his overcoat anymore, he still knew if word got out Michael Conners was spending time in the 14th precinct again, someone might think it newsworthy. At the very least, his noted presence could be a warning to the person he was attempting to track. Anonymity had become a very helpful tool to him. That didn't help his distaste for the buttoned uniform.

While there hadn't been any cameras or reporters following his entrance and exits, he couldn't help but feel he was being watched at times. It felt like eyes were burning a hole in the back of his head. He had to forcibly remind himself not to look around. He was sure it was just a bout of paranoia. There was no reason for anyone to care about some injured desk cop.

That was a reasonable and logical conclusion, but it didn't help his feeling of being watched. It made him more and more uneasy. He'd covered the only window near his little makeshift office with newspaper so no one could look in and see when he was walking to the break room to eat his meals or to the bathroom.

The cops had something of a mixed reaction to him. Many of those who had been around for a while treated him with a combination of respect and weariness. The stories of his work around the precinct had led to his name being well-known, but he'd very rarely worked with anyone who wasn't Lawrence. So, most of them had nothing but outside information in regards to who and what he was. But whatever he was, he was clearly important enough to be given preferential treatment by the lieutenant. He was an outsider, and set apart from them even if they appreciated his abilities and practices.

The newer cops treated him with either dismissal or outright distain. Anyone who had passed their probationary period carried an air of superiority where he was concerned. On paper, he was supposed to be an expert transferred from another precinct to advise the lieutenant on a confidential case, but those who had been around for a while liked to whisper and soon enough his true identity became common knowledge within the station.

The door to his little supply closet opened up and Guston walked in, slightly flush which meant something had gotten under his collar. It forcibly reminded Conners of his brief stint as a police detective. More than once, he'd done something that drove the lieutenant crazy just to see that particular shade on the man's face. Now though, it sent a shiver of worry through him.

"What's wrong?"

"We've got another message."

He dropped an open envelope on Conners' desk and the broken man slowly examined the letter and envelope.

"This is high-stock paper," he said. "Not a lot of people use this and very, very few would use this for something as mundane as an anonymous message."

"You figure it's someone with some old money then?"

"Most likely. No idea why someone with money like that would be interested in taking out what remains of Kingston's men though. Is this how they normally contacted you?"

"No, they constantly changed up their messages. The most common was a call from a burner phone through some type of voice modulator, but the messages were so short they were never much good for extra information."

Conners flipped open the letter and saw it listed an address towards the north end of the city. A quick run of the address revealed it was an old office building scheduled for demolition. Conners felt a slight apprehension as he examined the letter. The supply closet around him disappeared in a flash of flame. He could smell the burning wood and feel the rush of searing heat wash over him. Kingston screamed, cursing him as he burned to death. Conners' heart started pounding in his ears and he looked down to see his right hand trembling.

He knew this was all in his head. None of it was real. So he shouldn't be struggling with anything, and he forced himself to breathe. It didn't matter that his chest hurt and he could feel the air catch in his throat.

"Well, guess I'll go check this out then," he said, reaching for his cane and straightening up. "I'll text you if it turns out to be anything good."

"Excuse me? I certainly hope you don't think you're going there alone!"

"Why not?"

"Aside from the fact that you half-died last time Kingston's men were involved? Listen Conners, I won't sugarcoat it for you. You're a right pain in the ass, and I think you enjoy that part of it. But, the fact is that you're a good worker and as much of a headache as you can be, you're reliable and you have twice the guts of most of my staff. I know why Bill liked you so much, and neither he nor I want your time here to end on a coroner's table. I'll be with you. Can't trust anyone else here with this. Not until I know more anyway."

Conners nodded, not sure if he trusted himself to speak. That little speech was by far the kindest thing Guston had said about him in the entire time Conners had known the man. He had taken the time with police resources to confirm Guston had been Bill's previous partner. He wasn't sure how to absorb that information. He did feel more than a little touched Bill had cared for him enough to write a recommendation to his previous partner despite their arguments.

The lieutenant drove them through the streets in one of the station's cruisers and had insisted the both of them don protective vests under their shirts. Personally Conners found it more annoying than anything. For all his struggles and pains over the past eight months, he wasn't afraid of what might happen. It wasn't that there was no risk. It was simply that the risk played out much like a math calculation in his mind. There was no panic or stress associated with the danger, just numbers.

The fog that filled the streets gave Conners the uncomfortable feeling of being blind, as if there were eyes all around just out of sight. He felt sure that someone was watching, even if that made no sense and he had no idea why they would be interested in an ordinary uniformed cop.

When the lieutenant stopped the car in front of the building, they saw the sign on the front door that warned of the forthcoming demolition. Guston threw Conners a sideways glance but Conners didn't respond and shouldered the door. It wasn't locked but had rusted a little. Still, it gave way after a little force. The interior looked even worse than the outside, with cracked and stained concrete. What windows existed were either too dusty and stained to see through, or looked straight into the brick wall of one of their neighbors.

"Can't imagine why this place would be scheduled for demolition," said Conners, jokingly. "It's basically every frat's dream place for a party with tetanus free of charge."

"Glad you're at least finding some humor in this, every hair on my neck's standing on end."

Guston reached for his waist and drew his service pistol. The lieutenant may not be in the field as much as his uniformed officers were anymore, but he was still an accomplished shot and Conners was glad the man had insisted on coming. The dark-haired cripple limped towards the end of the entrance hall where there was an elevator that had a note taped to it. The paper was of the same stock as the note the lieutenant had received.

Loft.

"You don't think that's a trap?" asked Guston.

"Most likely it is."

"So what do you want to do?"

"Spring the trap."

The lieutenant rolled his eyes and appeared to bite back a retort. Had this been before his fight with Kingston, the lieutenant would've pushed the issue. However, Conners' injuries and experience appeared to taper the man's combative nature. Conners was forcibly reminded of his trip to Richards' office after Bill's murder. That memory sent another wave through his aching head.

A courtroom pitted him against the most dangerous woman in the world.

The flash of a machete in the noonday sun.

It was getting harder to stay upright and he leaned on his cane.

The bang of a pistol and a child with blonde hair and bright blue eyes.

Fire. Flames. Kingston screaming and cursing him.

Her dead body.

Jessica Lawrence's dead body.

He felt himself sag against the wall of the elevator as sweat pooled on his brow and under his arms. His brain felt like it was tearing itself to pieces and it bellowed out for action.

Danger! Danger! Deadly warning!

Yet his body would not respond and his eyes could find nothing to combat or anything he could use to defend himself. The air grew heavier and heavier until he was sure he would suffocate from the pressure.

Focus! he snapped at himself.

With an effort that put his weight training to shame, Conners reeled back and slapped himself across the face as hard as he could. He could tell he'd done a decent job, because it stung and he knew there would be a red mark. Guston was staring at him with concern but fear of either the note or Conners relapsing kept him from vocalizing any concerns. It wasn't an elegant solution, but it helped bring the proper world back into focus, and he could stand upright again… well, closer to upright at any rate.

The elevator slowly clanked and rocked its way up the building until it stopped, having traveled as high as it could. Conners threw the lieutenant a sideways glance as the doors very slowly creeped open. Without even realizing he was doing it, Conners began to analyze the scene that opened before him, as if the elevator doors were instead curtains spreading to put on a play for an audience of two.

The room was mostly bare, with several bedsheets covering the windows and the singular piece of furniture being a couch in the center of the room. He tried to see if there was anyone or anything on the couch, but it was faced away from them and it was impossible for him to tell. The place was wide open and only a central pillar interrupted the vast emptiness.

Worst possible place for a fight, Bill mentioned. *No cover, save the couch and the pillar. Quick way to get taken out by a sniper. Must be why the squatter put up the sheets.*

The lieutenant began to take a step forward, but Conners glanced down and instantly spotted the trap he suspected may lie in wait. It was a tripwire, and while he doubted it was attached to a bomb, there were several easy enough traps someone could set up to kill cops or intruders. He pointed out the wire and pressed his back up against the side of the elevator before pressing the *open* button.

The lieutenant mirrored him and Conners struck the wire with his cane. The telltale *twang* sounded and there was the sound of something falling. Half-a-second later, a knife supported by a broom handle swung down and poised in midair at eye-level.

"Nasty," muttered Guston.

Conners nodded his agreement and drew *Sherry* carefully keeping his eye out for other homemade traps. Luckily, the open structure limited the tenant's ability to set anymore presents for them. They moved forward in sync, and reached the couch as one. Conners swung around it in as wide an arc as he could while keeping his gun trained on any assailant who might be lying in wait. The furniture was unoccupied.

"I don't get it," said Guston softly. "Why bring us here for…"
Bang!

The gunshot cut him off as the projectile flew through Guston's right arm. The lieutenant fell back behind the pillar and sunk to the ground. Conners took just a split-second to analyze the situation.

Four figures had entered the room from the fire escape, and they all held guns: three pistols and a shotgun. Their stances weren't military or police-based, but they were well-practiced and far better with their weapons than most street thugs. Their clothing was mostly black, but nothing that would draw much of an eye on the street, just enough to suggest unsavory behavior, but nothing extremely criminal.

The pistols all seemed to be of a similar model, and with muzzle brakes fitted on the end. The shotgun hadn't been the weapon responsible for Guston's injury.

They don't want to cause excess noise if possible, he heard Lawrence suggest in his mind.

Sherry *would draw plenty of attention,* Bill noted.

Conners placed one hand on the rim of the couch, using it for leverage to volt over the furniture and duck behind it for cover. He spared a quick glance at Guston. He was injured, but not seriously. He was radioing the station for backup, and his training was starting to take over. Something was sticking in the back of Conners' mind.

Something was wrong... had been wrong. Well, something *aside* from the fact that he was being shot at. It took him a moment or two, but eventually it *clicked* in his whirling brain. He'd moved fine... normally even. He hadn't been limping since they'd entered the room. He hadn't drawn *Sherry* with his left hand. He hadn't been leaning on the cane, even while he'd carried it. He'd jumped over the couch without issue. In the moments when his mind was distracted, when he was analyzing... his leg didn't hurt.

The realization almost brought a tear to his eye until he heard the *crack* as a gunshot hit some concrete.

Leg later! Fight now! Lawrence berated him, and she was right.

He threw himself around the far end of the couch, where they wouldn't be looking for him and had half a second to see the group approaching. Luckily, to his adrenaline-laced brain, half a second was equal to a quarter-minute: plenty of time to take aim and loose a couple of *Sherry's* bullets.

Bang! Bang!

Two shots, center mass. He could tell from the way the man took the first bullet that they'd worn vests, but the vest was relatively light, and his group was close enough that his second shot tore through the fabric and floored the man. Conners ducked back and saw several shots hit the floor where he'd been a moment ago.

One down, said Bill.

Guston peaked around his pillar and fired three times with his pistol before there was a loud *blast* from the shotgun and Guston moved back into his hiding spot, holding his wounded appendage and scowling. Even from this distance, Conners could see the blood that meant two things. One: the shotgun was firing pellets instead of slugs, and two: the lieutenant had been hit again. Conners motioned for the man to join him behind the couch and stood to provide covering fire.

His remaining four shots sent the men scattering but didn't connect properly. He ducked back down as Guston scattered to his spot.

"Not great," Guston said, pulling out some bandages to try and stop the bleeding. "I'm getting shot to pieces. You hit?"

"Not yet. Backup coming?"

"Two minutes."

Conners nodded and began reloading while Guston fired blindly to keep their assailants at bay. He got two bullets out before the man with the shotgun popped up over the couch. Conners expected him to point the long weapon at him, but the man didn't. Instead he was brandishing a small weapon in his left hand. Conners didn't recognize it for a long moment, until the man pointed it at the policemen and fired. A thin dart flew out and hit the man in the leg, and he realized what kind of gun it was.

They brought a tranquilizer gun? he couldn't help but question.

They're here to catch, not kill, Bill pointed out. *They won't kill you, only incapacitate.*

Conners dropped *Sherry* and swung the weighted cane at the man's head. However, the assailant expected the move and ducked under his blow. Conners brought the cane up and over his head to swing again, but he heard the tranquilizer go off again, and before he bring the weapon down on the man, he felt the strength drain from his fingers and legs and he fell backwards, right into the arms of one of the other assailants.

He fought to stay conscious, and commit their faces to memory, but it was like trying to keep water in his hands. The harder he tried to hold onto the details the faster they left him. Then he was floating, drifting through space. It was nice, and peaceful.

Couldn't I just stay like this? he pondered to himself. *This is... this is actually quite nice.*

Why can't you? asked Lawrence. *Why can't you just stay like this? Just stay numb... stay quiet.*

Could you? Bill put forward. *Could you actually hide away? Is it in you to do that? Is it in you to give up, even if it might not be time for you to give up? Could you stay here?*

Are you ready to rest?

He knew then that he couldn't give in. And there was surely nothing that was going to hit him that would break him. There *was* nothing that could break him. Not when he was given a mission from the God of man... or was there?

Chapter XL: Not Alone

For a long, long time, Conners wasn't aware anything had changed. Actually, he supposed it hadn't: not exactly. He'd gone from lying down and staring at nothing in nothingness to lying down and staring at nothing in nothingness, only now he was awake. He hadn't been entirely sure of that at first. Eventually his back legs started to go numb and he felt the pain from lying on what he supposed must be concrete. He wasn't sure if he'd gone blind or was just entrenched in darkness. In either case, the blackness surrounding him was absolute and unrelenting.

He guessed he'd been conscious for just over a couple hours, though of course there was no way for him to verify that. Deciding he had nothing else to do, he stood up. Once this resulted in no change to his vision, he decided to walk forward. He had no idea what constituted "forward," but made his best guess. He'd once heard people lost in the forest tended to wonder in circles. What if he walked in what he thought was a singular direction only to wonder aimlessly in circles nonstop?

"Well," he said aloud. "Even if I *do* wonder in circles nonstop, how exactly is that any worse than not knowing where I am right now?"

He seriously considered the question for a long moment.

"I suppose it's not worse," he answered himself.

He walked *forward* as much as he could given no visual cues, and walked until he slammed into something very hard. He backed up a step and reached out to feel whatever he'd just smashed his nose into. It too was very hard, and seemed to be concrete.

"A wall," he said to the blackness.

The blackness said nothing back, which he thought was more than a little rude. What was far less rude was the minimal bit of information the wall was giving him. The wall had a slight inward curve to it. Curious, Conners began to follow the curve. He moved steadily, if a bit more slowly to avoid slamming his already sore nose into anything.

The curve remained so steady it took him several long minutes to realize that he actually *was* walking in a large circle... at least he *thought* he was walking a circle. Determined to prove this theory to himself, he took off one of his shoes and slowly scooted around the room until he happened to find his shoe again by accidentally nudging it with his foot.

Still, the knowledge pleased him because he'd ascertained something: he was in a round, concrete room about ten feet in diameter and it was either pitch-black or he was blind. It was nothing especially helpful but it was something, and that knowledge in and of itself provided him a strange type of comfort. The fact that he could function (even if it was in a limited capacity) meant he wasn't done: not yet.

Are you ready to rest? Even in the darkest valleys and loneliest nights, I shall be with you, and I love you.

Well, it was plenty dark and lonely now.

Conners found the wall and slunk down to lean against it. He was very tired, far more than he should've been from his brief excursion of the room. He forced himself to try and clear his mind in order to pray. He didn't even really know what he wanted to pray for; so he prayed for those he loved. He prayed for his parents. He prayed for the lieutenant, and the other cops at the fourteenth precinct. He prayed for Bill and Lawrence's souls, even if he had no idea what good praying for the dead might do.

As that melancholy thought slid idly across his brain, he heard a noise to his right and turned. As he opened his eyes, he realized how stupid it was to turn and look for whatever had caused the noise. However to his surprise, he *did* see someone sitting next to him. Several powerful emotions immediately rose and began to battle each other, creating a hurricane of pain within his chest.

The first pang that reared its head was the surprise. It was a mixture of shock, awe, and pleasure. He was shocked to see anything, let alone see a person with such clarity. Also, seeing them meant he wasn't blind, which was a pleasurable realization.

The second emotion was the fear. Whoever was next to him could've been an enemy, at the very least they knew more about this situation than he did, and he *had* been abducted. He had no reason to trust whoever had appeared next to him.

The third and fourth were joy and love. The person who had sat next to him was none other than Bill. It was Bill undeniably. He wore the same thick mustache and his hair was roughly parted to the left. He grinned at Conners just the way he used to before…

The fifth was pain. Bill was dead... *had* been dead for several years. He was dead, and Conners hadn't been able to do anything to help him.

"Hey old man," he said, leaning back against the wall.

"Hey kid," Bill said.

"This is new."

"You do realize you're telling yourself that?"

"Just let me go with it," Conners said, smirking slightly. "It's helping. You look good, old man."

"Being dead will do that to you. Come on kid, you didn't call me up to talk about how I still look good while you're beginning to age."

"Guess not," Conners mumbled. "So you want to talk about it?"

There was really only one thing that Conners could think about and it wasn't as if he could try and mount a breakout when he was still so weak and had so little information.

"Let's lay it out," said Bill. "Someone's been taking out Kingston's men over the past several months."

"They're skilled," Conners supplied. "They know how to leave little evidence behind and avoid being caught by either the mob remnants or the police. That speaks to experience and knowledge."

"They also have enough drive and patience to continue the work for several months, but never get so eager or daring as to take on more than a few at a time. That means a lot of passion and patience. Likely they have to scout out targets for several days or at a week at time to find the right moment to pounce."

"That means time," said Conners. "Someone who doesn't live lavishly or have a demanding job: if they could maintain one at all."

"So you're looking for someone who's reclusive, but connected or wealthy enough to run a scheme like this."

Conners pondered this. He could come up with a small handful of names that might have the money and time to kidnap him like this, but he had trouble linking any of them to the kind of motive that could stretch to this level. After several long minutes of struggling with his sluggish brain, he gave it up and turned back to Bill.

"Hey Bill," he said so softly the sound didn't even reach his own ears. "Does it hurt?"

"What kid?"

"Dying... does it hurt?"

Bill let out a long sigh and looked up.

"Only for a second... depending on how you die of course. But after the shock sets in, and you start to go... it's a lot like going to sleep after an exhausting week of work and travel. You know how sometimes you get so tired you couldn't even reach the bed, and you just pass out on the couch because that's as far as you can go?"

"Right."

"It's a lot like that... Then, it's peaceful."

"How's heaven, old man?"

Bill smiled sadly.

"You do know I don't actually know anything you don't know, right?"

"Humor me."

Conners saw Bill roll his eyes and adjust himself slightly on the concrete.

"It's a wild ride, kid. Been enjoying myself for the first time in a long while."

"That... that sounds nice. Save me a seat up there, ay? Don't know how much longer I'll be, but time is a construct of the living and all that."

"Already got your name on a piece of paper... both of them, in fact."

That made him laugh a little. As the laughter lifted his spirits, it helped push down the dread that had been slowly creeping in on him. The darkness wasn't so bad, just so long as there was still a small bit of light. So long as he had that speck of light, he could laugh in the darkness... so long as it stayed lit.

He didn't know exactly when it had happened, but when he next looked around Bill had left him. He was by himself again, although not quite alone. Jesus had promised he would be there even in the darkest valleys.

He couldn't help but notice how incredibly tired he was. His brain still felt fuzzy, like someone was smothering it with a pillow. He was so very tired. So despite the poor conditions, he passed out and found himself drifting into the land of dreams almost instantly.

~*~

When he woke up, he couldn't remember what he'd been dreaming about, his mind had clearly been struggling with something, because he had a pounding headache. The second annoyance was he still couldn't see anything. He was almost famished, to the point hunger was starting to gnaw at his belly. He hadn't been this hungry since he'd escaped the hospital after losing his memory. When he'd been doing his vigilante work as John Black, he'd often been short of cash, but he could at least get ahold of some ramen or peanut butter sandwiches.

As his stomach protested loudly once more, Conners felt like he was punched directly in his eyes and pain exploded in his head. Out of reaction, he shielded his eyes and rolled away from whatever had just hit him before trying to chance a look from behind his fingers. The red-orange glow of his fingers greeted him. As much as his eyes hurt, he was relieved to realize this meant that he hadn't truly been blinded—only kept in the dark for an extended time. That was a relief he didn't realize he'd needed.

He heard something heavy *thunk* to the concrete floor. As carefully as he could, Conners began the slow process of peaking through his fingers. He saw that a small square about the size of a postcard had opened up in the ceiling, and it was from this hole that the light had assaulted his senses. Only he came to see it was not a miniature sun as his injured eyes suggested, but a simple glass lantern lit by a candle. It gave him the uncomfortable feeling of being stuck in the victorian era.

Looking back down, he saw in the center of his underground cell, there was a small tray with bread and overripe fruit resting on it, as well as a bottle of water. Before he was even aware of commanding his body to move, he'd reached the tray and drank half the bottle of water. It was lukewarm and tasted slightly metallic, but to him it was as precious as an oasis in the Sahara.

Then he tore into the bread. It too was old and partially stale, but he was so ravenous he barely had time to taste the food as it made its way into his system. He only stopped when he nearly threw up.

Your stomach shrank, he heard Lawrence chastise him. *You'll make yourself sick if you don't pace it.*

If they wanted you to starve to death, they wouldn't bother feeding you, Bill added.

He forced himself to stop, despite the fact his brain was screaming at him to consume everything and anything in front of him while he could. As he stopped, he felt the most peculiar sensation. It was like a prickling all over his brain, as if his mind itself had gone numb. It took only a singular moment for him to realize what this meant.

Whoever took me spiked the food with some kind of drug to slow my brain and cause visions. Some type of hallucinogenic would be the most likely agent.

His brain slowed things down for him while Bill and Lawrence considered his options for him. Bill spoke first.

Option 1: Refuse the food. It will drive you past the point of hunger, but you've been there before. You'll survive, and you can use your brain to formulate a plan. It's going to take some time and be unpleasant. Still, whoever took you clearly wants you alive and wants to have you slowed and unable to function. Sooner or later your opportunity will present itself.

Conners mauled this over while Lawrence provided her counter-argument.

You're going to starve if you don't eat. You're already to the point you were when you were homeless. Plus, you've already eaten some of the food, and you can tell it's already in your mind. Even if you were to throw up now, you wouldn't have your full mind back, and you'll be weak as well as slower. Besides, you weren't completely useless on these drugs. Over time you could build up a resistance and then find a way out while not being too weak to fight.

He considered this and as he tried to decide between his freedom and a stated hunger, he heard Vito speak in his mind.

Choose the middle road, son. There's always another way. Ignore the fruit, it's sure to be filled the brim with the stuff. Keep the bread and water and ration it out over a few weeks. You'll never be fully affected by the drug and you won't be starving.

His father... the liar, coward, and traitor.

Do what's right, kid.

Protect your life, Conners.

There's always another way, son.

Conners scowled and looked down at the bread in his hands. Finally settling on a course of action, he removed his under shirt and wrapped both the bread and water in it before setting it against the wall where he'd slept. The fruit he squashed and spread along the base of the opposite wall. Aside from creating a more pleasant aroma than his own stink, and distracting any bugs away from his bread and water, it would be good to see if there were any cracks or breaches in the concrete that he might be able to exploit, even if he couldn't tell how he might do that at the moment.

The actual acts of his father's advise was perhaps the easiest to carry out, but listening to him churned his stomach far more than the hunger or aging food could do. His days passed monotonously. He would fall asleep to the sounds of Lawrence and Bill arguing in his head, even while his father encouraged him. Then he would start his day by sipping a small bit of the water and eating a bite of the bread, using the ritual as a chance to practice communion. The bread was the body of Christ, which was broken for him, and the foul water was as close to wine as he would have for the blood that was shed for him.

"Father," he muttered to himself. "Protect me in this evil place."

And so his days lingered on. The one bit of grace left to him was that they did not close the trapdoor in his ceiling. For whatever reason, he was to be left the light. They even replaced the candle when it got low. He couldn't escape the feeling they were prepping him for something, even if he couldn't hazard a guess as to what.

Conners also attempted to keep some type of a workout regimen, and tried to keep a system of how long he'd been awake in this place. Both failed miserably. His body was too weak to keep up any workout, even cardio. For a while he was able to track the passage of time by the growth of his beard and greasiness of his hair, he lost track after the first week.

So he waited, he prayed, he ate, he drank, and he slept. Before very long, his bread and water ran out. However, he was given more the following day and so was not left wanting much. It was still hard, far harder than he'd hoped, but it was possible. He also *was* starting to build up a resistance to whatever they'd laced the food and drink with. Although he noticed it was far more potent in his water than in his bread. It pained him because the water was by far the more tempting of the two. Still, his father's plan—cowardly as it might be—was working.

So he kept the course. He discarded the fruit by throwing it at the ceiling and stowed his bread and water against the wall, covered by his shirt. He was fully prepared to spend most of the next several weeks trying to find a way to scale the walls somehow. The following "morning" as he thought of his situation, his schedule was interrupted. He was about to head to his daily allotment of bread and water, when there was a sliding sound from above him, and a thin ladder *thudded* to the ground a few feet away.

Before he could even move to start ascending it, a thin figure began climbing down the ladder. There could be no mistake. Whoever it was, was here for him.

Chapter XLI: Visitors

Conners looked up in a slight daze as a woman dressed in a black button-up shirt and dark grey slacks slowly descended the ladder and stopped before him. He could see she wore a fashionable pair of shoes that didn't have an elevated heel, which was smart. Climbing a ladder in heels would not be fun.

He'd never met this woman before, at least not as far as he could remember. She had shoulder length orange-red hair and vibrant blue eyes. Her face was beautiful, in spite of the three scars that were clearly visible, even by the dim candlelight. Two started just below her left eye and traced their way down her face and neck before disappearing into the folds of her shirt. The third was a shallow mark that started at the base of her lip and stopped at the point of her chin. The marks were very old but displayed prominently.

She displays them like a badge of honor, Bill muttered.

Yes, Vito agreed. *But is she proud of the scars, or does she view them as a victory over what caused them?*

He slowly stood up and saw she was studying him just as intensely as he was studying her. He was quite sure he'd never said two words to this woman in his life, but there was something uncannily familiar about her. However hard he tried to connect her to someone in his life, he couldn't quite place it. There was something to the slight smirk she wore and something in her eyes that screamed at him but he just couldn't tell what they were saying.

Suddenly, it occurred to him that even with his brain's ability to slow moments down, this woman had been standing before him for nearly a full second and he had yet to say anything. He mentally prepared himself.

Showtime.

"Are you the maître d? I think I'd like to lodge a formal complaint or two in regards to the atmosphere and the room service."

His voice was hoarse and soft, betraying the nonchalance he was attempting to put forward.

"Oh you are wonderful," she said softly and reached up to touch his face with two spider-like fingers. "You're *exactly* how I thought you'd be. You really are quite an impressive specimen, Michael Conners."

Her voice was soft and excitable, like someone who felt they were on the verge of a major breakthrough in their field of study.

"I think it's considered rude to use someone else's name without giving your own," he said, willing his weak body to prepare for a fight, though he was having trouble enough summoning the energy to talk.

"Oh," she said, seeming truly abashed at his jest. "I'm so sorry. My name is Elizabeth. You'll have to forgive me. This is a big moment for me. You see, I've wanted to meet you for many years now. I confess I was often curious what you would think of me. How do I measure up to your expectations?"

She posed for him, sweeping her hair back. But he was truly lost.

"I have never met you before and didn't know you existed before now. How would I have had any expectations of you?"

She scowled and it threw her scars into sharp relief. Suddenly her slightly cheerful and playful demeanor vanished, replaced by a vicious glare full of resentment and hate. Quick as a blast of lightning, she slashed out at him and her fingers were curled like tiger claws. Instinct took over and Conners fell to his left, away from her slash. Reacting more from intuition than conscious thought, he used the momentum from his dodge to spin around Elizabeth and kneed her in her lower back. The blow caused her to break one of her nails against the wall.

She turned and glared at him as he backed up and assumed a defensive posture. However, as quickly as her animalistic posture had appeared, it vanished and she looked at him almost playfully.

"Oh, you *are* marvelous. You haven't missed a step. I can see why she was fascinated with you. But you really did win that one in the end. I can't explain how grateful to you I am for that."

"Pretty strange way to show gratitude," he said, still on the defensive.

"Such a witty mouth," she said, smiling just a little too wide. "I'd like to bite that smart lip of yours."

Her words sent a chill through him like a cold blast of air on a winter night. She viewed their interaction as some type of foreplay, even if she didn't mean it to end sexually. This was a method of playing for Elizabeth. The problem was Conners still didn't know the name of the game or what his expected role was.

"Why would you be grateful to me?" he asked, hoping to throw her off. "You said I 'won that one.' What did you mean?"

That did stop her for a moment. He could see a mixture of confusion and hurt on her face. Whatever it was he'd done, Elizabeth clearly thought he should've known about it and somehow related it to her.

"You... but you set me free..." she said softly.

"Ok," said Conners softly. "I set you free. Don't suppose you'd consider returning the favor."

He pointed up at the trap door to illustrate his point. She seemed to seriously consider his offer for a long second before she shook her head violently.

"Nope. Can't do it. If I let you free, you'll leave. Won't you?"

"And I can't leave?"

"I don't want you to."

Trying to follow her logic was bizarre. It was as if half her mind was still that of a child, and didn't form complex thoughts. The other half seemed to be that of a sociopath, understanding right and wrong, but not caring about them. Nevertheless, he knew it was in his best interest to play along with whatever game she wanted to run on him. It was easier to see a possible path now that his mind was a little clearer.

"And what do you want from me?" he asked, watching her carefully for any sign of another attack.

"I want..." she began confidently, only to drop off. "I want you... No, I want you to give me... I..."

She didn't finish, but began to pace quickly, and Conners could see he'd struck a nerve. Whoever this lady was, she might be capable of building a plan and executing it, but she wasn't someone who considered her own desires much. She'd wanted him here. That much was obvious. But she wasn't clear on exactly *why* she wanted him.

Time to poke the bear a bit, kid. Just be careful.

"I mean, I'm sure you know why you wanted me, right? What was the reason?"

Elizabeth clutched at her head and *hissed* like a snake poised to strike.

"Because you were... *his*. You took her away and you were his."

"I understand," said Conners, wondering vaguely if he'd *ever* told a larger lie in his life. "So why would you want me? What do I mean to you?"

"EVERYTHING!" she shrieked and flew at him.

He held his arms up defensively and caught her before she could claw at him again, but the momentum knocked him to the ground and she began to reach for him desperately. She was stronger than he was after his long stretch in the small hole. He had the benefit of practice and clarity. So he was able to keep himself from suffering serious injury.

After striking at him for a minute, she sprung back, as if she'd been burned by contact with him.

"I'm sorry," she said, as the shadow of anger passed from her. Conners didn't drop his guard an inch. "You have to understand what he meant to me."

"He who?" asked Conners, wondering if this were related to Kingston or some crook he'd help lock up.

Elizabeth looked up at him and her eyes were filled with disbelief and sorrow.

"You don't even know? But... how could you not know? Why wouldn't he have told you? Surely, he told you! He must've told you! You just weren't listening!"

He swallowed his retort and backed up a step, which seemed to shake her slightly. She gazed at something he couldn't see roughly waist-high before she suddenly spun on her heel and ascended the ladder.

"Hey!" he shouted after her, but she didn't slow. "Wait!"

He summoned up every bit of his energy and chased her up the ladder. He was right behind her for a second when she struck back suddenly and her shoe caught in him the nose and he heard it break, spewing blood down his front and putting an unpleasant copper taste in his mouth. Despite the pain he held onto the ladder and continued his ascension, albeit a step behind Elizabeth.

When she reached the top of the ladder she sprinted forward and Conners clambered up after her. He got a quick glimpse of the room above his cell, except "room" was the wrong word for it. It was almost like a hallway that stretched on for perhaps fifty feet. It was lined not with doors and walls, but the iron bars of a holding cell, and it reminded him uncomfortably of a castle's dungeon room. It wasn't even lit by electronic lights, but by dim candles like the one above his one cell. He could see no other trap doors that could lead to a room like his.

Elizabeth was already at the far end of the hallway of cells and as he started to give chase, a rough pair of arms latched around his arms and torso and yanked him back.

Stupid! Stupid! Bill's voice berated him. *Always check your surroundings for threats. I taught you better than that!*

He tried to stamp on the feet of his captor, but he was too weak to do damage to the man without a weapon. Then he felt a small prick in his neck and his vision quickly faded to black.

~*~

When he came to later, he didn't immediately open his eyes. He could already feel the familiar flooring of his cell under his back. He could feel the familiar dulling of his brain and his senses, and knew he'd been drugged again. From the feel of things he'd been given a double dose. They'd also apparently given him some nutrients. He could feel the blood in his veins pumping as his body was repairing much of the damage done during his imprisonment.

The next thing that hit him was the smell, and it was beyond horrid. It was stronger than almost any other scent and yet he was able to place it immediately, even with his dulled senses and thinking power. After all, nothing else in the world smelled quite like a burning man. The strange, sulfuric smell of the burnt hair would cling to his nostrils and one whiff of a flaming, blood-lined liver would haunt anyone to their dying day.

Conners knew it because he'd smelled it once before, and so he knew exactly which of his demons had decided to torment him well before he opened his eyes and sat up. Still he did so, more to feel his muscles and relieve the stiffness in his back than anything else.

Before him stood the shambled, burnt remains of James Kingston, clothed in a pure black suit made of silk. Beneath the suit he sported a blood-red shirt with an open collar and a pair of shined leather shoes covered his feet. Had Conners not already known it was Kingston, the face would've been indistinguishable. In fact, there wasn't a true face at all.

The head was completely blackened, looking more like burnt oak than skin and flesh. What few wisps of hair remained only served to add to the horrid sulfuric smell. In spite of his charred flesh, no one could mistake the look of pure loathing that filled every speck in Kingston's infinitely deep brown eyes. He watched Conners as one watched a fencing opponent, marking every inch of movement.

"I don't want to talk to you," Conners said, rubbing his eyes angrily.

"Hello John," said Kingston. As he spoke, flecks of charred skin broke and fell from his lips and face. "Been a while. I've been really, really busy since you murdered me."

"Killed," Conners corrected without thought. "There's a difference."

"Yes," Kingston said, loosing a horrible, hallow laugh that sounded like it come from his black soul more than his lungs. "There is a difference, and you're a murderer. What is it like to be a serial killer? I might not have even managed that one... at least not directly."

"I don't know how many people you murdered. I only know you were too dangerous to be left alive."

"But that's not why you killed me... is it? I had people removed or killed to further my business. I killed who I had to in order to get paid. Why did you murder me? Because I killed your little girlfriend and you got angry. In a way, you're even more a murderer than I am."

"SHUT UP!" Conners shouted and swung at him.

His fist went straight through Kingston's head and collided with the wall and he felt two of his knuckles break.

"Losing your grip, John? That's really a shame. I always thought you would've been a worse threat than all that. Through everything I did to you, I always took you seriously. Perhaps that was my greatest mistake."

"Even I can't begin to calculate the amount or magnitude of your mistakes," Conners snapped, holding his damaged hand.

"No... in your current state I suppose you can't. How horrible is it: having that great mind and being unable to access it? That's got to feel like cutting off your balls."

Kingston laughed again and Conners scowled and covered his ears. This of course did nothing to block out the horrible sound since it originated from inside his own head. He felt hot tears begin to work their way down his cheeks. All the while, Kingston laughed.

"Your life is one designed in flame, John. You lost your boss to fire, you lost your love to fire, and you purged my life with fire. You should burn yourself down too: just finish purging the whole lot."

Conners slammed his head against the wall hard as he could. He felt a small trickle of blood join the tears falling down his face.

"I'm sorry," he whispered softly.

He could've been apologizing to God, to Bill, to Lawrence, to the child he shot, to Kingston, to himself, or to all of them at once. He knelt and wept, holding his head in frustration and pain. All the while, Kingston laughed. Unable to do anything to stop the horrible sound, Conners simply knelt in his little cell and waited for the tormenting sounds and smells to pass. Slowly—very, very slowly—they did.

He had no idea how long he knelt like that, but judging from the pain in his knees it had at least been a few hours. When he finally straightened, his legs protested. He slapped them several times to get the blood flowing.

You can do this, kid, said Bill softly. *Just focus yourself. Be smart. Adapt. Overcome.*

As Conners looked around, he realized he was once again visited by someone. After another moment, he realized Elizabeth stood before him. She was studying him as if he were an animal safely contained behind glass or bars.

"Trying to make sure you didn't damage your prize?" he grunted, sneering at her.

He saw she held a long syringe with what he could only assume was a very generous dose of the hallucinogenic she'd been using on him.

"That brute was a bit rough with you earlier, my dear. I'm sorry about that. I had to make sure you weren't reacting poorly to the direct dose. However you seem to be functioning very well. Much better than expected."

My dear? Lawrence echoed. *She's actually enamored with you...*

Conners looked up carefully and could see that Lawrence had a point. Elizabeth's pupils were dilated and even in this dim lighting, her face was a little flushed. She *did* intend to drug him, but even in that act there was a strange touch of tenderness and caring in her face. Elizabeth considered herself to love him. This began to spark an idea in his mind, and he forced himself to reply.

"Funny that. I would've said my mental capabilities were lessened."

"Oh no Conners," she said, smiling wide as she approached him with the needle. "We both know it would take far more than this to stop you completely."

NOW! The chorus of voices sounded in his head, and Conners reacted like lightning, moving so fast he actually hurt himself a little. He reached up and grasped her wrist with both of his hands. He saw shock fill her face. Whatever she'd excepted, it wasn't for him to resist her. He didn't give her time to think over his burst of resistance either. He twisted her wrist as hard as he could. She winced and dropped the syringe.

Instead of reaching for the makeshift weapon, Conners knelt and bit the palm of her hand as hard as he could. His jaw ached from the sudden unexpected use. Nevertheless, he could feel the tell-tale copper taste in his mouth that meant he'd drawn blood. Elizabeth reached down for the syringe and Conners reacted on impulse as she opened her mouth to scream.

He couldn't say exactly *how* he knew it would work… maybe he'd had no clue. Instead of attempting to silence her with his hand, he swept down in a flash and pressed his lips against Elizabeth's and kissed her with as much strength as he could muster. If she was surprised or repulsed by his action, she gave no sign. Instead, she returned his kiss. He felt her reach up and run her fingers through his hair right as his left hand found the syringe.

He doubted she ever even felt the needle enter her neck until he'd already injected the drug into her system, and after a long moment, she collapsed onto the stone ground.

Chapter XLII: The Impossible

Conners stopped and stared at Elizabeth's limp body for several seconds. He didn't have a plan. He didn't even have a clue as to the best step to take. He hated being lost, but there was little hope for it. He carefully retrieved the syringe: now empty. Still, the needle could be used as a weapon if he were precise. His body wasn't up to a straight fight with anyone stronger than Elizabeth, even if his brain had been working properly.

Quick as he could manage, he head up the ladder. As he reached the top he spun around quickly, putting all his weight on his hands and arms so he could fight with his feet. Just like last time, there was a large man. Despite his focus on battle, Conners' mind observed the man in a split-second.

He wasn't very tall, but clearly weighed much more than Conners, even before his kidnapping. He wore a navy-blue suit with a white button-up shirt which was open at the top. His hands were scarred, and Conners spotted both the hunting knife and the pistol at the man's waist. The man's dirty blonde hair and mustache gave him the unfortunate appearance of being permanently out-of-place regardless of his surroundings.

The man reached for him and Conners kicked out as hard and high as he could. If he'd been at his full strength, he likely would've broken the man's jawbone. As it was, the man was knocked over as his chin split and a splattering of blood covered the white shirt.

Out of instinct the guard reached up and covered his chin and Conners reacted quickly. He flew forward and slid the syringe into the man's left ear as deep as he could reach. The man screamed and rolled on the ground in pain, but Conners didn't hesitate. Utilizing his distraction, he reached down and grabbed the knife from the man.

The briefest of regrets came over him as he looked at the man he'd just assaulted. However, he had no choice but to neutralize the guard and he couldn't leave the man behind, even badly injured. Steeling his heart, Conners plunged the hunting knife into the man's neck, just below the jawline and angled upwards. After a second of struggling, the man fell limp and hit the ground: dead.

Conners took a long second to center himself. When he was ready, he finished searching the body.

He'd briefly considered taking the man's clothes, but aside from finding it distasteful to wear the clothes drenched in the blood of a man he'd just killed, they would never have fit him. He did take the man's pistol, a set of keys, and found he'd been wearing an earpiece. Curiously, Conners inserted the earpiece into his own ear and heard chatter between a few different people.

"...taken up near the stairway. Any word from the boss?"

"Not yet. Relief should be here in about an hour. Just sit tight until then."

"Not sure why we have to guard them so much anyway. He's so drugged up he couldn't find his own ass, and she snapped a while ago."

That was interesting. It meant there was someone else held here too. Not that Conners exactly felt he was in any position to mount a rescue, but he certainly couldn't leave anyone in this horrible place. Checking the guard's pants, he found what was easily the most valuable gift: a cellphone. He quickly dialed the lieutenant's desk number from memory. The phone rang for several seconds and Conners would've sworn the phone was making things difficult on purpose.

"Lieutenant Mark Guston."

"Never thought I'd be so glad to hear your voice," Conners mutter quietly into the receiver.

"Conners?!"

He heard the lieutenant hastily pull the phone up and off speaker.

"Where the hell have you been? I've had people out for months trying to find you. Everyone's been losing their minds!"

Months? We've been out a long time, kid.

"Things are bad," Conners said. "I was held captive but I've made my way out, still trapped in the building though. I'm weak and drugged so the sooner you start tracing this call the better. I'm going to go silent now but I'll leave the line open for you to trace. Soon as you can, send SWAT and an ambulance. There's another hostage here somewhere and she's likely in as bad a shape as I am."

He could hear Guston start to protest, but he muted the phone and used the light from the screen to look around the hallway he'd gotten up to. During his brief excursion up the ladder last time, he thought he saw several cells lining the walls, and looking around it was clear he'd been correct.

His eyes had long ago adjusted to little light, and the cellphone was practically a beacon for him as he passed cell after cell: all empty. It wasn't until he was at the last four he finally hit something. Despite the phone's bright light, he almost didn't see the figure at the back of the cell, since they were curled up in the far corner, wrapped in black clothing.

"H-hello?" he called out. His throat scratched as he spoke and he felt out dehydrated he was. "Can you hear me?"

"Go away," said the figure.

Her voice was even worse than his, and it was so faint he could've missed the words altogether. Even as soft as the words were, they sounded dead and hallow: as if they'd been said without thought or processing. Even computers could "talk" with more inflection in their voices. He reached for the ring of keys he'd taken and after a fair bit of trial and error, he found the correct one. With a good heave, he finally slid the door back and cautiously walked in.

"Listen," he said, reaching out for the woman. "I was trapped here, but I just knocked Elizabeth out. We have a chance to get out of here but we have to leave *right now*."

"Just leave me alone already," she hissed at him, and he could hear the tears in the tone of her voice, even though it was still low and hallow.

You can't leave her, kid. She's a victim. She needs help.

Nonsense, you tried and she doesn't want to go. There's always another way. Besides if you try and drag her along she'll just get both of you shot. Save yourself.

Shut up! he snapped mentally.

"Hey. I know this place is horrible but I really am here to try and help you. I'm not just going to leave you here."

He stopped maybe two feet away from her and knelt carefully, trying to present as non-threatening an image as he could, though he was fully aware in normal society he would've stuck out immediately. Still, she couldn't have thought he was one of the guards once she actually saw his face.

As he knelt down though, he saw her shift quickly and deliberately. One of her feet swung around and came right at his head. Out of instinct more than anything else, Conners fell back and assumed a defensive stance, though not one that might seem like he was trying to threaten her. He was prepared for a follow up on her assault. After all, the guards had mentioned she "snapped." But he never could've prepared for what the cellphone's light revealed.

She crouched before him, ready for combat. Her green eyes were narrowed and practically came to life at the prospect of a battle. Her hair reached the base of her spine, and while he couldn't easily discern the color with his little light, he knew it was normally dark auburn. Her skin was only lit by the phone's pale glow, but he knew the tan hue of it perfectly. He knew her lips and nose. He knew every detail of her face because he'd been seeing it over and over and over ever since he'd killed Kingston.

"L-Lawrence?"

It was impossible—illogical. Yet there she was. She was dressed in dark and dirty clothing, she was covered in dirt and old injuries, she was paler and thinner than he knew her to be, and she had never glared at him with such murderous intent. But it was unmistakably her.

Am I still hallucinating?

"Get away from me!"

She sprung forward and kicked at him again. Completely thrown by her appearance, he didn't think to defend himself. Her kick caught him hard enough to snap his head to the side and send him skidding to the ground. The cellphone was knocked out of his grip and he tasted blood again.

"Lawrence! What the hell?"

"Shut up!" she shouted and kicked out at him again.

This time though, he was ready for the attack and dodged it. He sprang to his feet, putting his guard up.

"It's me: Conners!"

"I don't believe you!"

He was stunned at the venom in her tone. She'd never been that harsh as far as he'd heard. He could see the pain in her eyes and the mental strain in her reaction to him. He knew that whatever form of Lawrence this was, she was extremely weak and pushed past her breaking point. She'd likely been through a treatment similar to his own, though from the sight of her it had been far longer than his few months.

She faced him with the determination of a soldier. She was set to go down fighting. He couldn't blame her for that. He still wasn't sure *he* was sane. Lawrence had always been strong, but the human mind and body could only take so much before they broke. Lawrence had clearly been through hell.

They drugged her too, Bill pointed out.

Play this one carefully, son.

"It's really me, Lawrence. I know they've done horrible things to you in here, but I can help you. I've always been there to help you, haven't I?"

"You're dead!"

That was hard to combat. He knew he was alive of course, but he'd been sure she was dead until about a minute ago… and he wasn't entirely sure he hadn't lost his mind. She flew at him again with a flurry of kicks he had to duck and slide away from. He'd seen her in the gym enough times to know her style of kickboxing. That combined with his mind's tendency to break down movement meant he could avoid her blows, even as weak as he was. While his fight or flight response was screaming at him to attack her back, he pushed it down. He had to reach her. If he couldn't she would… die.

"I thought you were dead," he said softly. "But you're not, right? And if we're not dead, then we need to work together and get the hell out of this place."

"I'm not going anywhere with you!"

He growled slightly. He had no time to do this the right way. He would do whatever could be done to help her, but there was no telling how long it would be until Elizabeth woke up. They didn't have very long before reinforcements showed up regardless.

"How could I prove it's really me?" he asked. "You can ask me anything, anything at all. I'll prove it to you!"

She ran at him and leapt up. He was expecting a roundhouse kick, but she delivered a strong double swing kick. Due to his body more than his brain, he managed to block the blow. It still sent him to the ground and he could feel the stone brick ground had scraped his back hard enough to draw blood.

"You're a hallucination… or some demon. There's nothing you can tell me that will fool me."

Conners sighed mentally. She was right of course. Resigned to the only plan he could think of he locked eyes with her.

Please God, guide me here.

"You're right. So how about I tell you something you know I'd never say if I were just in your mind? Lawrence, I lost everything when I thought Kingston killed you. It killed a part of me and if *I'm* not the one hallucinating right now it will be a miracle of biblical proportions. You have always been my very best friend. I'd do anything I could to help you."

"That doesn't..."

"And I love you."

That stopped her cold. He saw a thousand thoughts pass behind her eyes in a fraction of a second. He saw hope, fear, danger, desire, anger, and many more emotions fly by as she stared: dumbstruck. The moment the words hit his own ears, he knew he should've said them a long time ago. They were possibly the truest words he'd ever spoken.

"You... you don't..."

She didn't finish the thought, but she did lower her guard. Slowly he approached her and reached out to take her hand. She flinched and reached back to strike him. He didn't dodge her blow, but rolled with it a little to lessen the damage to both her and himself. It still hurt, but she didn't break away from him.

"I promise I'm not going to hurt you. I just want to get us out of here. I know it's scary, but after that we can take all the time we need to. I promise you."

She scowled and for a moment he could tell she was about to hit him again, but she didn't. Instead, she spoke in a slightly shaky voice.

"Y-you're not real."

"I'm really here," he said, and despite his preservation instincts, he kissed her knuckles. "I'm really, really here and I'm not going to leave you."

"You're really here?" she repeated, her voice full of pain and disbelief.

"I promise."

"What are you going to do to me?"

"For starters, try and get us out of this place. I've hopefully got some rescue on the way, but I need you with me on this or we'll both get killed. Can you work with me, please? I need you."

"You need me?"

"I always needed you."

She didn't respond for a very long time, but stared blankly at a spot about waist-high behind him. He saw something in her change.

The pain gave way to action and drive. Her fearful face grew grim, and she took on the role of a warrior. Now was the time for combat. She was ready to fight. He didn't want to pull her into danger, but he wouldn't stand a good chance alone, and if he was going to get her anywhere, it was better she was fighting with him.

"I need you, too."

He lifted her chin until she was looking into his eyes.

"I promise you I'm here: no matter what."

There was another long pause, one that seemed to stretch on for a frighteningly long time. However, she did eventually move. It was a motion so small, anyone else might've missed it, but he saw it clearly. She nodded. She was still very ill, but she'd agreed and she was alive. It was a start.

Carefully, he led her to the entrance of her cell. As he walked through it, he felt her hold back. She stared, lost for a long time at the threshold. She viewed it as if crossing it were equal to crossing a canyon by a rope bridge. He understood her hesitation. Soldier or not, breaking captivity seemed impossible and unbelievable. She had to have accepted her captivity and likely had suffered for longer than he had. Given her attitude he wouldn't have been surprised if she'd hallucinated something similar to this scenario before.

"I've got you," he said, as gently as he could given his urgency.

She's actually alive.

He couldn't help but allow his heart to jump for joy, and it beat so loud he could actually hear it in his ears. She was *alive.* He'd accepted she was dead. He'd been sure she was dead. He'd seen her body, but she wasn't dead.

It could be a trick, he heard his father say.

Don't start! he mentally shouted. *I do not need paranoia or doubt right now. One step at a time.*

Still, he couldn't help smiling a little to himself. She was *actually* alive.

His voice appeared to snap her out of her revery and she followed more willingly, albeit slow and careful. Conners stopped at the door at the far end of the hall and opened it less than half an inch. The light that poured in blinded him. He was forced to squint for several long seconds before he could even start to make sense of what he saw. His eyes felt like he'd just been hit by a flashbang.

He saw what looked like an extravagant kitchen. It was clearly well-stocked and the fruit and bread that stood on the counter made his stomach growl in demand. He couldn't hear anything on his earpiece nor did he see anything in the kitchen. So after several seconds he moved forward, tugging Lawrence along with him. He quickly pulled her to the island in the middle and crouched down behind it while grabbing a couple pieces of fruit.

"Here," he said, selecting an orange and handing it to her. "Eat something that's not drugged. We can't go too fast or we'll puke, but we need some nourishment."

Lawrence stared blankly for a second before she began to peel at the orange with chipped nails.

"I like oranges," she whispered softly to him, as if she'd only just realized this.

"Yeah," he said softly, peeking over the island for any intruders while he worked on his banana. "I remember you like nanche, but I doubt they have any here. Besides, they smell so strong we'd be found out for eating those."

"You remember my favorite fruit?"

He looked over at her.

"Well yeah. I remember tons about you. You're my best friend."

"I just... I haven't thought about things like that for so long... Your beard's longer."

He paused for a second, unsure if it was better to explain his captivity, dismiss it, pull her back to the present moment, or acknowledge it. He also didn't know what state of mind she was in right now. She wasn't attacking him or holding back anymore, and he was grateful for that. She seemed to be acting in a stunned compliance. It was like the rules of physics no longer applied to her world and she had no choice but to go with it.

She needs to know that you're real: that you and her can still exist as people.

"Yeah," he whispered softly. "Thought I might try the whole viking thing. Now I just have to braid it and shave the side of my head."

She didn't laugh, smile, or roll her eyes, but he could tell his little gag connected with her, because her eyes lit up just a little. Footsteps began to approach them and Conners ducked down behind the island again, placing a hand on Lawrence's shoulder to help keep her steady. Then, he heard both in the earpiece and just outside of the kitchen, "Think I might've heard a noise from the kitchen. Checking it out."

He felt his heart stop as terror gripped him. He tried to force himself to act but his body wouldn't move. They'd surely be found. There was no hope of escape. Lawrence would be captured. He'd be captured. They'd be killed or shoved back in their cells and drugged all over again.

FOCUS!

Conners went to reach for the pistol he'd taken from the guard, but it wasn't there.

Bang! Bang!

He turned slowly and saw Lawrence standing in perfect form, gun extended. The guard she'd just shot slowly hit the floor and everything suddenly exploded with action. While the earpiece was flooded with chatter, Conners stood and pulled Lawrence out of the kitchen, sprinting for what appeared to be a dining room.

The small bit of saving grace was he'd also heard sirens heading up the street. They ducked into the adjoining room, which turned out to be a huge dining room capable of seating at least a dozen people at a huge mahogany table.

"You with me?" he asked Lawrence quietly.

"They won't take us," she said with all the resolution she could muster.

"We just need to delay enough time for SWAT to break the doors down."

He briefly considered shooting out the window and trying to jump out of it, but it was a bad thought. If either he or Lawrence had been in good condition, it might've worked. But as weary as they were, they were having a hard enough time just moving from room-to-room. There was no sense revealing their position if they didn't have to.

We can do this, he told himself. *We have to do this.*

Chapter XLIII: Cavalry

Conners looked over at Lawrence to try and gauge her condition. She was knelt with two hands on the pistol she'd taken from him. While she wasn't aiming yet, her eyes were taking in the room around them and the two entryways. In a heartbeat, she could aim and shoot in the modified weaver style most policemen learned to use. That wasn't as bad as it might be. While she was definitely defensive and had her nerves on a hair trigger, she wasn't treating *him* as a threat and she hadn't lost her discipline.

It could certainly be worse, but don't let your guard down, Vito sounded.

Conners drew his knife and tapped Lawrence on the shoulder before mouthing, "Follow me."

She nodded and he crept to the opposite archway, trying to make as little noise as possible. Despite his determination to focus his diminished brainpower on their escape, he couldn't help but notice the extravagance of the home around them. It was clear whoever Elizabeth was, she was wealthy. The floors were high quality hardwood and he doubted he could've afforded even the dining table nearby.

As he peaked around the corner he saw a huge foyer with an actual chandelier that had to be at least ten feet across. It hung down from the huge thirty-foot high ceiling. A large carpeted staircase circled the chandelier to bring the bearer up to the second-floor balcony. Next to the bottom of the staircase was a huge, ornate door Conners could only guess was the main entrance.

Unfortunately, there was a barrier in the form of a thug with a rifle atop the steps, his weapon trained on the door. Conners couldn't be sure from this distance, but he thought it looked like an AR-15. All assault weapons were illegal for the public in Chicago, and an automatic rifle was illegal in most of the country, but somehow Conners doubted the legality of the gun was much of a sticking point for this man.

"Hey!"

Conners heard the voice from behind them only a split-second before Lawrence fired, and her shot hit the man squarely between the eyes. He couldn't decide if he was relieved she was the one shooting or not. Her aim was certainly better than his would've been, but there was something disquieting in the killer glare she had as she pulled the trigger.

It's wartime, son. Do whatever keeps you and her alive for now.
Boom!

With a huge slam, something collided with the front door. Apparently Lawrence's shot was the final straw for the SWAT team's lineup, and they began battering down the door. The door was clearly solid and had possibly been reinforced because it didn't give in.

"Quick!" Conners hissed. "Think you can take down the one with the rifle before they break in?"

Lawrence peeked out and took aim. Conners watched as she steadied herself and took careful aim.

Bang! Bang!

They watched as the guard clutched his chest and fell forward, rolling over the railing before he smashed against the ground. Conners looked around, trying to take as much in as he could all the while his earpiece exploded with people shouting at one another. Had he been in a better state, he might've been able to decode what they were saying, but at the moment it was just extra noise. So he tossed the earpiece and ran up to take the rifle.

He scooped it up. As he turned to return to the dining room he heard another *bang*. Pain exploded in his right shin and he limped as quick as he could before letting his mind run a scan on the injury. He tossed Lawrence the AR-15, and her training took over as she checked the rifle quickly before providing covering fire.

- *Entry wound, but no exit: bullet's still inside of my leg.*
- *Wound isn't bleeding too badly: bullet is acting as a plug.*
- *Chances of hallow point bullet: unlikely: damage would be worse.*

Hopefully Guston brought an ambulance. Little else to be done about it right now.

He grabbed the pistol from Lawrence and gestured towards the table.

"Help me flip this!"

She looked confused for a second, but then it clicked and she helped him tip the wooden table over and they dragged it until it was diagonally covering the corner and providing protection for them.

"We just have to hold out a bit," he explained, checking the pistol. "SWAT should breach any second and help us withdraw."

"Copy!" Lawrence said, popping up to fire a small volley of shots.

Four bullets left, he thought after checking his pistol.

It was far from ideal, but it could've been a good deal worse. He heard commotion in the kitchen and could hear several men thundering down the prison hallway where they'd been only a couple minutes ago.

They're collecting Elizabeth before the cops can breech, Bill pointed out.

We could help hold them down there. I didn't notice another way out and SWAT shouldn't take long.

Bad idea, Vito remarked. *You're already injured and outgunned, there's no way of telling what shape Lawrence is in, and just because you didn't see another way out doesn't mean there isn't one. Let the cops do their job and you do yours. Stay alive for now.*

Another man came running in from the kitchen and they both shot quickly. Conners hit the man right between the eyes. The guard's shot exploded against the table in the same second and he mentally thanked God for the foresight. As he ducked back down two more men came sprinting in from the other side of the dining room. Lawrence quickly shot one and sent the other fleeing.

Boom!

Another assault on the door broke the lock and sent it flying open, and he could hear the heavy footsteps of the SWAT team. He carefully reached up to help pacify Lawrence and collapsed against the wall.

"We're all right," he said, letting his exhaustion and weariness fall over him. "We're going to be all right."

His vision slowly began to fade away as he lost consciousness. When he came to, he was laying in an ambulance and he could feel the EMTs working on him. He forced himself to check his surroundings as best he could, and saw the lieutenant, still in his vest.

"H-hey lieutenant," he said, trying to smile. "Glad you got my message. Is Lawrence going to be all right?"

Guston smiled back, but Conners saw the lie behind it.

"She's sedated right now. Just rest. You've been through a lot and I'll need to get your report once you're well enough. For now, just let these guys do their jobs, ok? I've got you set up at the hospital, so the press shouldn't bother you."

"What about…"

"Lawrence will be in the same room as you. It was something she was quite insistent on. But both of you are in rough shape. Get some rest and we'll worry about everything else later."

"What about Elizabeth?"

"Later."

Conners let that pacify him for the moment, and fell into the world of sleep as the medication kicked in.

~*~

When he next woke up, he knew he was in a hospital. It seemed fitting: the number of times he'd woken up after a trauma only to realize he was in a hospital bed. This was only the third such time since he'd tried to stop Kingston from robbing the bank years ago. He could tell he was still incredibly weak, but in much better shape than he'd been for… however long he'd been in captivity.

They'd cleaned him up and dressed his wounds. From the feeling of it, they'd fished the bullet out of his leg, which was a relief. He forced himself to look around the room and saw Lawrence sleeping in a bed several feet away. She was incredibly thin and her face bore the kind of exhaustion that could've killed someone. Even in her sleep, she was tense and on edge. It was like she was prepared for an attack at any second.

She's been tormented for a long time, kid. She probably is *ready for an attack at any second. Who knows, she might not even know if what she just went through was real.*

I'm not even sure it was real. But I'm not going to just leave her after I got her back.

He climbed out of the bed and collapsed as soon as he tried to stand upright.

- *Muscles are weak and suffering from lack of nutrients.*

He latched onto the IV stand that was delivering what was doubtlessly a small mixture of drugs into his system, and used it as a walker to help cross the room. It was slow going and hurt far more than it should've. It made his rehab after being burned seem like a cakewalk, but his reward was also far greater than it had been then.

He reached Lawrence's bedside and sat in the chair there, breathing like he'd just run a marathon. Slowly, he reached up and touched her hand with his, noticing how his own hand was even more slender than it should've been, and it was shaking.

I guess I'm not in good shape either. Elizabeth kept us just a breath away from death. We're gonna have to deal with her once we can. But it'll be a while before either of us is in a fit state to attack a staircase, let alone someone as dangerous as her.

That gives you some time though, kid.

Time for what?

To figure out who she is.

How would I know who she is?

I'm telling you that you do *know who she is. You just can't quite put the pieces together yet.*

Can't you just tell me?

If I could, you'd know, wouldn't you?

He sighed and snapped himself out of his mental conversation, instead focusing on Lawrence. It felt so good to see her, even as much as it hurt to see her so injured. The fact she wasn't dead was confounding him, but he could wait. The fact she was alive at all was something to be grateful for, and so he let go of his curiosity.

Instead, he kept hold of her hand and prayed for peace and healing. It felt good to pray with Lawrence, even if she wasn't aware of what he was doing. It felt like something he should've always been doing, only he'd been too foolish to realize it. He didn't know how many hours he sat there, but eventually his exhaustion overcame him and he passed out with his head on the side of her bed.

He was awoken by a nurse entering the room and groggily sat up.

"Well, well," said the nurse, smiling softly. "Welcome to the land of the living, Mister Black."

"T-thank you," he said, stifling a yawn.

"You're supposed to be resting in bed."

"I am resting," he protested. "Does it matter if I'm horizontal when I do it?"

She glared at him, but he could tell it was more in jest than serious.

"If you're going to be difficult, we can restrain you."

"Bit calloused to say that to a prisoner, isn't it?"

"We're here to help you, John. Just don't fight us too much on that, please?"

He nodded, and looked at Lawrence.

"Is she going to be all right?"

The nurse hesitated for a moment.

"She wasn't in a good way when she got here. She's been through an awful lot, not to downplay your own problems, of course. She was very weak and appears to have been under some nasty drug for about a year. We cleansed both of your blood and you're getting nutrient treatments right now, but she's going to need some therapy and help if she's going to recover mentally. For now we're just trying to get your bodies back to being at least half-functional."

"She'll recover," he said softly, although he wasn't sure if he was talking to himself or the nurse. "She's going to recover from this."

The nurse nodded, but he knew it was merely to placate him.

"Well, in the meantime I need to get some vitals and bloodwork from you both."

He complied and let her draw the blood without protest or remark, instead focusing on Lawrence's sleeping face the whole time.

So I really wasn't dreaming or hallucinating it? She's really alive? Sure, she's in a bad way, but alive.

Despite what he understood and everything in front of him, it still seemed impossible she was actually alive. It felt uncomfortably like half of him was experiencing life before Kingston's death, and half of him knew life would never be as it had been back then. It was like having his mind torn in two all over again.

Never was one to do things the easy way.

~*~

He stayed at Lawrence's side for the whole of the next day, excusing himself only to shower and attempt to eat food, which it turned out was mostly jello. Apparently solid foods were not part of his approved diet yet. If he weren't still weak and tired, he would've seriously considered attempting another breakout just for a hamburger.

As he resettled into his seat he heard Lawrence stir. She'd been asleep since he'd woken up and he hadn't attempted to rouse her. He knew more than most the danger of interrupting a mind trying to recover after a trauma. She looked at him for two full seconds before he saw her brain register what she was seeing. When she did, she smiled wide enough that her bottom lip cracked a little.

"You're really alive?" she asked, slurring her words in a croaky voice.

"I feel like I should be asking you that."

He reached over for the cup on the side table and put the straw between her lips so she could take a drink of water.

"What happened?"

"Again," he said smirking a little. "I think I should be asking that. I saw your dead body. I *saw* Kingston over your body."

Her smile vanished and was replaced with a scowl, which was followed by one of the greatest expressions of pain he'd ever seen. It was as if someone had just stabbed her in the chest, and he saw tears begin to leak from her eyes as she gasped, trying to catch her breath.

"Y-you didn't see *me*. You probably didn't realize it at the time… After I left your parents' place, Janice and I were talking things through. She was concerned and wanted to help."

Conners felt a sudden stab of guilt as he realized he had never even tried to contact Janice during his recovery. Not that the two of them were exactly close but he'd been too self-absorbed and withdrawn to even think about reaching out to anyone they might've mutually known.

"When some of Kingston's thugs found her… Well, they couldn't tell the difference between us. I spent a while trying to figure out where they would've taken her. I didn't even think about the damn apartment until it was too late. By the time I got to it, the place was blown up and cops and ambulances were swarming it. Later I heard you and Janice had both died in the explosion, even though they'd thought she was me."

Conners grabbed her hands as they shook.

"He called me," he explained. "He used Janice to bring me to the apartments, and we both thought she was you. I… lost myself when I thought you were dead. I set up an ambush for him and blew the apartment up. I half-caught myself in the explosion and had to spend a long while being nursed back to stable condition."

He explained regaining his memory and briefly covered his recovery period afterward, though he left out his meeting with Jesus.

Lawrence was still grieving the loss of her sister and hardly needed to be reminded of the aspects of the afterlife.

"So," he said softly, trying not to sound like he was accusing her. "You were taking out Kingston's men while I was laid out?"

Laid out… certainly sounds a lot better than moping and pissing.

"Yeah. I knew I couldn't stop them as a cop. So I sort of took a page out of your book. I did the research and work on my own, tracked down the thugs, and either incapacitated them or just left a tip for the cops along with whatever evidence I'd gathered. It was working pretty well until that bitch caught me and knocked me out. Next thing I knew she had me in some sort of dark hole and drugged me over and over and over and over and…"

He placed a hand on her shoulder and she snapped herself out of it. She reached up and rubbed the tears out of her eyes.

"I remember," he said and kissed her hands. "Her name's Elizabeth and she's got some sort of focus on us; though I'm not exactly sure why yet. She said some things, but I'll need to go over all of it later. Hopefully the lieutenant caught her before she escaped. I'm sure he's going to want to talk to us about all this too."

"Think he's going to press charges on my work?"

"No," said Conners, firmly. "He didn't want to bring everyone into it before and you've earned a little cover. Besides, I doubt they *actually* have proof of any illegal activity. Even if they did you and I should be able to make things work out."

"So, you're sticking by me even with all of this… mess?"

He smiled softly, trying to reassure her.

"I'm by your side for as long as you want me there."

She smiled for a second time since seeing him.

"I saw you over and over… I had hallucinations and I saw you coming to rescue me, but you never did. Well, I suppose you did now."

He didn't know how to respond to that. How *did* you respond to the torment and torture of someone you loved?

"You… you told me you loved me," she said softly. "Did you actually say that?"

"I did," he said, looking right into her emerald eyes. "And I do."

Chapter XLIV: Explain

Conners groaned and sat up from the bed. He didn't usually sleep on his back but the hospital bed was hardly practical to use any other way. So he'd only been sleeping in bursts of a few hours at a time. The doctors had attempted to put him on sleeping medicine but he'd adamantly refused. After spending what he'd learned was several full months being repeatedly drugged and underfed in Elizabeth's underground hellhole, he refused to take anything that would dull his brain.

Still, he was mostly recovering. He could stand up and walk around their room without completely exhausting himself by this point, and Lawrence was even able to move a little. She'd been in worse shape than him, and while the adrenaline of their chance for escape had carried her the few rooms they'd moved, her body had refused anything more after they were rescued.

They both had frequent nightmares, Lawrence more than him. He barely slept long enough to dream, and he suspected his past traumas were helping him deal with his most recent one. Bill had once pointed out that it was extremely difficult to mentally break someone twice, which was one of the reasons the military trained people in the way that they did. He'd already suffered through a complete loss of identity, his murder of a child, losing a father figure, having his life put in danger several times, and being blown up to the point he'd technically died. After all that it was possible his brain just worked with trauma in a different way.

Lawrence was strong. She always had been, and while she'd been through more than her fair share of pain and suffering, it was clear this was cutting far deeper than anything else had.

He did what he could to help her, even if it felt like it wasn't very much. The biggest thing was reassuring her he was not actually dead. If he was honest, he appreciated this gesture just as much as she did, because he still often felt *she* might be dead and he was just suffering some elaborate hallucination. He held her hand through the several tests the hospital ran on her. Lawrence was *extremely* uncomfortable being touched by anyone else and more than once he'd felt her tense up as if to strike at the nurses.

The pair of them spoke to a psychologist and therapist frequently as well. Over the course of the two weeks since escaping Elizabeth, they'd met with the therapist a total of six times, each time as a pair.

Lawrence refused to be treated apart from him and he didn't want to lose track of her either. They were assured the sessions could slow down once they were released, but for now it was important they talk through as much as they could, as often as they could manage.

It helped them to speak about everything as a pair. When one had been pushed to the limit or to tears, the other would take over and speak for a while. It was natural for them to trade responsibility and protect each other in this way. Although, when he considered it, things had almost always been that way between them. Ever since Bill's death they'd always worked to help the each other, even if they completely disagreed with the other's methods.

However, things were going to be a bit different today. They were finally deemed to be in a fit enough state to allow the lieutenant and John's parents to visit today. Lawrence had been fretting about it no matter how much he'd tried to help keep her calm, and he could understand. He'd practically grown up skirting the edges of the law and following his own code more than anything else, but Lawrence was relatively new to it and suddenly she'd have to defend herself to her former boss. It was enough to put anyone on edge. Their best hope was that at his core, Guston was a decent man.

They spent the day distracting themselves, mostly by recounting moments from their lives before meeting one another. Lawrence was particularly interested in Conners' history as John Black and pestered him with as many questions as she could think of. Likewise, she shared her history with him, explaining what it was like to grow up in her family.

"My dad always had a huge gambling problem. He was already a recovering addict when my mom started to date him, and he swore off it after Janice and I were born. That lasted maybe five or six years before he found his way into a high-stakes poker game. Mom was furious and they separated, although I don't think they were ever actually divorced."

"What happened with your dad?"

"He was in and out a lot. When he was doing really well, he'd stop by and give us gifts and things. He always gave mom a fair amount of money too. I think he was trying to buy his way back into her good graces, but she'd always just put it in a fund for Janice and I and send him away again. Honestly that wasn't too bad, all things considered."

"And what about when he *wasn't* doing well?" Conners asked, recalling far too many cases involving gambling debts.

"Well, then things got... rougher. He'd still call mom up, but when he was struggling it was like Janice and I didn't exist. He'd refuse to talk to us and that always bothered me. I just wanted to say hi to my dad but if he was down and out the only thing he wanted was money. Luckily mom knew better than to give him any."

"Your mom must've loved both of you an awful lot," he said, smiling softly. "Can't be an easy thing to protect your kids from your husband's addiction."

"We used to hate her for it, because we sometimes wanted to call him or visit ourselves, but she never let us. The most we were allowed to do was write a letter she would mail. Every once in a while we might get one in return, but not often. We used to talk about that a lot, and say how mean she was being. It wasn't until high school I realized she was protecting us from him. When Janice and I saw what sort of people he would get involved with, it stirred us both to chase criminals in our own way. I became a cop, and eventually made my way to sergeant detective, and she became a lawyer."

Conners chuckled at that.

"Dinner conversations must've been riveting in your house."

She smiled, and he took pleasure in the motion. She was smiling more often and occasionally he'd even gotten her to laugh. But most of the time her face held a permanently pained expression, not unlike a soldier who had just seen their friends die in a firefight.

"There were the occasional arguments over procedure and protocol. You know how it is; lawyers always argue whatever they can on behalf of clients, and cops want to get results and view procedure as a block sometimes."

"Wow, and here I thought I was the wild one when I met you."

That made her laugh, and he cherished the sound as if it were sung by a choir.

"You were such an annoying prick then! I couldn't decide whether to help you or arrest you."

"I remember, and I'll have you know I'm *still* an annoying prick, thank you very much."

She shook her head at that and looked into his eyes with her bright emerald orbs.

"Yeah but you end up growing on a person."

"Like a damn fungus."

They both laughed as the door opened and Doctor Hughes walked in. Hughes: their primary care physician was a slightly pudgy man with a prominent bald spot and a small pair of oval spectacles that sat just a little too low on his nose. Still, as far as either of them were aware, he was a fairly skilled doctor.

"Mister Black? Miss Lawrence? Sorry to interrupt, but Lieutenant Mark Guston has just arrived to speak with you. I just need to check you guys real quick before he's allowed in."

Conners obediently held out his arm for the doctor to attach the sensor and blood pressure device. He'd heard one of the nurses name the device once, but the name was so ridiculous he couldn't even remember it, let alone spell it.

After it was determined a questioning from the lieutenant wasn't likely to harm them, the doctor nodded and glared at the door. Conners could tell whether or not the doctor knew exactly who they were, he'd been told that they weren't criminals and he didn't approve of the lieutenant pressing them when they were still comparatively weak. It made him respect the man just a bit more.

"Thanks doc," he said, nodding to try and assure the man.

Hughes left and Guston came in afterward, dressed in his police suit and hat. As the lieutenant approached them, he could feel Lawrence tense up and she gripped his hand very tightly. He quickly thought through a few things he could say to help lighten the mood a little. After all, it was his long-standing specialty to poke a bit of fun at people.

"Full attire," Conners said to Lawrence, smirking softly. "Either there are press around or we're getting medals."

Her mouth twitched at that and he felt her grip loosen just a bit.

"Honestly," said Guston, removing the hat and sitting near them. "I'm still shocked either of you were alive. I've been trying to come see you since you were admitted, but apparently you were both in critical condition and weren't cleared for anything that didn't have a warrant attached… and I'm not sure I wanted that."

"We appreciate that," said Conners.

"Yeah," said Lawrence, and her voice cracked. "It's… I'm glad to see you, lieutenant."

For the first time since entering the room, Guston smiled back and Conners allowed himself to relax a little.

"It's a relief to see you too, Lawrence. We were all sure you were dead. Then, after Conners got taken, we were sure *he* was dead. So, care to explain how you two apparently became immortal and why you only choose to grace us with your presence now?"

"We made a wish on this set of seven magical spheres from Japan," Conners said, though the joke was lost on both Guston and Lawrence. Sighing, he looked at Lawrence. "Should I start or you?"

"You first, please. I'm still a bit... everything, I think."

He nodded and a flash of concern flew over the lieutenant's features.

"They really did a number on you two, huh? I know you were both extremely weak when we found you, but you didn't really explain exactly what..."

"In time," Conners said, firmly. "Let me think for a minute. I guess it's good to go back to the day Lawrence's mother passed away..."

And so he talked and talked and talked. Lawrence was mostly silent and spoke only to verify what he'd said or correct a detail here and there. To his credit, Guston didn't interrupt or present a line of questioning. In fact, for the first time since Conners had met him, the man didn't act as a police lieutenant. Instead, he listened as a friend and let them say all that needed to be said.

When Conners finally finished explaining everything up to their holdout in the dining room of Elizabeth's manor, Guston rubbed his chin in deep thought.

"And you have no idea why she singled you out?" he asked.

"As for me," Lawrence said. "I think she is trying to fill the power vacuum Kingston left behind when he died."

That's a kind way to put it, Conners heard Vito say. *Sounds more like he died of natural causes instead of being burned alive.*

Shut up!

"When I started to catch the men she was using I guess it put me on her radar. She didn't seem to know I used to be a cop or anything. She never spent much time with me or spoke to me. I don't know if she even had a plan for me. She's..."

"Unhinged," Conners finished. "She had some type of fascination with me I haven't been able to explain yet. The trap you and I hit was likely intended for me. I know we took some precautions but it was hardly possible to keep my involvement in that case a complete secret. So, when we answered the call, they took me. When I woke up I was in Elizabeth's basement."

"Right. We explored that. Apparently there was a secret exit. How long were you down there?"

"Ever since she took me, I think."

"I'm honestly surprised you never found that exit yourself. You never seem to miss things like that."

"Well to be fair, I was drugged to the gills and hallucinating. It made it really hard to think properly, even if I could've seen anything. Things got… bad, to put it mildly."

"Well, I'll admit there's a bit of a mess involved there," said Guston rubbing his head. "But I don't think it should be anything that can't be handled. What are your plans, sergeant?"

Lawrence did a double-take. Conners couldn't help but remember this was the man who had fallen out with Bill due to a disagreement where the law was concerned. He'd broken off his relationship with his partner to uphold the law, and it was clear that decision had hung over him for the entirety of his career. More than once Conners had wondered if Guston had regretted the action. He still wasn't sure of the answer, but the lieutenant had apparently decided he hadn't liked the results enough to repeat them.

"How do you mean?"

"I mean do you intend to resume your work at the fourteenth precinct? There's a lot of things that would have to be taken care of before you were cleared for duty."

Conners took note and appreciated that the lieutenant used the word *before* and not *if*. The reality was after a trauma like the one they'd been through, they'd both need a full psychological work-up and several clearance tests before they were anywhere near cleared for active duty. Considering the damage that had been done, it was even entirely possible they may not be cleared. There were certain things the human mind just couldn't come back from and remain whole. As it stood, Conners wasn't sure if he or Lawrence *could've* resumed work, let alone if they wanted to.

"I don't want to go back to being a sergeant detective," she said softly. "I don't think that I can. I appreciate that you would do what you could to help me, though. I know it can't exactly be making things easy on you."

Guston smiled softly and nodded as a warm gesture.

"You're *always* going to be one of mine, sergeant, regardless of the path you chose in life. I look after my team."

Conners respect for the man rose, and for perhaps the first time since meeting him, he saw just a flash of the influence Bill must've had on the man. Guston certainly could be a total ass and had far too much personal ambition for his taste, but he did have his decent areas. While he wasn't entirely sure if he was flattering himself, Conners couldn't help but feel his influence on Guston had played a small part in that.

Nevertheless, the established joker in him couldn't help but push the situation just a little. Besides, he was still focused on trying to help lighten the mood a bit for all their sakes.

"Awwww, am *I* one of your favorites?" he asked with a slight drawl.

"You are the one I want to throw into a wood chipper."

Conners smiled and once again he felt Lawrence relax just a little. They might just be all right in the end, even if there was still an awful lot of work left to do.

"Well, I can't pretend I understand all of this yet, and at some point I'll need a signed statement from both of you, but I have enough to move on with for now. In the meantime, just focus on getting better. We'll handle Elizabeth. We've already got a fair few rocks to turn over so she won't be able to stay hidden for long. Oh and before I forget, Conners your mother wanted to see you if you're still feeling up to a visitor."

"Lydia?" he asked, slightly confused. "Vito didn't come, too?"

Guston suddenly stiffened, and it felt like the temperature in the room dropped several degrees. It took the lieutenant four seconds before he started to speak, and when he did his voice carried a stiffer, more official tone to it.

"That's the other reason why I wanted to come talk to you first, Conners. Your father had a hard time of it after you were taken, and unfortunately suffered a heart attack on October third last year. He didn't survive the ordeal."

"Vito's... dead?"

"I'm sorry, Conners."

He sat in a blank stupor, and didn't know what he felt. He wasn't sure if he was in pain or grief or denial. The only emotion he could work out clearly was the incredible crushing guilt that weighed on his heart like a lead brick.

Chapter XLV: Plans

Conners lifted himself from the new mattress he'd selected for himself and removed the bedsheets that were still too new to be comfortable. After spending a few days speaking to Lydia, they'd been released from the hospital, and the trio had found themselves in a strange position. Neither Conners nor Lydia wanted to return to his childhood home, and had put it on the market and sold most of the belongings inside. They'd barely talked about it. The entire process was handled by some ambitious—albeit capable—realtor.

He didn't keep anything from his bedroom except his laptop, a few choice case files, and a shoebox of old photos taken when he was too young to remember much of anything. They were usually of Vito and John Black. He had a hard time thinking of himself as John, even though he knew he was… or at least who he *had* been. But after being Conners, it was hard to return to being John. After Vito's death, that became impossible.

He still wasn't entirely sure how he was supposed to feel about his father's passing. The two had been both drastically different and very similar to one another all at once. Both had skirted the law, only in different areas to different ends. Both had followed their own code and done what they determined to be right, and neither could fully accept the other's beliefs. Still, through all that, John did love his father, and Conners felt like he'd lost the man before he'd fully come to know him.

He shuffled his way to the bathroom only to be greeted by a closed door and the sound of the shower running. Lawrence had risen before him and beaten him to their shared bathroom. He didn't mind much, but it was an adjustment from what he was used to. He'd spent most of his life doing things practically on impulse. So, he had to learn patience and consideration where having a roommate was concerned. The alternative was for he and Lawrence to separate and neither were fans of the idea.

While they didn't sleep in the same room, they spent most of their time together. Lawrence had woken only two nights ago sobbing and crying for Janice, to which he'd been able to do nothing more than hold her and try to help calm her down. She wasn't the only one struggling either. More often than not, he had nightmares. Sometimes it was Elizabeth, sometimes Kingston, sometimes Richards, sometimes a child in a back alley with a bullet hole in his head. He tried to maintain. He tried to deal with it. It wasn't going well. Either he spoke in his sleep or Lawrence was simply in tune with his pains, because usually when his nightmares woke him up, she was there and would try to help relax him. He loved her for it.

They still had regular check-ups with the doctor and saw their therapist every Thursday. Their bathroom medicine cabinet held a plethora of anxiety pills, mood stabilizers, supplements, and sleeping aids. Physically, they were certainly healthier than they'd been in Elizabeth's captivity, but they were still considered malnourished and underweight by the doctor.

He decided to pass the time waiting for the coffee pot to finish brewing by flipping idly through the channels, and found himself stopping on the local news. While he had historically despised the news and its manipulation of the general public, he'd felt disconnected recently. It felt good to be connected to the world, even if it was in so rudimentary a form as the local news.

Police have yet to issue a statement regarding the death of one Patrick Teller...

Ignoring Vito's warnings of the danger the story might present for him, Conners leaned forward, enraptured. The reporter went over the few details of the case they had access to. The facts were almost entirely useless to help procure a lead without inside information. However, the photographs of the store where the murder had taken place sent several alarm bells ringing in his head, and he paused the program to try and examine the scene more carefully. He didn't realize Lawrence had exited the bathroom until she sat down next to him on the couch, fully dressed.

Like a rush of cold water, her presence made him fully aware of the pressure in his bladder and he flew to the bathroom. He left it a couple minutes later, drying his hands on his pants. He found Lawrence staring transfixed at the television. The glow on her tanned skin made her appear paler than she really was. She was looking better than she had in the hospital. She was far closer to being whole, even if she wasn't there yet. She'd cut her hair to shoulder length: shorter than she'd worn it as a detective, though she'd abandoned the ponytail. The lost weight brought her cheekbones and chin into a higher prominence, but her eyes were perhaps the thing that most fascinated him.

Sometimes they were wild and fierce. She was like a hunter tracking her prey across the field. At other times they displayed her panic and fear. She reminded him forcibly of a scared child watching their parents fight, unable to do anything more than hope to go unnoticed. Sometimes, in the quiet moments around the apartment when neither could find the words, she looked like a wounded animal, ready to accept her death. She bore the grief of her lost family. Her sister and mother were both dead, and her nephew was living with his godparents. She hadn't been able to face seeing him and Conners didn't press the issue. Finally there were the rare (though they were becoming more frequent) times when she would would smile or laugh, and all the old wonder and excitement would make her emerald eyes light up.

Staring at the television, those eyes were narrowed and focused. She looked like a chess player anticipating an opponent's move and formulating a response. It was still displaying the picture he'd frozen the image on. Instead of turning his focus back onto the television, he focused on her.

Her gaze was intense and focused, and almost grim. However, within that glare, there was a lot of the emotions he knew in himself when he worked a case. There was the excitement, the hunger for answers, the desire to solve the puzzle, and the hope of catching a killer. He saw she would *always* be something of a detective, no matter what her job title was. He supposed he understood. He couldn't completely expel Conners from himself either.

"See anything?" he asked softly.

She breathed in sharply. It was the first time either had broached the subject of casework in the present-tense. Even when he'd chosen to take case files from Lydia's house, they'd never discussed the matter. Without any declaration, the idea of working a case was taboo. However, the mutually-imposed embargo on that subject made no sense. They were detectives: investigators by habit. They'd always sought the most dangerous beings the city had to offer for the chance to right a wrong. There was no sense in pretending otherwise.

"The picture," he reiterated. "Anything stick out to you?"

She waited another second before responding.

"There's no cameras pointing directly at the spot where Teller was shot," she began slowly. "But since the perp never hit the cash register that means Teller was truly the target."

"And?"

"There's one of those fish-eye mirrors above the bathrooms."

"Exactly."

"If the department could get their tech guys to clean up the footage a little, they might get a better image of the guy's face. Not definite, but it's something to work off of."

He smiled at her, and she smiled back at him, both flush with the victory of their discovery. He pulled out his cellphone and looked at her.

"Want to make the call?"

Lawrence pulled away just slightly, and he couldn't blame her. While Guston had been as good as his word and kept Lawrence from being formally charged with any criminal activity, it was also clear she preferred to keep some distance from the police aspect of her old life. Again, he could sympathize. He could remember his repeated efforts to shut Guston out of his life and refuse casework over and over and over.

"It's no problem," he said, as a slight fear jumped into her eyes. "I can do it if you want."

He dialed the number for the tip hotline and left a brief message indicating what he and Lawrence had noticed, and then hung up. Even if he'd wanted to do more, the case wasn't with the fourteenth precinct and while his name might carry a little weight, he wasn't sure he wanted to bring Conners back from the dead.

He didn't want to bring Conners back from the dead… yet.

That was an interesting feeling, because the implication was clear and unavoidable. He wasn't done, however much he might want to be at times.

Are you ready to rest?

He hadn't considered the question for a little while, but he knew his answer hadn't changed. He was not ready to rest. There was work to be done. He was still a soldier in the field and he hadn't received clearance to leave just yet.

So soldier, he heard Bill say. *Pick up your weapon and serve.*

Conners walked to the closet where he'd stuffed his boxes and files and pulled out one of the cases at random, and brought it to the kitchen table. Without saying anything, Lawrence walked over and poured them both a cup of coffee before sitting next to him at the table, and looking over the facts of the case with him.

He knew in that moment they would resume their work, even if it wouldn't be exactly as it had been. Lawrence likely would never be a cop again, but that certainly didn't mean she couldn't be a detective. Legally, he still held all rights to Knighthawk Investigations, and could hire whoever he pleased. Of course, he would bring Lawrence aboard the split-second she asked, but it had to be done carefully. Both he and Lawrence had their share of enemies and he wanted to build everything back up before making any public declarations.

They poured over the case file for most of the morning and early afternoon, skipping over lunch entirely. For a few hours, it was almost like things had been before Janice had died. For a few hours, Conners was a private detective and Lawrence was his police sergeant friend, and they joked and laughed together as if they weren't both bearing the marks of captivity.

It wasn't until a sharp *knock* snapped them out of their joined musings Conners checked the clock. It was past three in the afternoon. He carefully opened the door to find Lydia standing on their doorstep with several food items in her arms, which he dutifully took from her. Despite their protests, Lydia showed up at least three times a week to cook dinner for the pair of them and check up on their state of mind. Had he been more insistent, it was possible he could've made her stop. But she had already lost him for several years and only recently lost Vito; he didn't have the heart force the issue.

"You wouldn't believe the day I had at the store!" said Lydia as a way of greeting.

This was hardly unusual for her. Conners would've sworn his mother was attempting to get put on a reality show about the woes of everyday life. Sometimes the bank was causing what might've been a minor issue; only to her it was ridiculous and unacceptable. Other times she would mumble and complain about the poor service at a restaurant, despite the fact that the waiter or waitress was clearly busy. To her credit, Lydia was always polite and would joke slightly with any of the workers, but the moment they were out of earshot she'd start up. Today, it was apparently something to do with the employees at the grocery store.

"So I went to buy the noodles for tonight…"

Long and wide, Conners' mind provided without provocation. *She must be making lasagna.*

He mentally scolded himself and attempted to turn off his deductive mindset while his mother rattled on about how they'd clearly made a mistake in the sticker price of the noodles, and then she'd had the worst time trying to her coupon code accepted. All the while he merely nodded and listened politely. Lawrence replicated his actions but he could tell she carried as little interest in the conversation as he did.

"It's just the most ridiculous… What is that?"

She cut herself off mid-stride and pointed at their kitchen table. Conners followed the gesture and saw the notes from the file he'd unearthed.

"Oh," he said, feigning a nonchalance. "Just some notes from an old case. Lawrence and I were just taking a look over it. Nothing major."

Please let that be the end of it, he mentally pleaded.

"Hm," Lydia hummed curtly. "Well, that'll be enough of that."

"What do you mean?" asked Lawrence, and Conners was surprised by the force in her voice.

Lydia was slightly taken aback too, but only for a moment. She quickly recomposed herself and explained.

"Well, that casework was all too dangerous for you two, dear. I mean, you both went through some horrible things because of all that."

Conners fully expected Lawrence to back down. She hadn't done well with confrontation ever since they'd started to recover, not that he blamed her. Lawrence didn't back away. If anything, there was even more strength in her when she spoke.

"Missus Black, I care about you and I respect that you care for both me and your son, but this work is important to both of us. We used to help a lot of people."

Lydia didn't intend to back down either.

"I have both of your best interests at heart. John tells me he's encountered multiple killers, cultists, thieves, and rapists since he started this… vigilante crusade of his. I can hardly imagine you've had it any easier. No, the two of you will do much better once you choose a more mundane line of work."

"I can't speak for Conners," said Lawrence. "But I certainly don't want to spend time stocking shelves or crunching numbers for some company for the rest of my life. I didn't get through Elizabeth's crap just to sit on my ass. I'm going to do something."

"It's John!" insisted Lydia. "And as much as I regret reminding you of it dear, you've not been cleared for active duty. You can't just go back to being a cop until you are, and the lieutenant was quite clear on that."

"I'll go into the private sector if need be," said Lawrence, and Conners had never heard a firmer declaration from her. "I'm a detective, Missus Black."

"Whatever you decide to do is your choice, of course," said Lydia, the ice in her voice practically visible. "But I'm quite sure John is hoping to resume something a little quieter after his father's passing. After all, there's no sense in making your loved ones worry all the time."

Conners, who'd finally had enough of being spoken for, stepped forward.

"Mom, that's enough," he said, firm but not unkind. "I know you love me and you want to keep me safe. I know you're scared of the world since I was taken and dad died. But I need to help people. What is my life worth if I sit and refuse to use the gifts I've been given?"

"You died! More than once, if I have to remind you. I cannot hear that I have lost my son *again*. I can't. I won't."

Conners stiffened.

"Mom. I love you, and I am sorry. But I am going to return to work as soon as I'm medically cleared. I'm going to fix what things I can."

"Why do you have to try and do everything? Why isn't what you've done enough? Why can't you think of yourself and your family for once?"

"Like Vito did?"

That stopped her cold. Conners had never criticized Vito in front of her since he'd regained his memory. Not once. Out of a desire to preserve the relationship that had rested perilously above a pit of spikes, they'd never broached subjects they disagreed so heavily on.

"Vito put us ahead of the law. He put us first. It might've been done because he loved us, but it was wrong. A lot of people in this city relied on Bill and later on me when they couldn't convince or trust the police, or when the police couldn't close a case. No offense, Lawrence."

"None taken," she said, placing a hand on his shoulder. "Missus Black, I will go into business with your son. If we have to do this without your blessing, we will. But it would be better for him and you if you could support us on this."

Lydia was quiet for a long while. She didn't move, but her hands were white and shaking. Finally, she only managed to stutter for a couple seconds before she slowly turned and walked out of the apartment, leaving her ingredients on the counter. Conners waited two seconds after she left before shutting the door softly.

"It'll be ok," he said, speaking to himself. "She needs some time to accept things. Losing my dad was really hard for her. All the same, it's better that she knows now. When I go back, I would want her to know before instead of after. She deserves that."

Lawrence nodded and hugged him from behind.

"We."

"Sorry?" he asked, confused.

"When *we* go back, not you."

"So you meant that? You really want to work with me?"

She laughed and hugged him tighter.

"Conners, as far as I know I'm the only person alive who *can* work with you. I already used to work with you. This is really just going to save some money and time. Besides, I've got plans and I need to be there before you find a way to ruin them."

"First, I can always find a way to ruin plans. You know that. Second, what *exactly* are your plans for my business?"

"Well, our business needs a new location large enough for us to live in and work out of. I'm definitely thinking some hardwood floors, and how do you feel about taking on a few new people?"

"We're going to need a bigger place… Think we could get a fireplace?"

Chapter XLVI: Students and Teacher

Conners peeked over the collection of over twenty hopefuls that had passed whatever reasonable test he'd put forth to help weed out their new employees. As it turned out, Lawrence hoped to turn him into a teacher who could help usher in the new age of Knighthawk Investigations.

Conners had made a quick call to Paul Boston. The man had accepted Conners' resurrection with the same oddly detached air he'd presented when his late wife had passed. However, he'd seemed excited at the prospect of turning Knighthawk Investigations into a true firm. Within a few weeks, they'd found a location for the new office and made the press release revealing his status and the revival of the company.

For a while, they were bombarded with requests for interviews and pressures from different brands and companies. All of these Boston and his team swiftly handled. Conners had been clear that he didn't want to change or compromise who he was, and he'd been promised that he wouldn't have to. He also demanded both and he and Lawrence could run things as they saw fit. Boston agreed in exchange for the right to use the company if there was a case that deserved it, 12% of the company, and some bragging rights as their wealthy backer. Never being one who cared about the credit for his work, he'd agreed.

Then had come casework which had lasted into the new year, and it was actually a huge change to get back on the streets again. They hadn't had any murder cases, or worked with the fourteenth precinct yet. They'd cleared quite a few cases of theft and three missing persons cases.

Then, they'd announced their competing internship program. Conners and Lawrence agreed they would take on a total of four students between the two of them, and they'd had more applicants than he could've imagined. Luckily, a quick questionnaire had weeded out plenty of the would-be students. The remains were a large mix of men and women of different ages, races, and backgrounds. Several were either ex-cops or private detectives who either didn't like their old boss or had been released for some reason or other. Honestly, as long as they had the right heart and mind for investigation, he didn't care why they'd left their old jobs.

Teaching was difficult for him. So he was determined to make the hiring as simple a process as possible. Potential cases were building up and he had hopes to put his new team onto casework once they got into February. With any luck they might be ready to go out on their own in a few months… with occasional oversight, of course. Then after enough time had passed and he was ready, he might be able to actually retire from the field and consult on the cases purely within his own company. That would be fun.

Still, if he was going to make sure these people could handle the cases and demands of Chicago, he might as well have fun with it.

"All right!" he called out and the collection of students stopped and looked to him. "I'm Michael J. Conners and you all are officially my bitches until you quit, are fired, or can actually pull your own weight. I am going to demean, embarrass, and occasionally belittle you and your efforts when you fail. I will ask you to keep impossible hours, skirt the edge of the law, and solve problems the rest of the city cannot. Any problems with that, there's the door. See yourself out."

None moved.

Can't blame a guy for trying.

"All right then. Trial by fire it is… or theft in this case," he said, tossing a stack of copied files down onto the table. "Everyone take a copy of the file and split yourselves into two teams based on… let's say people who take cream or sugar in their coffee on one side and those who take their roast the way God made it on the other."

He heard Lawrence quickly stifle a laugh behind him. One young man came up to him. Without meaning to call it up, Conners saw the man's application fly before him.

Jim Longworth.

He was an aspiring detective who wasn't without promise, but he had a tendency to be a little too fond of women and golf for Conners' tastes. However, he'd made it through the vetting process and wasn't incapable as a detective. Still, something about the young man put Conners off just a little. He had a flavor for dry humor and sarcasm, but if anything that only made Conners see a bit of himself in the man. No, there was something else about Longworth that ever-so-slightly unsettled him.

"I don't actually drink coffee," said Jim, smirking.

Conners could tell whether or not Longworth was lying, he was using Conners' arbitrary guidelines to unsettle him, and so Conners fired back just as quickly.

"Then you're with the heathens. Join the cream and sugar team."

Longworth looked disappointed, but dutifully grabbed one of the copies and stood amongst his assigned group.

"My dear... something or other: Lieutenant Mark Guston has been the subject of a theft. Someone appears to have stolen his Medal of Valor, and while it hasn't turned up in any pawn shops or known black market sales, it has indeed gone somewhere. The team who comes the closest to the answer by sundown wins. Good luck!"

They scattered like flies fleeing a spray of raid. Only after the last of them left the room did Lawrence finally speak up.

"Did someone *actually* steal the lieutenant's medal?"

"Of course not, but it'll take them a while to get over that false bit of information and in the meantime I'll see how willing they are to work together and annoy the lieutenant, two very important pieces of information."

"Day one: jerk them around?" she asked, but he could see the smirk behind the question.

"Not like I'm going to stop once they're hired; might as well get them used to it. Meanwhile you and I have an interesting case."

"Lay it out for me, Sherlock."

"Does that make you John Watson or Irene Adler?" he asked, winking. "Last night we got an e-mail from Henry Wilton. He used to be a data analyst for some major drug company."

"Used to be?"

"Well, apparently they're getting ready to release a new antipsychotic that can help make a patient more passive and stop things like hallucinations with almost none of the negative effects that causes many patients to dislike their treatment. Problem is: Wilton discovered in about ten to thirteen percent of people, the drug actually can act as a depressant and increase suicidal thoughts and behaviors."

"Oh very nice," said Lawrence. "Can't imagine causing their patients to become depressed and suicidal was exactly a hit with the company."

"According to Wilton, they consider the percentage to be a small enough outlier that they're going to proceed with the release anyway, and refused to release his findings on the study. Mr. Wilton has a son with schizophrenia, which is what drew him to that area of study in the first place. He's become something of a whistle-blower."

"That would explain why he's no longer there."

"Exactly. Ever since, Wilton's been preparing to release his findings to the FDA. He's become convinced someone is tailing him. Today is the day he's making his delivery, and he's asked for us to deliver and protect him in an attempt to dodge his tail."

Lawrence nodded as a smile passed over her lips.

"And since when have you been known for your discretion?"

He walked up and kissed her cheek.

"Adversity makes strange bedfellows and all that."

"Well you've certainly got *strange* covered at least."

He nodded and allowed himself a moment of gratitude. In moments like this, it was almost as if Kingston and Elizabeth had never happened. It was just Lawrence and he spending time together, solving cases.

Conners reached up and put *Sherry* in his hip holster as Lawrence put her personal firearm under her left arm. They both hid a collapsible security baton in a pocket of their coats and Conners slid a number of other items including his lock pick set into his many pockets. It was like gearing up for war, and he loved the call of the battle.

They head outside and Lawrence punched the address into her phone while they climbed into her wine-red muscle car.

"So what do you think the chances are of this guy actually having a tail?"

"I'd bet someone from his old company wants to stop him from releasing his findings. But it's entirely possible his nerves are just causing him to be paranoid. Either way, once he makes his delivery intact, we have a payday and can see how the preschool class is doing."

"You really think they'll work out your wild goose chase?"

"They'd better. We can train them to see and understand, but not to think."

Conners enjoyed the time they spent driving to meet with Wilton. They joked with one another, reminisced over the past, and speculated over how their class of interns were doing. It felt... well, not exactly normal. But it felt more human than anything else had for far too long. It felt good. His blissful moment was interrupted only once when he gave in to the urge to check his phone and see if Lydia had contacted him.

She hadn't so much as sent him a text.

He honestly wasn't surprised, but still felt guilty. She hadn't handled the restart of Knighthawk Investigations well, and it wasn't difficult to understand why. He knew in his heart it was the right thing to do. But after struggling to rekindle a relationship with his parents, it hurt to put strain on what was already fragile. He knew Lydia loved him, but that didn't mean she was willing to accept his choices.

You could reach a compromise… or lie, he heard Vito whisper in his ear.

Shut up! Conners scolded his father's voice.

The change that had taken place in his brain since finding Lawrence was a little strange. She no longer appeared in his mind meetings as she used to, but Bill and Vito had taken somewhat opposing roles. They offered different solutions to the problems he encountered. Bill took the stricter, more morally upstanding path even if it was harder or sometimes harsh. Vito meanwhile was more compromising, often searching for some type of middle ground or workaround. This led to him routinely holding conversations with his own brain for up to a couple hours at a time.

He didn't bring it up in his therapy sessions because the only solution possible was meditation or to medicate his brain. He already did the first and refused the second, so he saw no benefit in revealing the workings of his mind. Besides, as inconvenient as it was at times, he really liked hearing Bill's and Vito's voices. They were both a father to him and he missed them both dearly.

What's the plan with Wilton, kid?

Lawrence and I drive him to a garage and change vehicles to throw off any trackers. Beyond that, just keep an eye out.

Why not simply deliver the papers yourself, son? If the concern is over his life, no one has any reason to suspect you.

I might be able to take a light stab at what he's uncovered but it's important and he can explain it. Besides, a long-standing employee has more credibility than a recently-revived PI.

They parked the car and Lawrence readjusted her mirror so she could clearly see the front door of the hotel where Wilton was staying. Conners texted the man that they'd arrived and he walked out of the revolving door less than five minutes later, clearly nervous and excitable. He climbed into Lawrence's car and Conners saw the man had actually handcuffed the briefcase to his wrist, which was ridiculous because it wasn't a particularly hard case to pick.

"Hello Mr. Wilton," Conners said, sticking out his left hand to shake the man's free hand. "I'm Michael J. Conners and this is my associate and good friend, Jessica Lawrence. We're going to make sure you don't wind up accosted or dead within the next hour."

Wilton didn't seem to think much of Conners' barb by the glare he threw at him, but he nodded all the same.

"The moment we arrive safely I'll transfer my payment to your company, detective. It's true you've handled dangerous things like this before?"

"A drug company tailing a whistle-blower? No. But I have had plenty of tangles with mafia thugs and leaders, cultists, and street gangsters. So, I'm confident we can handle whoever they might send after you."

That appeared to relax the man slightly.

"Good, this is just… really important."

They traveled in relative silence, Lawrence focused on the roads while Conners practically kept his head on a swivel, keeping constant note of which cars had been traveling on the same path for more than a few blocks. It was strange because without even meaning to, he found he was able to visualize a bird's eye view of a single block around them and the cars within that space.

As they continued their journey through the city, Conners was forcibly made aware of the presence of a sleek, navy luxury car that had stayed with them for a total of eight blocks. He wouldn't have noted it except that it only appeared after another red truck had turned away after following them for eleven blocks. It was a primary rule of tailing someone: where you can, bring multiple vehicles.

Subtly as he could, Conners tapped Lawrence's elbow and flicked his eyes to the rear-view mirror. She nodded softly enough that Wilton wouldn't notice and shrugged her left shoulder just enough that he could see the weight of her pistol under her arm. Conners leaned back and doubled-checked that he had *Sherry*, handcuffs, and his security baton on him. His heart began thudding and he had to breathe deeply to keep himself from going into an adrenaline rush. That ability might prove useful if a full-on fight broke out, but suffering a rush early would only raise his heart rate and flood his brain with endorphins he couldn't use, leaving him drained for when a fight actually did start.

Lawrence pulled into the parking garage with the navy car still a couple car lengths behind them. That morning, they'd borrowed three cabs from Joe just in case they had to switch to duck a tail. Sure enough, the blue car pulled right in behind them. Only as they started to move up the cylindrical ramp did he turn back to Wilton.

"We're being followed by a dark blue car," he said, pulling out *Sherry*. "Lawrence is going to cover you and lead you to another car before driving you out of here while I cover you both. Understand?"

"Wait! They are following me? But what do we do if…"

"I already told you exactly what to do: follow Lawrence. Do what she says. Other than that, shut up and keep your head down."

Wilton gulped visibly and tightened his grip on the briefcase, despite it still being handcuffed to his wrist. Still, he steeled himself and nodded. Conners placed his hand on the handle of the door and glanced at Lawrence as she parked.

"I exit first," he said. "I'll distract them and see if there isn't a way to end this without a shot being fired. Leave when you think you have a clear chance."

She nodded again and he could see the same furious focus that had grabbed her in Elizabeth's manor. His heart thudded so hard it physically hurt as he pulled on the handle and opened the door. He walked into the open air, feigning a calm he didn't come close to feeling as four suited men exited the navy blue car.

"Gentlemen," he said, examining them closely.

They were clearly *not* representatives from the drug company, at least not directly. They bore guns and even from this distance he could make out the gang tattoos each bore. He mentally filed them away for his future report. What didn't help was his heart was still attempting to run a marathon in his rib cage, and small bits of adrenaline kept hitting him and made it hard to think.

Focus! he heard Bill scold him.

"Detective," said one of the men, giving a mocking bow. "I heard you were dead."

"I tried it. Wasn't for me."

"Well then," he said, reaching into his chest pocket. "Let's avoid any unpleasantness."

Sheer panic flooded his brain. He saw fire licking around the edges of his vision, and Elizabeth's face swam before him like some perverse slideshow.

You're in danger, he heard Vito. *You need to run. You need to run! You need to run!*

Conners ordered his body to raise *Sherry* and duck behind a car for cover, but it didn't move. He didn't move. He tried again to give the command, but again his body refused to act. His mind panicked and sent a burst of adrenaline through him, and a simple thought hit him.

I've frozen up.

That was the simple answer. He felt the fear and a flash of the old dangers hit him and he froze. The man who had reached into his pocket pulled out a pistol and he could already see the blonde hair and blue eyes of a child.

You are about to die! Run!

And his legs miraculously obeyed the command. He flew behind a nearby van just as the man lifted the pistol. Conners drew *Sherry* and he heard tires screech behind him as Lawrence and Wilton took off. It took the group of gangsters a long few seconds to figure out what had happened.

"Get back in the car and follow them."

Conners slid under the van and fired two shots, one of which hit the tire of the luxury car. Before he even knew what he was doing, he was running. He sprinted up the stairs to the next level. Behind him, he heard the men curse and begin to debate what they should do next. Once he was above them, Conners quickly tried several handles and eventually found a minivan left unlocked. He quickly popped the trunk and hid himself inside. He prayed Lawrence was already far enough away that they didn't know where she was or what she was now driving. All the while he grew more and more frustrated with himself.

Why had he frozen up just because of a little danger? He'd faced far worse than that bunch several times over. Kingston and Elizabeth had been worse than that. Even Hunter had been worse than those goons. Yet, he'd frozen up. The danger had come, and he was hiding in a trunk.

You're not ok, kid. But you're human. You need to keep tackling this.

He let out a deep breath, and allowed himself to shudder in the trunk.

~*~

It was over an hour before he allowed himself to leave the safety of the trunk and check his phone. Lawrence and Wilton had safely made their journey, and Wilton was busy revealing everything he'd discovered. Lawrence was making her journey back to the garage to retrieve both him and her car. The four gangsters, whoever they might've been had disappeared by the time she was able to return the cab. Luckily, there were no bullet holes they might've had to explain to Joe that evening.

So, Lawrence sat with him as they waited for the police and he explained what had gone down. He didn't hide or excuse his actions or behaviors. He wasn't sure he could've hidden it from her even if he wanted to. She didn't chastise or critique him for his fear. She merely listened and held him while he grew frustrated with his own inaction. When he'd finished, she told him she didn't blame him for his fears. It helped a little. She was arguably one of the only people who knew exactly why he was freezing up, and she didn't blame him for it. It helped, but he still spent the rest of the day wrestling with it in his mind.

I'll do better. I have to do better next time something like this happens.

Chapter XLVII: Burn Baby

Conners sat back and examined the four surviving students standing before him: his elite team, such as they were. After over two months of an intense internship, he and Lawrence had finally been able to agree on their new employees. Four total people had passed whatever insane task Conners had been able to set for them and had enough promise to be worth mentoring into proper detectives.

First was Jim Longworth. Personally Conners still had issues with Jim, but he was quickly showing the most promise in the field. He was also overconfident and had a tendency toward laziness, but he was good at putting together puzzle pieces and had just enough instinct to dig in the right places without burning himself. Regardless of his mixed results, Lawrence and he agreed to keep Jim.

Second was Harriet Powers. She graduated college two years ago with a degree in criminal forensics and decided to try and apply her skillset in a practical way. She was a real genius with numerical and logic problems. She could often solve a problem in those fields even faster than Conners could. On the other side, she struggled to understand the slightly illogical patterns of human behavior, so she sometimes had trouble completely putting a case together where the human element was considered. Still, he knew she had to be on the team.

Third was Kenneth Newberry. Kenneth was a born-and-bred Chicago boy who had spent most of his life trying to live in an area of the city flooded with gang activity, and finally saw an opportunity to help start a change with Knighthawk. Having grown up learning that cops could be just as corrupt as criminals, Kenneth was a master at considering possible motives and finding suspects. He had a tendency to get stuck on a suspect and sometimes leapt to conclusions without finding a proper trail of evidence. Despite this tendency, he was an easy pick.

Last was Josh Lowery. He was an eighteen-year-old who had heard of Conners' exploits prior to Kingston and was eager to join the team as soon as they'd opened the internship. Josh was someone who soaked up lessons and information like a sponge and was always excited to learn something new. He was a little too excitable for Conners' taste, but he also had arguably the most important skill in a team: his ability to communicate and understand his co-workers.

Josh was able to seamlessly work with any of the other three, and could help them work with one another without Conners having to step in and yell at the group. So, while he wasn't yet the strongest investigator, he was indispensable to the group as a whole.

All-in-all Conners was pretty happy with his group. They'd proved capable in most of his testing, but today came a real challenge. There had been an arson call he'd picked up on a scanner. The case wasn't with the fourteenth precinct and normally arson wasn't a high-profile caseload. The saving grace was arson cases could often be like an iceberg, with there being a lot underneath the surface of a seemingly simple case. That combined with the difficulty of usable evidence made it a good chance to guide his new learners.

Conners walked into the new office space that had been put together for them. It was almost disconcerting to walk into the large room, see the people working in it, and think of them as *his*. The room had several windows next to a large bookshelf piled high with several reference books he'd thought would be useful study material. Two desks had been pushed up against either of the far walls with their backs facing each other. All four of his students had placed different personal effects on their desks. It created an odd contrast because while Harriet and Kenneth were fairly neat and kept only a few choice items around them, Josh and Jim sprawled items across their workstations like they were attempting to claim their territory with belongings.

For the most part, they'd proved to work well enough together. There had been a few arguments, mostly between Harriet and Jim. Harriet was strict and had a very difficult time bending from her process, which Jim had quickly picked up on and teased her about. Luckily Josh had a cool enough head to help keep the two in line most of the time. As he entered what he'd come to think of as the bullpen, the four stopped and looked away from their computers to meet his gaze. Josh even took off his headphones which Conners took as a compliment. The youth used to work nights as a DJ and almost always wore headphones in the office.

"Got a case for you today," he said, holding up the four copies of the file. "We're going to be delving into an arson case picked up by the local police early this morning."

"All right," said Josh smiling. "About time you put us on an open case, boss!"

"Couldn't you get something more exciting?" asked Jim, leaning back in his chair. "Arson's bottom-rung kind of work. We should be closing murder cases, or helping Vice or something."

Conners resisted the urge to growl and raised an eyebrow.

"You wanna work with murderers and drug dealers? Become a cop. You wanna learn how to close cases quickly and effectively? You do what I say."

Jim looked as though he was about to object, but managed to bite his tongue.

"Ok then," Conners said firmly. "Josh, go grab your car. I'll meet you guys at the site."

Josh nodded and began rummaging in his bag for his car keys while Conners texted Joe to send him a cab. He'd already decided ahead of time to travel apart from his students to scenes for a while. For one thing, it gave them a chance to talk and discuss things without fear of being overheard by himself or Lawrence. Not that he suspected they were plotting anything, but it was important they have a chance to bond and relate without feeling the pressure of their bosses. Aside from that, Joe's cabbies were far quicker than most citizens when it came to navigating the traffic of the city, and he wanted to get a head start on the case. That way, he could focus on guiding them instead of merely solving the case himself.

He managed to spend the better part of an hour slinking around before he heard the sound of Josh's car entering the neighborhood. Truth be told, he wasn't a car person and couldn't tell the sound of most motors apart. However, the kid's speaker system and choice in music meant he could practically pick Josh's car out of rush hour lineup based purely on noise. He walked up to a house that had been reduced to little more than ash. It was protected by a line of police tape and one very bored officer. Conners showed up near the car just as his students were exiting the vehicle. He didn't have a definite culprit but was able to pick up at least a few good leads and was eager to see how many threads his team could find and pull on.

The officer perked up at the sound of the engine and when he saw Conners, his eyes widened.

"You're that consultant, right? What are you doing here?"

Conners rolled his eyes and heard Josh's car doors shutting behind him. It wasn't exactly hard to pick him out of a lineup. Chicago wasn't full of men wearing graphic t-shirts and converse under long coats who walked around crime scenes like they owned the place. He couldn't help but mentally smile at this choice of shirt that afternoon.

It read: *My people skills are just fine. It's my tolerance to idiots that needs work.*

"It seemed a lovely spot for a date and I just want to get to know you a bit better," he said sarcastically before explaining. "I'm here cause the house behind you was just raised to the ground and Chicago's finest have yet to produce a perp."

"But we didn't call you."

"No, but I'm not your lapdog. I called your captain on the way over, and he agreed I'd be consulting on this case."

He felt Jim and Kenneth smirk at his banter, and he was forcibly reminded of his first case with Bill. The cop spoke into his radio for a second confirming Conners' claim. He sighed heavily when they confirmed what he'd said.

"Fine, but don't damage any of the evidence, and you're to report back to me or the detectives with anything you find."

"Damage the place anymore than a fire?" asked Jim softly. "How would we even manage that?"

"All right guys," he said, gesturing around him. "Show me what you can do."

They nodded and immediately split up and began searching in their own ways. Harriet had already unearthed her laptop and began searching for any records of crimes that might indicate arsonist behaviors while Josh and Kenneth were searching through the burnt remains to find a starting point. Jim was scanning the houses around them, pondering which of them could be considered of interest or canceled out as likely suspects. He had to admit, it gave him a strange combination of emotions to watch them work. He was forcibly reminded of his early attempts at crime solving. Only now he could see how foolish he must've seemed to Bill as he tried to solve Larry Kurtz's murder. Yet, there was also a sense of pride for what they were able to do, and hope for what they could become.

After about an hour of their searching, he let out a sharp whistle and they all looked up.

"All right, what have you all got?"

"There's a man at the end of the block named Martin Flatly," said Harriet, pushing her glasses back up slightly. "He was convicted in 2008 for setting fire to his own car. Seems worth talking to."

Jim scoffed and Conners forced himself to breathe before lashing out.

"What's funny about her idea?"

"The cops would've talked to him already," said Jim, matter-of-factly. "No point wasting our time in doing what they've already done."

"Right and wrong," said Conners. "Yes, obviously the police will have already questioned Flatly and the fact they haven't held him or charged him means they've found nothing concrete, but it's stupid to dismiss him based on that. Our job is catching what they often do not or will not. Understood?"

Kenneth, Harriet, and Josh quickly responded positively. Jim bit his tongue and looked as if he'd caught the smell of something foul.

"Jim!" Conners snapped, lowering the tone and raising the volume of his voice. "Do you understand?"

Jim looked Conners squarely in the eye, and had he not been so frustrated with the young man, Conners would've admired his steel nerves.

"I understand, even if I think it's a waste of time."

"Until you're taking cases on your own, your time is mine to waste."

"Yes sir," growled Jim.

Conners considered shouting the kid down, but pulled himself back. He didn't want to build an echo chamber and it was important his team was capable of thinking and acting independently.

"Kenneth? What have you found?"

"The house was smaller and less pristine than the surrounding houses. Several of the patches in the yard are bare and there are marks from where his truck was usually parked on the grass. The house could've been seen as an eyesore by the neighborhood making it a target for someone looking to lash out."

"Very good," said Conners, impressed by Kenneth's insights. "Josh?"

"Always double-check the most obvious idea. We should check if he had fire insurance and what he got paid for it. In all likelihood it's not insurance fraud because the house is in a good area. The lot alone would sell for a decent amount. So there likely isn't a need to take a risk getting caught just for insurance, but always good to be sure."

"Exactly," said Conners, glad at least one of them had brought up the insurance angle. "How do we proceed?"

Josh pondered the question for a long moment.

"If we're seen questioning the neighbors it could easily shake up or tip off whoever might've committed the arson. Best split up and tackle as many houses as we can. I would recommend Harriet visit Flatly while the three of us each choose a few houses we think most likely to view the house as an ugly target. Then we reconvene and can check on the insurance angle."

"Great plan. You three split up and take three houses a piece, marking anyone who sticks out to you. Harriet and I will question Flatly."

He felt more than saw Jim had a question on the tip of his tongue, but he held it back. As Conners and Harriet walked down the street, he pulled out his cellphone and dialed Lawrence.

"Hey Conners," she said, with cheer in her voice. *"How are the children doing?"*

"Oh, you know them: they don't like sharing their toys. Still, they're growing up quick enough."

"Well don't stay out too late. You're taking me out tonight."

"Am I? This is news to me."

"We agreed to try and engage in the outside world at least once a week."

"So you're just going to spring dates on me?"

"Exactly, gives you less time to try and find an excuse not to go."

He couldn't help but smile at her words.

"Sounds great. See you tonight."

"Have fun."

Harriet knocked sharply on Martin Flatly's door. As they waited for him to answer, Harriet nodded pointedly to the fire-pit on the side patio of Flatly's house. Conners nodded in understanding and his mind began spinning quickly, putting together different facts about the house and the man who lived within it.

The door creaked open and a single bright blue eye peeked out from just above the chain latch.

"You're that private detective," said Flatly in a high-pitched voice. "You're here because you think I started that fire."

Conners examined the man as well as he could through the crack. His clothing was expensive, though shabby, and his hair was greasy and unwashed. It was not the image of a man who took good care of himself. What was more interesting was the bandages wrapped around both his hands. Clearly his love of fire had burned him more than once.

However, the burns weren't the wounds of a man who made careless mistakes while committing arson. This man started fires all the time. He just couldn't stop himself from touching the flames. It was clear the fire he had been touching wasn't a huge one, or he would have multiple burns all over his body, instead of just his hands. He had been dealing with small fires: several matches and his fireplace most likely.

"Actually," said Conners, trying to relax himself and Flatly at the same time. "I don't. You've been burning yourself. With someone who has as much respect for fire as you do, I have to figure it's not from a large house fire."

Flatly flushed, but Conners also saw a small flash of relief.

"I just... the flames are so beautiful that I can't... but I don't want to hurt anyone or anything. So I just keep to my little fires, where it's safe."

Harriet threw a glance at him, but he kept his focus on Flatly.

"I believe you," said Conners honestly. "But the people who set that fire did hurt someone. So if you know anything that might help us—anything you didn't tell the police you should tell us now."

Flatly looked down nervously, but then glanced back up.

"I saw a red truck parked next door the night of the fire. No one there drives it. I didn't want to look like I was trying too hard to make sure I wasn't a suspect."

"Thank you," Conners said and tried to smile.

Martin shut the door sharply and Conners tugged on Harriet's shoulder to get her moving back down Flatly's driveway.

"How did you know it wasn't him?"

"Flatly is too careful," he explained. "He burns himself but not badly enough to be from a large fire. Anyone who has that great a respect for fire would never be careless enough to burn themselves on an illegal fire. You have good instincts, but you need to learn to look past the statistics and see the individual."

Harriet nodded, but looked slightly crestfallen. He understood her frustration because she was a perfectionist and someone who saw anything less than complete accuracy as a failure. He'd have to be sure to talk with her later on so she didn't get too deep into her head.

When he regrouped with the other three, they each delivered their report. Josh and Kenneth each managed to speak to three separate house owners, but Jim was by far the most enthusiastic despite having focused on only a singular suspect.

"I found someone a little way up that's been trying to sell his house for the past few months, and apparently that burnt place was driving down his house's value. The next-door neighbor said he heard the husband and wife fighting for several months. Wouldn't be surprised to learn they were trying to get divorced and sell the house to separate."

"Did he own a red truck?"

"Yeah…" said Jim, slightly confused. "Saw it in the driveway. Why?"

Conners groaned internally. He'd hoped Jim had been wrong so he'd have a better excuse to chastise him for not following orders. But, in the end Jim's hunch had been right.

"Shame Flatly didn't pan out," said Jim, pointedly, and Conners instantly reversed his decision to forgive Jim's arrogance.

He might be skilled, but he certainly wasn't able to work with his team or learn from what he was taught. He likely would make a fine detective in his own right, but he had no business on the team.

"Jim," said Conners, curtly. "Go back to the office and clear out your desk."

Jim stared at him like he'd sprouted a second head.

"What?"

"I've had enough of you. You can't work with others, you're arrogant, and you refuse to consider anything outside of your own ideas. You still want to be a detective? Then go to the police. You can work by yourself and close cases well enough, but there's no place here for you."

For a long moment, he thought Jim would refuse. But the youth eventually growled and spun around to walk back to the main road and find a cab. There was silence for a long few moments.

"Come on, team," said Conners, determined not to let them shy away. "You guys need to examine a truck for proof of arson."

Eventually, the young investigators responded. After an hour of work, they had a convincing report to deliver to the policemen. That evening when he reached the office, Jim's desk was clean and empty. Conners reached over to the young man's nameplate and chucked it in the trash bin in full sight of the other students.

"I can teach you guys how to solve cases," he said firmly. "But I can't teach you how to learn or how to work together. You keep doing as you've been doing, and you have nothing to worry about."

Chapter XLVIII: Opening Bids

Conners smiled at Lawrence as she lay her head on his shoulder and they both flipped through a few cases. It had been almost six months since he'd fired Jim, and the rest of his students had flourished well over the half-year. Most days it was difficult for him not to brag about them. Once more, he appreciated how Bill must've seen him during their time together. The office they had been living and working out of was huge. Compared to the little office of Bill's he'd started in, Knighthawk Investigations was practically a manor.

While he and Lawrence had always intended to live in the building, their trio of students spent far more time in the building than anywhere else. Kenneth had even gone so far as to change his residency to the office and let go of his old shoebox apartment, moving what he didn't need constant access to into a storage unit. All three slept in a set of bunks more often than not. They usually ate and worked all in the building, leaving mostly for casework or to shop for essentials. Conners and Lawrence weren't exactly surprised either. Part of their draw to the candidates had been an obsession with their work.

Harriet was the only one who faced some interference as her mother and father liked to check-in on her. More than once, her mother had expressed her frustration when they'd dropped by unexpectedly only for Harriet to be working in the field. When Conners had approached her about it, the young woman insisted they would grow accustomed to it and she didn't want a lighter work load. It helped their drive to see that they were having true impact on the city too.

They'd each grown to the point that he let them tackle or at least start work on a smaller case without his help. Several businesses, including the police came to them regularly and his trio of students grew to be almost as recognizable as he and Lawrence were. Still when cases were either dangerous or complicated, he would guide the trio or take the case personally. Sometimes they could receive praise or thanks, and these he would share directly with them as a group. Any valid issues or complaints he had, he brought up to them privately. In these private sessions, he'd made sure to be understanding but bring them along. He learned how to work with them. He let the cases reward them, and he was their guide.

From what Conners had heard, Jim had gone to work for the twelfth precinct, and Conners had made a mental note to give the place some breathing room ever since. He had little doubt Jim would find a way to flourish and do well amongst the cops, but what he needed was a team who was willing to listen, learn, and work well together. Whatever Jim's other qualifications might be, those were not among them. That didn't stop the slightly awkward feeling everytime he entered the trio's work office and saw the empty desk and small filing cabinet that was now blank.

"What about that insurance swindle case we got Tuesday?" asked Lawrence.

"Boring," said Conners, tossing the file towards his ever-growing pile of cases he'd take if nothing more interesting came along. Said pile was so large it was close to claiming a drawer of his filing cabinet all by itself. "Oh, here's a nice one: double homicide from last week."

"Cops already closed it," said Lawrence.

"Damn. Since when was a cop actually capable? Present company excluded, of course."

"If you want to solve murders yourself, you can't put them on the back burner all the time," said Lawrence, in a sing-song voice. "Not everyone in the world is willing to wait for you to show up and do their job for them. Not everyone even likes having you around."

"*You* like having me around."

"Yeah, because I was one of the very few cops that worked well with you. And as far as I can tell I'm one of a half-dozen people that actually likes you. Can't imagine why."

He kissed her on the cheek before peeking back at another file that had been in his inbox.

"Now *this* is more like it!"

He stood hastily and snatched the phone up to call the team into the study. They dutifully arrived a minute or so later. Josh's hair stuck up slightly around his ears, which meant he'd been listening to his music full-blast prior to his call, doubtless just loud enough for Harriet to actually be able to discern the song, which explained the slightly irritated edge in her gaze. Kenneth's clothes were rumpled and the specks of sand in his eyes indicated he'd been asleep when Conners had called.

"By my royal decree," Conners said in a high-pitched British accent. "Thou three shall inquire as to the location and dealings of a racket of the sexual nature, believed to be taking place within our very own city."

"We get to break up a sex trafficking ring?" asked Kenneth, reaching for the file.

"Fine, spoil all the grandeur of the moment," Conners muttered. "Yes, we're going to scout and see if we can't track down a warehouse supposedly being used to smuggle several women into a sex slavery ring run by some Russian gangsters. It's suspected many of the women stolen were split into different packs, then sent to several different cities prior to their auctions. The sellers could maximize profits and minimize losses if one of the groups were discovered, and the feds suspect Chicago is now hosting one such group."

"If the feds are on it, this is high profile, yeah? You sure they'll let us in on this?"

"They aren't inviting us in. Lieutenant Guston of the CPD is assisting and is calling for all hands on deck. He might be reluctant to include us. But if we get the right place, he gets the credit and a nice feather in his cap courtesy of the United States Government."

"What do we get?" asked Kenneth, jokingly.

"We get to stop the organized selling and rape of several women," said Harriet, formally but with a slight edge to her tone.

"Fair point," said Kenneth, handing her and Josh the file. "So what's our first move, boss?"

"Cops are convinced there's a warehouse near the lake they might be using, but I disagree. I want you guys to scout anywhere that might be big enough for a ring like this, then discretely scout them, and check in if you find anything worth digging into. You should go armed, but don't engage if you can avoid it. These guys aren't the kind to shy away from disposing of someone who sticks their nose in too far, clear?"

They nodded and ran off to gear up and search the internet for any large storage places that might fit the profile before they could begin whittling down likely suspects. Conners walked over to the hanging hook where his trusty trench coat sat and threw it over himself before glancing back at Lawrence and noting her slightly too-stiff posture.

"You ok?" he asked reaching out to touch her shoulder.

She initially stiffened at the touch and then her eyes found his and she relaxed a little.

"Not exactly good memories where kidnapping and abuse are concerned," she said, trying to smile at him.

Conners nodded and kissed her forehead.

"Stopping bad guys, yeah?"

The simple message seemed to reach her as she looked up and grabbed his hand before kissing his knuckles.

"I love you," she said, very softly.

He felt his heart rise just a bit at that. It was the first time she'd said it. In a way, he'd never *needed* to hear it. He knew he loved her and he knew she loved him, and that was fine. They'd never discussed it or raised the idea of marriage. He had thought about it a few times. It has hard not to when they spent almost all their time together and didn't like to be separated for very long.

Still in her admission, he felt his heart grow just a little lighter. He had to force himself to relax so he didn't grow overexcited and reckless. Recklessness and sex ring smugglers wouldn't mix well.

"I love you, too."

He saw some of the same tension he felt slide off her shoulders. Neither of them had *completely* recovered from what Elizabeth had done to them. As their therapist had pointed out, it was possible they would never fully recover: only learn to cope. Conners hadn't had another episode like the day in the parking garage, but he also hadn't been placed in the same level of danger since then.

Dutifully, Conners slid *Sherry* into the holster at his waist and straightened his long overcoat. Lawrence mirrored him by grabbing her favorite brown leather jacket and placing her pistol under her left arm.

"So if the kids are going to stakeout some warehouses, what are we doing?" she asked.

"First, we'll eat some lunch that neither of us has to cook or lie about. Then I figure we can do something normal couples do until the kids dig up a promising lead."

"And what exactly do *normal* couples do?"

"I have no idea," he said, smirking. "So we'll fake it 'til we make it. Right?"

~*~

Later that day, as the sun turned a deep shade of orange and began to set behind the towering buildings of the city skyline, Conners and Lawrence walked up to the small patio his trio were camped out on. Josh and Kenneth were eating either half of a sub while Harriet was staring intently at a nearby storage facility that was listed as belonging to a plastics company that no longer operated in the city at all. The payments had dutifully continued, and they agreed it was a likely hangout for illegal activity.

"Any word from the cops?" asked Josh as Conners took a seat next to Harriet and pulled out a monocular from one of his many pockets.

"They're doing several sweeps throughout the day. If things move at a steady pace, they'll be here in a couple hours. Until then, we just keep an eye out for anything suspicious."

"Well so far we haven't seen anything," said Harriet, whose eyes were glued to the storage building. "Granted we've only been here for about thirty minutes."

They spent the next couple hours taking it in shifts to watch the building. The trio had picked a good spot and there was even a sub shop nearby for when they got hungry. Conners was most of the way through a Philly Cheesesteak when he heard Kenneth give a start and Lawrence whistled at them.

"What we got?" he asked, peering over the ledge.

"Group of gangsters just pulled up," said Lawrence.

Conners pulled out his monocular again and saw three dark, luxury cars had pulled over just in front of the building. Two men in slick, black suits exited the lead car first, followed quickly by several men Conners took to be underlings. He couldn't recognize any of the faces or tattoos. But being that they were supposed to originate from another state, he hadn't really expected that he would. Then a large man in the back looked around cautiously before heading to the trunk of the car.

He popped the trunk open and started pulling out women, as if it were some horrid moving day. The women were all thin and their hands were bound. Conners hissed angrily and looked over at Lawrence, who was already unearthing her pistol.

"We're out of time," she muttered and began moving carefully towards the building the gangsters were entering.

Conners turned to the trio.

"Stay here. Call the police and keep an eye out. Under no condition are you to go near that building."

He reached for *Sherry* and began to follow Lawrence. He could already hear his mind dissecting the threats.

- *Total number of foes: Even dozen.*

They're bound to be on edge, keeping an eye and ear out for the police. Whatever you do, it'll have to be before the police arrive. Too many sirens and they'll try to disappear or kill the girls. You'll need to be careful and quick, kid.

We could just cut off the exit route, suggested Vito. *Keep you and Lawrence safer while stopping the escape. Let the police take the brunt of it.*

Too dangerous, Bill interjected. *You've never been able to trust the police 100% when things were dire. Do the right thing.*

Conners nodded to himself and his world began to speed up while his father diagnosed the building. They managed to reach the back door without incident, which he picked quickly.

- *Old and uncared for: no power or heat.*
- *Mostly comprised of sheet metal and rusted through.*
- *Could create a place for a sniper.*
- *Lawrence is a better shot than you and sniping keeps her relatively safe from any return fire.*

"Take the east wall from out here," he said. "This place is barely held together. You can find a hole and cover me while I'm inside."

He saw the instinctual rejection in her eyes, but she considered his words. In a split second he saw she knew he was right. She nodded before retreating to the wall he'd indicated. Conners took a deep breath as the lock *clicked* open. He cracked the door a hair and peered inside as best he could. The rising moonlight created just enough light to see by, but not enough to make out any details.

Light could be a great diversion, he heard Bill say and Conners quickly took out his phone and set a delay so it would flash and take a picture ten seconds after he pushed the button. He slipped inside the building like a shadow. He carefully took a strong flashlight out of his pocket but didn't activate it yet. He saw several figures muscling the girls into a truck trailer in the middle of the room.

Carefully, Conners placed his phone at an angle against a crate and pressed the photo button before moving as quickly and quietly as he could away from the place. Sure enough, after ten seconds, there was a bright flash. He heard several gunshots and saw the area where he'd placed the phone light up with the spark of impacting bullets.

Outside, he heard the sound of Lawrence's pistol unleash and saw three of the figures fall, clutching wounds. He had to admire her work. Even at a distance, she'd managed to hit her targets accurately. None of those she'd hit were dead: at least yet. They were out of commission though. Conners mentally placed the gangsters where he'd seen them as the flash had gone off.

He quickly popped up and fired *Sherry* twice before ducking down again, and he heard a scream as one of the men fell.

Eight still in fighting condition, his brain let out.

Conners quickly tapped the button on his flashlight twice which caused it to flash rapidly. In morse code it was actually blinking out S.O.S. However, in that moment he was more concerned with the disorientating and distracting light. As the blinking started, he slid the light across the warehouse and sure enough, a hail of bullets followed the light.

Lawrence and he both responded with their own shots and five more men hit the ground.

Three more.

The next response wasn't more gunfire. Instead he heard a voice directing the other two.

"Stop! This isn't the police!"

They appeared to follow instructions, because Conners could see them lowering their weapons.

"Who's there?" called out the man who had given instruction.

Conners trained his weapon on the speaker before calling out, careful to project enough so that his voice would echo and reverberate. It wouldn't do to give his position away in an exchange of dialogue.

"Michael J. Conners!" he said firmly. "I'd ask your name, but I don't bother myself with soon-to-be dead men."

Of course, he wanted to arrest the men if possible, but he wasn't going to let them hurt Lawrence or the girls they'd brought out.

"*Shit!*" he heard the leader swear harshly.

"What's the big deal?" asked one of the men, and Conners could see he was carrying a rifle. "Sounds like it's just one guy."

"Shut up you moron!" the leader snapped. "This is the one who took out Kingston and Richards."

Despite himself, Conners couldn't help but feel a touch of pride at the knowledge his work and reputation had put some true fear in the heart of this man. After a moment the leader addressed Conners again.

"I'd heard through the grapevine you were dead."

"Well can't trust those grapevines," said Conners moving along his hiding spot. "Besides, too many scumbags trying to move their sex-slave ring through my city."

"Look. Clearly, you have us at a disadvantage. But we can work something out here, right? How about we just leave here, you can have the girls in one piece, and we all just go our own way?"

"Fine. First, you need to put those weapons on the ground!" Conners bellowed and he saw the man gesture to his followers before they put the guns down.

Conners walked forward, *Sherry* at the ready and he heard a sound across from him as Lawrence entered the building. As they grew closer, he saw them look at Lawrence with confusion. He tossed a bag of zip-ties to her and she quickly moved from man-to-man, tying their hands up while he covered them with his revolver.

"But you agreed to let us go!" said one of the men who hadn't been injured.

"And you kidnap and sell women. I think my sense of fair trade bottomed out. You want to cut a deal? Talk to the police."

The leader looked up at Conners and growled.

"They warned me about you when I suggested Chicago. You really are a particular kind of bastard, aren't you?"

Conners smiled at the thought that Bill would've liked the description.

"If you ever do get in contact with your boss again, tell him eventually I'll catch him too."

"Conners!" called Lawrence as she opened the trailer and began helping the girls out of it.

Together, they kept an eye on the kidnapped girls and criminals until they heard the sirens of the approaching police. While the SWAT team began formalizing the arrests and bringing in the EMTs to treat the women, Conners couldn't help but replay his breach.

He hadn't frozen or hid from the danger. He'd done his job and done it well. More than that, he'd become more than just a detective in the eyes of both the citizens of the city and the criminal forces that wanted to work within its boarders. He moved to where Lawrence was nursing a small cut on her forearm.

"You good?" he asked, gesturing to the cut.

"Course," she said, and grinned at him. "Kids are outside explaining. There will be a fair bit of statements and explaining to hand over, but shutting down this shipment should go a long way."

"Good," he said and kissed her softly. "Lawrence, I'm really glad I have you with me."

"Yeah, I guess I like you enough to keep you around. Besides, you're pretty comfortable to hug."

He smirked slightly but continued onward.

"I'm being serious."

"That's a new one."

"Well, first time for everything. But jokes and all that aside, I wanna ask: will you marry me?"

She didn't stiffen or move away from him. Instead, she closed her eyes and slowly leaned her head on his shoulder.

"Hardly a romantic spot to ask that, Conners. But I suppose it took you plenty long enough to ask. Course I'll marry you."

He would've sworn his heart was physically swollen from the happiness that filled it.

Chapter XLIX: I Do

The next six months were some of the most taxing in Conners' life. While the kids had become almost competent and were able to handle several cases on their own, his own life had become a bombardment of wedding plans. Throughout his entire life, Conners had never put much thought into his furniture, clothing, or appearance. Now, half a year had been dedicated to answering several seemingly unimportant questions about his wedding day.

Lawrence was nearly as fried as he was. It seemed quite a simple idea at first to get married, but then they'd made one possibly fatal mistake: they'd agreed to tell his mother about their engagement. She was thrilled of course, but it meant what *was* going to be a simple, quiet affair had been spread and grown far past what either of them were ready to organize.

So, they'd decided to hire a wedding planner. All they'd have to do was answer a few questions which neither particularly cared about and their planner would handle everything. That had quickly become complicated because apparently his wedding was something half the city had an interest in. The mayor himself had insisted on having their wedding in Ping Tom Memorial Park. The Chinese-themed park covered about thirty or so acres, and it seem like they were going to have to pack every square inch of it with one citizen or another.

And of course, having so many attendees meant they needed to work with a few different catering companies. Then there was the concern over audio and video services, which he hadn't even planned on prior to the overpacked arrangement. The mayor seemed insistent on using their wedding as something of a publicity stunt, which meant they at least didn't have to pay much for the majority of the services. Still, these services *did* require an absurd amount of planning and organization.

Luckily, tomorrow was his wedding day, and it would be as much a relief to be done with the planning as it would to actually have married the woman he so desperately loved.

Because of the unending list of details that had to be decided, both he and Lawrence occasionally took a simple case just to get out of the office and away from the planner for a few hours. Conners had been chasing a man who had been stealing cars in high-end neighborhoods for a few months. The police had yet to successfully collar him. Conners had managed to rent a car with a remote start, and left it running on a popular street. The thief didn't realize until he'd stepped on the brake to change gears the key was not actually in the ignition. So, Conners had been tearing after him for a couple blocks.

The thief was a young man in his early twenties with long dark hair and visible tattoos on his forearms. He was fast, but not particularly bright or forward-thinking, and Conners intercepted him by cutting through a narrow alleyway. As he landed on top of the would-be car thief, he felt his phone *buzz* in his pocket. Growling, he cuffed the youth and slid his thumb across the phone to answer it.

"Hello?"

"Hey," he heard Lawrence's exasperated voice come through. *"Just wanted to make sure you've got your suit picked up for tomorrow."*

"My jeans and t-shirt? Yeah, all good."

He heard her stifle a laugh and was reminded in a quick second why he loved this woman.

"You going to be home tonight?"

He considered it for a second, but knew his mind would be far too excitable to allow him to sleep a wink.

"Not tonight. Supposed to be bad luck to see the bride before the wedding and all that, right?"

"Are you kidding me? Everything is bad luck. Speaking about bad luck is bad luck. Just... I'll see you tomorrow then, all right? I love you."

"I love you," he said and ended the call.

"You getting married?" asked the kid Conners was currently pinning to the ground.

"Shut up. This isn't a moment between you and me. Don't steal cars!"

He dropped the thief off to a couple of officers from the tenth, encouraging them to take credit for his collar. All he'd really wanted was the distraction.

As Conners let his mind drift over his arrest, he found himself irrevocably drawn to everything he'd done since escaping from the hospital after Kingston's assault on him. He remembered trying to be cold and calculating. He remembered his shooting an innocent child, and the penance he'd tried to pay back ever since. He remembered the day he'd met Bill, who had become nothing short of a father to him.

You ended up being one of the good ones in your own right, kid.

He let his mind cast over Bill's relationship with Richards.

She still contacts me every once in a while: Kelsey, my ex-wife. I always tell myself I won't answer when she calls, but it's hard to completely cut out someone you loved, however screwed up they might be.

He couldn't help but wonder at the influence that crazy woman had ended up having in his own life as well. She'd killed his father figure. She'd become obsessed with him, nearly causing him to betray Lawrence and break a few serious laws.

Obsessed.

That word echoed in his mind for a reason he couldn't quite seem to put his finger on. He let it ring through his subconscious again.

Obsessed.

He still couldn't quite explain why that was significant to him, but another quote from Bill came to his mind.

I always wanted a little girl, but by the time we had a home ready, the affairs had begun and afterwards… Well, things never lined up right, I guess.

And suddenly another voice struck him, but it did not belong to Bill.

You don't even know? But… how could you not know? Why wouldn't he have told you? Surely, he told you! He must've told you! You just weren't listening!

Conners ran his fingers through his hair and closed his eyes, desperately trying to focus on Elizabeth's face. He saw the deep scars and the hungry, deranged eyes. Behind those, he could clearly remember the structure of her nose and the shape of her mouth. He could remember the curve of her eyebrows and the distinctive chin she bore. He knew those features very well, and as he placed them, his mind felt as if it had been dunked in a bucket of ice.

Half of Elizabeth's features matched up perfectly to Richards' face. The resemblance was undeniable when he truly compared the two in his mind's eye. Elizabeth could have taken her mother's place with a bit of make-up and hair dye. Actually, come to think of it, she had taken her mother's place regardless. The other half was a face he would've been thrilled to see anywhere else, and the resemblance was just as undeniable.

Elizabeth was Bill's daughter: one he never knew he had, because Richards would've seen any number of opportunities to use her own child against the man she was obsessed with. Elizabeth was (genetically) Elizabeth Scott. She was the child Bill had always wanted but never could've known he had. While Bill had been pushed through pain and regret due to a marriage he couldn't repair, his child had been tormented and punished by his own ex-wife.

A sudden pang of understanding and pain flew through him and in a split-second he felt a connection to Elizabeth he couldn't brush off no matter how desperately he wanted to. The scars that had stood out so clearly on her face made a frightening statement in combination with her narcissistic mother. Elizabeth had served as a constant reminder of all that Bill was. Even in Richards' kindest moments, she would've merely been grooming the child to serve as a form of revenge.

Elizabeth is just as obsessed with you because you took away her mother, and her tormentor. You took away the father who abandoned her: and the man she always heard about but could never know. You saved her and stole everything from her, kid.

"She wants the connection with her father I had," Conners said to himself. "She feels like I stole her father. But you never knew she existed. If you had, I wonder if you would've taken me in at all..."

He hailed a cab from the main road and took it to what used to be the Howling Wolf Apartments. What was left of the building after he'd defeated Kingston had been bulldozed and converted into a newer, low-income apartment building. It meant what had once been a nearly abandoned street had a bit of life in it again. Mostly it was poor families or singles trying to maintain a life in the bustling city, but it was a nicer sight than the place had been before.

He gazed up at the building for a while, letting his mind draw imaginary lines to convert the building to what it had been back when it was his apartment. He could clearly see where his bedroom window would be, though now it was only brick wall. He recalled the late nights spent climbing in and out of that window utilizing the fire escape. He remembered the hours spent playing his guitar while he thought about his targets. More than once he'd gotten into arguments with the neighbors due to playing late. The memories made him smile softly.

It's the Black habit to end up being a pain in the ass, he heard his father say.

Conners started to walk towards the park. It was a long hike to make, and snow flurries had started to fall, brought into sharp relief by the spotlight. Conners wrapped his trench coat a little tighter around himself and pulled a scarf out of one of his many pockets to help keep out the cold. Chicago was more his home now than it had ever been.

He was born and raised several times within the city limits. John Black was born in Cook County Hospital, which was now closed. Michael Conners awoke in Northwestern Memorial Hospital with a bad head wound and a complete lack of any human understanding. Several years later, he had been brought back to life at Weiss Memorial Hospital after setting fire to an apartment and blowing himself up. Finally, Conners and Lawrence had been nursed into a semi-fit state after Elizabeth had drugged them to the gills and starved them for months by the staff of AMITA Health Saints Mary and Elizabeth Medical Center. Four different hospitals marked four distinct points of his life.

Really, he'd been four different people throughout his life. First he'd been the impulsive, angry avenger. Then he'd become a self-centered man who learned how to have a heart. Next he'd been the wounded veteran: almost damaged beyond repair… almost. Now he was… What was he, exactly? All of these things and none of them all at once. He was wiser and more experienced than he'd been as a teenager. He had more compassion and more understanding than he'd used as an emerging detective. He was far stronger and more determined than he'd been as a damaged man. He was… he was everything he needed to be. Not that it made the journey easy or pleasant, but it occurred to him he never could've been who he was without all of his experience. Years ago, he never would've taken on his trio and trained them up. Luckily, they'd ended up working out very well and were almost capable.

The night carried on, past midnight into the early hours of the morning and still Conners walked. The city might not have noticed the change of the time as far as the bustle of traffic was concerned. The sidewalk was largely unoccupied and there was plenty of space so the few people he did pass didn't have to physically bump against him. Still, even though they were only lit by the streetlights and surrounding windows, and were at a decent distance from him, his brain continued to deduce facts about the people and send them to him of its own accord.

- *Slight limp in the left leg: bad cartilage in the knee.*
- *Heavy smoker—recently picked up marijuana again: hiding the habit from his family.*
- *Recent argument with her child, trying to keep a cool head about it.*

He didn't know if he would ever be able to completely switch off that part of his brain, and he didn't think he would want to if he could. Deductions and reasoning were a part of him as much as his ability to ignore the lettering of the law when it was the right thing. His mother, Guston, Joe, the trio, and Lawrence were all vital pieces of his life. They were part of who he was.

Eventually, Conners found himself walking by a coffee shop and decided to stop and rest while he sipped from a truly disgusting cup of coffee. While he rested and sipped, he watched the world around him. It was a world that would keep spinning around regardless of what he did, and yet his actions in it were pivotal and went much farther than he'd have thought. It was as beautiful as it was horrifying.

He wasn't sure how long he spent at the little table, but as six in the morning rolled around, he dialed Josh's number and had the kid pick him up with his suit in the back of the car. Josh was already dressed up in a shirt and tie Conners couldn't have been paid enough to wear. As always, his car blared some type of music that mostly consisted of bass. Josh drove Conners to a public rest area where he quickly showered, shaved, trimmed his goatee, and dressed for his wedding. More than a few people cast him a suspicious glance at his emerging in a fairly nice suit, but they didn't decide to approach him about it. One of the benefits of living in a large city: there was always someone around crazier than you, so your level of crazy was considered acceptable.

He climbed back into Josh's car and they reached the already overcrowded streets almost an hour before the ceremony was due to start. Conners moved through the throng of people, and was waylaid every few steps because what felt like half the attendees wanted to shake his hand and say something, which made him regret that they didn't decide to just go down to city hall and do the official work without a ceremony. Eventually he reached the gazebo. It was easy to see the color scheme he and Lawrence had hastily chosen through arrangements everywhere, but honestly he couldn't have cared less if every single napkin and streamer clashed horribly. Truth be told, the wedding planner had done a good job of making everything look good, given what little they'd really cared about.

They attached his microphone and battery pack which he quickly tested and got cleared by a man with grey hair and a long beard who was running a soundboard. For the umpteenth time, Conners ran through the vows he wanted to use in his head. Suddenly he heard a voice that was not his own ring out across the crowd.

"All right!" called Harriet. "Places people! The bride is arriving."

Conners took his place at the podium and clasped his hands behind his back looking at the temporary screen his bride was approaching from. Lawrence slowly entered from behind the screen and the lieutenant took her arm as she moved down the aisle. The late morning sun mirrored her form and helped veil her face as if she was a dream made real.

Her pure white dress made her beauty radiate all the more. He forced himself to breathe normally. In spite of his attempts to remain calm, Conners could feel his pulse quicken as she approached him in what appeared to be slow motion. As she reached him, he could see the smile dancing on her lips and the slight mist of the tear she was refusing to let run. She was lovely, and he couldn't have asked God for a better partner.

"Ladies and gentlemen," began the minister. "We are gathered here today to celebrate the joining of Michael Conners and Jessica Lawrence. They will join together under the gaze of God and become one. The bride and groom have elected to write their own vows."

"Jessica…" he said and let her name ring out for a moment. "From the first day we met, you have always been my friend and companion. You saw through any guise I put up, almost instantly. You were and are a constantly beautiful thing in my life. You've saved my work, saved my life, and helped lead me to God to save my soul."

He felt himself starting to tear up slightly at the intense emotions he'd put into these words.

"I love you… and I can say it no other way. I don't easily connect to people. I don't always understand the way they behave or the reason they do certain things. But I connect to you, and I know if I have you as my wife nothing else matters. You'll be by my side, and I'll be at yours. I will serve you faithfully as your husband until my dying day."

She squeezed his hands softly and he was forced to take a moment to wipe the tears out of his eyes. He could hear several members of the audience mumbling in approval and breathed just a little easier.

"Michael J. Conners," Lawrence said, and he listened to the words she'd prepared just for him. "I met you as a smartass who was too clever for his own good. But underneath that, I could see there was someone who desired to help people. You are a good person and a good man. I have been proud just to know you. I never loved another person like I love you. I do love you. I love that when you walk into the room, my world stops for a moment. I love that you'll stop at nothing to do the right thing. I love that you can make my day with a kiss, and calm me down with banter. You are the only man I could ever let into my life like this, and I love that too. I want to be there every day of your life, as a devoted and loving wife."

Josh held up the wedding ring to Conners, just like they'd practiced. Conners took the small golden band from the kid's hand.

"This ring, which has no ending will ever be a sign of the love I have for you."

He placed the ring gently on her finger and she reached to Harriet, pulling out a similar band.

"With this ring," she said. "I take you as my strength, my anchor and my husband."

"By the power vested in me," said the minister. "I now pronounce you man and wife… You may kiss the bride."

Conners took just a split-second to look carefully upon the face of his new bride. It was perfect. She'd barely used any makeup, just enough to amplify her own natural beauty, and she was all the lovelier for it. She was looking at him as if he was the only thing that existed in the world.

He leaned forward, making sure to put all his love for this woman into the action, and pressed his lips to hers. It was as if lightning struck the universe in that moment. The world ceased spinning and he could see stars behind his closed eyelids. He even heard the thundering and slowly realized it was the crowd around them cheering and clapping. Slowly, he pulled away and opened his eyes.

Jessica Lawrence: now Jessica Conners—his *wife* threw her arms around him and hugged him tightly. He let himself laugh. Happiness flooded through every inch of his body and made him weak at the knees. It was a second when everything was perfect in the world.

Bang!

The gunshot pulled Conners right out of his dreamlike state. He and many of the gathered policemen looked around quickly, but Conners knew his eyes found her first. Even at this distance she was unmistakable.

Elizabeth Richards stood at the far end of the seated crowd, with a pistol held straight up in the air.

Chapter L: The Challenge

Conners stared at Elizabeth and heard the policemen who were attending or serving as protection leap into action. Many were shouting for her to drop the gun, but Conners could already see she wasn't there to hurt any of the attendees. She was there for him. He was her obsession: her final challenge.

"Everyone," he said, allowing the microphone to carry his voice out clearly. "Please, let's all be calm. This is something personal between her and I."

He could see some of the police were inclined to listen, several seemed intent on stopping her either way, which he couldn't fault. Lieutenant Guston shouted out for them to form a perimeter and keep the attendees safe, and they moved to obey. Elizabeth didn't try to move or stop them from forming their circle around her. She had no intention of escaping. This was her final act, one way or the other.

Conners took off his microphone and battery pack and stepped towards Elizabeth when he felt Lawrence tug on his sleeve.

"If you get a chance to take her down, take it. You know what she's like."

Conners nodded and kissed her cheek. He moved for Elizabeth, and removed his tie and undid the buttons of his jacket to allow him to move with more freedom. The redhead across from him had already dropped the pistol and was holding twin dueling sabers.

Very old school challenge, he heard his father say. *Surprised she didn't come here and throw down a gauntlet.*

It had been more than a few years since Conners had practiced any swordplay, and he had little doubt Elizabeth would've studied the base of her challenge. He approached her slowly, and saw how she never took her eye off him. She was angry, lost, and in deep emotional pain that kept her from being clear about her own life.

You're hardly one to start throwing stones in that area, kid.
Fair enough.

"Well Elizabeth," he said, letting his voice carry to her. "Afraid you've missed most of the main event, but the afterparty should be starting up soon. There's catering and an open bar for over twenty-ones, I believe."

"I'm not here for your ceremony. Although, I am happy you two got married. Always beautiful when two broken people try to repair each other."

"Wouldn't know," said Conners, solidly. "What's it like to know everything you wanted ends in complete failure?"

"I'm not done. Not by a long shot."

"Give it a minute. I believe you and I have unfinished business, yeah? You want to get back at me for what I did to your mother or my relationship with your father?"

"I don't care about *her*. But you stole my inheritance. I should've inherited William's company and things. You stole them from me."

Conners couldn't help but regret he didn't have *Sherry* with him at that very moment.

"*Bill...*" he said firmly. "...never knew you were his daughter. Your mother hid it from him and he took me on as his student and successor. I'm sorry you never knew your father but I had nothing to do with it."

"All the same!" she snarled and threw one of the sabers at him. "You stole my rightful inheritance and I've come to lay claim to it."

Conners caught the saber deftly. He knew he didn't have to fight her. He could easily call for the lieutenant to send his men forward and never have to fight Elizabeth. For all the excuses he could make, the truth was actually very simple. He *wanted* to face her. He wanted to prove Bill was right to choose him and he wanted to prove he could overcome her. He wanted this confrontation as much as Elizabeth did.

"So be it," Conners said and they lifted their sabers in perfect synchronization.

His heart sank slightly when Elizabeth assumed her stance. She'd clearly practiced fencing often and he recognized the stance of someone who trained in saber style. He'd studied some fencing after receiving Bill's sword cane, but that was several years ago and he'd trained with a foil. It was a completely different weapon with a different grip and different attack style. His old footing and stances might be somewhat helpful but that would be the only part of his training he could reliably use.

He dropped into the old stance, and let his body remember the training it had gone through. Nevertheless, his grip was a little awkward and he felt odd with his offhand at his hip instead of curled behind his head to keep balance. Elizabeth smirked at him.

"You could just admit I deserve father's name, and your wife doesn't have to become a widow. Your mother doesn't have to lose the last of her family."

She didn't wait for his retort and struck out with a flurry of blows. Conners fell back and circled to the left to fend her off. She wasn't holding back either; his arm stung slightly as they separated. Conners glanced around and saw many of the gathered police had their hands on tasers or non-lethal weapons. He threw up his arms to deter anyone who was getting excited. He already saw the reporters who had come with hopes of little more than a fluff piece hastily taking pictures and writing wildly.

He focused his attention on Elizabeth and his mind slowed her movements down for him as adrenaline flooded his system.

Guide me through this, he called out to his mental guides.

She favors attacking from our right, his father noted. *We can circle around and hit her from behind if we're quick and careful. Her training can also be her undoing. Saber fencing is all focused on upper body strikes. Fight dirty and strike at her feet when you can.*

Elizabeth is in pieces over the state of her parentage, kid. She's not prepared for any sort of mental needling. If you challenge her linage to me, she'll lose composure. You'll have to draw this out a little. Outlast and enrage her.

Conners struck out and Elizabeth knocked his blow aside. As she drew her weapon in to respond, he used his momentum to kick out hard. His foot landed in her shin and the moment he felt the ball of his foot make contact, he pressed all his weight into the attack. Elizabeth *hissed* in pain as her knee buckled and she knelt down. This brought her face by Conners' right hip and he quickly improvised an attack. He lifted his right leg in a high-step, bringing his knee into her face.

As Elizabeth let out a cry of pain, Conners leapt back, creating space between the two of them. After a sharp breath, he reassumed his stance.

"That was cheap!" she shouted as a small trickle of blood fell from her nose.

"Your mother was one of the dirtiest cheaters who ever lived, and you couldn't even learn how to win properly. Bill should be relieved he never had to teach you."

She snarled and leapt up, spinning the saber around wildly. He fended off her attack and fell back again. However, he couldn't avoid the blows completely and he felt her weapon tear through the jacket and shirt on his right forearm and a sharp pain tore through him as blood began to spill from the wound. He could already feel his grip on the saber weakening and he tried to retreat.

But his dig at Elizabeth had unleashed the fury of a hellish woman and she was not intending to give him any reprieve. As she slashed out again, his mind brought the world around him to a near-stop and he was forced to see the similarities between the pair of them.

I know you, Elizabeth, he thought, and he could feel her pain too. *I know what it is to be so lost that you do whatever you can to belong, even if you disagree. I know what it is to fall and feel like there is no bottom to the pit you find yourself in. I know what it is to hate yourself so deeply you refuse to let anyone see the person you really are. I know what it is to be truly alone, and feel as if you deserve to be alone. I understand what it is to be empty inside.*

He threw his saber up to block her attack and as the blades rang out across the park, he felt his grip give out, and he dropped the saber as his fingers refused to hold strong. Elizabeth did not stop and continued swinging forward, and it was all he could do to duck under or dodge her attacks.

"All your words, all your achievements and you can't measure up to my abilities!" she screamed, nicking him across the collarbone.

"Everyone!" called Guston, but before he could give an order Conners heard the tell-tale sound of a taser launching its hooks, and Elizabeth stiffened before falling over.

Conners looked over to see who had fired and saw Jessica standing over Elizabeth. Her face was hard, but she was perfectly in control of herself.

"He doesn't have to match you," she said, just loud enough for Elizabeth to hear. "Because he's not alone."

Conners turned to the lieutenant and nodded. At least a dozen officers moved forward to arrest Elizabeth. He didn't watch and instead went to Jessica, who had now released the taser she'd fired.

"You ok?" he asked softly, kissing her.

"I'm ok. Are *you*?" she asked indicating his cuts. "That was really stupid, you know?"

"I'm fine," he said. "It was stupid, but important. You knew that before saying 'I do,' right?"

She smiled softly, and kissed him back. Conners took her hand in his, admiring the feel of their wedding bands. He looked over to see the lieutenant and a few officers loading Elizabeth into the back of a police car while reporters were circling around snapping pictures and asking questions as fast as they possibly could.

"I think our lives are a bit insane," he said, so only Jessica could hear.

"Dear, my life has been nothing but insane since the day I met you. But I'm happy to accept that. Just promise me you won't get into a near-death situation with anymore arch-enemies."

He chuckled slightly.

"Never know. I do seem to piss people off with some frequency."

"Yeah, and yet for some reason I still love you."

"I love you, too."

He stopped for just a second and it was as if he could see Bill and Vito standing amongst the gathered crowd. He could see Bill's plaid shirt and work boots standing in stark contrast to the suits gathered around him. He could view his father with his cane and stern eyes that hid his inner smile. He knew them almost as well as he knew himself, because they were always with him.

Except they weren't: not properly. He took a deep breath and considered his mental guides. They had been brought there because he'd needed them. He'd had them both in the moments he was broken and hurt, but he had been healing. He was better than he'd been when he'd left his father and rejected the wrong he'd been birthed from. He was better than he'd been when he was seeking redemption through Bill. He was whole, and now married to the woman he loved. He could understand his mind. He could accept who and what he was in a way he never could before.

And so, he did something he never thought he would've been able to do. He took in his mental images of Bill and Vito and whispered in his mind.

Thank you. Thank you both for everything. I love you both.

And with that admission, he let them go. He became solely himself.

Epilogue: Twenty Years Later

Beep! Beep! Beep!

Conners groaned as he rolled over and slapped the top of his phone repeatedly, trying to stop the infernal noise. The early morning sun streamed in through their bedroom window and he could already hear the noises that meant breakfast was being prepared in the kitchen down the hall. As he lay his head back on the pillow, his feet were suddenly assaulted by something cold and wet and he curled them up, quickly stuffing them beneath the comforter.

"Sienna!" he snapped at the pug that was enthusiastically licking his feet. "Stop it! You mutt!"

Their dog, Sienna, had recently turned seven and still had as much energy as when she was just a pup. She had taken to sleeping in their bed until Conners' alarm went off, at which time she would assault his feet until he got out of the bed.

"I'm getting up!" he informed her as she bounced around excitedly. "I'm up!"

He swung his feet out of the bed and sat up to put on his slippers. He righted himself and looked over at the small collection of pills he had to take each morning according to one doctor or another. He put the pills into his mouth, and took a quick swish of water to down them all in the same gulp.

Conners opened the bedroom door and moved down the hallway. As he did, he allowed himself to examine the photos that lined the walls. He relived each moment briefly, and was filled with pride, happiness, and laughter at the moments from their lives.

As he reached the living room and saw into the kitchen, he saw three figures gathered within it. The first was his beautiful wife of twenty years. She was bent over the stove, which was emitting a small haze of steam that carried the smell of frying eggs, bacon, and sausage. The second figure was Josh, who was (as ever) dressed in some utterly ridiculous fashion and listening to whatever music was big in the club scene. Truthfully, he'd turned into an impressive detective, and Conners was happy to have him heading Knighthawk Investigations. By now, all of his three students were heading their own teams, and had quickly become known as a real force in the city.

Last was his and Jessica's beautiful daughter, Lily. No matter how old she got, Conners couldn't help but see her as his young child, exploring the world with the same distinct lack of caution as her father. Lily never shied away from anything, and had gotten herself into trouble a fair few times by refusing to stay out of something that interested her. She was fiercely intelligent, and far more compassionate and understanding than he'd been at that age. That was largely due to her mother's influence.

"Turns out he was smuggling the stuff in the bean bag chairs," Josh said, clearly finishing a description of a case they'd been working on.

"Makes some sense," Lily said, shrugging. "Not like anyone in their right mind opens one of those things."

"I *seem* to recall," said Conners, feigning confusion. "That *someone* agreed to not ask about casework anymore, in exchange for her first car. And I recall that *someone else* promised to stop telling my daughter about the disturbing acts of the criminals throughout the city when he became head of my company."

Josh smiled and leaned back.

"Firstly, once I took over the company, it no longer was *your* company. So that deal is null and void anyway. Secondly, the story wasn't disturbing at all. Was it Lily?"

"No, it was just interesting. It's fine dad. Besides, most parents would be grateful to have a daughter that was so interested in their line of work."

"Lily," he began, joining them at the table. "Sometimes I wish you'd take after your mother and actually listen to instruction once in a while."

"Well, you have yourself to blame for that," said Jessica, swooping down and kissing him on the cheek. "As is the case with so many of the problems in your life, my dear."

"And here I thought we'd agreed to share all our problems some twenty years ago."

"You made your problems into my problems *long* before we were married."

"What exactly is this group attack today?"

Lily smiled and jumped up, excitedly.

"You're still taking me today, right?"

"Taking you? Where?" he asked, exaggerating the question.

"Dad! You promised to take me to Depaul today for my interview! Rachael and Paul are both going, and if we're late there's no way I'm going to get in."

"Lily," he said holding up his hand. "Relax. You've had a perfect G.P.A. since you were born. You're going to be fine, and we're not going to be late."

They ate breakfast together, laughing and sharing stories about what was going on in the morning news, though Conners was careful to give anything related to open cases a wide birth. That didn't stop Josh from critiquing the actions of the detectives working on a store robbery that had taken place in the night.

After he ate and got dressed, he walked with Lily to his car. Thankfully, he'd managed to pick up driving during their twenty years of marriage, not that he hadn't scared Jessica.

Lily hopped in the car and Conners took just a moment to stop and examine the world around him. He could clearly see the prominent figures from his life. He could see those who had made him who he now was.

He could see Vito and Lydia, the doctors who had first treated him when he'd awoken in the hospital, Hunter and his cronies, Bill, Guston, Richards, and Kingston. He saw Elizabeth, who last he'd heard had been brought to a long-term high-security prison with behavior health services. He saw Josh, Harriet, Kenneth, and even Jim, who had moved down to Florida after some incident with his captain. As he looked over these people, he couldn't help but thank them all for the roles they'd served in his life and during his time of growth.

Despite all of that, he still wasn't completely ready to rest, because now he was the growth in so many other people's lives.

"Dad!" called Lily impatiently from the passenger's seat. "We need to go, or we're going to be stuck in the traffic!"

"I'm coming! I'm coming!" he shouted out, and moved towards the car, ready to approach yet another chapter in his life.

THE END

Made in the USA
Monee, IL
07 March 2023

29060369R00249